THE NIGHT OCEAN

PENGUIN PRESS

NEW YORK

2017

THE NIGHT OCEAN

Paul La Farge

PENGUIN PRESS
An imprint of Penguin Random House LLC
375 Hudson Street
New York, New York 10014
penguin.com

Artwork on pages 17 and 27 by the author

Sources for other images:
Page 181: Ancestry.com
Page 374: John Hay Library, Brown University

Library of Congress Cataloging-in-Publication Data

Names: LaFarge, Paul, author.
Title: The night ocean / Paul La Farge.
Description: New York : Penguin Press, [2017]
Identifiers: LCCN 2016043484 (print) | LCCN 2016051643 (ebook) | ISBN
9781101981085 (hardcover) | ISBN 9781101981108 (ebook)
Subjects: | BISAC: FICTION / Literary. | FICTION / Historical. | FICTION /
Mystery & Detective / Historical.
Classification: LCC PS3562.A269 N54 2017 (print) | LCC PS3562.A269 (ebook) |
DDC 813/.54--dc23
LC record available at https://lccn.loc.gov/2016043484

Printed in the United States of America
3   5   7   9   10   8   6   4

DESIGNED BY AMANDA DEWEY

This is a work of fiction based on actual events.

For Robert Kelly

I say to you againe, doe not call up
Any that you can not put downe.

—H. P. LOVECRAFT,
The Case of Charles Dexter Ward

I.

A RESULT AND A PROLOGUE

1.

My husband, Charlie Willett, disappeared from a psychiatric hospital in the Berkshires on January 7, 2012. I say *disappeared* because I don't believe he's dead, although that would be the reasonable conclusion. Charlie's army jacket, jeans, shoes, socks, and underwear (though, strangely, not his shirt) were all found at the edge of Agawam Lake the day after he left the hospital. The police say Charlie's footprints led to the edge of the lake, and nobody's footprints led away. Even if Charlie could somehow have left the lake without leaving tracks, they say, it's hard to see how he would have survived long enough to reach shelter. According to the National Weather Service, the overnight low temperature in Stockbridge was 15 degrees, and Charlie didn't have an extra set of clothes: the girl who gave him a ride swears he wasn't carrying anything. What's more, no one denies that Charlie was suicidal. The last time I saw him, in Brooklyn, he told me he'd taken a handful of Ambien, just to see what would happen. What happened was, he slept for twelve hours, had a dizzy spell in the shower, and sprained his ankle. "My life is becoming a sad joke," he said, "except there's no one around to laugh at it." He looked at me entreatingly. I told him there was nothing funny about an Ambien overdose. It could kill you, if you took it with another depressant. "Thanks, Miss

Merck Manual," Charlie said. "I'm still your wife," I said, "and you're scaring me. If you really want to hurt yourself, you should be in the hospital." To my surprise, Charlie asked, "Which hospital?" I thought for a moment, then I told him about the place in the Berkshires.

Two days later, Charlie was on the bus to Stockbridge. He called me that evening. "I feel like I'm in high school again, Mar," he said. "The food is terrible, and everybody's on drugs. I nearly had a panic attack, trying to figure out who to sit with at dinner. Who are the cool kids in an insane asylum? The bulimics look great, but the bipolars make better conversation." "Sounds like you'll fit right in," I said, and Charlie laughed. He sounded like himself, for the first time in months. What had he sounded like before that? Like himself, but falling down a well in slow motion: each time I saw him, his voice was fainter and somehow more echo-y. That's something Charlie might have said; normally, I am more cautious with my descriptions. I have never heard anyone fall down a well. "Are *you* on drugs?" I asked. "I start tomorrow," Charlie said. "Wanted to call you tonight, in case there's anything you want to ask before they erase my mind." "Don't joke," I said. I thought about it. "What's your favorite nut?" I asked. "Oh, Mar," he said, "you know the answer to that one."

Charlie called again two days after that and told me they had him on 2 milligrams of risperidone—which was more than I would have given him, but never mind—and it made him woozy. "But the characters, Mar," he said, "the characters!" He was taking notes in his journal, for an essay he planned to write about his *downfall*. "Take it easy," I said. "If they think your journal is antisocial, they might confiscate it." "I am," Charlie said. "I've only got enough energy to write for, like, five minutes a day. The rest of the time I watch *Lost* on DVD." He didn't talk about his therapy, but I didn't expect him to. We had always respected each other's privacy. "How long are they going to keep you?" I asked. Charlie said, "They're saying a couple of weeks." I said I would visit as soon as I could, probably the next weekend. Then, afraid that Charlie would draw the wrong conclusion, I clarified: "I just want to know you're all right, and that you aren't making the doctors miserable." Charlie said it was his job to make the doctors miserable. Then he said, "Just kidding. My job right now is to make a world I can live in." I wondered if he'd picked that phrase up in therapy, and what dopey therapist could have fed it to him. What Charlie needed was exactly *not* to make a world. He needed to figure out how to live in the one that exists. All of that took probably two seconds. "I'm happy that you're doing well," I said, and Charlie said, "Thanks." We hung up.

That was on January fifth. On the seventh, Charlie forced the lock on his door with a bit of plastic, climbed a cyclone fence, and hitched a ride with a Simon's Rock student named Jessica Ng. He told her he was meeting friends at Monument Mountain, for an Orthodox Christmas celebration, and she, the fool, dropped him on the shoulder of Route 7. He waved, cheerfully, she said, and walked into the forest. It's all in the police report. For the police, and Charlie's mother, and more or less everyone else, the last sentence of the story will be written in the summer, when Agawam Lake warms up, and Charlie's body rises to the surface. Only I do not believe he is dead.

This, you'll tell me, is pure wish fulfillment. I feel guilty that I didn't save Charlie from suicide, so I've constructed a fantasy in which his suicide didn't happen. It's possible. Just because I am a psychotherapist doesn't mean that I'm immune to delusional thinking, and I *do* feel guilty. I lie awake wondering whether, if I'd acted differently, Charlie would still be here. If I hadn't pushed him away in that last conversation; if I had been more patient, more understanding; if I hadn't moved out when I learned about Lila. Or, I tell myself, because I *was* patient, *was* understanding, maybe my mistake was to keep my thoughts too much to myself. When Charlie came back from Mexico City with evidence of Robert Barlow's miraculous survival, I could

5

have told him the evidence didn't add up. When he went to *see* Barlow—the person he thought was Barlow—I might have said what I felt, which was, that the story was too good to be true. Even though I know what Charlie would have said: "Mar, you're being mistrustful. I know it's hard for you to remember, but there are people out there who aren't crazy." And I would have sulked, because I hated when Charlie called me *mistrustful*. It made me feel small, and it wasn't true. My real mistake, I tell myself, when midnight comes around, and I get out of bed to drink a glass of wine and listen to the BBC, my mistake was that I believed Charlie too much. Then I remind myself that I loved Charlie because he was so unbearably easy to believe.

2.

This is not the story of our marriage. Still, I want to note some things that happened early on, because they make what happened later easier to understand. Charlie and I were set up. His friend Eric was dating my friend Grace, and so, in accordance with the law that every young paired-off person in New York City has to pair off his or her friends, Grace threw a party in her Hester Street studio, and Charlie and I were invited. I didn't want to go. This was in 2004, when I was doing my residency at Weill Cornell, and I reserved my free time for sleep or reading the novels that piled up on my little glass-topped table. Also, the night of the party was very cold. But then I thought, Marina, if you don't leave the house, you're going to spend the rest of your life alone, or, worse, you're going to marry a doctor. So I put on about six layers of clothes, and, feeling like one of the old *Star Wars* action figures Charlie collected—I didn't know about them yet, but now, eight years later, Charlie images are what come to mind—I took a cab to the Lower East Side. As soon as I got to the party, I wished I hadn't come. Thirty of Grace's art-school friends were crammed into her studio, holding drinks close to their chests and shouting at one another over a mix CD. It was like being in college again, and I felt a kind of despair, watching all those people pretend that time did not exist. But it was so cold out that I didn't go home right away, and while I was leaning against the wall, wondering if *I* had changed since college, Grace came up to me and shouted, "Marina! I need your help! I left my inhaler somewhere, and now I can't find it."

With a familiar mild irritation—Grace was always losing things, always asking for help—I headed toward the bathroom. My path was blocked by a large plastic rabbit, spray-painted gold, and while I stood before it, wondering what it was doing there, a boy asked if I knew where the rabbit had come from. "Probably from a gallery in Williamsburg," I said, and the boy, who was, of course, Charlie, laughed. He told me he had seen a rabbit just like this one, once, in Memphis, and he'd discovered that it came from a chain of restaurants called the Happy Rabbit. The chain was founded by a Chinese immigrant named William Lee, and the amazing thing, Charlie said, although I didn't know his name yet, the amazing thing, he said, was that Mr. Lee actually *served rabbit,* because he believed that, in the future, nuclear war would make it impossible to raise beef cows or even sheep. "Like many other people," Charlie said, "he was preparing for a future that never happened." "Or at least one that hasn't happened yet," I said. Charlie grinned. It was as if he'd thrown a football into some trees, and I had not only caught it but thrown it back to him. "Actually," he said, "I'm not sure this is one of the Happy Rabbit rabbits. But it could be." He was skinny and stooped, with a scraggly goatee and hair clipped close to his skull. His skin was light brown. He wore a green army jacket over a blue paisley shirt and red pants: a motley outfit, I thought, as if he were protecting himself by playing the fool. He wasn't the man I had dreamed of meeting, but my dreams were confused, and the men I did meet were often good-looking jerks. And then it was midnight, and everyone else had gone out to a bar. We were still standing beside the rabbit. Suddenly, Charlie asked, "Is it all right if I kiss you?" I said he might as well. "What do you mean, I might as well?" he asked. "Well," I said, "no one knows when that nuclear war's going to show up."

But this isn't the story of our marriage. It's not the story of how quickly Charlie moved in with me and stood Han Solo and Darth Vader on my bookshelf, in front of D. W. Winnicott and George Eliot. It isn't the story of how we got married at City Hall, with Charlie's mother and my brothers as witnesses, because my parents refused to come down from Connecticut to watch me marry a *schvartze;* or how we posed in front of a photomural of the Statue of Liberty, and Charlie remarked that the statue was exactly the wrong symbol for people who were getting married, and I punched him in the ribs. What's important is that I loved Charlie because he made life lively. When I met him, he worked as a fact-checker at the *Village Voice,* and in his free time, he wrote profiles of people who could have been famous, or should have been famous but weren't, because of some stubbornness in their character, or some flaw in the world. He didn't make a lot of money, but that didn't matter, because I was making enough. After my residency, I was an attending for two years at Mount Sinai, then I went into private practice, doing analytic psychotherapy, which I believe in, and which I'm good at.

What Charlie was good at was immersing himself in obscure and beautiful facts. He loved the people he wrote about in a way that I sometimes envied but would have been afraid to imitate. As a therapist, you get to care deeply about your patients, but you can't *love* them without sacrificing the neutrality that makes therapy work. For Charlie, there was no limit. When he was writing about an employee of the Oakland Department of Motor Vehicles who had invented a purely rational language and was, so far as anyone knew, its only speaker, he learned the language. He and the DMV employee conversed in it; I listened with amazement as Charlie clicked and clucked into his phone, scribbling notes on a steno pad balanced on his knee. But when

I read his profile of the language inventor, I understood why he had put so much effort into the research: I could *see* the DMV employee standing at the breakfast bar of his bachelor's apartment (he'd invented his language, he said, as a way to make sense of things after a bad divorce), eating a Baby Ruth and licking chocolate from his fingers. "Was that what you were talking about? Candy?" I asked. "Uh, no," Charlie said. "Actually, I intuited he was a Three Musketeers kind of guy." "You *intuited*?" "Yeah," Charlie said, "sometimes, when you get deep enough into someone's head, you can kind of see things. It's like you become them, and you're seeing the world through their eyes. Of course, I asked him about it, after I wrote the first draft. Baby Ruth. I was pretty close, right?"

Why was Charlie the way he was? As we got to know each other, I couldn't help coming up with some hypotheses. His parents were both professors at Columbia, his father in English, his mother in philosophy. When Charlie was ten, his father, who happened to be black, was accused of sexually harassing several of his female graduate students. He cried racism, but Charlie's mother, who happened to be white, left him anyway. Charlie's father died of a brain tumor before the charges were resolved. These events, coming one after another, sent Charlie into what I would have called a serious depression; he called it his *passage through the underworld*. He lost interest in doing anything, and in seeing anyone he hadn't known before his father died. The only exception to this rule was Dungeons & Dragons, which he started playing when he was twelve and played more or less nonstop until he turned seventeen. "I had the little figurines and everything," he said. "Even my nerd friends were freaked out. I had to play in the back room of a hobby shop in Midtown, with these Asian kids from Stuyvesant, and some guys in their thirties who were probably repressed sexual predators. But that was how I met Eric—he was as messed up as I was, or more so. We used to take the bus together, to D&D tournaments in New Jersey and Pennsylvania and so on. We'd stay up all night, come back on the bus in the morning, and go straight to school. It was like we were on drugs, except that we didn't even drink. And we did super well in the tournaments. There was this one time, we were playing through the Tomb of Horrors, and Eric and I were the last two survivors." "So what happened?" I asked, trying not to smile. "I killed him," Charlie said. "The first-place prize was a twenty-dollar gift certificate. A man has his priorities." "I meant, why did you stop playing," I said. Charlie blushed. "I went to Princeton," he said, "and met a girl named Megan, who was into Pablo Neruda. Long story short, I turned over a new leaf and became the outstanding writer of nonfiction whom you see before you."

Traces of the old Charlie were still easy to spot. I don't mean that in a judgmental way. Nothing has led me to believe that people can change their deep selves; the best we can do is to fit our dispositions into the real world, and Charlie did that. His profiles didn't make him famous, and they certainly didn't make him rich, but they were a joy to read, even if you had no interest in the things his almost-celebrities were almost famous for. He took their obscurity and lit it up with his caring. The only sad thing about his work, I thought, was that it was connected to his father: as if he were still trying to salvage his lost, flawed dad, who had spent his professional life looking for traces of colonialism in the poems of Sir Thomas Wyatt the Younger. I didn't tell him that, but I wonder if anything would have been different, if I had. Probably Charlie would have grimaced and said, Mar, you're a great therapist, but you're not *my* therapist, so please, shut up. But maybe it would have sunk in, anyway, and he would have been more cautious when he met L. C. Spinks. Actually, I think he must have known, by the end, that he had to let his father go. I think his disappearance was a way of letting go: not a great way, but the only one he could imagine, at that point. More wish fulfillment, you'll say. Maybe so. The most terrible of my midnight thoughts is that Charlie took L. C. Spinks with him to the bottom of Agawam Lake, not in reality but in his heart, and that my husband is there now, deep in cold water, curled around the memory of the worst father he'd ever known.

3.

L. C. Spinks came into our lives thanks to Charlie's friend Magnus, whom I still see sometimes, sitting in a café on Avenue B, or walking his dog in Tompkins Square Park. I avoid him. Magnus is, or used to be, a poet; he published a book in the 1970s, and one of his poems was turned into a song by the Holy Modal Rounders, whose music Charlie tried to explain to me, in vain. At one point, Magnus taught classes at City College; now, as far as I know, he lives on disability and the remains of an inheritance. He is walrus-shaped, with a shock of white hair and a gnawed walrus mustache. Charlie used to say that Magnus looks the way Theodore Roosevelt would have looked if Roosevelt had come of age in Greenwich Village in the 1950s, but that tells you more about Charlie's powers of idealization than it does about Magnus himself. I don't know how the two of them met. What I do know is that Charlie was planning to write a profile of Magnus, but then, one day in the summer of 2006, the two of them started talking about H. P. Lovecraft, whose stories, it turned out, they both admired.

"Who's that?" I asked. "You don't know?" Charlie said. "Only the greatest American horror writer since Poe." Lovecraft was the author of "The Call of Cthulhu," *At the Mountains of Madness,* and other works I hadn't heard of. His stories, Charlie said, were about a universe inhabited by powerful alien beings, who feel about humanity the way a person coming home from a long trip might feel about an infestation of spiders. "Sounds cheerful," I said. "I got a kick out of them in junior high school," Charlie said. "In fact," he went on, blushing, "Eric and I started a Cult of Cthulhu. We sewed ourselves black robes, and walked up and down Broadway in the middle of the night, holding signs that read THE END OF THE WORLD IS NIGH—GIVE TO THE CULT OF CTHULHU. In retrospect, it was suicidal, but nothing bad ever happened to us. I think we must have been so weird that people left us alone. A half-black kid and a Puerto Rican kid, stumping for Cthulhu! We could have been poster children for the city of New York." "You didn't really believe in Cthulhu, did you?" I asked. "No," Charlie said, "but it was so much fun to pretend we *did* believe, it was a lot like believing. I'm sure," he added, when he saw my worried expression, "if Cthulhu had actually appeared, I would have been scared shitless."

Magnus, who knew everything about everything, or pretended to, told Charlie that he had met one of Lovecraft's friends, a fellow named Sam Loveman, who owned a used-book shop on Fourth Avenue. Those were their real names, Charlie said: Lovecraft and Loveman, which was ironic, because if there was anything they didn't know about, it was love. Anyway, this was in the 1970s, when Sam Loveman was very old, and Magnus was looking for books by the English writer Hubert Crackanthorpe, a realist who had drowned himself in the Seine at the age of twenty-six. Loveman turned out to be a Crackanthorpe fanatic, possibly the only such person in the world. He immediately became fond of Magnus. They'd spend hours in Loveman's second-floor shop, sitting on draftsman's stools, talking about their beloved, forgotten writers, and it came to light that Loveman had known H. P. Lovecraft in the 1920s and '30s. "What was he like?" Magnus asked, dazzled. "Howard was a real New England gentleman," Loveman said, but as their conversation went on, he revealed some things about Lovecraft that weren't exactly pleasant. Lovecraft had hated the Jews, black people, Asians, Arabs. He had despised women. "In the end," Loveman said, "I think the only person he ever cared about was Bobby Barlow, and even about him, I'm not sure." "Barlow?" Magnus asked. "Robert Barlow," Loveman said, with a kind of bitter sadness mixed with puzzlement. "He was Howard's literary executor. You don't know the story?" Magnus shook his head. "Well," Loveman said, "Barlow was a *very* assiduous fan who lived in Florida. He wrote letters to Howard, and they became friends. Finally, in the summer of 1934, Barlow invited Howard to visit him, and Howard went. He stayed with Barlow for two months. But what you have to bear in mind is that Howard didn't stay with *anyone* for two months. He was too attached to his precious old furniture, his books, his dear Providence. The other thing that makes the episode unfathomable is that Howard was forty-three when it happened, and Bobby was all of sixteen, and *not* good-looking." "You mean they were lovers?" Magnus asked. "No one knows," Loveman said. "No one dared to ask Howard, and Barlow vanished. I heard he went to Mexico and died there under unhappy circumstances." "Oh," Magnus said. "If they *were* lovers, and I'm not saying that they were," Loveman continued, "then that was the stupidest thing Howard ever did. Although in truth, it was probably the most endearing thing, too." "How do you mean?" Magnus asked. Loveman patted the stack of books on the desk beside him, as though to reassure them of something. "Don't you see?" he asked. "If he really did love Bobby, at least that would mean he was human." Sam Loveman died soon after that, but the story of Lovecraft and Barlow remained in Magnus's mind, hard and small, like a seed. He thought of doing something with it, writing a sequence of poems, maybe, but he lost interest. "Which is the tragic pattern of my life," Magnus said, rubbing his finger across his mustache. "If only I'd known how to hold on to things, I'd be immortal." "And that's the story," Charlie said. "I'm going to look into it." "I bet you will," I said.

So Charlie set out on the path that would lead to the shore of Aga-wam Lake, but I don't believe his journey ended there, and I have reasons for not believing it. There's the note he left on his bed in the hospital, which read: *Do not disturb me, I wish to sleep for a long time*—an absurd message from a literal point of view, since Charlie wasn't *in* the bed, but a meaningful one to anyone who has read his book about Lovecraft and Barlow. There's the fact that Jessica Ng keeps changing her story. Did she leave him on a side road, by an abandoned farm? Did she leave him within view of the lake? Did she leave him *at all*? And, finally, there's the image I am looking at as I write this, a photograph of a stretch of nearly black sand, and, beyond it, an indigo ocean. It showed up on my phone a month ago. I cried when I saw it, then I laughed. It's just the kind of thing Charlie would do.

II.

AN ANTECEDENT
AND A HORROR

1.

Howard Phillips Lovecraft, Charlie soon discovered, was even stranger and more forbidding than Magnus had made him out to be. Lovecraft was born in 1890, the only child of Winfield Scott Lovecraft, a silver salesman, and Sarah Susan Phillips, the daughter of a rich Providence merchant. When Howard was three, his father was committed to the Butler Hospital for the Insane, following an episode of paranoid delusion, and Lovecraft went to live with his grandfather. He had a bookish, solitary childhood, which was marked by a fondness for eighteenth-century English literature and the tales of Edgar Allan Poe. He disliked games and had few friends, but he did enjoy building cities out of blocks and enacting their decline and fall.

Lovecraft's grandfather died in 1904, and Lovecraft and his mother moved to a smaller house. Lovecraft found the change so deeply upsetting that he contemplated suicide: he really was attached to familiar places and familiar things. Also, his mother sounds like a terror. She was pretty, vain, and nervous; she dressed the infant Lovecraft as a girl—a fact of which critics have made much over the years—and told people that her son was so ugly, he shouldn't be allowed outside in the daytime. In the end, though, Lovecraft decided that life with Susie, as she was known, was better than no life at all. There were so many things he wanted to know: What would Shackleton and Scott find in the Antarctic? What about Africa, and the vast gulfs of space? He studied history and science, especially astronomy, about which he wrote a column for the *Providence Evening News*. He dreamed of becoming a scientist, but when he was seventeen, he suffered from mysterious seizures and withdrew from high school. For several years, Lovecraft did nothing at all; then, in his twenties, he published a magazine called *The Conservative,* in which he advocated "total abstinence and prohibition, moderate, healthy militarism as contrasted with dangerous and unpatriotic peace-preaching, and the domination by the English and kindred races over the lesser divisions of mankind." "Uh-oh," I said, when Charlie told me about this. "It gets worse," Charlie said.

Lovecraft lived with Susie until 1919, when she, too, was committed to the Butler Hospital for the Insane. She died there in May 1921. Six weeks later, as if his heart had been released from servitude to her, Lovecraft met Sonia Greene, a Ukrainian Jewish immigrant, at a convention of amateur journalists in Boston. Sonia was seven years his senior and had a teenage daughter by a previous marriage. She was not attracted to Lovecraft, but she admired his writing. What Lovecraft felt for her is not known, because she burned his letters, a whole trunkful of them, before she left for California in 1935. However, it doesn't seem to have been a passionate attachment. Lovecraft never kissed Sonia, never said he loved her. When he wanted to express affection, he wrapped his pinky finger around hers and said, "Umph." They were married in 1924, and he moved into her apartment in Brooklyn. The two years that followed were difficult, to say the least. Lovecraft placed wordy ads in the newspaper, announcing that he was available to revise and edit works of prose and poetry on any subject, but no one hired him. He tried selling magazines door-to-door, but he had no talent for selling. He didn't *believe* in selling. It wasn't gentlemanly.

Meanwhile, Sonia sold women's hats, fed Lovecraft spaghetti, and brought him to meetings of her literary club. He became almost psychotic. By the end of 1925, he was writing to his aunt Lillian about the "loathsome Asiatic hordes" and "scarcely less undesirable Latins" of New York, "the clamorous plague of French-Canadians," and "the hideous peasant Poles of New Jersey," not to mention the Jews, who, he wrote, "are hopeless as far as America is concerned. They are the product of alien blood, & inherit alien ideals, impulses, & emotions which forever preclude the possibility of wholesale assimilation." "Whoa!" I said. "Maybe you should let this one go." "What," Charlie said, "and miss the chance to tell the world that Lovecraft had sex with a sixteen-year-old?" "Are you writing an exposé?" I asked. "Kind of, kind of," Charlie said. "You know, childhood hero with feet of clay. I appreciate his honesty, though. You don't have to read between the lines." "Wasn't his wife Jewish?" I asked. "Yep," Charlie said. "Old Howard was a complicated fellow."

In the spring of 1926, Lovecraft went back to Providence. His marriage to Sonia dissolved. He worked frantically, as if he were running away from something: in the two years following his return from New York, he wrote the stories "The Call of Cthulhu," "Pickman's Model," "The Strange High House in the Mist," "The Silver Key," and "The Colour Out of Space," and the novels *The Dream-Quest of Unknown Kadath* and *The Case of Charles Dexter Ward*. Because this last book ended up being the pattern, in a strange way, for Charlie's relationship with L. C. Spinks, I should say something about it. It concerns a young man named Charles Dexter Ward, a Providence native who is fascinated by the colonial past. While looking through old papers, he finds a reference to his great-great-great-grandfather Joseph Curwen, about whom no one has ever told him anything. He discovers that Curwen was a merchant who came to Providence from Salem around 1693 and lived there for a century without growing visibly older. Curwen performed sinister experiments in the cellar of his Pawtuxet farm, which finally upset the people of Providence so much that they raided the farm and killed him. Ward is eager to learn more. Why didn't Curwen age? And what were his experiments? He digs around in libraries and locates Curwen's house, where he finds secret papers that explain how to bring Curwen back from the dead. Ward performs a sinister ritual; there's a thunderstorm, and, poof, Curwen is back—but, unfortunately for Ward, his plans do not involve informing his great-great-great-grandson about eighteenth-century Providence.

If you don't know how the book ends, I won't spoil it for you. Let's just say that *The Case of Charles Dexter Ward* has been read as a parable on the perils of research. In the fall of 2006, I saw those perils more clearly than Charlie did. He said he hadn't forgotten what a problematic person H. P. Lovecraft was, but the more deeply immersed he became in Lovecraft's story, the more he forgot to ask questions about it, except the researcher's constant demand: *Tell me more.* Many of the things he learned seemed trivial to me—for instance, that Lovecraft had traveled with a black imitation-leather bag, or that he hated fish, and loved cheese—but Charlie recounted them with secretive excitement, as though, from these motes of fact, he were going to bring the man himself back to life. I said he was becoming too much like poor Charles Dexter Ward, and he laughed. "Just because my name is Charles?" he said. "Or actually Charles W.?" "You're freaking me out," I said. "Don't worry," Charlie said, "I'm in full *possession* of my faculties. *Mwahahaha.*" "Don't do that!" I said.

Charlie unearthed a certain amount of information about Robert Barlow, too. Just as Magnus said, Barlow and Lovecraft had corresponded, and Lovecraft visited Barlow in Florida twice, in the summer of 1934 and again in the summer of 1935. In between, Barlow and

Lovecraft met in New York City, and in the summer of 1936, Barlow visited Lovecraft in Providence. They exchanged hundreds of long letters, about art and politics and their health and the health of their relatives and their cats. (To Charlie's chagrin, only Lovecraft's letters survived. Lovecraft was not the kind of person who held on to other people's letters, apparently.) After Lovecraft died, in 1937, of cancer, Barlow wrote several reminiscences of Lovecraft; in one of them, he called his old friend a "closet Quetzalcoatl," which would have been more damning if *closeted* had been slang for *gay* back then. In another, Barlow wrote of his youth in Florida that "life, save for certain secret desires which centered on the person of a young man . . . was all literary then"; then he crossed most of the line out of the manuscript. In the published version, it read: "Life was all literary then." "Kinda sums it up, doesn't it?" Charlie said. "The official version plasters over the gaps, the secret doors leading down to sexual sub-basements . . ." "Sexual sub-basements?" I repeated. "Or something," Charlie said.

That was in October. Already, Charlie was working on his Barlow project to the exclusion of nearly everything else. But although the letters and memoirs offered up a great deal of circumstantial detail about what Lovecraft and Barlow did when they were together, there was a blank spot at the center of the story. No one could say—or, at least, no one *had* said—what they felt for each other. Even Loveman had never known if they were lovers. "So what's the story?" Charlie asked. "What am I even going to write about?" When he was feeling especially frustrated, he speculated that the truth about Lovecraft and Barlow had been covered up by somebody who wanted to protect Lovecraft's reputation. He talked about abandoning the Barlow project, about giving up writing completely. He'd always wanted to work on a fishing boat, he said. I had to laugh. My father has a thirty-four-foot sloop, and he offered once to take Charlie out on the Sound, but Charlie refused, on the grounds that he'd probably be the first black person to sail in Connecticut since the *Amistad,* and he wasn't ready to bear that historical burden. Ha, ha, ha. The truth is, he was terrified of anything he couldn't control.

Other things happened. My grandfather passed away. Charlie and I moved into a two-bedroom apartment in Brooklyn Heights, and talked about having a child. Then, one evening in November, Charlie came home with a flushed, triumphant expression. "What's up?" I asked. "There's a book," he said. He had found a reference to it in an article on the forbidden books of H. P. Lovecraft: imaginary books, which Lovecraft referred to in his stories. The best known of them was the *Necronomicon,* but there was also the *Culte des Ghoules,* the *Liber Ivonis,* the *De Vermis Mysteriis,* the *Unaussprechlichen Kulten* of Von Junzt. All of them full of powerful, secret knowledge—and all fictitious, which hasn't prevented generation after generation of Lovecraft fans from believing they are real. But, anyway, in this article, Charlie said there was a parenthetical reference, which was just the words *except, of course, the* Erotonomicon. The author didn't say what the *Erotonomicon* was, and, in fact, Charlie had the feeling that he, the author, had mentioned it as a joke, or that he had meant to delete the reference but forgot. "But," Charlie said, "the etymology is interesting. When I was a kid, I thought *Necronomicon* meant *the book of dead names,* but according to the article, it means *the image of the law of the dead,* or just *a book concerning the dead.* So the *Erotonomicon* would be the *image of the law of love,* which, you have to admit, is kind of intriguing."

At the beginning of December, Charlie went to Providence, to look some things up in the library at Brown. He was gone for three days and came back looking like an excited cadaver. He told me that he had read hundreds of Lovecraft's unpublished letters, in search of the *Erotonomicon;* but Lovecraft never mentioned it, and Charlie was beginning to think that the original reference had been one of the inside jokes that Lovecraft fans were always making when, pasted into an issue of *Canadian Fandom* from June 1952, he found this advertisement:

```
=========== DANGER ============
Have u lost your mind? Not yet?
*** Then u may want to read ***
****** THE EROTONOMICON *******
** Being, the Erotic Diary of *
** HOWARD PHILLIPS LOVECRAFT **
**** Edited by L.C. Spinks ****
** Write to Black Hour Books **
* P.O. Box 14110 Cooper Station
******** NEw York, NY *********
==== DO YOU DARE TO KNOW? =====
```

"Imagine my excitement," Charlie said. "If the *Erotonomicon* is genuine, then it contains exactly the information I've been looking for. The only problem is that it's impossible to find. Brown doesn't have a copy or even acknowledge that such a thing exists. I've been emailing with rare-book dealers all over the country, but they just laugh at me, as if I were some lonely teenager trying to buy a dirty book, or a book of spells, whichever they think is more embarrassing. Of course, the advertisement could be a joke, but I don't think so. Black Hour Books used to exist, and so did L. C. Spinks. He was a science fiction fan who lived in a little town in Ontario. I guess the question is, did he somehow find Lovecraft's diary? And if so, does it say anything about Barlow?"

I asked Charlie how he was feeling. "Why do you ask?" he said. "Because you look awful," I said. "I'm OK," Charlie said. "The only thing is . . ." He looked at me slyly. "I was wondering if you could maybe write me a prescription for Adderall? I'm becoming aware that this project is going to be an insane amount of work. On the plus side, it's the kind of story that sells. Which would be good, right? Since we're thinking of having a kid?" He fixed his eyes on me in a way that I found unsettling: it was as if he had read somewhere that this was how you convinced people you were sincere. Actually, the image that came to mind was of a stage magician, who keeps your attention focused on some irrelevant phenomenon while the trick happens elsewhere. But Charlie really did look worn out, and I worried that if I refused to write him the prescription, he'd get pills from one of Eric's programmer friends. Hoping the DEA wouldn't audit me anytime soon, I wrote a script for 20-milligram extended-release tablets. Charlie folded the slip and put it into his shirt pocket. "Thanks, Mar," he said. I told myself my intentions were good, but, in retrospect, I think it would be more honest to say that I was afraid.

Charlie didn't mention the *Erotonomicon* for weeks after that. I remember him talking about wanting to leave New York, to live in a big house somewhere in the country, a fantasy that struck me as being totally unrealistic. Charlie's idea of self-sufficiency was ordering food to be delivered. "So I know my kung pao," he said. "I still like the idea of more space. If we lived in a house, you could have a piano." I hadn't played since college, hadn't talked about playing; I was amazed that Charlie even knew this about me. "You're sweet," I said, "but I'm happy here. Aren't you?" "Definitely," Charlie said. But one night in December, I came home late, and he wasn't there. He hadn't left a message or texted to tell me where he was. This triggered some issues for me, and I became very anxious. I poured myself a glass of wine and watched TV, which helped, but not much. I drank another glass of wine. By the time Charlie came home, I was feeling hazy and sad. "Where were you?" I asked. Charlie said he and Eric had gone out for a beer in Chelsea, to celebrate a major victory. "And what was that?" I asked. Charlie looked at me warily. "Mar," he said, "have you been drinking?" "No," I said, but the mostly empty bottle was on the table in front of me. Charlie started laughing. He put his arms around me, and I clutched his skinny back and inhaled his wool-and-sweat scent. "Did you at least save me some?" he asked. "No," I said again. "Well, can we order pizza?" "No," I said; then I said, "Yes, but promise me that you'll never vanish like that again."

Charlie told me that he had finally gotten his hands on a copy of the *Erotonomicon*. He took a padded envelope from his messenger bag, and from the envelope he withdrew a slim blue clothbound book. I reached for it, but Charlie jerked the book back; then, realizing how weird that was, he handed it to me. I leafed through the first few pages, and a phrase in the introduction caught my eye: "I think, in the end, history will conclude that by publishing this book I have done H.P.L. a favor." How grandiose, I thought, and gave the book back. "Congratulations," I said. "Don't be grumpy, Marina," Charlie said. "This is a big deal." He replaced the book in its padded envelope, and put his hand on my thigh. "The pizza can wait," he said.

2.

It would be impossible to make sense of what happened to Charlie without talking about the *Erotonomicon,* so I am going to quote from it rather extensively here. Its story begins in 1925, when H. P. Lovecraft was living in New York:

Feby 2, 1925

Perform'd 3 times tonight ye YOGGE-SOTHOTHE
ritual, ceasing onlie when my Forces were entirely us'd.
Thought the while of *Belknapius,* with Longing.

In a footnote, L. C. Spinks helpfully observes that Lovecraft is writing in eighteenth-century English. He learned it from old volumes of Pope and Dryden and so on, which he found in his grandfather's attic as a child. At the same time, Spinks points out, this is the language of Joseph Curwen, the evil magus from *The Case of Charles Dexter Ward.* Was the diary written in the voice of Lovecraft's evil—but experienced—self? Or was the language a reminder of his happy childhood? Anyway, Spinks noted, all the sex acts were described in code.

Yogge-Sothothe is a being from Lovecraft's fiction: a collection of glowing spheres which is "the key and guardian of the gate" to the realms beyond the cosmos. It was also Lovecraft's word for masturbation, as I could probably have guessed.

As for *Belknapius,* a second footnote explains that Lovecraft was referring to Frank Belknap Long (1901–1994), a young writer who lived in New York. When Lovecraft moved to the city, he and Long became inseparable; they ate together, argued politics, shopped for books, took long walks at night—and all the while, the *Erotonomicon* revealed, Lovecraft longed for Long. This, Spinks wrote, was why he married Sonia and moved to New York, to be near his beloved Belknapius. But Long did not return Lovecraft's affections, so he looked elsewhere:

Feby 24

Down at ye Dockes againe this night, seeking Subjects
for ye Worke. No Shippe was in, so I tried y^e *Columbia-Streete,* where at length I found a Youth of Sullen & Poxy
Mien. In a Vile Shack in y^e *Warren-Streete* (aptly named!)
we tried a Lesser Summoning, but nothing Came. I was
Apologetick, & said great Fatigue must have caused my
Magicks to Faile, but the Boy was Unmov'd, saying that
not all Calls are Met with an Answer. *John Dee* himself
must from time to time have dropt a Syllable, and so
drawn a Blank. He beseech'd me to returne when my
Force was greater, and I said I surely would, tho' on
Reflection I think it best Not. The boy reek'd of *Tobacco,*
a smell that pleases me not, and which has oft and againe
hinder'd my Contact with y^e Outer Spheres.
   Y^e coste: $2.25.

Again a footnote. Sonia left New York at the end of 1924, to take a job at a department store in Cleveland; and Lovecraft moved into a board-inghouse on Clinton Street, in Brooklyn Heights. He lived on canned spaghetti and wrote nothing except increasingly outraged letters to his aunt Lillian in Providence. In one of them, Spinks says, he complained that a Syrian man lived next door, and "played childish and whining monotones on a strange bagpipe which made me dream ghoulish and indescribable things." Well, that's Brooklyn.

Unfortunately for Lovecraft, things only got worse:

Y^e 25 of May, 1925

A calamitous Day. Sought in ye Red Hooke a Body for y^e
Worke, and, chancing on a young Negro idling by the
Harbor, I brought him to my Chambers in *Clinton-Streete*. With a bottle of *Canadian Gin* which I hadde
from *Crane,* I induced him to perform the *Ablo* Ritual,
after the whiche he fell asleep, or seemed to, on my Cot.
Thinking to do the III. Ritual of the *Liber-Damnatus*
with him when he awoke, I settl'd to write severall
Letters I had for a long time ow'd. Then, damme, I must
have drows'd, for the next I knew, the Boy had vanish'd,
and with him, all my Suits except the thin blue, the
Flatbush Overcoat I had from Sonia, and *Samuelus's*
Radio, which he had entrusted to my Safe-Keeping. How
shall any of it be replac'd? If I could find the Boy, I'd
wring his Necke, and do *Ablo* again on his lifeless Forme.
    Y^e Coste: $4.00, 1 btl of Gin, and nearly all I own'd.

The footnote identifies *Crane* as Hart Crane (1899–1932), the Ameri-can poet, whom Lovecraft met through their mutual friend Samuel

Loveman, aka *Samuelus*. Crane was an alcoholic, and it's not surprising that he had bottles of gin to spare, even in the middle of Prohibition. The Ablo Ritual, according to Spinks, was another of Lovecraft's code words for sexual acts—in this case, probably oral sex. Spinks further remarks that the theft of Lovecraft's clothes was a turning point in his decline. By the end of 1925, he was writing things like:

> It is not good for a proud, light-skinned Nordic to be cast
> away alone amongst squat, squint-eyed jabberers with
> coarse ways & alien emotions whom his deepest cell-
> tissue hates & loathes as the mammal hates & loathes
> the reptile . . . Experience has taught the remnants of the
> American people what they never thought of when the
> first idealists opened the gates to scum.

I diagnosed psychosis; Charlie heard the true voice of the white American soul. Spinks was more charitable. It all came back, he said, to the Ablo Ritual with the Negro boy. "An encounter that could have put Lovecraft thirty years ahead of his time, morally speaking, became, in the weird logic of his imagination, a source of horror. But at the root of it was an act of love." Given that the *Erotonomicon* was published in 1952, I think Spinks overestimated the tolerance of his own era, but I'm not going to press the point.

Lovecraft went back to Providence in March 1926. His diary recorded no sexual encounters until the fall, when the Yogge-Sothothe ritual returned, followed almost immediately by an unconsummated meeting with a "young *Portugee* boy, no more than X or XI" in an alley off South Main Street. Spinks speculated that this might have been connected to the publication of Lovecraft's story "The Call of Cthulhu" in *Weird Tales*. "Success," he wrote, "posed as much of a threat to Lovecraft's image of himself as a reclusive New England gentleman as did sex itself." He could live without sex for months at a time, but when a crisis occurred—a story accepted, a story rejected, a visit from an out-of-town friend—he'd wind from South Main Street to South Water, "searching out the docks where the bay and sound steamers still touched," looking, in this "maelstrom of tottering houses, broken transoms, bubbling steps, twisted balustrades, swarthy faces, and nameless odours," for a companion with whom to do Ablo, or *Borellus*'s Ritual, or *Zaristnatmik*'s Ebony Boxe. Always with a boy or a young man, frequently of another ethnicity or race. Then he met Robert H. Barlow.

3.

Barlow was born in Kansas City, Missouri, and grew up on military bases in Kansas and Georgia. In 1932, his father, Lieutenant Colonel Everett D. Barlow, was discharged from the army for medical reasons, which probably had to do with his "delusions of having to defend his home against a mysterious Them," as one of Lovecraft's biographers put it. He moved his family to a house outside DeLand, Florida, about three miles from the nearest neighbors. Here Barlow played piano, raised rabbits, shot snakes, painted, drew, and collected weird fiction. In one of his reminiscences, he noted that, "I had no friends nor studies except in a sphere bound together by the U.S. mails and the magazines of fantastic stories for which Lovecraft wrote"; but through their correspondence, he and Lovecraft became friends. He asked for Lovecraft's autograph and sent news about High and Jack, his cats. He offered to type Lovecraft's manuscripts. He wrote stories and mailed them to Lovecraft, who returned them with enthusiastic comments. In the spring of 1934, Barlow invited Lovecraft to visit him in Florida, and Lovecraft went. He stayed with Robert and his mother (his father was visiting relatives in the North, and his brother Wayne was away at West Point) from May 2 to June 21. This is what the *Erotonomicon* had to say about his trip:

De Land
May 4, 1934

Ye gods, but the boy is young!* He is younger than
Galpinus† was when I met him in Cleveland. He is
slimmer, too, and seems to be *watching* me, as though
he were waiting for me to do something—drop my bag,
crow like a rooster, turn into a bat. I shall have to be
careful. Fortunately there was a youth at the *Arragon*‡
who knew what I wanted, the little adept, as soon as I
arrived. No sooner had I got my hat off and my
stationery unpacked then he was scratching at the door,
insinuating that he knew certain rituals which would
turn even the oldest flesh to stone. For $1.25—how they
are cheap down here! no morals, I suppose, to pay the
price of—I had an Ablo and *two* Nether Gulfs.§ That
showed him what old flesh can do! At least when it is
warmed by the Florida sun . . . The imp limped out
round-eyed, and offered to return in the morning with
another of his brotherhood. I was sorry to inform him
that I would be on the De Land bus before the sun came
up. Still, with his memory I may attempt to summon up
somewhat—only where? There is no privacy in this
house; though Bobby's bedroom and mine are separated
by a hall at one end and the upstairs landing at the other,

---

* Thankfully, Lovecraft had abandoned the eighteenth-century style by this point in the *Eroto-nomicon*. This footnote, by the way, is mine. Spinks's was much longer. I'm borrowing his form so as not to interrupt the flow of the text.

† Alfred Galpin (1901–1983), whom Lovecraft met in the summer of 1922. Galpin went on to become a composer and a professor of musicology at the University of Wisconsin.

‡ The Arragon Hotel, in Jacksonville, Florida, where Lovecraft had stayed on a previous trip, in 1931.

§ Active anal sex? Lovecraft refers to that act elsewhere as "the Outer Spheres," but, confusingly, he also uses this second term to mean orgasm.

he is liable to burst in at any time. Meanwhile his mother snores in the big bedroom downstairs. Possibly the shed by the lake will suit my purposes—if I can convince Bobby to leave me there by myself.

May 8

Bobby and I were in Yoh-Vombis[*] this afternoon, looking through his run of *The Fantasy Fan*,[†] when I could help myself no longer, and asked whether there might be a secret panel in the back of *this* closet which led to *another* closet, where he kept the truly accursed volumes of his collection. He professed not to understand what I meant: was I looking for something by Charles Fort?[‡] Yet I thought that in the back of his eyes—which are pale brown, by the way, and much magnified by his glasses—I saw some tremor of interest. "Nay," said I, "I was thinking of *The Picture of Dorian Gray*, or something of that ilk." Bobby was perplexed: "By Wilde? I don't believe . . . that is, I don't know who has forbidden it." "'Twas only a joke," I said. "Your old Grandpa has odd humors, sometimes." I am afraid that I went too far.

---

[*] This was the name Barlow gave to the closet where he kept his collection of weird fiction and poetry. It strikes me as sad that this material was literally housed in a closet. The name "Yoh-Vombis" comes from the Clark Ashton Smith story "The Vaults of Yoh-Vombis," which I haven't read.

[†] A popular fan magazine, published monthly from September 1933 through February 1935.

[‡] Charles Hoy Fort (1874–1932) was the author of *The Book of the Damned*, a compilation of phenomena, many of which were reported in scientific journals, but which science was utterly unable to explain. Lovecraft didn't care for Fort's work, but Charlie did. A copy of *The Complete Books of Charles Fort* still stands on my bookcase. On its creased cover, a collage of fish raining down on a Victorian street.

May 11

Fie on the fidelity of Ghu!* Today Bobby told me he
was going blueberry-picking with Johnston,† the
housekeeper's son, an athletic young man who stalks
around the Barlovian estate with a needless machete—
needless for the grounds, but handy when it comes to
protecting his "turf" from elderly visitors. I insisted on
going with them, despite Bobby's warning that the trip
would be muddy, difficult & possibly unpleasant on
account of the mosquitoes, snakes, &c. All those things
proved true, & the mosquitoes in particular were even
worse than Bobby made 'em out to be, but the Old
Gentleman persisted, driven half-mad by the thought of
what Johnston might get up to with Bobby if they were
left alone in a blueberry-patch. We spent a wretched
afternoon trekking through the swamp & jungle, Bobby
darting ahead, just a leg visible, a bit of shirt, nothing at
all, and Johnston, the brute, asking over & over if he
could give me a hand. Both of them were visibly
displeased by my company. And the worst was still to
come: when we were almost back to Dunrovin,‡ I fell into
a stream, and lost nearly all the berries I had painfully
gathered! I apologized 'midst scowls and grumblings and
was glad to be back in the semi-privacy of my room. Now
it is night, and Florida moths are burning themselves up
in my lamp—white moths which can lose a wing and
spiral somehow back into the croaking darkness.

---

* A reference to Barlow's short story "The Fidelity of Ghu," which was, at that point, unpublished.
† Charles Blackburn Johnston (1897–?), a painter.
‡ The name Lieutenant Colonel Barlow gave to his Florida house.

May 12

Remorseful, possibly, anent the outcome of our berry-
picking expedition, Bobby drove me to St. Augustine,
two hours distant. We forewent the old town, which I
had seen when I visited Canevinus,* and made straight
for the chapel of Nuestra Señora de la Leche—where,
according to improbable legend, the Catholics said their
first Mass in the New World. Indisputably true however
were the tombstones in the small graveyard next to the
chapel, which belonged to young people dead of the
plague a hundred years earlier. We sat on a stone bench
just beyond the cemetery railing and imagined what kind
of story might be told about these wretches—young
men & women dropping dead, covered in foul sores,
pustules, &c. Would a ghoul relish such meat? What is
meant, precisely, by a *ghoulish appetite*—do ghouls
prefer the fair? Bobby threw at me an oft-quoted line of
Poe's, *viz.,* that there is nothing more poetic than a
beautiful dead woman, and asked if I agreed. "A dead
one more than a live one," I said, in jest. "But Beauty,"
said Barlow, "do ghouls care for Beauty?"

 The Old Gentleman hesitated, as if he'd heard a
knocking on some long-rusted door . . . a door that *did
not lead to the outside, but to the crypt.* "I believe they do,"
he said. No one was present to see us. Bobby's eyes
grew to fantastic dimensions as his face approached the
surprised, suntanned face of an Old Gentleman who had

---

* Lovecraft's nickname for Henry S. Whitehead (1882–1932), Episcopal clergyman and author of
weird fiction. He lived in Dunedin, Florida, on the Gulf Coast.

for many years believed his kissing days to be over. Iä! Deesmess! Jeshet! BONEDOSEFEDUVEMA! ENTTEMOSS! We rose from the bench and followed a white shell-shard path into the woods.

May 13, Hour of the Goat

Rose late. Bobby had already gone out—to De Land to buy provisions, at his mother's request. He returned just before sunset and suggested we take the rowboat out, and I gladly acquiesced. We rowed to the far shore of the lake, where we moored the boat by a stand of Northern oak. There we found a dead heron, trapped under a branch in the lakeside mud. "Ugh," Bobby said, "what a stink." He asked me to help him carry it into the woods, but I could not bring myself to touch it. With a further grunt Bobby heaved it out of the muck himself, and, holding the dead thing close to his chest, carried it out of sight. When he returned to the boat I apologized for my cowardice. "It's unbecoming, I know," I said. "A gentleman should be the equal of every situation." "Even this one?" Bobby asked, and brought his face close to mine. "Halt," said the Old Gent, "desist!" "Why?" Bobby asked. The Old Gent took a moment to collect his thoughts. Why, indeed? Because the act is naturally repugnant to the overwhelming bulk of mankind— because it is merely cheap unrestraint, and therefore aesthetically ignominious—because sex is a prosaic mechanism, an aspect of purely animal nature, & separated from such things as intellect & beauty . . . Bobby interrupted me, & with fevered seriousness he placed his hand on the bony knee of the Gentleman, which had not been touched in that way since the year MDCCCCXXV, and not pleasurably, then. An indescribable chill penetrated my frame as he spoke in a low but sonorous voice: "Howard," he said, "you and I are going to *die*. We will be as dead as that heron. Why shouldn't we do what we want, if we enjoy it, and don't hurt anybody?" "Pleasure has many forms," replied the Gent, "and *this* is certainly not the highest of them . . ." "Reason all you like, Agrippa," he said, "but I don't see why the one form should exclude the other." Bobby touched my lips with his. "Why, but, but," sputtered the Gent, while Bobby giggled at his apoplectic tediousness and general mustiness of moral character. Then, with an interior thunderclap, Reason saw—there was no reason. Why in Pegāna's* name should we not enjoy our bodies—any less than we curry our horses, or nourish our slaves? Why not enjoy—*all?* With sudden vigor I rowed us into the center of the lake, where I made the boat go around in circles. Bobby giggled; he cackled; we both laughed like the madmen we had become. Mad with Reason! Drunk on Scientifickal Explanation! The sun set; grackles squawked and night-herons barked in the reeds. After what seemed like hours, Bobby wondered aloud if his mother would be looking for us. "I don't care," said the Gent with new-found brashness. "I am rowing until someone reproves me!" True to my word, I went on rowing until Mrs. Barlow came to the edge of the lake and hollered that we young 'uns had had

---

* A reference to Lord Dunsany's collection of fantastical short stories *The Gods of Pegāna* (1905).

enough fun for the day, and it was time to come in
and eat.

The *Erotonomicon* chronicled furtive kissing and cuddling in Barlow's bed and the closet Yoh-Vombis, where they "did Ablo" for the first
time, and Lovecraft "probed ye Outer Spheres" with "magickall Ease"—
the eighteenth-century dialect kept creeping in. Possibly it was a sign of
Lovecraft's discomfort with what was taking place, although at no point
after this did he suggest that he and Barlow should stop having sex. His
chief concern, and Barlow's, was the return of the Colonel, whose mental health had become even more precarious during his trip north. Many
was the night, Barlow reported, when his father had sat with a shotgun
on the porch, waiting for the squat, shadowy figures he had first spied in
the Philippines to emerge from the forest and try to slit his throat. What
would he do if he learned that his son was Lovecraft's lover?

Curiously, neither Barlow nor Lovecraft seemed worried that Barlow's mother would catch them—she may have had other things on her
mind. Charles Blackburn Johnston, the painter, was more observant:

June 4

Came down from an *Ablo*—my third in twenty-four
hours!—& found Johnston scowling in the sitting room.
"Where's Bobby?" he wants to know. "Sleeping," says I.
"At least I assume he is. We were up late, and there's a note
on his door, requesting that he not be disturbed." "We
were going to drive over to Daytona Beach," Johnston
said. "Don't suppose that would interest you. *You* don't
like to swim." Unruffled, I admitted that I do not enjoy the
sea. "Although I've had some very amusing moments by
the shore," I said. "What were you doing last night?"

Johnston asked, the villain. "Bookbinding," I said. "Bobby
shot a snake, and we've been using its skin to make
books." This was the literal—though hardly complete—
truth, and Johnston could find no way to refute it. "Tell
him I'm leaving at noon," he said, "and I'll have a dozen
bottles of cold beer in the trunk." I assured him that the
message would be relayed. Johnston went away, and I
tiptoed upstairs and scratched at Bobby's door. *"Entrez,"*
he said. He was sitting cross-legged on his bed, entirely
naked, with a glass of water in one hand and a copy of
Merritt's *The Metal Monster** in the other. "My dear
Mr. Carter," he said, "Have you got your *Silver Key?*"†

Johnston appears only once more in the *Erotonomicon*. Lovecraft's attention was entirely focused on Barlow: they went to Silver Springs,
where Barlow

proposed we try a *joint* Yogge-Sothothe—in a glass-
bottomed boat! We were on the far side of a green-tufted
island, out of sight of our fellow pleasure-seekers, but,
"Ye Gods," I exclaim'd, "what if we are observ'd from
Below?" "'From Below' would make a good title for a
story," quipped Bobby. I told him not to be foolish.

Despite Lovecraft's squeamishness, the two of them *did* write a
satirical story, "The Battle That Ended the Century," a spoof of their
friends in fandom. According to the *Erotonomicon,* it was composed the

---

* A novel by Abraham Merritt (1884–1943), serialized in *Argosy All-Story Weekly* in 1920.

† The reference is to Lovecraft's stories "The Silver Key" (1926) and "Through the Gates of the Silver Key" (cowritten with E. Hoffmann Price in 1932–1933). The main character in both stories is Randolph Carter, who seems to have been a kind of alter ego for Lovecraft.

way Valmont wrote his famous letter in *Les Liaisons dangereuses:* with Barlow's typewriter balanced on Lovecraft's naked back. Then they parted. The Colonel would be returning soon, and Barlow's mother advised Lovecraft to be gone before he came home. Barlow, too, seemed to have lost his enthusiasm for the Silver Key and Nether Gulf; he went off alone to shoot snakes in the forest, or rowed alone to the middle of the lake and wrote in *his* diary.

On June 21, 1934, Lovecraft took the bus from DeLand to St. Augustine, where he stayed at the Hotel Rio Vista, two blocks from the Florida School for the Deaf and Blind. The *Erotonomicon* records his reaction to the sudden separation:

> . . . did *Yogge-Sothothe* in my room, then I felt a wave of terror, as though I had stepp'd into a great gray-green Ocean, and the combers were rolling me in their troughs. Your Old Gentleman has been a solitary character for much of his life, but, Pegāna! I have never until now known what it is like to be *alone!!!*

Lovecraft consoled himself with familiar things:

> June 28

> Return'd to the *Arragon.* I fear'd the *Kid* who came to me at my last Visit would be Absent, & trembl'd somewhat at the Knees when I saw him pushing a Mop thro' the Lobby. This time he came unask'd. He sooth'd the Old Gentleman, who had fallen into a Melancholy Way. Just before daybreak we visited yᵉ Outer Spheres. He left my room soone after, but there lingers in the bed an Odour, as of Cinammon. Yᵉ Coste: *nil!!*

4.

Lovecraft saw Barlow again at the end of December, when they met in New York. Lovecraft was visiting friends, and it wasn't until the early hours of the thirty-first that he and Barlow were alone:

> . . . but when *finally* Bobby shuts the flimsy door of his
> hotel room, he goes to his satchel and pulls from it a
> mess of paper! "Howard," he says, "I've written another
> story. Will you read it?" I sat down at the desk, sighing,
> with pencil in hand. Well! Three hours passed before
> Grandpa had finished improving Bobby's mediocre tale
> of the last man on an arid world—and by then the lad
> had fallen asleep. I added to the end of the story a few
> heartfelt sentences about the futility of human endeavor,
> by way of reproach.

The incident had no ill effect on their friendship. In June 1935, Lovecraft visited Barlow again in Cassia, the village where Dunrovin was situated, after what had become a customary stop in Jacksonville. This time Barlow's father was home, and Lovecraft notes with amused relief that they had no reason to fear him:

Dunrovin

June 10, Year of the Lizard

The Colonel came out of his room at dinnertime, &
professed to be very pleased to meet the Rhode-Island
Gentleman about whom his son had been raving all year.
Physically he and Bobby are almost of different species—
the Colonel is stout, big-shouldered, worn, obviously,
with time and care, & sports a mustache of 1912 vintage.
He resembles his son chiefly about the eyes, which are
narrow and suspicious. For some time we kept the
conversation to the weather, the proliferation of rats in
the trees—"strange, short-tailed rats," the Colonel said,
suggesting an inclination to the weird!—and the
excellence of Mrs. Barlow's cooking. However as the
meal drew to a close I ventured to ask about the
Colonel's health. "Sir," he said, "if I may speak freely, it is
poor. I can read the signs as well as any man—they tell
me I will die on October seventh." Poor fellow! I think he
really believes it. However, Mrs. Barlow saved the
evening from gloom with a bottle of brandy, of which,
needless to say, the Colonel was the only partaker. In a
quarter of an hour he and I were animatedly discussing
Chancellor Hitler's chances of saving Germany from
economic collapse; twenty minutes after that we were
singing "In Enterprise of Martial Kind."* Sad, curious
man! Bobby looked sour. Said he would not do Ablo nor
anything else in the house—we must find a place
outdoors.

---

* From Gilbert and Sullivan's operetta *The Gondoliers* (1889).

Lovecraft and Barlow spent the summer of 1935 building a cabin on the far shore of the lake, by the stand of oak trees they had visited the summer before: the Druid-Grove, Lovecraft called it. They made love in the grass, in the cabin, on the lake, at night, after Barlow's parents had gone to bed. It was an idyll, an almost unbelievable suspension both of Lovecraft's self-loathing and of the world's judgment of his behavior. "I am for the time being really alive & in good health & spirits," he wrote to his aunt Lillian. "The companionship of youth & artistic taste is what keeps one going!" On June 17, Lovecraft and Barlow visited Black Water Creek, three miles from Dunrovin:

> It is hard to convey the effect of a scene like this . . . The black, silent glassy river with its cryptic bends—the monstrously tall cypresses with their festoons of moss— the twisted roots clawing at the water—the ghastly, leaning palms—the black, dank earth . . . everything to suggest some exotic world of fantasy . . . We did the Ebony Boxe on the riverbank, then lay on our backs & watched menacing clouds skulk from treetop to treetop. Bobby proposed that we collaborate on a story set in this place, & I readily agreed. We decided that it will be about a degenerate family of swamp-dwellers, who, whilst hunting possum or some such, stumble upon a ruined temple where far more ancient *and far more degenerate* beings dwell . . .

Even better, on July 9, the Barlows invited Lovecraft to stay past the summer's end:

> The whole family is in favor of the Gent's staying on. Mrs. Barlow made a vague, timid suggestion that I could

help Bobby prepare for college, which he will attend next year. A flattering overstatement of the Gent's academical abilities, I am afraid! But they were all so kind & insistent that I said I would give the proposition careful thought—it would mean separation from my books & files & familiar home things. In the meantime, Bobby asked if I would help carry his printing press out to the cabin. It was a warm day even by the Gent's standards, & we were both dripping by the time we had the press in place beside Bobby's desk. "Now there's hardly room for a man to stretch out in here," I said, "you've got it as snug as the cabin of a ship." "I'll bet there is, though," Bobby said. He indicated a spot on the new-cut plank floor. We made an Elder Sign* & promptly fell asleep.

The invitation was all the more tempting because Lovecraft hated the cold. What was more: in Florida, he would have Barlow's company and the Colonel's, too. They knew a lot of the same songs. On the other side of the scale was Lovecraft's attachment to Providence, the city where he had been born and where his deepest attachments lay. "I *am* Providence," he had written to his aunt—but he wrote that when he lived in New York. Now he was in a place that made him happy. Could there be a Florida Lovecraft? What would that person be like?

---

* Spinks notes that in Lovecraft's novella *The Shadow over Innsmouth* (1931), the author described the Elder Sign as "somethin' . . . like what ye call a swastika"; but he drew it elsewhere as a single line with shorter lines branching off, like a bare tree. So, mutual oral sex? Why am I guessing at this? Maybe it's just that, after what happened to Charlie, I want to pin everything down.

July 11

I have accepted Bobby's invitation. Can it be? Is the Old
Gentleman to be forever divorced from his native land?
"It isn't forever," Bobby points out, "and besides, you're
not so old." Yet the decision cost me sleepless nights.
I do not want to repeat the ghastly rashness & idiocy
of 1924!* I must be sure I can *belong* here, which means, I
think, not being *useless* or *idle.* I am like a man who,
having once fallen into quicksand, watches every small
variation of the ground for signs that he is about to sink
again. "But Howard," Bobby says, "if you knew
everything that would happen, how could it be an
adventure?" Ablo, Aklo,† rest. Nether Gulfs. Rest.

With this decision, a remarkable transformation occurs. Its most
visible sign is that Lovecraft starts eating fish. In the third week of July
alone, he tries mackerel, flounder, swordfish, and marlin, and asks Barlow's bemused mother if he can have them each again, so he can decide which is most delicious. He puts on weight. Barlow drives him to
DeLand to buy new collars—but instead he buys new shirts, of the
"short-sleeved button-down variety." He reads the Colonel's copy of
the *West Volusia Beacon,* which never used to interest him. Even more
surprisingly, he visits the West Volusia Historical Society, where he ap-
plies for a job as a "front-desk man." In New York, in the middle of the
Roaring Twenties, Lovecraft could not find work; here, in DeLand,
where he is a Yankee outsider with no résumé and no references other

---

* I.e., the year Lovecraft moved to New York City.
† Performing oral sex, presumably, rather than receiving it.

than the seventeen-year-old Barlow and his deranged father, he gets the job right away.

July 24, 1935

This *morning*—ahem—saw Grandpa at his post in De Land, fitted out in his freshly ironed shirt and worn but newly polished wing-tips! Bobby, who had been loitering in the coffee shop on Main St., came in around eleven. "I wonder if you can help me," he said. "I'm looking for something that used to be here a long time ago." "That's our business," I said helpfully. "What was this thing called?" "I believe its name was *Howard*," he said, giggling. "Of course," I said. "The Old Howard, it's called around here. Built by the Spaniards in 1638, it stood until just last year, when a hurricane brought it down. You'll find the ruins about twenty miles down the De Land-Eustis Highway." "What was it?" Bobby asked. "Some kind of fortress?" "No one knows," I said. "Its construction was highly peculiar. For one thing, it had no doors." "No doors? Then how did people get in?" "Either they were born there," I said, "or they didn't get in at all." With that I shooed him out, but he returned at five o'clock to drive me home. He proposed a celebratory *Borellus,* but I declined—wanted to stretch my legs before it was time for supper.

Lovecraft gave half of his first paycheck to the Barlows, and with the other half, he bought a radio. He listened to the news and discovered in himself a strange fascination for the game of "Base-Ball."

He planned to buy a car and asked Barlow to give him a driving lesson. Then:

July 30, 1935

The Jacksonville Kid has return'd. He came to the
Historical Society this afternoon, & profess'd himself
much Surpris'd to find me there. He was looking, he
said, for Documents pertaining to a certain Ancestor who
had been cruelly enslav'd by the *Spanish,* & work'd to
Death at the *De Leon* Sugar Mill.* I said, I was not sure
any Documents surviv'd from that Era, but any such as
we hadde would be in the Records Room. Normally it
was closed to the Publick, but as we had no other
Custom I thought he might enter, provided he were
Accompanied. Outer Spheres—*quietly.* Then I hurried
him out, before he could be Seene.

August 3

Iä Shub-Niggurath, the Black Goat of the Woods With a
Thousand Young! Iä Nyarlathotep, the Messenger, and
Yog-Sothoth, the Opener of the Way!! The Old Gent is
driving!!! At a secluded spot by the side of the De Land-
Eustis Highway: Ablo 1x. "This," Bobby said, "is why we
have cars." Against my will, I thought of Jacksonville—
only 2 hours distant, with an automobile.

---

* In De Leon Springs, about ten miles northeast of DeLand. According to Charlie, it is now a pancake restaurant.

August 4

In the afternoon Bobby and I made a return excursion to Black Water Creek. Bobby wanted to do the Box again, but the Old Gent could not summon up the strength for it, so we settled for the Aklo Password, which I was glad enough to give him. Then, as on our first visit, we lay back on the moss, & listened to mournful birds, which sounded like loons, tho' I wouldn't have looked for 'em in Florida so early in the year. "Howard," Bobby said, "are we ever going to write that story?" I said that *he* should write it, & I will revise it when he's done, though he hardly needs my corrections—the lad has come a long way since "Till A' the Seas."* "But don't you want to write it yourself?" he asked. "It's so much your kind of story." I informed him that the Old Gent may take a break from weird stories for a spell—they were never aught to me but an amateur pursuit, and I am done with amateurism for the time being. I kidded him about wasting time on stories when he could be studying for M.I.T., or Brown, until he rolled onto his side and started throwing pebbles into the water. "Careful, or you'll wake something," I said. "I wish," Bobby said, petulantly.

August 6

The Jacksonville Kid came in again. I told him to come back at the end of the day, when he could impersonate a janitor, & I could tell the Barlows I was working late.

---

* This was the story Lovecraft revised in Barlow's hotel room on December 31, 1934.

"I'm still looking for them documents," he said. I laughed and told him we'd turn the place upside-down until we found 'em. Ablo—no documents. Promised that I will come up to Jacksonville as soon as I am confident driving on the highway. But I cannot be seen with him too much, & not only on account of the color of his skin.

August 15

Return'd from Jacksonville to find Dunrovin cast into Gloom. Twas Mrs. *Barlow* who told me what had occurr'd: just an hour after I drove off, she heard a Frightful Cry from Bobby's room, & ran up to see what the Matter was. "Nothing," said he, in a trembling voice. "I was merely rehearsing for a play." Hearing no further Shrieks, she return'd downstairs, & did not think to look in on her Sonne until Evening, when she went up againe to inquire if he would eat. Getting no Reply, she try'd the Door, & found it lock'd. *Johnston* was summoned from his Mother's House, where he chanced to be stopping, & he broke it downe—& found *Bobby* on his Bedde, his Wrists considerably bloodied. There was a moment of great Feare, & the Doctor was summon'd from *De Land*, but as it transpir'd his Woundes were mere superficiall Cuts, that had produc'd much Blood, but no real Harm. Bobby claim'd it was all for his Play, a Mode, however extream, of assuming a Character. The *Doctor Medicus* advis'd Mrs. Barlow that he should be seen by an Alienist, & quit the scene. Bobby, much embarrassed by all the Commotion, excus'd himself, & went to his Cabin, having first Promis'd to doe himself no further Injurie. &

there I found him, supine on the floor by his Press, &
holding by his side a certain Notebook, property of
Mr. *Lovecraft*, of the *Rhode-Island & Providence Plantations.*
Hearing me come in, he op'd his Eyes, and murmur'd,
"You thought my story was *mediocre?*"

The next day, Barlow was contrite. He had overreacted, he said. He never wanted, or imagined that he had, Lovecraft's love exclusively to himself. What he wanted was honesty. Now that he had read the *Eroto-nomicon,* he felt that he and Howard could be better friends—that they could be real friends. But the spell which had kept Lovecraft in Florida was broken. On August 18, the Barlows drove Lovecraft to Daytona Beach, where they intended to spend a couple of weeks, probably at the advice of the psychiatrist who had seen Robert. They left Lovecraft at the bus station. As he had the year before, Lovecraft stopped in St. Augustine on his way North, and on August 20, Lovecraft's forty-fifth birthday, Barlow joined him there. Lovecraft's letters (quoted by Spinks, and verified by me) indicate that they visited an Indian burial ground "where the skeletons were preserved as they were buried," whatever that means, but there is no entry for the date in the *Eroto-nomicon.* Lovecraft left St. Augustine on the twenty-first and traveled directly to Savannah, where he admired the old buildings, charmingly arranged around a grid of little parks.

5.

Lovecraft and Barlow saw each other for the last time when Barlow visited Providence in the summer of 1936. He stayed in a boarding-house behind the apartment Lovecraft shared with his aunt, at 66 College Street, a situation which Lovecraft found trying:

> July 31
>
> Bobby scratched at the door shortly after A E P G* had gone to bed. Wanted to talk about his novel,† which I find unpromising. "Why," I asked him, "would a sane & mature artist wish to talk with a cheap & undistinguished prizefighter?" "I don't know," Bobby said archly. "Why do *you* think?" I let him know in no uncertain terms that the Grandpa who succumbed to his advances last summer is no more. A man of taste & dignity cuts that side of himself off as he ages, I said, & for an artist the responsibility is even greater, because his work will be

---

* Annie Emmeline Phillips Gamwell (1866–1941), Lovecraft's aunt.

† Barlow had begun a "monumental novel" (Lovecraft's words) in the fall of 1935. He abandoned it shortly after Lovecraft's death, and Charlie believes that he destroyed the manuscript. *Believed*.

read by many who do not know him. I advised Bobby to read *Hoxsie Sells His Acres,*[*] which is proof that the decent Anglo-Saxon spark still burns, even in the literary milieu. Bobby scoffed, & called me a hypocrite. I told him that he *must* not make a scene, & certainly not with Mrs. Gamwell sleeping just down the hall!! Threatened to throw him out bodily if he could not be calm. He retreated—wanted to be kissed—said he wouldn't have come to Providence if he'd known what a beast I had become. I had him out by 3 A.M.—at which point I returned to the ordeal of *Well Bred Speech.*[†]

However, the two soon reconciled:

Aug 1

A contrite Barlovius visited me after midnight. He had something to show me, he said: a photograph of Jules Verne on his deathbed, which he'd had duplicated from the negative at the 42nd St. Library in New York. We agreed that the old man looked quite majestic. "You see?" Bobby said. "Not everyone looks bad with a beard." "I never said anything of the sort," I replied. "It's a matter of the composition of the face—and the era in which the face finds itself. On *you,* for example, those whiskers are quite unbecoming." Bobby rubbed his mustache doubtfully. "Do you think so? I've gotten a lot of compliments on 'em." I chided him for the

---

[*] A 1934 novel in verse by the Rhode Island writer Christopher La Farge (1897–1956).
[†] A textbook by Anne Tillery Renshaw, which Lovecraft was revising.

abominable *gotten* and inwardly wondered whose
compliments he meant. "When I die—shave me," I said.
"You won't die," Bobby said. "Hypochondriacs like you
never do. You'll outlast everyone you know." He touched
my knee—I flinched. "Howard," he said, "can't we go
back to how things were?" "Impossible," said the Old
Gent. Bobby's nose twitched. He rose, & said, "In that
case, I'll be off." I saw him to the door, but at the thought
that Bobby now belonged to my *past* I lost the power to
resist him, & in a moment we had done Ablo. I felt the
warmth of it spread through my whole body, as though
he'd carried a phial of Cassia with him, & opened it in
my Providence room. Then I shooed him out, & told
him that in the future we'll have to meet in public, &
behave as friends. Yog-Sothoth'd, in memory of
encounters recent and ancient—all now equal in
non-actuality.

Aug 8

. . . on returning from the graveyard, Bobby said he felt
de Castro* had been spiteful toward him. "Is he jealous?"
Bobby asked. "Of your youth, possibly," I said. "He's
broken-down and penniless, and his wife has just died. If
you feel anything for him, feel pity." "I don't want to get
old," Bobby said. I told him he would feel differently
when he was Grandpa's age. "*If* I reach your advanced

---

* Adolphe de Castro (1859–1959), writer and translator. De Castro, Lovecraft, and Barlow had
visited St. John's Churchyard, in Providence, and composed acrostic poems on the name Edgar
Allan Poe, who had walked in the same graveyard ninety years earlier. In Lovecraftian circles,
Charlie said, this episode is known as the "Poe-session."

age," Bobby said. "Stop being morbid," I said. He laughed. "Howard Phillips Lovecraft has told me not to be morbid!" "Ssh," I said, "you're making too much noise. And if you think I am morbid, you haven't understood me at all. I merely think that I, we, all of us, are insignificant, from the cosmic point of view." "In which case . . ." Bobby said, and put on his sly-kitten face, which his whiskers only accentuated. The imp was impossible to resist. We tiptoed up the stairs to my bed-study-library, & did the Cryptic Seal of Ulthar. Afterward Bobby asked, "Howard, do you love me?" "Yes," I said. The Old Gent would have been lying if he said any different. Then in jest I took hold of Bobby's pinky finger and said, "Umph."

On August 15, Lovecraft and Barlow visited Newport. On the twentieth, Lovecraft's forty-sixth and final birthday, they went to Salem and Marblehead. Lovecraft had written about both towns in his stories (Salem was "Arkham," and Marblehead "Kingsport"); Marblehead in particular had made a lasting impression on him when he first went there, in 1922. Years later, he was still talking about the trip as "the high tide of my life," the one moment when he felt united with his environment, rather than alien to it. The return visit with Barlow was stimulating:

> Marblehead!! The gabled roofs, the fort overlooking the harbor, everything just as it was the first time I came here—the place does not change. It is the sole survival into the present of the untainted Anglo-Saxon world to which my soul and imagination belong. We walked down to Fort Sewall, where we stood a while, gazing at

the Salem Sound, & imagining that we were merchant princes, watching for our ships laden with cotton & molasses. I'd just begun to think of a story—history of a *New-England* family which passes on some unspeakable taint from generation to generation—when Bobby, whose mind was apparently running on a parallel track, asked, "What if my artist wanted to talk to the sea?" "I imagine he'd collect seashells," I said, irritated at having my thought broken off. "Or what," Bobby said, with characteristic agility, "if the sea wanted to talk to *him?*" "That's interesting," I said, "but the sea is too vague. It would have to be something *in* the sea, for the tale to have interest." "Figures swimming in the sea." "Figures gesturing from the waves," I suggested, "beckoning, perhaps." "And the artist must try to understand their meaning," Bobby said. "It's certainly better than your prizefighter," I said. Just then, as if to invite our thoughts further down this path, a harbor seal broke the surface of the shining water. We entertained ourselves with speculation as to what it might be trying to say, & decided it was telling us we'd stared at the ocean long enough, & should wander on in search of nourishment.

Aug 20, *later*

Ablo, Aklo, Outer Spheres. Bobby is asleep. I must write quietly—don't want him to find this notebook again!!

From this episode, Spinks wrote, came Lovecraft and Barlow's final collaboration, a short story called "The Night Ocean." It is about an artist who visits a resort town called Ellston Beach at summer's end to "rest a weary mind." He has been working on his entry for a mural competition; now it's done and he wants a change of scene. At first he finds Ellston Beach pleasant: the house he rents is less than a mile from town, but because it's around a bend in the coast, it feels secluded. He swims in the ocean, walks on the beach, and goes out for dinner. He finds the curio shops and "falsely regal theater-fronts" of Ellston Beach vaguely annoying, and returns to his cottage. The summer ends. The first mists of fall cover the sky, and the town empties out. The artist eats dinner in a hurry; for some reason he's afraid to be outside after dark. He mentions that there have been drownings at the beach—even swimmers "of a skill beyond the average" have been lost, and their strangely mangled bodies washed up onshore days later. No one thinks too much about this. Then one day the artist is out walking, and he's caught in a rainstorm. Something about the sky and the cliffs and the beach reminds him of a story he read as a child, about a princess who falls in love with, or is loved by, a sea king, but the memory slips away. He goes back to his cabin and puts on dry clothes, and then, while he stands at the window, watching the rain, he sees figures on the beach which were not there before. He goes out and gestures at them (so the idea of gesturing was reversed, Spinks noted), and they look at him, "as if they awaited some other action." But the artist doesn't know what to do, and eventually the figures vanish back into the sea.

The next morning, on his way to the village, the artist finds a hand tangled in some seaweed—at least it looks like a hand. It has fingers. He doesn't touch it. Days pass, in which the artist is troubled by "a perception of the brief hideousness and underlying filth of life," and meanwhile the ocean gets colder and colder, and the sky gets darker and darker. Finally, the artist decides he's had enough of Ellston Beach; and just then he gets a telegram, informing him that he's won the mural competition. It doesn't make him happy. He stays up late on a moonlit night, smoking a cigarette and watching the ocean, and sees a figure swimming "with horrible ease," and carrying something—a man, probably—on its shoulder. Then the figure disappears back into the ocean, and the artist leaves Ellston Beach, and we never find out what the figures in the ocean were, or what they wanted. The story leaves us with a sense of the futility of even trying to understand. We will vanish from the Earth, the artist says, but the ocean will be around forever.

6.

Barlow left Providence at the beginning of September. His parents had divorced, and he went to live with his mother in Kansas City, where he enrolled in art school. In October, Lovecraft climbed Neutaconkanut Hill, from which he had a marvelous vision of Providence, "a dream of enchanted pinnacles & domes half-floating in air, & with an obscure air of mystery around them," he wrote to Barlow. A few weeks later, Lovecraft was walking in the Squantum Woods when two kittens, one gray and one tortoiseshell, came out of nowhere and followed him, like guardians. The world seemed to be full of mysterious signs.

That winter, Lovecraft complained of a "grippe" which wouldn't go away. In March 1937, his aunt took him to the Jane Brown Memorial Hospital in Providence, where he was diagnosed with nephritis and intestinal cancer. He died on March 15, having first named Barlow as his literary executor. Barlow went to Providence to collect Lovecraft's papers, and took them back to Kansas City, where he let grief overwhelm him. He dropped out of art school and moved to San Francisco. His plans to publish Lovecraft's work bore scant fruit: a single letterpress chapbook of Lovecraft's commonplace book, printed in seventy-five copies. Before long, Lovecraft's friends August Derleth and Donald Wandrei took matters into their own hands. They started a publishing company called Arkham House and put out a fat, dense volume of Lovecraft's stories. At the same time, Wandrei and Samuel Loveman (who had his own reasons for hating Barlow) spread a rumor that Barlow had stolen Lovecraft's manuscripts, and he was excommunicated from the society of Lovecraft's friends.

For the second time, Barlow considered suicide, but instead became a poet, and entered the anthropology program at UC Berkeley. He moved to Mexico City, where he taught at Mexico City College and published so many books, papers, and pamphlets on the civilization of the Aztecs that historians of Pre-Conquest Mexico still remember the 1940s as the "Barlow decade." For a time, he seemed to have found happiness; then, in the fall of 1950, one of Barlow's students threatened to expose him as a homosexual. On January 1, 1951, Barlow shut himself in his room and took twenty-six tablets of Seconal. His body was not found until the next day, or possibly the day after, because he had left a note on his door, which read, in Mayan, *Do not disturb me, I wish to sleep for a long time.* There was no funeral. The *Mexico City Collegian* ran an obituary, and the *Mexico Quarterly Review* published a memorial essay; neither mentioned that Barlow had killed himself, much less why. The only frank report of his death came from William S. Burroughs, who, by one of those coincidences which sometimes make fact as rich and as strange as fiction, was Barlow's student. "A queer Professor from K.C., Mo., head of the Anthropology dept. here at M.C.C. where I collect my $75 per month, knocked himself off a few days ago with overdose of goof balls. Vomit all over the bed. I can't see this suicide kick," Burroughs wrote in a letter to Allen Ginsberg.

Meanwhile, Lovecraft had become famous. His books sold and sold; his reputation grew, and came, as the years passed, to resemble a cult. This was thanks, in part, to Derleth and Wandrei, who fabricated the myth that Lovecraft had been an aristocratic recluse, who roamed the streets of Providence at night but otherwise had nothing to do with the world. They did not speak, or let others speak, about the less savory aspects of Lovecraft's character: his racism, his anti-Semitism. They certainly did not speak about Robert H. Barlow. Spinks mentioned all these sad facts in his footnote to the *Erotonomicon*'s brief final entry:

Nov 12

Down in yᵉ *Packet-Streete,* a Lesser Summoning with
a Boy who spoke no English. I had to explain what I
wanted from him with *Signs.* Gave him $1.15. I have no
Idea how much he Ask'd.

7.

But it was all a hoax: the *Erotonomicon* had been written by L. C. Spinks. "I can't believe it, Mar," Charlie said. "Even though I know, I still can't believe it. Where did this freak get his information?" The *Erotonomicon* was published in 1952, and the first biography of Lovecraft didn't appear until 1975. When Spinks wrote his book, Lovecraft's letters to Barlow were still uncataloged and off-limits, in the vaults of the John Hay Library, at Brown. Even if Spinks *had* read the letters, they didn't have any sex in them. "It's *so* messed up," Charlie said.

In the spring of 2009, Charlie tried to figure out how Spinks had done it, but there wasn't much to know. L. C. Spinks had been an appliance repairman by trade; in his spare time, he wrote and published a fan magazine called *Pickman's Vault,* which consisted of lists of books and magazines that Spinks wanted to buy or sell, humorous observations about life in Canada, and some clumsy attempts at macabre fiction. One issue featured fake letters from various science fiction luminaries; it earned Spinks a reputation as a prankster in the otherwise placid world of Canadian fandom, but nothing about *Pickman's Vault* made you think that its author could also have written the *Erotonomicon*. How had Spinks done his uncanny imitation of Lovecraft's prose—and of Lovecraft's life? Charlie didn't know. He did, however, find a great deal of information about what happened after the *Eroto-nomicon* was published. When you knew what to look for, he said rue-fully, it was everywhere.

To put it mildly, history did not conclude that L. C. Spinks had done Lovecraft a favor by publishing the *Erotonomicon*. The first outcry came from Lovecraft's fans, who reacted with horror and disgust to the idea that their idol had had sex with young men, some of them Negroes. Bob Tucker, the editor of the long-running fanzine *Le Zombie,* wrote, "Why did it have to be BOYS? If it was girls, I could have cut him some slack, but as it is—I want to barf. I'm going to throw my *Weird Tales* in the incinerator this afternoon, and try to forget I ever thought this creep belonged anywhere except in jail, or the nuthouse." Tucker's reaction was typical. All over the United States, fans came up with ingenious ways to dispose of Lovecraft's books: on pyres, in chasms, over the sides of ships in international waters. Meanwhile, the U.S. Postal Inspection Service declared the *Erotonomicon* obscene. The New York police raided the offices of Black Hour Books and confiscated all unsold copies of the book—or at least all the copies they could find—but the harm to Lovecraft's reputation had already been done.

No one seems to have considered the possibility that the *Erotonomi-con* was a hoax. On the contrary: fans and critics alike found evidence, which had mysteriously been overlooked until then, that H. P. Lovecraft was a homosexual. There were no female characters in his stories—or almost none! His creatures had long, slimy tentacles! Also, Lovecraft frequently used the words *nameless* and *unspeakable:* What was that, if not a sly reference to the love that dared not speak its name? "Every-thing about HPL's stories is queer," wrote Forrest Ackerman, another well-known fan, "but this diary is the only tale he ever penned that's really frightening. Who knew? It turns out the horror was *him*." In Havana, a fan named Raul Bru formed an anti-Lovecraft society, which published two issues of a magazine called, predictably, *Hatecraft,* before it disbanded. In fannish circles, *Lovecrafty* (or just *crafty*) became a synonym for *queer.* And worse things were still to come.

In the fall of 1952, the *Erotonomicon* came to the attention of the House Un-American Activities Committee, which was, in those days, roaming the nation, looking in ever less likely places for signs of Communist conspiracy. Homosexuality was, as everyone knew, a gateway to Communism. When HUAC convened in Chicago, in September 1952, to investigate the influence of Communists in the labor movement, they also summoned August Derleth to testify. He was examined by Harold Velde, an Illinois congressman:

Mr. Velde: Mr. Derleth, did you have any idea that Mr. Lovecraft was a homosexual?

Mr. Derleth: I did not, because he wasn't.

Mr. Velde: Were you personally acquainted with Mr. Lovecraft?

Mr. Derleth: If you mean, did I ever meet him, then no, I didn't. We wrote each other letters.

Mr. Velde: But you believe that he wasn't homosexual.

Mr. Derleth: I don't believe he was sexual at all.

Mr. Velde: Mr. Derleth, I would like to read you a passage from Lovecraft's story *The Dream-Quest of Unknown Kadath*—am I pronouncing it right?

Mr. Derleth: Yes.

Mr. Velde: I am going to read a passage from this story, and I would like you to tell me what it makes you think of.

Mr. Derleth: Go right ahead.

Mr. Velde: "They bore him into that cliffside cavern and through monstrous labyrinths beyond. When he struggled, as at first he did by instinct, they tickled him with deliberation. They were frightfully cold and damp and slippery, and their paws kneaded one detestably. Soon they were plunging hideously downward through inconceivable abysses . . ." This fellow does use a lot of adjectives, doesn't he?

Mr. Derleth: . . .

Mr. Velde: ". . . abysses, in a whirling, giddying, sickening rush of dark, tomb-like air; and Carter felt they were shooting into the ultimate vortex of shrieking and daemonic madness. He screamed again and again, but whenever he did so the black paws tickled him with greater subtlety." What do you think of that, Mr. Derleth?

Mr. Derleth: It's from his Dunsanian period.

Mr. Velde: Pardon me?

Mr. Derleth: Never mind. It's a scene of horror. Carter has been captured by the night-gaunts, and they're taking him to the Peaks of Throk.

Mr. Velde: The peaks of . . . I see. Well, what do you make of all the tickling?

Mr. Derleth: This is ridiculous.

Mr. Velde: If I were trying to frighten someone with a story about a terrible monster, I think it's very unlikely that I would mention tickling.

Mr. Derleth: Well, you may not find it frightening, but I'll bet Howard did.

Mr. Velde: He thought it was frightening to be tickled?

Mr. Derleth: I guess he probably did.

Mr. Velde: And yet you're sure that Mr. Lovecraft wasn't queer?

Derleth, who was himself bisexual, engaged to a high-school student, and utterly terrified by the way events had turned, made the mistake of mentioning that many of Lovecraft's young correspondents in

New York City and elsewhere had been Communists at one time or another—at which point HUAC thought it might have stumbled onto a rich new lode of subversion. Weird fiction wasn't as glamorous as Hollywood, but people did read it, and the committee couldn't stand by while night-gaunts and such like tickled America's youth pink. So Lovecraft's friends and disciples were investigated. The ones who had jobs lost them, and they all suddenly found it impossible to sell their work.

It was as if the *Erotonomicon* were one of the forbidden books from Lovecraft's fiction, destroying or driving mad everyone who came into contact with it. The only person immune to the book's malign power was L. C. Spinks: him it made famous. After Derleth testified to HUAC, Spinks played the part of the apostate who had seen the error of his ways. He told Walter Winchell that he had published the *Erotonomicon* because he wanted people to know who Lovecraft really was. It was as if he had deliberately struck a blow against Lovecraft in the name of decency. And, in fact, as the *Erotonomicon* did more and more harm to more and more people, Spinks underwent a curious transformation. He spoke less about revealing the truth, and more about the dangers of "perverted horror"—i.e., the kind of horror fiction written by homosexuals, Communists, and other subversives. Four years before *The Invasion of the Body Snatchers,* Spinks wondered if horror itself was a plot to co-opt the minds of vulnerable young Americans. He appeared at dinner parties with Winchell, William F. Buckley, Whittaker Chambers, Roy Cohn, and so on. In photographs from that period, Spinks looks genial and bloated, the way you'd expect someone to look if he spent all his time being wined and dined by the right-wing intelligentsia of the United States.

The zenith of Spinks's fame came in February 1954, when he wrote an article for the *Saturday Evening Post,* in which he attacked Lovecraft, Derleth, Donald Wandrei, Clark Ashton Smith, Donald

Wollheim, C. L. Moore, Fritz Leiber, Robert Bloch,* and just about every other writer whom Lovecraft had ever praised, as degenerates whose art, if you could even call it art, made its readers into morbid cynics. In place of their tawdry, dangerous work, Spinks proposed, there ought to be a genre of "wholesome horror," which would thrill its readers with stories of men and women triumphing over monsters; or, in certain cases—stories for small children, or the feebleminded—over natural enemies such as bears and cold.

---

* Wollheim (1914–1990) was a notable science fiction writer and editor. C[atherine] L[ucille] Moore (1911–1987) was also a science fiction writer. Fritz Leiber (1910–1992) wrote a well-known series of fantasy novels; Charlie knew them by heart. Robert Bloch (1917–1994) went on to write *Psycho.*

8.

Then, in the spring of 1954, *Galaxy* magazine published a letter from a distinguished Mexican anthropologist named Pablo Martínez del Río. Outraged by what the *Erotonomicon* had to say about R. H. Barlow, Martínez del Río had hired a private detective named Edward Armstrong to find out whether the book was genuine. Armstrong began his investigation at the office of Black Hour Books on Lafayette Street, where he found a scene of total chaos: boxes were heaped everywhere, along with rolls of brown paper and scissors and bottles of rubber cement, bundles of advertisements for books such as *Lady Chatterley's Friends, I Was Hitler's Doctor,* and *Venus in Chains,* and plaster busts of Moses and Goethe (one each), as if the world's least tidy academic had agreed to share an office with the world's least tidy pornographer; although, in fact, it was probably just the aftermath of the police raid. From amid this jumble there eventually appeared a prim bald man in a red bow tie, who introduced himself as Samuel Roth. "At that point," Martínez del Río wrote, "a chasm of fakery opened beneath my feet."

Roth was a notorious *booklegger,* a publisher of illegal books, whose pirated edition of *Ulysses* had caused an international scandal in 1927. By 1954, he had been convicted seven times for publishing obscene material and served four prison terms. He ran a thriving mail-order business, which invented imprints one after another to stay ahead of the U.S. Postal Inspectors. The year before the *Erotonomicon* appeared, Roth had published *My Sister and I,* an incest memoir attributed to Friedrich Nietzsche, which was almost certainly a hoax. And Martínez del Río's letter went on: Roth told Armstrong that he had never seen Lovecraft's notebook, only a typescript. Nor had he met Spinks, who, he said bitterly, was avoiding him. I hear he's writing a memoir, Roth said, with Doubleday—*Doubleday!* But what can I expect, no one is grateful to a prophet in his lifetime. OK, Armstrong said, well, do you have an address for Spinks? Sure, Roth said, but don't expect him to reply. He combines the worst qualities of a hermit and a prima donna. He went into the back office and returned with a ledger, which he stuck under Armstrong's nose. Look at these royalties! he said. I thought the book was banned, Armstrong said. Ha, Roth said, all my best-sellers are banned. How do you think they become best-sellers? Look at that. Forty thousand dollars in sales—and not a word of thanks! Armstrong noted Spinks's address—a post office box in Parry Sound—and saw, beside it, the address of someone named V. Schmidt, in Bismarck, North Dakota. Who's this Schmidt? Armstrong asked. I have no idea, Roth said. Spinks just wrote to me and said ten percent of the royalties should go to her. Her? Armstrong repeated. Truly, I don't know, Roth said, and I don't care. This business makes me sick. I'd quit tomorrow, if anyone else had the courage to do my job. He slammed the ledger shut. I was meant to be a poet, he said. Have you read my poems? I don't read much poetry, Armstrong said, but Roth was already rummaging in a box under what in a normal office would have been the receptionist's desk. Here, he said, my first collection. You'll see, it's twenty years ahead of its time! Armstrong took it and stumbled downstairs, blinking as if he had stepped from the pages of a closed book into the light of the three-dimensional world.

What happened next, Martínez del Río wrote, was that Armstrong went looking for V. Schmidt. He took the train to Minneapolis, rented a car, and reached the Schmidt farm just as night was falling. At first the woman who answered the door denied that any such person as V. Schmidt lived there. But Armstrong, who was used to being put off, insisted, and finally the woman told him to wait. Violet! she shouted up the stairs. There's a very rude gentleman to see you! She showed him to a small bedroom with a sloping ceiling and a pink rag rug on the floor, and there, sitting at a battered Shaker desk, Armstrong found Violet Schmidt, an obese girl about twenty years old, whose gray eyes were magnified by glasses so thick they seemed like the closest thing to blindness. Armstrong asked her if she knew L. C. Spinks, and she burst into tears. Violet was a science fiction fan; when she was younger, she had written letters to Pickman's Vault. She bragged about her ability to mimic anyone's handwriting, and said that Spinks had asked her to forge the signatures of nearly every famous science fiction fan in America for a prank involving some fake letters. The letters were ridiculous, she said, but the signatures fooled everybody! So Violet was not entirely surprised when, in the fall of 1951, she got a call from Spinks, asking if she could do H. P. Lovecraft. A few days later, she received a package containing a typed manuscript, a twenty-year-old blank notebook, a sample of Lovecraft's handwriting, and several bottles of black Skrip ink. There was also a note from Spinks, with instructions on what to do: *Everything must be returned to me*, it concluded. Spinks loved pranks, and that was what she assumed this was. Violet was astonished to learn, months later, that the "rather disgusting" book she had penned had been published and that it was causing a sensation. She wrote to Spinks and mentioned that her mother wanted a new washing machine. They came to an agreement. Do you have anything to back this up? Armstrong asked. Any proof? I'm not dumb, Violet said. She lifted the folding top of her desk and took out a note from Spinks: *Everything must be returned to me,* it concluded. She showed Armstrong a bottle of ink.

That summer, every fanzine in North America demanded that L. C. Spinks explain himself, but Spinks stayed silent. Possibly, he believed he was so important that he didn't have to care what fandom said about him. He'd dined with Walter Winchell and written for the *Saturday Evening Post!* He had the attention of a continent. Why should he worry about some teenagers with overactive typewriters? What he didn't know was that one of the teenagers' fathers worked for the Postal Service. Mail fraud was a crime in Canada, too. Spinks was in the shower, singing an air by Carl Orff, when the Mounties arrived.

The hoax unraveled quickly. The notebook and typescript were found in Spinks's study; Edward Armstrong handed over the bottle of ink Violet had given him, and it matched the ink in the notebook. On May 12, 1954, Spinks's lawyer delivered a statement to the Toronto *Star,* in which Spinks said that the *Erotonomicon* was "a practical joke that went wrong," and apologized "if anyone's feelings were hurt"— quite an understatement. The *New York Times* ran a story about Samuel Roth's many crimes; and the drama of the *Erotonomicon* came to an end a week later, when Spinks appeared on Edward R. Murrow's TV program *See It Now.* Murrow had no idea who Lovecraft was, and he didn't care. To him, the hoax was simply the story of another group of Americans who had been duped into walking in fear, and another example of courage and good sense winning out in the end. What Spinks hoped to get from the interview is less clear. I watched the clip with Charlie: the Spinks who appears on Murrow's show is exhausted and bewildered, like a man who has walked into a fogged-in valley and has for many days been trying to find his way out. He's wearing a checked sports coat and a tie. It's hard to tell on the pixelated YouTube video, but it looks like his fly is open.

Murrow: Mr. Spinks, earlier this week you gave a statement to the Toronto *Star,* in which you confessed that you had made up a book called the Eroto . . . eroto something, am I right?

Spinks: [*Nods.*] It's called the *Erotonomicon.* And it's . . .

Murrow: Never mind what it's called. The important thing is that you destroyed the reputation, the posthumous reputation, of a writer named H. P. Lovecraft. Now the question I think most Americans want answered is, why did you do it?

Spinks: Why?

Murrow: Yes, why?

Spinks: I . . . I guess I . . .

Murrow: Surely you must have had a reason.

Spinks: Well, Mr. Murrow, I'm from a small town in Canada. And all my life, I've dreamed of having an adventure. You know, like going on a safari, or climbing a mountain, or fighting in a war. And I guess this book was my adventure.

Murrow: Do you mean to tell me that you ruined a man's reputation because you wanted an adventure? For shame, Mr. Spinks.

Spinks: Well, I don't know. I'm just telling you how it seemed to me at the time when I, uh, when I did it. I guess I just wanted to do something daring.

Murrow: So you defamed an innocent person. A man who had never done anything to *you.*

Spinks: I didn't think of that.

Murrow: I don't see how you could not have thought of it.

Spinks: Well, I didn't! I got caught up in the excitement of it, eh? You know, when you do something like that, you really feel, you feel like you're living. And when you're living you don't think about everything that comes to your mind. You just think about living.

Murrow: Mr. Spinks, I think you'll excuse me for saying that your answer is incoherent and unacceptable.

Spinks: You know, horror fiction has a corrosive effect on the minds of young children.

Murrow: And?

Spinks: Well, I just think it needs cleaning up.

Murrow: So you defamed Lovecraft in order to clean up horror fiction, am I understanding you correctly?

Spinks: I don't think I defamed anybody. I'm not sure. Yes.

Murrow: You deliberately wrote an obscene book to clean up literature. Mr. Spinks, even you have to admit that that's absurd.

Spinks: Is it? I mean . . . What does it mean, to know why you did something? Who knows why they do what they do? Do you even know why you're interviewing me?

Murrow: Yes, Mr. Spinks, I do. And I think this interview is just about finished.

The video is unsettling. It's like watching a soul dissolve into dust before your eyes—like watching a mask drop and finding no face behind it. The only way to understand it is to think that Spinks didn't care anymore about *how* he was seen; he only wanted to be seen. But, in fact, the last known photograph of Spinks was taken in front of the CBS studio on Park Avenue, before the interview. He is wearing dark glasses and looking anxiously at something that's happening up the street. A stranger's arm obscures most of his torso. It adds to the impression he gave in the interview, that he was someone who had never really been.

9.

Charlie tried to find out what had happened to Spinks afterward, but this proved strangely difficult. He published nothing after May 1954, and no one published anything about him. His name didn't appear in L. Sprague de Camp's *Lovecraft: A Life,* or in S. T. Joshi's thousand-page *I Am Providence,* or in the *Journal of Lovecraft Studies,* or *Studies in Weird Fiction,* or the papers delivered at the various Lovecraft conferences that had been held over the years. In the 1970s, it became fashionable for science fiction writers to talk about sex—but no one spoke about the sex scandal that had nearly engulfed Lovecraft's reputation. It was as if fandom had found the hoax too queer and decided to erase L. C. Spinks from its memory, Charlie said. And that wasn't all: Spinks himself had vanished. He wasn't listed in any public record anyone had seen fit to put online; there wasn't even a newspaper obituary to revive the memory of his hoax for a column inch or two. Charlie was certain that *someone* knew what had happened to Spinks, but every path he tried led to a dead end. "It's the riddle of the Spinks," he said. He wrote to S. T. Joshi, the Lovecraft biographer, to ask if *he* had any information about Spinks, and Joshi replied that he not only knew nothing about Spinks, but didn't want to know. In his opinion, far too much had been made of the question of Lovecraft's sexuality. Of course, it was interesting, the way anyone's sexuality is interesting, it excited a kind of prurient interest, but really, Joshi wrote, it was only one aspect of Lovecraft's being; and when you thought about the other aspects—his anti-modernism, for example, or his often over-looked talent as a regional writer, a kind of Faulkner of New England—his sexuality began to seem like one of the least distinctive things about him.

At the end of May, Charlie told me he was done looking for Spinks. "The more I look, the more his story unravels," he said, "and the more it unravels, the more I doubt my sanity. Anyway, it doesn't matter. I can end my Barlow project with Spinks's hoax. It's like, the lengths some people will go to, to fill in a blank spot. Then I say, whew, glad *I* know where reality stops and fantasy begins, and I'm out." Charlie grinned. His voice was warm and full. I thought with relief that I had heard the last of L. C. Spinks, but as a psychotherapist, I should have known better. Nothing in a person's life vanishes for good; it only drops out of sight, to return, as Lovecraft would have put it, when the stars are right.

III.

A SEARCH AND AN EVOCATION

1.

In order to go deeper into the world of his story, Charlie retraced Lovecraft's 1934 trip to Florida. In June 2007, he took the bus from New York to Charleston, Savannah, Jacksonville, and, finally, Daytona Beach. (There was no longer a bus station in DeLand.) He rented a car at the Daytona Beach airport and drove inland, past billboards which were like no other billboards he had ever seen before: advertisements for a law firm that specialized in divorce for men only and a gun shop that sold tactical arms; a warning that faking auto accidents is not child's play. The landscape between the signs was flat and drab green, streaked with white where a road led off into the forest. Malls encroached on the forest, with palatial strip clubs and bunker-like movie theaters, but to Charlie's delight, DeLand looked as if it hadn't changed much since the 1930s. Art Deco buildings in pastel blues and pinks and yellows boiled in the humid air. The storefronts belonged to grimly local businesses: a diner, a health food store, and a doll-repair shop, its windows populated by row upon row of armless, legless, or headless dolls. Lovecraft would have loved it here, Charlie thought. He ate lunch in the diner and drove on to Barlow's house, which he had located on the Internet. He was relieved to find Dunrovin abandoned: he had dreaded speaking to the people who lived there and explaining why he had come. On the other hand, the property was very clearly marked with NO TRESPASSING signs. Charlie parked in the driveway and got out of his car. His heart was pounding. The house where Barlow had entertained Lovecraft was two stories tall, and made of, or at least sided with, massive cypress logs. It looked very sturdy for a structure built by a paranoid lunatic, Charlie thought; or maybe Colonel Barlow's paranoia had contributed to the sturdiness of its construction. He walked quickly around the property, taking photographs which, when he looked at them later on, would turn out to be almost useless: a swath of lawn with Dunrovin in the distant background; a bush that mostly obscured the tumbledown red barn; a close-up of the shed which—in the *Erotonomicon,* anyway—Lovecraft had thought about using as a writing studio. The lake where Lovecraft and Barlow once rowed had dried up; its bed was choked with reeds. The lawn was speckled with seedpods and white sand. But the parts of the house that Charlie could see through the downstairs windows were intact, if mostly empty. The rooms were spacious and comfortable-looking. Indeed, a heap of sofa cushions on the living room floor and a new propane tank by the kitchen window suggested that someone might be moving back in. Charlie took a photo of himself standing by the front door, as a kind of trophy, and hurried back to his car.

The next day he explored St. Augustine and saw the chapel of Nuestra Señora de la Leche; then he returned to Dunrovin. As before, he walked the grounds, taking pictures, but then he decided that he couldn't leave Florida without making an effort to get into the house, and tried the front door. It was locked. He circled around reluctantly, as if he were daring himself, or even compelling himself, to do something he didn't want to do. There was a glassed-in porch facing the dry lake; one pane had broken and been replaced with a sheet of clear plastic. From where he stood, Charlie could see that the back door to the house was open, as if someone had just left. With the feeling that he was no longer merely doing something stupid but doing something stupid and dangerous, Charlie went inside. He switched his camera to video mode and started recording, aware, as he did so, that this was just what people do in horror movies. He circled through the down-stairs rooms: the kitchen was in poor condition, its floor covered in yellowish linoleum squares that were peeling up at the corners. The stove was rusted and the refrigerator absent. A dead water bug lay on its back in the sink. The next room to the right, or counterclockwise, was a sitting room, with blue walls and a fireplace, completely empty. Then the front hall, the locked front door, and stairs going up, which for some reason gave Charlie a bad feeling. The last, large downstairs room was the living room, Charlie thought; later he would deduce that it had been Mrs. Barlow's bedroom. It contained the sofa cushions Charlie had seen from the outside, a dining room chair, and a purple long-sleeved T-shirt. People come here, Charlie thought.

He returned to the kitchen, his heart beating rapidly. He wanted to leave the house, but the same force that had impelled him inside asked a question: *What's up those stairs, Charlie?* I'm not going up the stairs, Charlie thought. But he went back to the front hall and climbed the stairs, holding his camera in front of him as if it might protect him from whatever was up there. Immediately to the left was Barlow's bed-room, also light blue. The front of the room was under the house's eaves, and there were several closets, one of them lined with wooden shelves. This must be Yoh-Vombis, Charlie thought: the closet where Barlow had kept his weird-fiction collection. The amber shelves were empty, but there were pencil marks on the door frame, charting Bob-by's meager youthful growth. One mark was much higher than the others: *H.P.L., 6/7/1935.* Charlie shuddered. He imagined Lovecraft stooping beside Barlow in the small closet. The two of them so close, they could feel one another's breath . . . Up until that point, Charlie had been rooting for sex to turn up at the heart of his story. He figured that Lovecraft needed it, and Barlow wanted it, and where was the harm? Those pencil marks changed his mind. He would never know what happened for sure, he said, but after he saw Yoh-Vombis, he was rooting for chastity. He noticed a matchbook far back on one of the shelves, from a café in Montreal. It could not have been an authentic Barlovian artifact, Charlie thought, and, in fact, he had no idea how it had got there, but he pocketed it anyway.

He went back into the bedroom, and just then, something creaked downstairs. Charlie stood very still and held his breath. This was Florida, where they sold *tactical weapons*. Charlie was unarmed, and totally unthreatening, but he was a black man, upstairs in someone else's house. For some reason he kept the camera going, pointed at a blank wall. After a long time, he realized that he couldn't remain motionless in Robert Barlow's bedroom forever. He took a step toward the stairs. Nothing else moved. Driven by what struck him, at this point, as a completely insane drive toward completeness, Charlie went into the last room of the house, the bedroom that had been Lovecraft's. It was the counterpart of Mrs. Barlow's room downstairs, unfurnished except for a small pink bureau that had been pushed into a corner. He walked around to the hallway that connected Barlow's bedroom to Lovecraft's, went through Barlow's room one last time, trying to pull with him whatever ghostly impressions might linger there, and finally glanced at the screened-in sleeping porch, which Lovecraft had mentioned in his letters. Then he hurried downstairs and out of the house without bothering to document anything else on the grounds, got in his car, drove back through DeLand and its now-sinister Art Deco buildings, and on to Daytona Beach, where he found his way to a Chinese restaurant. He ordered a Tsingtao and drank half of it, and only then did he dare to look at the video he'd shot.

It showed an empty house in poor repair; the only strange thing about it was the duration. Charlie had been in the house for twenty minutes at least, but the video was only two and a half minutes long. He wondered if part of it might be *missing,* and decided that fear must have distorted his sense of time. And yet: that night, when Charlie was typing his notes about Dunrovin, in the safety of his hotel room, the cursor on the screen seemed to lag, as if it weren't just a pattern of electrically activated crystal dots, but an actual object, a tiny wall, which he was pushing through a resistant medium. Or, he thought, as if the cursor were dragging its feet, as if it didn't want to tell this story. He imagined Barlow standing there, pale, bespectacled, wearing a jacket and a tie, his dark hair combed straight back, shaking his head and whispering something, *No,* or *Don't!* Then the cursor leaped forward and a string of mistyped letters appeared all at once on Charlie's screen. CHKL;WWN. Cthulhu? Curwen? The ghost, which had never been there, was gone.

2.

At the beginning of December, Charlie found evidence that Robert Barlow might not have killed himself. It was in a history of science fiction fandom called *All Our Yesterdays;* the author reported that a collector named C. L. Barrett had run into Barlow in Florida in the early 1960s, years after Barlow's supposed death. Neither Barrett nor the author of *All Our Yesterdays* was surprised to find him alive. Science fiction fans had a tradition of faking their own deaths, as a practical joke, or as a way of quitting fandom and its various obligations. There was a word for it in fandom's argot: *pseuicide.* "So maybe that was what Barlow did," Charlie said. "Wouldn't it be amazing if he were still alive?" "When was Barlow born?" I asked. "In 1918," Charlie said. "So, right, he probably isn't alive anymore. But if he *was* . . . Mar, can you imagine?" I gave Charlie a hug. His excitement was completely out of proportion to the evidence, but his wish for Barlow's story to have had a happier ending was moving. It made me think of my own work: that fall I'd been reading about the psychoanalytic treatment of severe trauma, which was something I wanted to specialize in. It occurred to me that Charlie and I were both trying to rescue people from the past.

Then Charlie told me that he had bought a plane ticket to Mexico for the Christmas holiday. I was furious. My family vacations in Miami every Christmas, and I relied on Charlie to get me through it, especially that year, because my grandfather wouldn't be around to keep my grandmother in check. "Why can't you go some other time?" I asked. "I thought it would be easier to go while you were away," he said, innocently. "You'll be with your family, and you won't miss me." "Are you kidding?" I said. "First of all, I *will* miss you, and second, my grandmother is going to think our marriage is in trouble." "Tell your grandmother I love you madly," Charlie said. "*Madly* is right," I said. "What am I supposed to say? That you went to Mexico to look for a dead guy?" "Tell her I'm writing a book that's going to make us rich," Charlie said. "A Book-of-the-Month-Club Main Selection." I assumed he was kidding, although in retrospect, I'm not so sure.

Charlie flew to Mexico City the day before Christmas and came home on New Year's Eve. I was in bed with the flu. "How was your trip?" I asked. "Mar," he said, "have you ever seen fireworks from an airplane? It's crazy. All those stars and flowers and so on turn out to be three-dimensional. It's like flying over like the spores of some fantastic plant." "I meant Mexico," I said. Charlie said the city was sprawling and dangerous, like Los Angeles in the 1980s crossed with 1970s New York. It seemed to be falling apart and being rebuilt at the same time, sometimes in the same place: the rusted frame of an unfinished skyscraper, or the roots of a tree that had broken through the sidewalk in front of a newly renovated villa. The mild, dry air smelled of burning trash. Charlie took a cab to the apartment he had rented online, a modern one-bedroom in the Colonia Roma. Day after day, he rode the Metro from one end of Mexico City to the other, looking for evidence that Robert Barlow had not killed himself. He found nothing. Barlow's house in Azcapotzalco had been replaced by the press that prints the Mexican edition of *The Economist*. The old campus of Mexico City College was partly a hospital and partly a parking lot. Charlie did succeed in making an appointment with an American anthropologist who had studied with professors who had known Barlow. He waited in an Italian café for several hours, but the anthropologist didn't show up. When Charlie went back to his apartment, he found an angry email: the anthropologist had been in the café for hours, he wrote, but *Charlie* hadn't showed up. Charlie began to feel like he was in a Bolaño story, or even a story by Borges. What he was looking for existed in a parallel universe, which converged with Charlie's universe only in the pages of *All Our Yesterdays.*

He took the bus to the Desierto de los Leones, where Barlow's friend Pablo Martínez del Río, or Don Pablo, as everyone called him, had supposedly scattered Barlow's ashes, in the company of Barlow's mother and brother. Charlie took a tour of the old nunnery, which was impressively austere, except for the profusion of girls who had come there to be photographed in their *quinceañera* dresses, and their proud families and awkward boyfriends; then he set off into the forest. His guidebook warned him that people had been robbed in the park and that he shouldn't leave the main trails, but he completely forgot about this advice. He climbed higher and higher, up trails that were less and less well marked, until he was on a track of white scree among high, drab bushes. There he found a pair of men's olive-green pants, set out on a rock. It wasn't hard to deduce that there was a person nearby, but for some reason Charlie kept going, until, near the top of the mountain, he found an encampment, a ring of rocks and stumps around a burned-out campfire, with empty bottles littered all around, and a bag of trash hanging from a tree. At this point he started to think seriously about what *kind* of people might be living at the top of a mountain in a notoriously dangerous national park, miles and miles from the nearest paved road. He took a picture, another useless picture, of Mexico City filling the valley like a lake of smog, and started back down the hill, only he couldn't go very fast, because the scree kept rolling out from under his feet. When he was half a mile down the hill, in the place where the pants had been, and where the pants, scarily, no longer were, a man called to him from the bushes. He was speaking Spanish, and Charlie had no idea what he was saying, which was good, because the man started shouting, and if Charlie *had* understood him he probably would have broken into a run and fallen on his face. He walked as fast as he could down that path and all the other paths, and just before he came to the road that led back to the nunnery, he nearly ran into an enormous white bull, which was grazing in the trail. It was like something from a story by Flannery O'Connor. The bull was as nonplussed as Charlie was, and he got home safely. "Still, it was freaky," Charlie said. "If something *had* happened to me, it would have been as if I'd vanished into thin air." "That's scary," I said. "I wish you hadn't told me about it." "Hold on," Charlie said. "The story gets better."

On Charlie's last full day in Mexico City, he went to the American Embassy, in Cuauhtémoc. Without much hope, he explained to a neatly dressed male secretary in the records section—everyone at the embassy looked like a Mormon, Charlie said—that he was looking for information about a certain R. H. Barlow, an American citizen who had allegedly died in Mexico City on January 1 or 2, 1951. "Allegedly?" the secretary said. "That's what I'm trying to figure out," Charlie said. "I'll have someone check the files," the secretary said. "Can you come back in an hour?" Charlie killed time drinking Tecate at a bar nearby, which turned out to be a gay bar; why the U.S. Embassy should be right across the street from not one but actually several gay bars was, he said, anyone's guess. Then he went back to the records section, where the secretary was waiting for him. "I found the file," he said, "and I'm sorry to tell you that your friend is dead." He produced a faded green folder and showed Charlie the death certificate, which was dated January 9, 1951. It gave Barlow's cause of death as *congestión visceral generalizado*, generalized visceral congestion, which struck

Charlie as being the kind of thing you might say about a person who wasn't really dead. He turned over the previous document in the folder, an application for Canadian citizenship, which Barlow had submitted at the end of 1950. The Canadian consulate wanted to know if Barlow was a Communist. "I'm sorry," the secretary said, "but these files are confidential. You shouldn't really be looking at this at all." He closed the folder and took it back. "Why did you show it to me, then?" Charlie asked. "Oh," the secretary said, "this is Mexico. You'd be surprised how many people come in, wanting to know if people are really dead. We try to put the ghosts to rest." "Thanks," Charlie said. "Never say the United States government did nothing for you," the secretary said.

"Well," I said, "at least now you know." "Maybe," Charlie said. "What I want to know is, why would Barlow apply for citizenship in Canada? His whole life was in Mexico." "Don't go there," I said. "You're right, Mar," Charlie said. "I need a drink." He went to the kitchen and I heard him trying to get ice out of the ice tray. "How was your family?" he asked. "They gave me the flu," I said. I heard an ice cube skitter across the floor, a curse, the clink of a glass. "You know what's really insane?" Charlie called to me. "What?" I asked. I hoped he'd tell me that he was giving up his Barlow project, but what he said was, "I keep thinking, L. C. Spinks was Canadian."

On January 2, Charlie went back to the library, only to find out what he already knew: that Spinks had vanished. Everyone who had known him was dead: Samuel Roth, Walter Winchell, Roy Cohn, even Violet N. Schmidt, of Bismarck, North Dakota. He wished he had met Magnus ten years sooner. As it was, he was rooting around in a graveyard, and he couldn't even find Spinks's headstone. But this, he said, was his third clue. After weeks of fruitless searching, it occurred to Charlie that there might be no headstone, for the simple reason that L. C. Spinks was not dead. And yet there was no trace of him—*not as*

L. C. Spinks. With fingers that were suddenly too clumsy for their work, he searched the Canadian phone records for R. H. Barlow. There were many *R Barlows* in Canada, but only one who lived on Waubeek Street, in Parry Sound, Ontario. Charlie dialed. An old man answered the phone. "Mr. Barlow," Charlie said, "My name is Charlie Willett, and I want to ask you about the *Erotonomicon.*" There was a long silence, then Barlow laughed. It sounded like someone shaking a spray-paint can full of sand. "Well," he said, "I wondered how long that would take." Charlie asked if he had a minute to talk, and he said, "A *minute?* No, you'll have to come up." "I'm sorry?" Charlie said. "Come up," Barlow repeated. "OK, when?" Charlie asked, and there was another silence. It took Charlie a while to figure out that Barlow had hung up. Then he called me at my office and left a message telling me that he had to fly to Canada immediately. I called back as soon as I could. "Have fun," I said. I tried not to sound worried.

Charlie flew to Toronto and drove unsteadily through a snowstorm to Parry Sound, a resort town on the eastern shore of Lake Huron. Climate-wise, it was the opposite of DeLand, although in other ways the two towns were eerily similar. They were about the same size, with little picturesque downtowns that sold used things and handicrafts. *Remedial towns,* Charlie called them: they'd been held back a grade or two, but were trying to catch up. Waubeek Street ran between the water and the rail viaduct; it was easy to guess which house was Barlow's, because it was the only one on the block that was falling apart. The yard was a lumpy field of mysterious snow-covered objects, at least two of which appeared to be concrete birdbaths. Several half-full bird feeders hung from the trees. Charlie climbed the steps to the front porch and rang the bell, and a voice from deep within the house called, "Come in."

Holding the foil-wrapped bottle of Burgundy he'd picked up on his way out of the airport, Charlie stepped from winter into a season that exists only in the houses of old people, a hot, dry season that reeked of cat litter and mentholated spray. A plaid wool jacket and some hats hung on wooden pegs, beside an aluminum walker with tennis balls on its front feet. Immediately to the left was a staircase hung with interesting-looking photographs, but: "In here," the voice called. Charlie followed it to the kitchen, which was done up in faded greens and yellows. Barlow sat by the window. Charlie had expected him to be decrepit, but he looked robust, like an athletic seventy-year-old. He wore a brown sweater, creased slacks, a white open-collar shirt. A few strands of black hair were combed back from his wide skull. He was smoking a pipe; its smoke coiled complexly in the beams of winter light that shone through the parted chintz curtains. "Are you the electrician?" he asked. "I'm Charlie Willett," Charlie said. "I talked to you on the phone the other day." "Oh," Barlow said, "yes, of course. I didn't know you were . . ." "Here," Charlie said, holding out the bottle of wine, "I brought you something from Toronto." "Thank you," Barlow said. He smiled with real warmth. "Tell me," he said, "how did you find me?" Charlie told him about the clues: the mention in *All Our Yesterdays,* the application for Canadian citizenship, the Montreal matchbook he'd found in Yoh-Vombis. Barlow looked pleased. "You're very good," he said. "What about Kansas City?" "What?" Charlie asked. "Never mind," Barlow said. "Would you like something to eat?" "No, thanks," Charlie said. "Well, then," Barlow said, "I suppose we should get started. Do you have a tape recorder?" Charlie took out his phone. Barlow looked at it with wonder. "That's a tape recorder?" he asked. "Yes," Charlie said. "We don't have flying cars, but we've got great phones." Barlow winced. "Why do you say that?" he asked. "I just meant, reality never caught up with the old science fiction dreams," Charlie said. Barlow looked at him suspiciously. "No," he said, after a while, "from that point of view, we're still living in the past."

3.

CW: Just for the record, will you say your name?

RHB: My name is Robert Hayward Barlow.

CW: OK, Mr. Barlow. Where do you want to start?

RHB: [*Laughs.*] You know, I've thought about this moment for years, but I've never considered where to begin.

CW: I could ask you questions.

RHB: Yes, go ahead.

CW: Is the *Erotonomicon* real, or is it a fake?

RHB: I did my work well! It's the latter. Very much the latter.

CW: You made it up.

RHB: All, except the parts that are true.

CW: Except . . . Let's come back to that. I think I understand why you did it. You wanted to get back at Derleth, and Wandrei, and the rest of Lovecraft's friends. The book was revenge for what they had done to you.

RHB: Wandrei especially, and also Sam Loveman. I didn't care so much about Derleth, who was just trying to get Lovecraft published. We actually became friendly, years later.

CW: What I don't understand is why you took it back.

RHB: Who says I took it back?

CW: Don Pablo was your friend. He wouldn't have written that letter if you didn't want him to. Also, if you don't mind my saying so, there's no way in the world he would have sent it to *Galaxy*. He probably didn't even know what *Galaxy* was.

RHB: [*Laughs.*] Actually, he did. Don Pablo was a science fiction fan.

CW: Oh. But the investigation was a sham, wasn't it? You told Armstrong where to look. If there was a real Armstrong.

RHB: There was. A friend of mine in New York. He sold stoves.

CW: So, OK, why? You had your revenge. Why take it back?

RHB: Can't you guess?

CW: Tell me.

RHB: Howard! In the end, I loved him too much. I thought I didn't, but I was wrong. And when my scheme had succeeded far beyond anything I had imagined, and Howard was in danger of being really forgotten, I decided to end it. So I made myself into a cartoon balloon, and gave Don Pablo the pin.

CW: Were you in love with him?

RHB: Oh, a little. Don Pablo was dashing. Have you seen a photo of him? I'll show you one, if you like. My albums are in the study.

CW: I meant, with Lovecraft.

RHB: You don't know? Then that's where I'll begin. [*Pause.*] Where did you grow up?

CW: New York City. Why?

RHB: I grew up on army bases in Kansas, then Georgia, before we moved to Florida. Everywhere I went, I looked for people who were like me, and didn't find them. By the time I was seven or eight, I had begun to wonder whether I belonged anywhere, to any people in the world, and even if the world was worth belonging to. That feeling persisted until I found Howard's work. He was the first person I ever knew who believed as deeply as I did that the world was awful, absurd, and utterly indifferent to everything that had the misfortune to live in it. But there's a strange consolation to knowing that someone else shares your despair. Or no—not consolation. The word I want is *exhilaration*. When I read Howard's stories, I felt for the first time that I was not alone.

CW: I know what you mean.

RHB: Do you? Well. I wrote to Howard, and he replied. *Weird Tales* had just rejected *At the Mountains of Madness,* and he was very bitter about it. Despite that bitterness, or maybe because of it, he answered my questions patiently, and we started to correspond. I felt it absolutely: Howard was one of my people, or I was one of his. So, naturally, I wanted to meet him. He mentioned that he went to Florida sometimes in the summer, and I invited him to visit me in Cassia.

CW: Why did Lovecraft accept your invitation?

RHB: I suppose he thought my company would be congenial. I was a weird fiction fan; we had very similar taste. Also, you have to remember that Howard had no money. He couldn't afford to stay in hotels, and here I was, offering him a free bed for as long as he wanted it.

CW: So he came to Florida. What happened?

RHB: He got off the bus in DeLand, carrying his black bag . . . Do you know about his bag?

CW: Yes.

RHB: No matter how far he traveled, he took only one small black bag, made of imitation leather. It contained writing paper, underwear, and two shirts. Why should I carry more? he said. I don't need it. Of course, if I had a train of native bearers, or an elephant . . . [*Coughs.*]

CW: Are you all right?

RHB: Yes. Howard came right up to me. Barlovius, I presume, he said, and held out his hand. I remember thinking that he looked a little like Dante. His hair was more gray than I had expected, and he was wearing a rather old blue suit. Also, he had thick lips, not protruding ones, but broad, broad lips, which were purplish in color.

CW: You weren't attracted to him.

RHB: I wasn't thinking about that. I hadn't even considered him as a physical being until that moment. He was so much older than I was! And all this time, Howard was standing there, with his hand out. I shook it. Then he pirouetted on his foot, and said, Ah, DeLand! I had a memorable cheese sandwich here, in the summer of '31. I tried to take his bag, but he wouldn't let it go, and we stood there with both our hands on it. Then he laughed and let go. We got in my parents' old blue Ford, and I drove us home.

CW: Where Lovecraft met your mother.

RHB: Bernice, yes.

CW: I have to ask. How did your mother think it was OK for this forty-three-year-old man to live with you for, what was it, seven weeks?

RHB: Closer to eight. But you underestimate me. Bernice didn't know that Howard would stay so long. For that matter, neither did Howard. He had the idea that he would continue south to the Keys, and take a boat to Havana, if he didn't run out of money. I, however, had a different idea, which was, that Howard would keep me company. Each time he mentioned the Keys, I remembered one of the as-yet unvisited wonders of our region. Oh, the Spanish sugar mill in De Leon Springs! Oh, the old mission in New Smyrna Beach! I was the Scheherazade of Central Florida. Then I'd go to Bernice and inform her that Howard would be staying for another day or two. That said, I don't think she minded having him around. Unlike my father, he wasn't insane, and he had very good manners.

CW: Lovecraft must have wanted to stay, too.

RHB: Oh, yes. You can't convince people unless they want to be convinced.

CW: Tell me what the two of you did, when you were together.

RHB: Well, let's see. We went for a lot of walks. We'd walk on the highway to Cassia, which was just a general store and a pool hall, although for some reason there were two post offices, one in the general store and the other up on a hill, in a kind of shed. We had to stop by both, because Howard was always expecting letters, and we didn't know which post office would have them. We rowed on the lake behind my house. The Moon Pool, Howard called it, after the story by A. Merritt.* We went up to Silver Springs, to ride in the glass-bottomed boats they had there . . . You know, that was where they filmed the movie of *Tarzan*, in Silver Springs.

CW: What else?

RHB: We talked. Howard knew all the people I had been corresponding with, the weird-fiction authors and fans. He told me what they were like. I remember him complaining about Belknap Long's mustache. It makes Belknapius look like an anarchist, he said. Or, rather, it would, if it were entirely grown in. As it is, it makes him look like a Democrat! [*Laughs.*] We read to each other. Howard read his own stories aloud

---

* *The Moon Pool* was published in *All-Story Weekly* in 1918. My note—all the rest are mine. I wish I could say that I found their veracity reassuring.

very well. His speaking voice was high and thin, but when he read aloud it became deeper. Sepulchral, he would have called it. [*In a deep voice:*] "But by God, Eliot, *it was a photograph from life!*"* He could have been a wonderful radio host. Let's see. What else did we do? He watched me work on my letterpress. He encouraged me to make a business of it, putting out editions of weird fiction and poetry. If only I kept at it, he said, I could be the Caxton of the weird. Do you know Caxton?

CW: He printed Bibles, right?

RHB: Yes, very good! I remember one morning we drove up to St. Augustine. Howard had spent a month there, in 1931, and he knew everything there was to know about the old Spanish buildings. He led me around for hours. Finally, I said, Stop, please, stop! What's wrong? Howard asked. What's *wrong*? I said. My feet are coming off, that's what. Howard was contrite. Darn it, Barlovius, he said, you know I'm here at your pleasure. You have to tell me when I get to be too much.

CW: In the *Erotonomicon*, there's a scene at the chapel of Nuestra Señora de la Leche, where you and Howard kiss for the first time. Did something happen there?

RHB: Ah, the chapel. Have you seen it? Not very impressive, really. Just a Mission-style box, very plain inside, with a lot of novena candles, and prayers for fertility on slips of blue paper. La Señora de la Leche, you know, is the fertility aspect of the Virgin Mary. As usual, Howard wasn't satisfied until he had not only read every prayer, but found a nun to ask who had built the chapel, and when, and why, and who was buried in the cemetery next door. Then we sat on a bench by the

---

* The last sentence of Lovecraft's 1927 story "Pickman's Model."

graves. What do you think of this, Bobby, Howard said: The chapel was built on the ruins of an aboriginal mound, which was consecrated to a fertility goddess, but not one of your cleaned-up Christian ones. Ceres, maybe. Some people believe the Romans made it to the New World, you know! He pulled a story out of the air, about poor Spanish families with an unusual number of children, and a doctor who comes to vaccinate them, one August, at the time of the harvest. The children all resemble one another strangely, as if they had the same father, who was not quite human . . . [*Pause.*] I wanted to kiss his neck. You have to understand, I hadn't thought anything like that about Howard before. I knew that I was attracted to men, and I'd even had a sordid little affair with a medical student at Stetson.* But until that moment I had thought of Howard as an older brother, a very admired older brother, unlike my brother, Wayne, with whom I had more or less nothing in common. I hadn't imagined that I would be in a position to kiss him, any more than I believed that by saying the right words in the right order, I could summon Yog-Sothoth from beyond the stars. But I could, that was what I suddenly understood. I could! Howard was two feet from me. The sun had turned his skin an attractive pinkish brown. I could, but I didn't dare. Ceres? I said. That sounds promising.

CW: And then?

RHB: And then we bought ice cream cones, and ate them on the Bridge of Lions. You couldn't go anywhere with Howard without eating ice cream.

CW: Ah.

RHB: A few days later, I drove him to De Leon Springs, to see

---

* Stetson University, in DeLand, was founded in 1883.

the Spanish sugar mill. Howard was ecstatic. You know, Bar-lovius, he said, we think of this as the New World, but it's surprisingly old, in parts. He sighed. I think I could be content here. I could never imagine myself a Spaniard, of course, but I might be a renegade Englishman who had turned up in the middle of the swamps. I pointed out that the swamps were to the south of us. Don't quibble, Howard said. Allow an old man his delusions. We wandered through the grounds and went into the forest. You see, I said. Dry land! Impudent youth, Howard said. Half an hour later, we came to a clearing, and Howard asked if I wanted to rest. Sure, I said. We sat on some springy moss, which Howard stroked absently, as if it were a cat. Howard, I said, do you think it's strange that you're my friend? Why would it be strange? Howard asked. Because you're so much older than I am, I said. Howard laughed. You know, Barlovius, he said, when I think of my four-year-old self, I have to imagine him, the way I imagine the lives of the ancient Romans. But when I think of myself at your age, no transformation is necessary. I *am* that person, essentially, still. Why, do *you* think it's strange? I think it's strange that we're *friends,* I said. With the feeling that I was launching myself into a very powerful and very frightening obscurity, I took Howard's hand. Then, disaster. Howard jerked his hand out of mine, and stood up. What in Pegāna's name are you doing? he asked. When I didn't answer, he said, Let's go back to the mill. I want to look at it again before supper. I wanted to scream. I'd revealed myself to Howard, and he was disgusted. Now he would go home and tell all of our friends what had happened, and everyone would shun me. I was thinking of how to save myself, when Howard stopped at the forest's edge. Barlovius, he said, I'm sorry if I spoke too brusquely. You startled me. But I don't see that there's any need for *that,* between us. If it has a place anywhere! He gave a speech about all the various societies which had considered homosexuality a criminal offense, beginning with the Zoroastrians and concluding with the incarceration of Oscar Wilde. It took fifteen minutes. Which only goes to show that *it* is naturally repugnant to the overwhelming bulk of mankind, he said, by way of conclusion. As if I didn't know that already.

CW: Then what happened?

RHB: Howard stayed for nearly another month. We never talked about what had happened at De Leon Springs, and I tried to put it out of my mind. Howard apparently did the same, although now and then he said something that made me think he had judged me in a way that couldn't be reversed. Once, for example, we went to Daytona. We were standing on a corner by the beach, talking about the fearsome things that came from the ocean, or *might* come, when a young colored man—excuse me, a young *black* man—beckoned to us. He wore paint-streaked overalls, and his arms were white with plaster dust. He was leaning against a mailbox, with a can of beer in his hand and a bag of tools at his feet. I suppose he would have liked to be on the beach, but it was closed to colored people. To black people. I couldn't help noticing that he had beautiful golden eyes. You want to know what's out there? he asked. Howard looked at him with horror and shook his head. Take it easy! the stranger said. I'm too worn out to give you folks any trouble. Howard tried to pull me away, but I didn't go, and he ended up walking ahead by himself. What's out there? I asked. Well, the stranger said, before the crash, they were *going* to build houses, on land they took from digging the foundations for other houses, and dumped in the ocean. He told me a story about surveyors marking out streets, and dividing the seabed into lots that had been sold, according to the tramp, to some of the most respectable families in America. I thanked him for this information and rejoined Howard. You do like queer people, don't you? he snapped. I was just curious, I said. Weren't you? Not at all, Howard said. Perhaps it's a failing, but my curiosity is reserved for the larger currents of history. Individual particularities have always depressed me. He didn't say another word all afternoon.

CW: Huh.

RHB: I told myself that my desire for Howard was stupid and unreal. When I felt like I'd explode if I didn't *do* something about it, I made a drawing of a forbidden grotto, guarded by a toad-like monster, or a mountain temple, where naked slaves were devoured by horrible creatures with wings. Howard admired them, and I was delighted. Sex was nothing, I thought, when compared with the unspeakable customs of the toad-men! I drew maps of their country, and began an epic poem about them, which I annotated with colorful accounts of their language and customs. I was going to be the great artist of the toads.

CW: [*Laughs.*]

RHB: Well, *I* took it very seriously. [*Pause.*] In June, there was a rainy spell. Howard and I wrote a story together,* and I typed several of Howard's manuscripts. One day, he came into my room. I was trying to set some of Belknap's poems in type, but my type was all pi'd, and Howard found me looking under the bed for a capital M. I don't know why you don't

---

* The satiric "Battle That Ended the Century," which Lovecraft and Barlow published anonymously.

keep your room neater, he said. It seems to me you'd save yourself a lot of time, which you could use to actually print things. I told him that the spic-and-span chapter of my life had ended when we left Fort Benning, and that I wished never to revisit it. Howard looked unhappily at a pile of shirts with some string tangled in them, and a lump of bookbinder's wax. Where do you keep my manuscripts? he asked. I pointed at Yoh-Vombis. In there, I said. Sacred. Never to be disturbed. Never? Howard said. He took the wax and threw it at the ceiling, to see if it would stick. The truth is, he said, you can throw them out, for all I care. I don't know why you keep such worthless old things. The wax landed on the floor, and I picked it up. They aren't worthless to me, I said, and they're not even that old. Now will you look in that case for a capital W? [*Pause.*] When the rain let up, Howard told us he was leaving. Havana was out, but he wanted to visit Poe's house in Philadelphia on the way home, and needed to reserve funds for that. We'll miss you, Bernice said, a little dazedly. She didn't understand how he could have been with us for so long. Be sure to send us a letter now and then, she said. Oh, I will, Howard said. The next morning, I drove him to DeLand, to catch the bus. It was pouring, so we waited in my car. This is our last chance, I thought. Well, Barlovius, Howard said, I couldn't have asked for a better Virgil to show me around these lovely swamps. Forests, I said. I wanted to weep. Around these *forests*, Howard said. The bus pulled in, and the lights came on inside it. Looks like there are seats in the front, Howard said. A woman got off with her son, who was about six. He jumped into a puddle with a very serious look, as if it had to be done exactly right. I'm off, Howard said, thank you again. He took his bag and ran through the rain to the bus. I waited for it to depart. I thought he might run back to me: *Robert, wait, there's something I wanted to say . . .* But the bus left on time. I was so angry, I drove home at fifty miles an hour, which was ten miles faster than the Ford could go. I lost control of it on a turn and hit a tree. Luckily, the Ford was made of something very solid and got just a scrape. The tree was more seriously hurt. I told my mother the road was slick with rain.

CW: Honestly, I'm amazed that you remember all of this so well.

RHB: There are things you don't forget.

CW: When did you see Howard next?

RHB: That winter, in New York. He came down every year, for Belknap's parents' New Year's Eve party, which had become a kind of reunion of Howard's New York friends. Belknap's parents lived in an apartment on West End Avenue, and they did it up for the occasion, with tinsel and white and red streamers. A crowd of people stood around the big silver punch bowl in their dining room, shouting at each other in what seemed to be a foreign language, and breaking away now and then to grab a handful of cold cuts from one of the platters Mrs. Long had put out. The air reeked of cheap cigars and cigarettes. I didn't see Howard, and I didn't recognize anyone else. I was about to leave when Belknap came up and said, You must be the illustrious Robert Barlow! He seized my elbow and pulled me into the crowd. Fellows, he said, here's Barlow, emerged from the swamps of Florida. I tried to explain that I lived in a wooded area, but no one cared. Belknap poured me a glass of punch. Howard came up out of the crowd and beamed at me. Hail, Barlovius, he said, welcome to the frozen plateau of Leng!* [*Laughs.*] I had found my people. Before I knew it, this black-haired goldfish of a boy, who turned out to be Don Wollheim,† had led me to a corner of the living room, where he tried to recruit me for the Communist Party, which he had just joined. Every superior person ought to be a member, he said, looking over my shoulder, as if for a superior person who might be coming up behind me. I said that my artistic pursuits left me no time for politics, and Wollheim began to explain in a very superior way that politics *was* art, but then Sam Loveman came to tell me that Howard was looking for me. As he led me back toward the refreshments, he said Howard had told him all about me, and that he, Loveman, had expected me to be some kind of mad pygmy dressed in animal skins. He was pleased to see that I looked civilized. How old are you? he asked. Sixteen, I said. Oh, Loveman said, well, of course, Howard has many young friends. I found his tone insufferable. It was easy to guess that Loveman was gay, and that he was jealous. Howard told me about you, too, I said. Loveman stiffened. What did he say? he asked. I didn't answer. What did Howard say? Loveman asked again. His face was flushed. Nothing important, I said. We'd just found Howard. Were you looking for me? I asked him. I was, he said. In a low voice he went on, You have to be careful, Barlovius. These New York Jews will eat you alive if you don't stop 'em. They're like encyclopedias with teeth. What's that? Loveman asked. I was just saying that Belknap's mother

* A region of the imaginary world where Lovecraft's novel *The Dream-Quest of Unknown Kadath* (1927) takes place.
† See the note on page 70.

knows the importance of cheese, Howard said, pointing to the cubes heaped on a blue-and-white china platter. Stick close to me, Barlovius, he went on, we stand a better chance of getting at the eats if we go together. Loveman followed us to the cheese plate, and we talked for a while with an athletic young man who turned out to be the illustrator Hannes Bok.* Like Belknap, he had a wispy mustache, which made him look like Douglas Fairbanks with mange. Hannes was also clearly a homosexual, or not *clearly,* but obscurely, behind the tight-lipped gentlemanliness which was the pose we all adopted in those days. But there was no mistaking the way he looked at me. I couldn't believe my good luck. Not only to be with Howard, but to have found out that nearly all his friends were gay! Belknap wasn't, it's true, and I wasn't sure about Wollheim. But the others *were.* It was wonderful. To be among my kind . . . [*Laughs.*] Loveman's roommate Pat had spiked the punch, and Howard got drunk, only he didn't know it, because he'd never before had a drink, and no one told him. Meanwhile, Loveman and Pat and Hannes were talking about *Lady Chatterley's Lover.* They were making fun of the sex, the twining of flowers in Lady Chatterley's pubic hair and so on, and Pat said, louder than he meant to, For sure, that was scarier than anything in *Weird Tales!* Howard was outraged. Clearly, you don't know much about horror, he said. Horror is premised on the experience of what we *do not* and *cannot* understand, whereas what you're talking about is mere low-class smut, which every schoolboy has encountered before he's in long pants. The room fell si-

---

* Hannes Bok (1914–1964) was a notable science fiction illustrator.

lent. *Your* presence here, Howard said, pointing at Pat, is evidence that even the least intelligent of human beings can produce offspring, but that's no reason our reproductive biology should show up in literature. You're dead wrong, Pat said loudly, sex is human, and novels can't just ignore it. Why not? Howard asked. Shouting is human, too, but if you raise your voice in a library, you'll be shown out, or you ought to be. As for *humanity*, I get enough of it just taking the streetcar. What *I* want, when I sit down to read a novel, is wonder. I'd never heard Howard speak like that before, from the seat of his power, so to speak. It was majestic. Belknap whispered something to Pat, and Pat said, When you put it that way, I see your point. I like wonder, too. You probably mean the Wonder Wheel, down on Coney Island, Howard grumbled, but Belknap was already leading him back to the punch bowl. A quarter of an hour later, at Belknap's urging, Howard sang a comical song he'd composed earlier that day, which I don't remember, except that he rhymed *Cthulhu* with *toodle-oo*. It surprised some people who didn't know how the name was pronounced.* Then, suddenly, Howard sat down. Are you all right? I asked. Short of breath, he said. I ought to go out and get some air. I'll go with you, I said. We retrieved our coats and went out. It was a fiercely cold night, and the wind blowing from the Hudson made it even colder. Knots of people were marching up Broadway, laughing and singing "Auld Lang Syne." People threw firecrackers from their cars. The cold air refreshed Howard, and in a minute he was

---

* Lovecraft pronounced it *KOOT-u-lew,* whereas most fans pronounced it, and still pronounce it, *ka-THOO-loo.* To say the name Lovecraft's way, Charlie said, is like rolling the R's in *Mordor:* the mark of a fandom so refined that almost no one knows what you're talking about.

laughing at his *dizzy spell*. It must have been overindulgence in cheese, he said. I had no idea I had a limit! We all do, I said. Barlovius, you are wise beyond your years, Howard said. But honestly, what kind of idiot would call *Chatterley* honest, or frank? All that nonsense with the gamekeeper reeks of violets. You've read it? I asked, astounded. Of course, Howard said. When you lead a life like mine, you tend to read everything. We were walking downtown, with the vague idea of reaching Times Square. When we came to the triangle where Verdi's statue stands,* I made a clever remark about Lawrence and the operatic side of life, but Howard was no longer listening. Pegāna, I'm completely frozen, he mumbled. His blue lips could hardly form the words. Where are you staying? I asked. With Belknap, he said. You should have stayed there, too, you would have saved yourself three dollars a night. Belknap lived on One Hundredth Street; walking him back there was out of the question. My hotel is just up the street, I said. Does it have heat? Howard asked. Excessively, I said. Then point me toward it, Howard said. It was New Year's Eve, and no one wondered at all about two coated, hatted men staggering upstairs together. And my room was, in fact, very warm. I filled water glasses from the tap, and Howard sat on the bed in his coat, staring dully at the wall. Mark this night, he said, after a while, for I have cheated death! You don't even have frostbite, I said. Not where you can see it, Howard said. Take off your coat, I said, I'll warm you up. Without thinking, I leaned forward

---

* Verdi Square, on Seventy-Third Street and Broadway. I walk past it all the time, on the way to my office on Central Park West, and now I can't help imagining Barlow standing there, arm in arm with the white-faced Lovecraft. Was Lovecraft's face white? Was Barlow holding his arm? I don't know. As Charlie said, once you get deep enough into a story, you start seeing things.

and kissed his nose. Howard blinked. Bobby? he said. Yes, I said, and kissed his mouth.

CW: I thought the two of you were revising a manuscript.

RHB: Not that night.

CW: Did you . . . ?

RHB: I'll tell you in a minute. I have to use the washroom, and I see Xictli is hungry. Have you met him? Here, Xictli. Come. [*Gestures.*] No? Well, he's shy.

4.

CW: So, what happened?

RHB: Happened?

CW: That night. In New York.

RHB: Howard fell asleep, and so did I. When I woke up, he was gone, and I didn't see him until the next summer, when he came back to Florida.

CW: Your father was home that summer.

RHB: Yes.

CW: What was that like?

RHB: It made my work easier. My father distracted Bernice, and she didn't play hostess so much. [*Laughs.*] Or wonder what Howard and I could be doing.

CW: What did your father think of Lovecraft?

RHB: The Colonel identified Howard as an ally in the ongoing war between himself and Spain.

CW: Oh.

RHB: Also, they both loved Gilbert and Sullivan. I didn't make that up. My father wanted them to perform *H.M.S. Pinafore* at the community theater in DeLand, with Howard as Buttercup. [*Sings.*] *Buy of your Buttercup—poor little Buttercup* . . . Can you imagine?

CW: Not really, no. What was your work?

RHB: What?

CW: You said, the Colonel made your work easier.

RHB: Oh. Perhaps *work* isn't the right word. I wanted Howard to stay with us. That was the purpose of the cabin we built on the far side of the lake, so he would have a private place to write. And so *we* would have a private place to make love, or at least that was what I hoped.

CW: Did you? Make love, I mean.

RHB: We built the cabin. It was an enormous amount of work, because all the materials had to go *around* the lake, or else *across* the lake, in the rowboat. Charles Johnston helped with the framing, and left us to do the siding and the interior. I don't think he expected we'd ever get it done, but we did. Howard was surprisingly handy.

CW: Was there ever anything between you and Johnston, or between him and Howard?

RHB: [*Laughs.*] No. Charles was as straight as they come. His idea of fun was picking up blond girls at Daytona Beach. He couldn't have cared less whether I had sex with Howard or with a water buffalo. Really, he was a very agreeable person.

CW: Ah.

RHB: And . . . there we were. I kept waiting for something to happen, and it didn't. [*Laughs.*] The cabin was a disaster in that regard. Howard would row across the lake after dinner, and stay there all night, and I hardly saw him at all. I asked what he was doing, but he wouldn't tell me. Barlovius, he said stiffly, there are matters that belong to a gentleman's privacy. What, I said, it's not like I'm asking you about going to the toilet. Bobby! he said. From hints he dropped, I had the idea that he was working on a new story. He asked me to drive him to the library at Stetson, so he could consult some psychology textbooks. He went for long walks by himself in the forest. Meanwhile, I dropped hints to my parents that I wasn't prepared for college. I needed a tutor, I said, an educated person. Well. At the end of July, my father took Howard aside for a talk, man to man. What, exactly, were his prospects in Providence? Wouldn't he be glad to trade his revision work* for a steady job as a tutor? With some light singing duties on the side? The salary wouldn't be much, but the position came with room and board. When Howard told me about the offer, later that evening, I could have clapped.

CW: But he didn't stay.

RHB: A few days later, we went back to De Leon Springs. Seeing the sugar mill for the second time was very much like seeing it for the first. Howard lingered by the millstone, running his hands over its rough, pocked surface as if to draw the sweetness of the past out of it. After half an hour of this, he said something about how picturesque it was, and I said, Not if you were a slave who had to work there. Howard said that of course slavery had been a lamentable institution, but on the other hand, it was responsible for some great works. The Cyclopean pyramids of Egypt, not to mention the even more Cyclopean pyramids of the Aztecs . . . I said I had nothing against pyramids, but the people who made them should have been paid. You sound like Belknap, Howard said. Free

---

* Lovecraft made a meager living revising stories and poems for other writers, most of them amateurs.

lunch for everyone, and equality all around! Well, I said, I don't think some people should be the property of others on account of the color of their skin. I won't argue the case with you, my dear Barlovius, Howard said, but I do think you ought to distinguish your moral sentiments from your aesthetic ones. The lower levels of society may have fascinating customs, but that doesn't make 'em intelligent, or good. What do you mean, the lower levels? I asked. Well, Howard said, blushing with irritation, the lesser races. The Egyptians used African slaves—Nubians and such. I imagine the Aztecs relied on the subject races of their area. I don't know any Nubians, I said, indignantly, but the Negroes I *do* know are just as intelligent as white people, and every bit as good. I'm sorry to use that word but it was what we said at the time.

CW: No worries.

RHB: Howard told me to keep my voice down. Of course there are individual exceptions, he said, but if you were to visit New York, and see the masses of 'em there, you'd understand what I mean. The best thing that could happen would be for a kindly gust of cyanogen from the tail of some passing comet to wipe 'em out. *You* ought to distinguish being dramatic from being human, I said, and I've been to New York, in case you don't remember. I stormed out and went into the forest to brood. It was impossible, I thought, I couldn't be in love with Howard. He was a loathsome old man who didn't understand people. How could he? He'd spent his whole life with his aunts. But how could he have so little *curiosity*? I didn't understand, then, that Howard's prejudices were rooted in pain. His father went mad when he was just a little boy . . .

CW: I know.

RHB: . . . and his mother went mad, too, somewhat later. One by one, Howard had lost the people he loved, until all he had was his famous sense of himself as an eighteenth-century gentleman, with all the good and bad qualities that entails. He needed to believe that he was a superior being, or at least that he belonged to a superior race, because, in his heart, Howard was terrified that he was nothing at all. His prejudice was like a child making a wall out of sand, to keep the ocean out. The child keeps putting more sand on the wall, and the ocean keeps pulling it down, and the child knows that, in the end, the ocean will level the wall, but what can he do? All he has are his hands, and maybe a shovel or a pail.

CW: It's like your story.

RHB: My story?

CW: "The Night Ocean."

RHB: Ah, yes. Well, I suppose that was a story about Howard. He looks at the ocean, day after day, and he knows he'll never understand it, let alone master it, but there it is. The horrible ocean.

CW: That's funny. I always thought of the story as being about *you*. I thought you were the artist, and he was the ocean, the thing you would never understand.

RHB: Oh? Oh, well, yes, that also.

CW: Because the main character is a muralist, which was something you wanted to do, too.

RHB: Indeed. [*Laughs.*] It's funny how many ways you can read a single story. But I suppose that's the mark of a good work of art, isn't it?

CW: So they say.

RHB: I was still furious when Howard found me. I'm sorry, he said. I've become damnably insensitive in my old age. You're right, of course. When you consider humanity from a cosmic point of view, we're all equally insignificant. To a visitor from Betelgeuse, I imagine, we'd all seem like ants. Some black and some red, but ants just the same. I didn't say anything. Howard looked around, to see if there was anyone nearby, but of course there wasn't. Bobby, he said, I've been thinking about the evening we spent together in New York. Oh? I said. Well, he said, as you know, there's nothing *intrinsically* wrong with any human behavior, so long as it isn't dishonest, and doesn't cause harm. The problem is, and always has been, how it's looked on. In ancient Greece . . . Howard turned bright red. I can't stop thinking about you, he said. Pegāna, Bobby, what am I becoming? He made a strange sound, like a frightened rabbit. I can't stand it, he said, it's like some other entity has possession of my *mind* . . . He looked at me anxiously. I remember that you expressed some feelings in this place, last summer, he said. Do you still . . . ? Yes, I said. Howard sighed. He picked a blue flower from a jacaranda tree and handed it to me solemnly. I have it still. Would you like to see it?

CW: OK.

Sound of footsteps. Silence. Footsteps, then rustling of pages.

RHB: Here.

CW: Wow.

RHB: It used to be more blue.

CW: What happened next?

RHB: Starting that afternoon, I began to tell myself a story, and in this story, Howard and I were in love. We stayed in Florida for only a short time, then we moved to another part of the country. I imagined us in San Francisco, which I knew almost nothing about, except that it was far from my family, and had a lot of bookstores. In my story, we bought a house there, and invited our friends to visit: Belknap, and Price, and Ray Cummings,* and dozens of other people who, in reality, would never have crossed the United States to see a couple of homosexuals. We threw costume parties, and raised rabbits and chickens. We slept in the same big bed. I didn't tell Howard my story, because I didn't think I had to. I thought he was telling it, too. We sat in the rowboat without talking, or even rowing. We held hands. We didn't go on any more expeditions, except to eat ice cream in DeLand, and bump knees under the lunch counter. Where would we have gone? We had already found what we were looking for. [*Pause.*] One day, Howard told me he had thought of an idea for a novel, which he was thinking of calling *The House of the Worm*. It was about several generations of an English family, and the rise and fall of their fortunes. At the end of it, he said, the last male descendant emigrates to New England, where he has various misadventures and finally goes mad. It ends tragically, Howard said, but what I want to show, Barlovius, is the immense *connectedness* of human life. When you think about the way the same patterns repeat, from generation to generation, it's almost monstrous. Like in "The Dunwich Horror,"† I said. Howard was nonplussed. Not quite that, he said. I want to write about real people. Do you know Zola's novels? He talked excitedly about the research he'd have to do, to write this novel. He could do some of it in the New York Public Library, but the genealogical records he wanted were in London. Imagine, he said, the Old Gent in London! It's always

---

* E. Hoffmann Price (1898–1988) was a prolific pulp writer, whom Lovecraft had met in New Orleans in 1932. Barlow invited him to Cassia, but he never went. Ray Cummings (1887–1957) was a science fiction writer in Mount Vernon, New York. He visited Florida several times, but Barlow was unable to meet him, either.

† Lovecraft's 1928 story about a Massachusetts family that interbreeds with extra-cosmic beings.

been a dream of mine to get there, but I've never felt venture-some enough to make the trip. And now . . . I do! His face was flushed with happiness. I thought: all right, London. And I began to tell myself a story about that. [*Pause.*] But *still* nothing happened between us, sexually. And to make a long story short, I went out one night and had sex with the boy we had met on Daytona Beach, the one who believed in the houses in the ocean. Do you know who the Gullah are?

CW: Sure.

RHB: Island people, from Georgia, descended from slaves. They have their own language, which is quite interesting. Part African, part English, but not modern English: it's more like early nineteenth-century English, miraculously preserved. [*Sighs.*] It's funny to think that the past Howard longed for *does* exist, or did, but only in places where Howard would never have dared look for it. My friend's name was Luke, and his parents were Gullahs from Tybee Island. They believed all kinds of strange things—cities in the ocean was the least of it. Luke's grandmother was a hoodoo woman, who believed you could make someone go away by writing their name backward . . . Where was I?

CW: You slept with Luke.

RHB: Not *slept.* I drove to Daytona; we had magnificent, simple sex in the back of the Ford; then I drove home. Howard was awake when I came in, washing collars in the bathroom sink. Where'd you go, Bobby? he asked. I should have lied, but I was never good at improvising, the way Howard was. I had to prepare everything. So, like an idiot, I told him the truth. I thought if I made him jealous, he'd want to try the same things with *me.* But Howard just stood there, his mouth part-way open, rubbing his hand against the lip of the sink. Then he said: For someone as well-off as you are, Bobby, you have remarkably little breeding. He shut the bathroom door. I heard him cough, then water running in the sink, then, for a long time, nothing at all. He was still there when I went to bed.

CW: What happened?

RHB: Howard didn't come down until after lunch. He went straight into the garden and talked to Bernice about the orchids she was teasing from the ground. I joined them, but Howard wouldn't look at me. Finally I asked if he'd help me carry the boat into the water, and we walked down to the lake. I'm sorry about last night, I said. Please tell me that I haven't ruined everything. *Everything* would be an exaggeration, Howard said. He stood very stiffly, with his hands in his pockets. Even in DeLand, I'm sure there are people who aren't thinking about you at all. Will you forgive me? I asked. For what? Howard said. For hurting you, I said. My dear Barlovius, Howard said, you haven't hurt me, except insofar as it pains me to see you demean yourself. How old is your friend? My age, I said, seventeen. Oh, Howard said. He plucked at a strand of Spanish moss that hung from the branch of a live oak. You're both very young, he said, and . . . now we've got it in the water, I think I'll take the boat out. I watched him row to the far side of the Moon Pool, where he sat, holding the oars but not moving.

CW: He loved you.

RHB: I thought so. Howard stayed six more days, to prove I hadn't broken his heart. Then I followed him to St. Augustine, for his birthday, to prove that *I* believed I hadn't. We barely talked. I remember standing on the wall of the Spanish fortress, running my hand along the coquina stone of the parapet. Howard was walking below me, inspecting the foundation, just a little figure in a cheap blue suit. How useless this all is, I thought. [*Pause.*] My parents got divorced in the summer of 1936, and Bernice and I moved back to Kansas City. I went to see Howard that August, in Providence. We had been exchanging letters as if nothing were wrong. I thought . . . I wondered if he might have forgiven me, after all. But when I got to Providence, Howard was busy revising some awful book,* and he had no time. He was another person in Providence: older. He worried about money, and talked about it constantly. I hate to say it, but I found him dull. Even his skin had become dull, like an old man's skin. I tried to revive him with a plan to publish William Seabrook's travel books† in a uniform edition, but he was completely unmoved. They're all in print, he said, why bother printing 'em again? Because of how they'd look, I said. I think it would make a nice effect. There could be a Seabrook Library, bound in midnight-blue Morocco leather, and stamped in gold. Or would red be better? You would have trouble finding a question that interests me less, Howard said. I don't understand, I said. I thought you and Seabrook were friends? Robert, Howard said, what you don't understand is that *I* care about literature, whereas *you* care about books. I didn't speak to him for days. But at the end of the month, we took a trip to Salem and Marblehead.

CW: The famous Arkham and Kingsport.

RHB: You've done your homework. There were four of us on

---

* Anne Tillery Renshaw's *Well Bred Speech*.

† William Seabrook (1884–1945) was a journalist. His book *The Magic Island* introduced the zombie into popular culture.

the trip: Howard and I, Kenny Sterling,* and Sterling's friend
Roscoe, who was, I believe, a law student. We toured Salem
as a group. Sterling got on my nerves, and Roscoe was even
worse: both of them fawning over Howard, and at the same
time making themselves out to be very important, as if they
were the initiates of a cult, the purpose of which was to laugh
at how stupid everyone else was. What really bothered me,
though, was how much Howard enjoyed it. I thought at first
that he was going along with them, but then I saw that
he thrived on their attention, that it made him into something he very much wanted to be. I had a terrible thought,
that *this* was what Howard wanted from me. Not love, and
certainly not sex, but adulation. All this time, I had imagined
that he was drawn to me because we were akin to each other,
but now I wondered if he'd answered my letters so generously because he knew that I would save them, *because I was a
collector.* I wondered, bitterly, if he'd ever seen me as anything
other than an instrument of his posterity. Not that I would
have minded being that, necessarily, but it was so dishonest.
To use me that way and not tell me I was being used. When
we got to Marblehead, on the second day of our trip, Sterling
and Roscoe were in ecstasies. I think the desk clerk at our
hotel has webbed fingers, Roscoe said, tittering. Could he be
of the accursed race of fish-men? I have a strange foreboding
about the chowder, Sterling said. Careful, men! I told Howard I wasn't feeling well. But you have to see Marblehead, he
said. It's one of the wonders of New England, a place where

---

* Kenneth Sterling (1920–1995) was a fan who had met Lovecraft in Providence. He later became
a physician and worked (brave man) at the VA Medical Center in the Bronx.

the past has been harmoniously incorporated into the present. It won't be harmonious with my headache, I said. You go ahead. He and Sterling and Roscoe went out together, and I walked alone to the Old Burial Hill, which overlooks the harbor. I didn't want to see Howard ever again. I had my bag with me, and I decided I'd take the bus to Boston, then back to Kansas City. After that, I didn't know. I could see cars nudging up and down the streets of Marblehead, but they had nothing to do with me. Nothing had anything to do with me. I thought of throwing myself from a cliff, but there wasn't a cliff nearby. I sat at the foot of a big spruce tree, and I was still there when Howard scrambled up the path, out of breath. Barlovius! he said. Thank all the gods! I went back to the YMCA to see if you were feeling better, and they told me you had left. I did leave, I said. I see that, Howard said, but why? I just stared at him. Aha, Howard said. Do you mind if I sit down? So we sat there for a while, then Howard said, At your age, Bobby, you naturally imagine that what you feel is important. When someone slights you, you want to murder him! And when you think you're in love . . . When you get to be the Old Gent's age, however, you'll understand that everything you feel has been felt before, over and over, until it's as worn out as my 1917 overcoat. Really, it's comical. Each of our so-called individual emotions is just a repetition of something that has been felt countless thousands of times before, by countless others. From *that* point of view, it's hard to put much stock in feeling. Do you see my point? Forget it, I said. It was a hot, cloudless day, and you could see quite far. What's that? I asked, pointing to a black speck on the horizon. I think it's Bakers Island, Howard said. Unless it's a hitherto unknown island, where mysterious lights blink in a code that the cryptologists at Miskatonic University* have yet to crack. When they do crack it, I said, it'll say, *Howard, come home.* Howard laughed. What would I do without you, Bobby? he asked. I shrugged. Find another acolyte, probably. I'm sure Roscoe or Sterling would be glad to oblige. Possibly, but would either of them do *this*? Howard asked. He took my hand. I was stunned. Careful, Mr. Lovecraft, I said, someone might find your behavior low class! Howard laughed again, less happily. He looked out to sea, and said, I wonder if I'll ever get to England. Let's go, I said, impulsively. We'll set you up in the British Museum, and you can write your book. I'd like to see Scotland, too, Howard said. I hear their castles are exceedingly ancient and gloomy. We'll find the gloomiest one, I said. Then we'll go to Paris, and see the Catacombs. Howard looked at me with amazement. Barlovius, he said, I think you're serious. Absolutely serious, I said. Howard tightened his grip on my hand. I was sure he would say yes—it was clear to me that he wanted to go. But after a single, beautiful moment, in which I imagined the two of us living together openly in Paris, or if not there then in Morocco, a moment in which I imagined that love and even happiness might exist in this world, Howard asked, How do you propose we pay for this trip? We'll work our passage across the Atlantic, I said, and hitchhike the rest of the way. Ah, Howard said. You expect me to stand in the roadside dust, with my thumb out. Why not? I asked. And sleep in the woods, Howard said, and warm my hands at a campfire. Sounds like fun,

---

* A fictitious university, which figured frequently in Lovecraft's stories. As a teenager, Charlie made himself a Miskatonic U. student ID, which, he said, got him in to more than one bar.

I said. What about Mrs. Gamwell? Howard asked, meaning his aunt. Would she come with us? I hadn't thought of it, I said. I couldn't leave her alone, Howard said seriously. She's getting on in years. What if something happened to her while we were away? I had just had the pleasure of spending three weeks next door to Mrs. Gamwell, and she seemed able to take care of herself. You'll write her letters, I said, the same as always. What about my things? Howard asked. I'd miss them if we were gone too long. Now you're teasing me, I said. England is full of things. France, too. Yes, but they aren't *my* things, Howard said. And what if one of us fell ill? I don't speak a word of French. We'll worry about that if it happens, I said. No, Bobby, Howard said, I can't. I'd be too afraid that something would take away all the pleasure I might get from such an expedition. I realized two things then. The first was how great a part fear played in Howard's life. Not the cosmic fear he wrote about, but ordinary fear, that his luggage might get lost, or that French food wouldn't agree with him. I did not love Howard any less for this, but I did feel sorry for him, and I didn't want to be like him. That was the second thing I understood: I wanted to live. I looked out at the flashing Atlantic, flecked with tiny sails, and promised myself that I would cross it. To Howard I said: All right, have it your way. What about an expedition to find some ice cream? Howard smiled. It may be perilous, he said, but, nothing ventured, nothing gained. The Miskatonic University Ice Cream Expedition of 1936, I said. We were still holding hands. Howard wrapped his pinky around mine, and said . . .

CW: Umph.

RHB: Umph. Then we walked back to town, and joined Roscoe and Sterling.

CW: Was that when you wrote "The Night Ocean"?

RHB: What? No, that was earlier. After Bernice and I moved to Kansas City, in July of '36, I fell in love with a boxer, and while he was training, I'd wait for him in the public library. I must have written it then.

CW: But it's all about the ocean!

RHB: Yes? Well, I probably missed the ocean. I used to love going to Daytona Beach.

CW: . . .

RHB: What can I tell you? Now that I think of it, though, I did show the story to Howard, before we went to Marblehead. He made a few changes, but on the whole he admired it. You know, Barlovius, he said, you would be one of the best weird writers of your generation, if only you applied yourself. I thought he was scolding me, and out of sheer perversity, I decided not to write any more weird fiction. [*Laughs.*] Later, after Howard died, I realized that he really had liked the story, but it was too late. I couldn't go back. And, in fact, "The Night Ocean" was the last story I ever wrote.

CW: The end of an era.

RHB: One rarely knows that at the time. What I remember is that Howard and Sterling and Roscoe and I spent a pleasant afternoon in Marblehead. Now that I knew Howard loved me, I didn't mind them so much. We walked along the shore that night, looking for the phosphorescent jellyfish which Sterling assured us would be there, but they weren't, and the next day Howard and I went back to Providence. He opened the door to his apartment and groaned sepulchrally, Here's the mail. A few days later, I had to go back to Kansas City. Howard walked me to the bus station. It was very much like our first parting, in DeLand, two years earlier, only this time it was Howard who was downcast. You know, Robert, he said, I'd be glad to see you settled here, one day. I don't think Mrs. Gamwell would like that, I said. She couldn't stand me, because she knew just what I was. I don't live my *entire* life to please Mrs. Gamwell, Howard said, only most of it. I imagine that a gentleman of my age should have the right to choose his friends. I promised to think about it. In fact, I couldn't imagine living in Providence, which struck me as being a city of aunts. I wanted to see Paris. I know what that means, Howard said. You'll be halfway to making a decision, then a butterfly will appear, and you'll run off to look for your net. Not necessarily, I said, blushing. We reached the bus station. Used to be a stable, Howard said, if I'm not mistaken. The property of a man named Peaslee, who owned all the hansom cabs in Providence. He held out his hand. Good-bye, Robert. He waited until the bus door closed, waved once, solemnly, and walked off. The bus route wound down toward the river, and as we turned onto Exchange Street, I had a view of College Hill, lit by the afternoon sun. For one long moment, I saw the city the way Howard always had, as a dream-city, where the colonial past curled like a cat, sleeping in a doorway, which might wake up at any moment, stretch, and come back to life. The buildings shone red and white and gold; the blue air hung over them like an upside-down ocean. Then the bus turned again, and the hill vanished. I had the ridiculous thought that this vision had been Howard's parting gift to me, and now that it was gone, I had lost him, too. I told myself not to be stupid, but of course I was right. Howard died six months later, while I was in Kansas City.

5.

Here, unfortunately, Charlie's phone ran out of memory. For the rest of the story, he had to rely on the notes he'd scrawled while Barlow spoke, which he fleshed out later with facts he'd gathered from his own research. The spring of 1937, Barlow told Charlie, was a gray epoch of grief. He ruined everything he touched. He enrolled in the Kansas City Art Institute and studied with Thomas Hart Benton, the great muralist, but after Howard died, Barlow lost interest in painting. What could a mural do? Wasn't art merely a consolation for the artist and his bourgeois friends? At first Benton appreciated his rebellious spirit, but Barlow never finished anything, and Benton got tired of him. So Barlow quit art school. He went to Mexico to learn Spanish, then he moved to California—not to San Francisco, where he had imagined living with Howard, but to Lakeport, a small resort on a large blue lake surrounded by towns. He stayed with the Beck brothers, Groo and Claire: two handsome redheads who published a magazine called *The Science Fiction Critic*. Claire had a mania for bathing and walking around in tight-fitting underwear. Groo was surly. When it got cold, he sat by the fire, reading *Amazing Stories*, listening to the radio, petting his dog, and eating walnuts, all at the same time. In their company, Barlow began to dream again. The Becks had a letterpress, and he used it to print Howard's commonplace book. He thought Lakeport might become what Cassia could have been, a haven for artists. There were empty houses all around where his friends could live. He wrote to Clark Ashton Smith, a writer and painter whose work Howard had admired. Smith lived in Auburn, north of Sacramento; Barlow imagined him as a pillar of this new California community, this utopia of the weird. He was going to rally everyone under the black banner of *Lovecraft*. He ignored the letters from friends in New York, who said Sam Loveman was telling everyone that he, Barlow, was a thief. He also ignored the nagging letters from Wisconsin, where Derleth was waving his own Lovecraft banner, pompously, and, Barlow thought, somewhat comically. He had never met Derleth, but he had a mental picture of him: a stout fellow in a plaid jacket, with a face like an insurance salesman's. Not weird at all, he thought. Barlow was still deciding which of the Beck brothers to fall in love with when Clark Ashton Smith sent him a postcard, to say that he did not desire to see Barlow, or to hear from him, ever again.

It was as if someone had taken a meat cleaver and cut out Barlow's entrails. He knew that Derleth was exasperated, and Wandrei and Loveman hated him, but until that moment, he hadn't realized how much they hated him, or what evil they were capable of. They had taken Lovecraft from him. And Lovecraft was, in a way, all that Barlow had. Now that he was banished from the society of Lovecraft's friends, he had no idea how to go on living. He went to San Francisco and rented a room at the YMCA on Turk Street, where he wrote poems about flowers and sleep and trumpets and caves and Howard and Aztec gods who were really just Howard in disguise. There was something about the order of a poem that appealed to him, something about its compactness. It was like pulling a noose tight around the world, but even Barlow could see that tightening a noose was not the same thing as living. Every night he went up to see Clyde, the third and oldest of the Beck brothers, in his apartment on Telegraph Hill. Clyde was in the middle of being divorced by his wife; he spent a lot of time sitting in an armchair by the window, smoking a pipe and reading William Butler Yeats. He and Barlow got drunk often. Once, they went to a Mexican restaurant where Barlow tried to speak to the waitress in Spanish, only to discover that she was Irish—"black Irish," Clyde joked. He was studying Celtic literature and everything looked Irish and gloomy to him. Clyde's company probably kept Barlow from killing himself, but even so, after a while Barlow got tired of him. Being slandered had awakened his capacity for hatred, and like any new emotion, it came out wildly. He hated men with beards, then he grew a beard and hated men without them. He hated the fans who wrote Lovecraft memorials in their putrid little magazines, and he hated the millions of human beings who didn't know who Howard was. On the anniversary of Howard's death, he dragged Clyde to a German restaurant: he wanted to drink to forget, but he talked about Howard all night, and wouldn't let Clyde change the subject. What he really wanted, he thought, was to enrage everyone, so they'd be like him, and love him, finally, for what he was.

Groo Beck moved to San Francisco in the winter. He had grown a beard for the World's Fair,* which made him look like an Irish Jesus, and Barlow fell in love with him. They moved into an apartment near Clyde's. It had only one bedroom, and one bed, which folded out of the wall. Barlow and Groo named the bed *Montresor,* after the villain in the Poe story. Each time one of them folded it up, they would shout, "For the love of God, Montresor!" as if somebody were trapped within. That was the most fun Barlow had with, or in, the bed. But there were other games to play: Groo and Barlow dressed as cowboys

---

* I.e., the Golden Gate International Exposition, which was held on Treasure Island in 1939, to compete with the better-known 1939 World's Fair in New York.

and outlaws, and roamed North Beach, looking for strange things to eat in the Italian groceries. They threw olives at the harbor seals and lurked in Golden Gate Park, making weird birdcalls. Barlow thought he might be coming to life again, that San Francisco might have saved him, but really he was just a guest at a costume party. When he figured out that all the people he knew there, who claimed to have discovered their true, free selves, were, in fact, dressed *as* people, he became frantic. He wrote poems about love and gardens and vines and sleep, but they didn't release him from the feeling that he was not living. Was the secret to try harder, or not to try at all? *Was* there a secret? Trolley tracks winked at Barlow like prostitutes. The Golden Gate Bridge waggled its fingers. Over here, it whispered, your people are here, at the bottom of the Bay. He told Groo that he was going crazy, and Groo told him to see a doctor.

With a rationality that struck Barlow, in retrospect, as being totally miraculous, he took Groo's advice and met with a warm gray woman named Barbara Mayer, who had an office in the youth center on Eighteenth Street. He told her everything. "How do I go on living?" he asked. She rolled a sucking candy around in her mouth. "Well," she said, "is there something you want to do?" "I want to live," he said. "Robert," she reproved him, "living is not an activity. Why don't you go back to school?" He thought that might be all right but didn't know what to study. "What about business?" Barbara asked. But after what had happened with Derleth and Wandrei, Barlow knew all he wanted to about business. "What about anthropology?" he suggested. He thought that by learning about different people and different languages he might forget his own problems. Barbara looked him over. "That's not a bad idea," she said, "but you're going to have to shave your beard, and please, *please,* stop wearing spurs."

Barlow took courses at the Polytechnic Institute, in Spanish and anthropology and European history. At first he didn't bring his books to class, or take notes. When he lost interest in what his teachers were saying, he went to Golden Gate Park and took a nap on the lawn. Sometimes he felt like he was playacting and sometimes he felt like he was falling through space, and everything around him was also falling, with incredible speed, but lightly, and this seemed like it would go on forever. He got C's and C-minuses on his midterms. Barbara twisted her hair into a knot and secured it with a pencil. "Robert," she said, "it doesn't seem like you have much aptitude for these subjects. What if we put you in a trade school? You could become a commercial illustrator." Maybe I really am nothing, Barlow thought. Maybe I deserve nothing. Then he heard an exasperated little voice, which was himself, shouting that everyone else can do this, and, in fact, everyone *does*, and why, Robert, why not you? So he began the almost impossible work of loving the world.

He enrolled at Berkeley and studied with Alfred Kroeber, whose famous friendship with Ishi, the last of the Yahi Indians, was two decades past. Kroeber was a firm and distinguished Yorkville German who claimed to be in favor of fun but never had time for it himself. He worked his students hard. The worst mistake you can make, Kroeber taught, is to see another person through the lens of your prejudices. And the *second*-worst mistake is to think you aren't looking through the lens of your prejudices. It was a paradox, to which the answer was, to know your subject as specifically as you could. To know it as if it were your own life. For a long time, Barlow hated it. He didn't understand why Kroeber made him sort bone fragments, or learn the names of plants, or, memorably, make fire with sticks. Barlow wasn't going to do any of those things. He was going to study handsome young men with queer customs! And yet Kroeber saw something in Barlow that Barlow himself had not seen. He invited Barlow to his house in the Berkeley hills, a big construction of weathered redwood that, like

Kroeber himself, gave the impression of being precisely what it was. Here Barlow met Kroeber's daughter, Ursula: at the time, a wide-eyed eleven-year-old whose favorite pastime was to let grown-ups imagine they were educating her.* "Robert," she said, "tell me about the pyramids!" "They were burial chambers, Ursula. Vast burial chambers." "I know that, Robert, but why are they *pyramidal?*" "I don't know, Ursula." "Well, Robert, *I* have an idea. You know that four is the number of death, in China and Japan . . ." She loved science fiction and was surprised to learn that Barlow had been friends with Lovecraft. Although, she said, she didn't much care for Lovecraft's work. It was frightening and somehow inhuman. Ursula gave Barlow an insight into her father: Kroeber, she told him, had been married once before, to a pretty, dark-eyed woman whose photos were still to be found in his study. "She died of tuberculosis," Ursula said, "a long time ago, when my father was still working with Ishi. You know who that is, don't you?" Barlow knew. "Well," Ursula said, "when my father's first wife died, my father went to see Ishi, who was making arrowheads in his room in the museum. Ishi didn't say anything, he just smiled at my father and went on making arrowheads. He knew my father was sad, and this was his way of consoling him. Imagine? Ishi had lost everyone, his whole tribe, but he could still console my father. It makes you wonder who was *saving* whom, doesn't it?" "I suppose," Barlow said. "My father still misses her," Ursula said. "Now, look at this story. I got to the part where the spacemen land on Mars, but I can't decide what the Martians look like. Why do people always imagine them as green?" "Probably so they stand out against their background," Barlow said. Ursula looked at him reproachfully. "Robert, that's very stupid! What creature would evolve to stand out against its background?" Barlow

---

* This was the fantasy and science fiction writer Ursula K. Le Guin (1929–): the K stands for *Kroeber*.

helped her with her stories, and in return, she helped him to understand what he was doing. Anthropology wasn't ant-work. It was a way of laying up consolation against the time when you would be bereft.

While he was at Berkeley, Barlow fell in with a group of poets who called themselves the Activists. Their idea was to get rid of denotation as much as possible and just have language connote things. Under their influence, Barlow wrote jagged, crystalline poems about plains and stars and dead knights who were of course Howard. His fellow Activists encouraged him, but he detected pity behind their encouragement. They thought of him as an apprentice and imagined that he needed *them;* but it was clear to Barlow from the start that *they* were the ones who needed *him,* in order to think of themselves as teachers. He was just playing a part, but he did like how the Activists kept their poems brief. It was a way to tighten the noose so much, you could almost mistake it for the neck. Still, he was relieved to go away in the summers, to Mexico City, where he learned Nahuatl from the great scholar Wigberto Jiménez Moreno. He loved it there. In Mexico, the past was strange and the present was indifferent. You could do what you liked. If you wanted to, you could sleep with men, so long as you didn't demand that anyone care about it. Even the land was indifferent; even the sky. Barlow had made many friends in the small tangled society of Berkeley poets, but he longed for space and quiet, and a respite from the terrible optimism of Americans, even American poets. He wanted to be among people who knew what it was like to have your guts cut out. By the end of 1942, he had sent all the Lovecraft manuscripts he'd ever possessed to Derleth, with the exception of one: the notebook in which Howard had written "The Shadow Out of Time." It didn't matter, because the story had already been published. In 1944, Barlow moved to Mexico for good.

6.

Mexico consumed Barlow, and it liberated him. He told Charlie about his adventures among the Tepuztecs, the Copper People, who lorded it over the hills of Guerrero until Cortés came, and who still believed their king would return from the stars; and he spoke about his *other* adventures, in the *fichera* bars of Mexico City, where bands bleated out rumbas and boleros in semi-darkness, and he swung in the arms of handsome men to whom he was as strange as if he'd been a ghost. He had a lover, a soft-drink importer named Martín, who bought him a Packard and a villa in the northern suburb of Azcapotzalco. It had a lovely garden, full of jasmine and tuberose, and Martín referred to it as *the boudoir*, or sometimes, when he was angry, as *the hospital*. Barlow called it the Casa de Tlaloc, after his favorite of the Mexican gods: Tlaloc was the god of rain but also the lord of Tlalocan, the verdant paradise inhabited by the spirits of the drowned. Barlow's paradise was work. He translated old Nahuatl documents that the Spaniards had preserved, records of the tribute paid by various peoples to their Aztec masters, chronicles of the city of Tula, legends, genealogies. He wasn't exactly saving these people from oblivion—the Spanish codices were safe, unless the war jumped the Atlantic—but he liked to think that he was bringing them into the present. Certainly, if it hadn't been for Barlow, many facts about their strange and terrible lives would have been forgotten. It was tedious, painstaking work, which would go nowhere for months before suddenly resolving itself into an article, or the chapter of a book; but Kroeber had trained him for that. The problem was how much material there was. When he thought of all there was to translate, and how slowly he had to go, he really did despair, as if he had put out to sea in a rowboat, headed for France, and when he was halfway across the Atlantic, a bird flew up with a message, telling him that what he wanted was in Australia. Barlow's consolation was that he was making wonder real. Or rather, he wasn't *making* anything: he was finding real wonders. The world contained them and always had. Six days a week, twenty-nine days a month, Barlow went to bed with a headache and a sour feeling in his heart, as if he'd been trying to animate a huge dead body with his own blood. The seventh or thirtieth or thirty-first day, he sprang up, his heart pounding, as enchanted by the fact that he was Robert Barlow, in Azcapotzalco, D.F., Mexico, as he would have been by a talking fish, or a horse with wings.

He was, he had to realize, no one's apprentice. He was a teacher. It amazed him. And when the war ended, and soldiers started showing up in his classes—big-shouldered; older, in some cases, than he was, but just as selfish as six-year-old children—that was even stranger. Barlow worked day and night to shovel what he knew into the cooling furnaces of their minds, and he was often infuriated by how coolly they took his instruction. He explained to them what Kroeber had taught him about loss and consolation, but the students were utterly uninterested. They wanted merely to be thrilled. So Barlow tried to thrill them, with stories of sacrifice and conquest, extortion and pride, and sometimes it worked, but most of the time teaching, too, left his heart sour. It made him feel that his body was too small, too frail; that his spirit was withered in a way that became obvious when it tried to lift the weight of authority. He envied Don Pablo's apparently effortless charm, his Oxford accent, his cape, his spats. He complained to Martín about this, and Martín asked the obvious question: "What has *he* written, Robert? Who hears his accent, on paper?" "Maybe I should live on paper," Barlow said, bitterly. "If you did," Martín pointed out, "I couldn't kiss you." But Barlow slid away. "Hold on," he said, "I'm almost done with this chapter."

Always, always, he was holding something. He held his students' attention when they drooped, sleepy with cheap beer, sunlight, tennis. He held a dictionary in his lap. He held the Culhua Mexica* in his head, the way a politician holds his constituents: he knew the provincial governors, the secretaries, the tax collectors, the high priests, and he tried to keep track of what they all wanted, so that he could read between the lines of their letters, which were full of strange formalities and equally strange abruptnesses. He held Martín's sorrow in a ball in his hand: *Robert, if I were disgraced before my children, I would have to kill myself.* When he was awake, he dreamed of putting it all down. When he was asleep, he dreamed of releasing metal spheres which flew out over the ocean and returned to his hands. This, too, made him sad: it was a dream Howard had had in Cassia. He told it to Barlow at the dinner table, which they had moved outdoors, into the shade of some trees. The truth, however, was that Barlow thought about Howard less and less. A curtain had fallen between him and his memories of the two summers in Cassia, the trip to New York, the Providence visit: only four meetings in all, so few, compared with the dozens and dozens he'd had with Martín; and then another curtain had fallen in front of *that* curtain. The distant past drove out the recent past. In the sum-

---

* This, Barlow believed, was the proper name for the Aztecs. It was what they called themselves, to link their society to the culture that had flourished at Culhuacán. Charlie couldn't help noticing that *Culhua* also sounded a little like *Cthulhu:* as if Barlow was searching for Lovecraft in the Mexican past.

mer of 1946, Barlow wrote to the library at Brown, offering them all
the papers he still had from Howard's estate, and his own weird fiction library, if they would send him a Chandler & Price 12×18 press,
with motor for AC current, 110–120 volts, 50 cycle, with three chases.
He wanted to print a newspaper in Nahuatl, so the Nahua could learn
to read their own language. Maybe there could be a Nahuatl revival,
he thought, a new flourishing of the old culture. Maybe the Nahua
could pick up where he would inevitably leave off, when his strength
gave out.

In 1948, Barlow kept the promise he'd made to himself years earlier and crossed the Atlantic. He consulted *certain ancient manuscripts*
in the British Museum library, with a wry smile on his face; then he
went over to Paris and did the same in the Bibliothèque Nationale.
Once, in Paris, Howard flickered to life in the seat next to his and
looked over his shoulder. "My god, Barlovius, what language is *that*?"
he asked. "Surely it must be the Pnakotic tongue, in which the priests
of Easter Island recorded their most terrible secrets." "It's a list of
grain deliveries," Barlow said. "Although the Spanish priest who copied
it seems to have mixed in a recipe for corn gruel." "Amazing," Howard
said. Then he asked, "Barlovius, what's wrong?" "Nothing," Barlow
sighed. "It's just so hard to love the world." "Why bother?" Howard
asked. "After all, there's nothing especially lovable about a billowing
collection of atoms, spiraling around in compliance with laws that
have nothing to do with us." "So, what do I do?" Barlow asked. "Whatever you want, so long as you don't embarrass yourself," Howard said.
"But, Howard," Barlow said, "if I'm just a collection of atoms, why
does it matter whether I embarrass myself?" "Because people remember," Howard said. "And by the way, Barlovius, the light in here is very
dim; you should be careful of your eyes." Then he was gone. Barlow
finished his work at the library and went out to get drunk and find
someone who would hold him, no matter what it cost.

When Barlow returned to Mexico City, he found a letter from Martín, who had left him, and a garbled telephone message from Paul Murray, the dean of Mexico City College, congratulating him on his new chair—only, his secretary, Castañeda, had thought to add, the chair never showed up. He assumed the new responsibility as gracefully as he could. The only good thing that came with it was Don Pablo's friendship: at first Don Pablo wanted Barlow's support for his expeditions in search of Ice Age artifacts in the Valley of Mexico; then, when he discovered that Barlow had written weird fiction, he confessed that he, too, had once dreamed of being a fiction writer. He invited Barlow to his villa, where he proudly displayed a complete edition of the works of Edgar Rice Burroughs, re-bound in green leather. Don Pablo told Barlow that for many years he had intended to write a great epic, about prehistoric men who build cities out of ice, and ride mastodons into battle, but he, who once rode with Pancho Villa, had never had the courage to begin it. All he had for his pains were a map, a sheaf of incomprehensible notes, and an encouraging letter from J. R. R. Tolkien, with whom he'd been friendly at Oxford. "Ridiculous, isn't it?" Don Pablo asked. "Not at all," Barlow said, at which point Don Pablo befriended him unconditionally, without prejudice toward his middle-class background or his hungry, furtive glances at Mexican boys.

Don Pablo was the last of Barlow's fathers, and the best. He took Barlow to lunch at the Jockey Club: an *impersonation,* he explained, of the Paris institution, of which he was also a member. Over a bottle of Sauternes—Don Pablo liked sweet wine, which, he readily admitted, was a blemish on his character—he whispered to Barlow about the failings of the Mexican aristocracy: this one was feebleminded and that one, a bigamist; most of them were stealing from Alemán's government, and more than a few were stealing from one another. An old man glaring at his consommé had once had sex with a sheepdog. Don Pablo hated them all amiably; it broke his heart to see the Revolution come to this. Barlow, drunk, felt a thrill of insideness. He was out of his depth, but at least he was among the initiated. Don Pablo offered to put him up for membership in the Jockey Club, but Barlow was wise enough to refuse. "I'm more comfortable around dead people," he said. Don Pablo roared with laughter. "Robert, these *are* dead people!" he said. But he didn't make the offer again.

In December 1949, there was a period of cold rain, and a new student appeared in Barlow's Mexico at the Time of the Conquest class, soaked, with water dripping from the brim of his gray hat. His name was Bill, and he'd briefly done something vague in the army, which entitled him to an allowance of seventy-five dollars a month, so long as he was enrolled in an accredited university. Mexico City College catered tacitly to his kind: it was common knowledge among the faculty that if all the enrolled G.I.s showed up for class, there wouldn't be room for them. Leeches like Bill kept the institution going. But here he was in Barlow's classroom, wearing a sodden gray double-breasted suit, and asking, in a remote voice, as though he were talking back to the radio, whether it was possible to see a human sacrifice anywhere in Mexico. A few of Barlow's students stifled giggles. "This is a class in history," Barlow said. "If you're looking for sensation of that kind, may I suggest that you read the newspaper." "Wel-l," Bill said, "I could do that, but I like to take a running start at the present. If the answer is no, just say so. I don't mind disappointment." Barlow looked at him again. A gaunt kid, or not a kid, with round spectacles: he looked the way Barlow imagined himself looking, if he were taller, and dead. "They happen every day, on every street in Mexico City," he said. "Just keep your eyes open, and you're sure to see one." There was a flash of exchanged consciousness between them: Barlow couldn't put it any other way. Bill came up after the class was over. "Enjoyed that," he said. "Sorry if I caused you any trouble." Immediately, without warning, Barlow was in a sexual panic. "Not at all," he said, gripping his notes. "As a matter of fact, I think you're right. There's a lot of past in the present. And," he added, without really knowing what he was saying, "there are surprisingly forward-looking moments in the past, too. The Christians call them *prefiguration,* but I like to think of them as signs that humanity does, now and then, make a correct guess about something." He'd never actually thought of it before. Bill smiled in an absent way. "You go deep," he said. "Most of the philosophers I know are drinking men. How about you?" Barlow blushed. "If you plan to take my class," he said, "please get yourself a copy of Bernal Díaz's *Annals of the Conquest of Mexico.*" But the name of the book was *True History.*

Bill never returned to Barlow's class, but Barlow saw him hanging around the bars of the Colonia Roma, always in a suit, often the same suit, looking like the world's filthiest junior partner in a law firm. Once, Barlow waved at him, and Bill looked up, incuriously, and went back to his conversation with one of the other leeches. His folded legs didn't quite fit under the table, Barlow noticed. After that he tried to avoid seeing Bill, and even changed the streets on which he walked, so he wouldn't pass any of the bars where Bill might be found. But one morning Barlow was reading the paper in a café called Lola's, around the corner from the college, when Bill came in and sat down next to him at the counter. He smelled like he'd urinated on himself. "Morning, Professor," he said. "Good morning," Barlow said stiffly. "Haven't seen you in school much." "And yet I have been learning," Bill said. "Cosmic secrets disclose themselves to me on a near-daily basis." He didn't say what they were, though. He just sat there with his elbows on the counter, looking placidly at Barlow, as if he had caught him in a butterfly net. "Where are you from?" he asked. "All over," Barlow said, "but my people are from Kansas City." "Kansas, or Missouri?" Bill asked. "Missouri," Barlow said. "I'm from Saint Louis, myself," Bill said. He clucked his tongue. The sound was like a coin falling into a vending machine. "Say," he said, "did you ever run across a fellow named Herb Wiggers? I knew him in Saint Louis, but I think he was in Kansas City before that." Wiggers, Bill said, had been a dentist, only he collected all the teeth he pulled and kept them in teak boxes, lined with green felt. Once a month he drove the boxes to a hotel in Chicago, where he swapped them with other tooth collectors. "Looking for rare ones, mostly," Bill said, "abnormal teeth with the wrong number of roots. Or animal teeth. You'd be surprised how many people have one or two animal teeth. It's a holdover from the earliest days of mankind. Crocodile teeth, even snake teeth. He had quite a collection. I wonder if you ever saw 'em." "No," Barlow said. He was sure Bill was lying, but wanted to see where his story would go. "Pity," Bill said. "With your interest in history, I think you would have found Herb Wiggers's collection enlightening." He coughed: another coin. "Actually, in Chicago, it wasn't just tooth collectors," he said. "There was a podiatrist with a lovely collection of little toes, pickled in formaldehyde. The gems of his collection were a pair of toes from a fellow with webbed feet, like a duck. The poor man couldn't wear shoes. But the tragic thing, Wiggers told me, was that the guy was afraid of water, and never learned to swim." Bill coughed. "The other fellow Wiggers liked to talk about was Dr. Benway, the famous Chicago proctologist. Maybe you've heard of him? No? Well, Wiggers said, *his* collection was a sight to behold . . ." Bill had a coughing fit. When it passed, he took a paper napkin from the dispenser and blew his nose. "Suppose I've taken up enough of your time," he said. "Would you buy me a beer before you leave?" Barlow summoned the counterman and ordered Bill a beer. Bill followed the transaction with wide eyes. "You speak Spanish?" he asked. "We're in Mexico," Barlow said. "Sure," Bill said, "but you don't need it."

Barlow left Lola's thinking that Bill was a horrible clown who must have come to Mexico to die. But at the end of the day he walked by the restaurant again, drawn by a desire, the outlines of which he already more or less knew. Bill was draped over a backward chair, looking at his hat, which had fallen to the ground. The other chair at his table was occupied by a stocky, dark-haired man named Dave Tercero, who wore two heavy silver bracelets on his wrist. He was talking about a plan to import television sets into Mexico and make a fortune selling them to the city's America-loving upper class. "They'll go crazy for television," he said. "As soon as one of them has a set, they'll all have to get one." When Barlow came in, Bill smiled at him with a kind of warmth but didn't say anything. He looked like he was about to die of boredom. "I'm sorry to interrupt," Barlow said, "but don't you think it would be a good idea to wait until Mexico has a television station?" Dave glared at him. "Hell," he said, "I don't think it matters much. They can just look at 'em while they listen to the radio. Anyway, who are you?" Barlow was about to introduce himself when Bill took a .45 automatic from his coat pocket. "How many shots do you think it takes to kill a hat?" he asked. "Fuck, Bill," Dave said, "put that away." "I should think one shot would do it," Barlow said, "provided it was well placed." "I reckon that's true," Bill said, "but it would require an unusual caliber of marksmanship. For your average citizen, how many shots would it take? To be *sure*?" He rested the automatic's barrel on his forearm and took aim at the hat. Dave said, "I've got a police record. Take care, you two." He walked the length of the bar, growing shorter and darker with every step. Bill was still looking at the hat. "Fire!" he said, and pulled the trigger, but the safety was on. He shrugged and put the gun in his pocket. "How much money have you got?" he asked Barlow.

They went over to the Bounty, on Calle Monterrey, and drank tequila. The bar's nautical theme, which consisted of two hurricane lamps and a many-handled wooden ship's wheel, inspired Bill to talk about *The Tempest*. Prospero, he said, was the character he admired most in Shakespeare, because he drowned his magic book at the end of the play. "Hell of a way to kick a habit," Bill said. He wanted to drown *his* books, but he hadn't written them yet. He owned some books, but they had been impounded by the New Orleans police. They would have taken his car, too, he said, but he had put it up on blocks. Then, on his lawyer's advice, he took it down again, and drove straight to Tijuana. His crimes included possession of narcotics and a desire to witness the end of the universe. He had a very clear idea of what it would look like. The Sun would turn to iron, and the Earth would freeze. Crab-like insects would crawl out of their holes with a clattering sound, like ladies in high heels swarming into a department store. The stars would go out. And he, Bill, would button up his coat, make his way to the New Orleans police headquarters, and take a shit in their waiting room. "In my version of that story," Barlow said, "the last man dies of thirst."* "Oh?" Bill said. "Thirst, a terrible way to go." They kept drinking, first at the Bounty, then at a *pulquería* Barlow knew about, where few Americans went. Waiters came around like morticians, and served them grilled octopus and rice. Bill didn't eat. "Who are you," Barlow asked, "Count Dracula?" "I'm from an old American family," Bill said.

Darkness enfolded the universe. Barlow threw up in a Mexican toilet, which was something he usually tried to avoid. He was leaning on the sink when Bill came in. "Putting on your face?" Bill asked; then, without waiting for an answer, he unbuckled Barlow's pants. "What are you doing?" Barlow asked. Bill propped him against the wall. "Life-saving procedure," he said. He knelt and took out Barlow's cock. "Talk to me in Spanish," he said. "I've been wondering what it would be like to suck a Mexican's cock, but I haven't got around to it yet." So Barlow

---

* A reference to Barlow's story "Till A' the Seas," which he had either revised or not revised with Lovecraft in a New York hotel room on New Year's Eve, 1934.

said something in Spanish, about the tribute Cortés had demanded from Montezuma; then, because he hadn't come yet, and because he could, he continued his monologue in Nahuatl. He was Montezuma, consulting his priests: Should they give Cortés what he had asked for? Could they get rid of him with inferior goods? Then he was the priest of Tlaloc, the rain god, counseling Montezuma not to give Cortés anything. "Your only safety lies in absolute refusal, my lord," he said. "From this point forward, I counsel you to practice absolute silence, and absolute refusal." Finally, Barlow came, although not powerfully. Bill patted his crotch. "You speak that lingo beautifully, whatever it was," he said. "I am the best of them that speak this speech," Barlow said, "were I but where 'tis spoken."

He didn't see Bill again for weeks, then Bill appeared suddenly outside the college's main building, on Calle San Luis Potosí, and fell into step alongside him. "My wife is sick," he said. Barlow had never heard that Bill had a wife. "She has terrible asthma," Bill said, "and she needs the Smith, Kline and French inhalers, but they don't sell 'em here." "That's too bad," Barlow said. He was sure Bill was about to ask him for money, and he had the sour feeling again. Life used you. There was no part of it that didn't take something away. "I was wondering if you happen to know a good American doctor," Bill said. "Somebody who could order her inhalers from the States. Only, he'd have to do it under someone else's name. Neither of us is supposed to be here. There are warrants out for us in New Orleans, I think I told you that." He smiled sweetly at Barlow, as if they were pals in some *Huckleberry Finn*–type novel, doing mischief on a summer river. "I'll pay whatever it costs," he said. "I just want her to be all right." Barlow felt as if he had been embraced. Some trust was possible, some caring. "I know a doctor named Márquez who might be able to help you," he said. "He isn't American, but he knows where to find things like that." Of course he did: he was Martín's doctor. "If you tell me how many you need, I'll see if he can get them for you." "As many as he can get," Bill said. "She goes through 'em. The air here isn't what you'd call high-quality." Suspicion flickered through Barlow's mind: if Bill's wife was an asthmatic, why had they come here? But so many forces pressed on a person's life. Why had Howard lived in Providence, when he couldn't stand the cold? People rarely chose the easy way for themselves. "Do you need cash up front?" Bill asked. "I'll tell you what they come to," Barlow said. "Solid, Professor, thanks," Bill said. "Hope to see you around."

Dr. Márquez's office was on the far side of the city, in the Colonia Merced Balbuena. Barlow took an afternoon to visit him. He still had the Packard, and he liked driving around, finding his way through the city's mesh. It was the bodily equivalent of learning a language. The more Barlow drove, the more he felt at home, and, at the same time, the more the city disappeared, in the sense that he stopped noticing it. The paradox was well known in anthropology: to see something, you had to be outside of it, but when you were outside of it, you couldn't see it for what it was. He knew the answer, too; it was Kroeber's answer. Work. Barlow never stopped wondering if there might be another solution. What, for example, if you didn't do anything at all? What if you just sat somewhere, and waited, to see what would come? Like a hermit crab in its shell, Barlow thought, although he didn't know if that was what hermit crabs did. Wait until food was in reach, take it, and put it into your mouth. The rest of the time: rest. He had the feeling that Bill would approve of this way of living, and in a strange way he thought Howard would have approved of it, too. It was gentlemanly. Then the traffic on the Avenida Insurgentes intensified, and Barlow got tired of waiting. When he got to Dr. Márquez's office, he explained irritably that he was trying to buy inhalers for an asthmatic American friend. Dr. Márquez smiled and said he would arrange for them to be delivered to Barlow's office. If illness were a grand hotel, Barlow thought, Dr. Márquez would be its concierge.

"Would you like me to send something for your nerves, too?" the doctor asked. "Is something wrong with my nerves?" Barlow snapped. "Oh," Dr. Márquez said, "it was our friend Martín, who said . . ." Barlow scowled. "I'll be all right."

When the inhalers arrived, Barlow took one from the box, to see what was in it: pure benzedrine. He doubted Bill's wife had asthma but declined to pass judgment. Try not to see other people through the lens of your prejudices, he thought. Try to remember that you always do. He wrapped the box in Christmas paper and left it with his secretary: a present out of season, for Mr. Burroughs, who would be calling. He went back to work. The spring departed and the summer came in, hot and dry. Barlow's garden withered, despite the efforts of the Nahua boy, Juan, who was supposed to be taking care of it. At some point that summer, the tiny magazine *Tlalocan,* which Barlow had been publishing, more or less single-handedly, since 1944, as part of his slave-like effort to make the Nahua aware of their lordly past, came to the attention of Diego Rivera. Rivera read the first issue of Volume III with great interest, and in August he invited Barlow to the party he threw every year on the anniversary of Leon Trotsky's assassination. This was the tenth anniversary, and everyone was expecting something spectacular. Barlow wished he could not go. He didn't want to meet all the personalities who would surely be at the party, didn't want to compare himself with them and come up, as always, short. He was happiest at the edge of the crowd, looking in. Also, the party was on the twenty-first, the day after Howard's birthday. Barlow would have liked to drink wine all day and pass out, as he'd done every other year on August 20; but Rivera's invitation meant he couldn't.

The result was that on the twenty-first, Barlow was miserable. He drove to the college to catch up on paperwork, which was what he did when he was miserable, because why would he ruin any other part of his life with paperwork? Dean Murray was talking to a Mexican in a colonel's uniform in the courtyard. Barlow hurried around them and spent the day writing evaluations of his faculty, who were the most eminent anthropologists in Mexico, although no one at the college seemed to know it. *Fulfills his departmental responsibilities thoughtfully,* he wrote, his pen drooping with boredom. *Complaints that Professor Gaos assigns too much reading are, in my opinion, unjustified.* At the end of the day, Barlow went to the men's room and looked at himself in the mirror. He looked perilously tired, and very young, and washing his face didn't help with either condition. He rubbed witch hazel on his neck, straightened his tie, and drove south to Coyoacán. A line of taxis and limousines was backed up outside the Casa Azul.* Rather than wait, Barlow circled the block and parked on a quiet, tree-canopied street some distance away, which felt like a defeat. With an angry grunt, he took the inhaler he'd reserved from Bill's shipment out of the pocket of his linen jacket and pressed it to his lips. Bitter gas filled his lungs, and green spots fluttered in the trees, like luminous parrots. Fuck, Barlow thought. He got out of his car and hurried to the party.

The garden of Casa Azul was hung with lights in the shape of red stars and yellow skulls, as was fitting for a holiday halfway between May Day and the Day of the Dead. Hundreds of people were making the sound of Barlow's heart. He talked with a polite stranger, who turned out to be the Canadian cultural attaché, an attractive, sandy-haired Ottawan named John French. They compared notes on Mexican food. Had Barlow tried *chapulines?* Yes, and more: the Tepuztecs ate silkworm grubs. "My god, grubs! What do they taste like?" "Like snake, only mealier," Barlow said, smiling. "But, when in Guerrero!" French gave Barlow his card and said they must have lunch. "You can be my Virgil in the underworld of the tortilla," he said. Why does

---

* The house Rivera shared with Frida Kahlo (1907–1954), who had inherited it from her parents. Now the Frida Kahlo Museum.

everyone want me to be their Virgil? Barlow didn't say. Why can't I be Dante, for once? He looked for Diego Rivera and found Dolores del Río, the film actress, who was shorter than he expected, and mostly covered in a gray shawl. He kissed her hand ceremoniously. She was one of the few people who would be capable of receiving the gesture unironically, Barlow thought, and he was right. He felt himself growing closer to that blessed *within* he was always looking for. "I have a friend named del Río," he said, "Don Pablo, the illustrious anthropologist?" "Oh, yes, he was my cousin-in-law," Dolores said, her eyes wide with remembered empathy. "My first husband, Jaime, admired him very much. He was so *macho*. Always climbing mountains, or fighting wars. How do you know him?" "We teach together at Mexico City College," Barlow said, and a little of the light went out of Dolores's face. "So many studious people!" she said. "I wish you all well, but my heart is with those who *do*." "Teaching *is* doing," Barlow said. He was immediately sorry he'd said it. This was his problem: when he felt himself being pushed away, he got angry and broke things. But Dolores del Río was looking at him with interest. "What do you mean?" she asked. Barlow undertook a vehement, confused account of his literacy project. Dolores listened with interest; then she took Barlow's hand and kissed it. "I take back what I said," she said. "My heart is with anyone who has passion. Now, if you'll excuse me, I have to find my friend."

She left Barlow in the dark of his incensed spirit. He wanted to thank Rivera and go home, but instead, unpleasantly, Dean Murray appeared. He had very clearly come up to Barlow but acted like someone who had been importuned. "Good evening, Professor Barlow," he sighed. Murray had played football in high school and come to Mexico with the Catholic Charities. He was completely out of place in this bohemian crowd. "Was that Dolores del Río?" he asked. "Yes," Barlow said. "What illustrious friends you have," Dean Murray said, although he didn't seem at all envious. "You know," he went on, lowering his voice, "three-quarters of the people here are Communists." Barlow couldn't help giggling. "*Chez* Diego Rivera," he said, "what can you expect?" Murray frowned, unsure whether he was being laughed with or at. "Yes, exactly," he said. "It's a pity that so many intelligent people should have gone over to the other side. But then, this is a nation of peasants." He took Barlow's arm. "Robert," he said, "what would you say if I told you that I work for the United States government?" "I'd say you must hold an appointed office, rather than an elected one," Barlow said. He had no idea why he was even speaking. His lips were numb, and his body itched with impatience to be somewhere else. He took out a handkerchief and wiped his forehead. "Ha, ha," Murray said, "the Barlovian wit, sharp as ever. Robert, I'm serious. Now that the Soviets have the bomb, it's an entirely different game we're playing here. Did you know that an atomic explosion turns sand to glass?" Barlow did know that. He'd read about it in *Amazing Stories,* in the mid-'30s, years before the bomb was invented. When *El Diario* printed the news about Hiroshima, Barlow had been sickened but not surprised. "Deserts of glass," Murray was saying, "think of it, Robert. The variety of creation reduced to a single, terrible thing. That's the Soviet ideal, wouldn't you say?" "What about Coke?" Barlow said. "What about Fanta?" "Phantoms?" Murray said, confused. "The orange-flavored soft drink," Barlow said. "Oh, yes, Fanta. What about it?" "Soft drinks have replaced *horchata* and *tepache* almost completely in the Mexican market," Barlow said. "Seventy-eight percent penetration, if I'm not mistaken." Murray shook his head. "Robert," he said, "the time when we can afford to quibble amongst ourselves is long past." But just then someone started playing the accordion, and someone else was playing an upright bass and singing. Barlow pulled his arm free of Murray's grip. "Excuse me," he said.

Red stars, yellow skulls. Barlow spun and jumped, waving his arms, until the people around him clapped with amusement. He knew he was acting like a fool, but, he thought, like a *holy* fool. He was doing it so no one else had to. I am the center, he thought; then he thought, I am the sacrifice, offered every year at this time to Xiuhtecuhtli, the old fire god. He kicked his heels together. He'd go gladly if it would save anything, but finally he was exhausted. He staggered to a chair under a tree. Something man-sized and black hung by a rope from its limb. Had there been an execution? Had he been spared? "Are you all right, my friend?" someone asked: a friendly giant in a tweed jacket and gray shirt. "Yes," Barlow said, then for some reason he started crying. "What is it?" the enormous man asked. "It's just so much work," Barlow said. The man gestured and a woman came up. "What's wrong?" she asked. "Why is he crying?" "He's an artist," the man said. "I don't know who he is, or what he does, but he's an artist." "*Pobrecito,*" the woman said, and patted Barlow's head. Barlow pressed his face against her thigh, which was encased in hard, buckled leather, like armor, and wept. "I'm sorry," he said, "I don't know what's happening." "It's all right," the woman said. "You're just lucky you're here. I tell Diego, this is the best place to cry in all of Mexico." "Oh," Barlow said. He wiped his nose. "Er, yes. I'm sorry." "It's all right!" The woman laughed. "But if you're feeling better, I'm going to keep the rest of our guests from breaking down."

After a while, Barlow stood up. He felt as if he should feel like an idiot, but he didn't. Instead, he felt radiant and rather proud of himself. He circled the crowd and got a plate of grilled pork and rice. He was sitting by the garden wall, chewing, when Murray found him again. "Are you all right?" Murray asked. "Mm," Barlow said. He didn't stand up: couldn't. And didn't want to. Murray said, "I wish you wouldn't call attention to yourself like that." Barlow wondered if sitting on the ground was really *calling attention to yourself,* then he understood that Murray was referring to his dancing. "Sorry," he said. "I don't know what came over me." "Well, be careful," Murray said. "You already have a reputation." "I do?" Barlow wiped his fingers on the dirt and stood. "I don't enjoy repeating stories," Murray said, "but I've heard that *you* have been seen with our Mr. Burroughs." "Yes?" Barlow said. "You know he's a morphine addict," Murray said, "and a homosexual?" "I had no idea," Barlow said. "He took an interest in Bernal Díaz, and I've been trying to give him some context. I like to do that, especially for our veterans." "Stop it, Robert," Murray said. "Don't you think we owe it to our fighting men?" Barlow asked. Murray looked at the ground and shook his head. "Please," he mumbled, "try to see the bigger picture. Wasn't your father a colonel in the army?"

Barlow was about to say something true but blasphemous about his father, when a bell rang out. Rivera was standing on a chair, by the tree at the other end of the garden. "Friends," he said, "you know we are here to mourn, but also to celebrate. We mourn the death of a great man, a great thinker, a great lover of the poor, who could have set the world on a better path than it now follows." "Lover!" Murray coughed into his hand. "The man led the Red Army!" "Ssh!" someone hissed. "We mourn the triumph of the stupid and the mean. But we also celebrate their impotence. No great man can be killed, friends, no great man is ever truly dead!" With that, Rivera pulled the black cloth from the thing that hung in the tree: a three-quarter-scale replica of Trotsky in papier-mâché, sculpted by Rivera himself, with wild white hair and a goatee and the eternal round glasses. The pants of his brown suit were tucked into high gray socks. "No one who gives, dies!" Rivera shouted. "No one! They give and give!" As he spoke, people ran up out of the crowd with axes, Barlow would never know where the axes had come from, and, truly, it didn't matter; they jumped in the air and struck Trotsky's shins, his arms, his buttocks and stomach, and as they beat him, his body fell apart, and small red lozenges tumbled from it: candy and firecrackers. The garden exploded. People were dancing. Barlow slipped away from Murray and walked quietly to his car, afraid to make a noise or even a gesture that would disturb the sudden perfection of the world.

7.

A week later, Barlow drove to Oaxaca. He stayed for three days in the mountains, in the house of a weaver he'd met the summer before; then he drove the terrifying road to the ocean, where he rented a cottage on the beach, a mile from town. He had brought Revueltas's *Los Días Terrenales* but couldn't read it. He didn't remember ever having been this tired. He'd put off the next issue of *Tlalocan* and was trying to shift *Meso-American Notes* onto the back of his student Fernando Horcasitas, who was becoming a promising anthropologist in his own right. Meanwhile, Barlow had been writing an article on the Aspects of Tlaloc in the Late Postclassic Era for months. There wasn't anything difficult about it: only another crossing of another wide sea of fact. Was he ill? Dr. Márquez said no and prescribed Seconal. You must treat yourself gently, Márquez said, and here he was, flat on his back, unable to rest or read. Was someone coming up the beach? Barlow felt as though he was waiting for someone but he wasn't. He was just desperate for interruption. And, frustratingly, everything around him was unbroken: the yellow-white sand curved gently north and south; the flat Pacific reflected a cloudless sky. Beneath it, he thought, lay Tlalocan: a peaceful place, where no one asked you to do anything. A boy was coming up from the town, dragging a sack of coconuts. He approached Barlow slowly, like a figure in a nightmare. *"¿Coco, señor?" "¿Porque no?"* Barlow dug in his pockets but all his money was back in the house. *"Disculpe,"* he said, angry at himself. The boy shrugged and went on, his sack making a broad slug trail in the sand behind him, although so far as Barlow knew, there were no more houses in that direction. He, Barlow, lay on his blanket and closed his eyes. He thought about inviting the boy to his house and slipped into a lascivious dream of what might happen if he did. But the boy did not come back. After a long time, Barlow stood up, folded his blanket, and with *Los Días Terrenales* tucked under his arm, returned to the house. He lit the stove and heated the pot of beans he'd left soaking that morning. He ate them out of the pot and smoked a cigarette. The ocean turned pink, then deep blue. As soon as it was dark, Barlow lay on the corn-husk mattress his host had grudgingly provided and fell asleep.

In September, Barlow took up his classes and departmental duties with a reluctance that bordered on repugnance, as if he had put on a coat that belonged to a person recently dead. Don Pablo was organizing another expedition in search of Ice Age remains; Horcasitas was supposed to have been reading manuscripts all summer, but hadn't read any of them. And Dean Murray invited Barlow to sit on the Student Life Committee, which was tasked with finding ways to keep the students from killing themselves in car accidents. Would it help if the college threw more parties? Should alcohol be served? And if not, what was to be done? Theatrical presentations? Parlor games? Barlow wondered if Murray had been testing him at Rivera's party, feeling him out for some completely different role. Only what would he have been testing? Scratch a professor and you find a paranoiac, Barlow thought. But scratch a dean and you find a con artist. He went to the committee's inaugural meeting: after two and a half hours, it was decided that the students would put on some short plays by Tennessee Williams.

No wonder, amid such excitement, that Barlow often found himself thinking of Bill. He hadn't seen him since the beginning of the summer, when Bill came to the office to collect a box of inhalers and accepted Barlow's invitation to dinner. He had been living in Mexico City for half a year at that point but had never eaten Mexican food, unless you counted steak *a la Mexicana.* So, after they'd had a few drinks, Barlow herded him to his favorite *taquería,* at the edge of the Barrio Chino. It was nearly eleven o'clock, but the bright yellow restaurant was full of families eating dinner: beefy, placid men not letting go of the necks of their beer bottles, for fear that they would be swept away in the table's general chaos; women darting their heads from side to side, like birds; plump children sipping from goblets of lime *agua fresca,* or, more often, from wasp-waisted bottles of Fanta and Coke. The meal was not a success. Bill picked at the mound of *carnitas* on his plate, smoked a cigarette, and, when Barlow had paid the check, sprang up from his chair and strode out into the night, his head down, his legs pulling straight forward, like a bank robber walking away from a heist. Barlow ran after him. "Didn't you like it?" he asked, pathetically. "Sure," Bill said, "I'm just careful of what I eat, on account of worms. Did I ever tell you about my friend who had tapeworm? The way he knew he had it was, he was eating four steaks a day, and still losing weight. So he went to the croaker, and the croaker said, Either it's cancer or you have *la tenia,* and there's an easy way to find out. He told my friend to pull his pants down, and spread his cheeks, which, obligingly, he did. Then the croaker reached into his pocket and took out a little piece of cheese, and held it in front of my friend's asshole. Just stay still, he said. And, sure enough, within five minutes, the worm stuck its head out, to see what was going on. So the croaker grabs a pair of tongs . . ." They were walking toward the Alameda Central. As soon as they stepped into the park Bill pressed his mouth to Barlow's. He had thin lips, and tasted of vodka. They stumbled across the dark lawn, into a thicket, where they had sex. Then they lay on the dirt and thought separately. "Thanks for the tour," Bill said, finally, standing up. "You want to give me a lift home?" Barlow dropped him outside a nondescript apartment house on the Calle Monterrey, where his wife either was or wasn't sleeping, if he really did have a wife; then he drove back to Azcapotzalco. Juan the Nahua boy woke up when he came in and leered. "Where have you been, *señor?*" he asked. "Working," Barlow said, stiffly. "In the garden?" Juan asked. Barlow looked at him. "You have leaves on your jacket," Juan said, and giggled.

Thinking, in Barlow's experience, rarely made anything happen; but at the beginning of October, Bill came to his office. He was even thinner than he had been in the spring, and his hair was greasy. "Howdy, Professor," he said, in a skeletal voice. "How's the world treating you?" "It leaves me alone," Barlow said. "Don't it?" Bill said. Then, without any other preface, he asked, "Are you still in touch with that doctor friend of yours?" "Your wife is suffering?" Barlow asked, somewhat acidly. "Wel-l," Bill said, "to be straight with you, Professor, it's more for myself. I'm having trouble getting H of any quality." "H?" Barlow said. "Horse," Bill said, "heroin, junk. Nobody'll write for me, except a Chinaman, whose scripts are only good in your more disreputable pharmacies. The quality suffers, as you can imagine." Barlow stiffened. "Mr. Burroughs," he said, "I'm an anthropologist, not a drug runner. Isn't there someone else who can help you?" "We're all in the same boat, Professor," Bill said. "They're cracking down. What we need is someone who comes on as a legitimate medical patient. Someone with dysentery, for example. Or if you could pull off an abscess? I knew a guy once, in Houston, who could fake an abscess. He learned the trick in Calcutta—" "What *you* need?" Barlow interrupted. "How many of you are there?" "Just me and Old Dave, primarily," Bill said. "Dave's old lady has a habit, but we can leave her out." "No," Barlow said. "Even if it could be done, I wouldn't do it. You need to cure yourself of your addiction." "Heard that from a lot of people," Bill said. "Didn't think I'd hear it from you." He looked at Barlow with unfocused curiosity. "Say, Professor," he said, "you aren't putting the bite on me, are you?" Barlow was furious. How could Bill think he wanted money? "You'd better leave," he said, "and, please, don't come to my office again. I don't wish to have any further contact with you." He was paraphrasing Clark Ashton Smith, but felt quickly that wielding the meat cleaver was little better than being struck by it. Unfathomably, Bill sat where he was, his legs folded at an angle to Barlow's desk. "You probably think I'm some disgusting addict," Bill said. "But, Professor, I want you to know that I'd kick H in a second if there was anything better out there." He looked at Barlow, as if he expected him to say what that better thing was.

As soon as Bill was gone, Barlow wished he hadn't lost his temper. The two of them were similar people, Barlow thought. They were both unsatisfied, both looking for some mysterious *more:* so the most ridiculous and catastrophic chapter of Barlow's life began. He got a prescription from Dr. Márquez, filled it in Cuauhtémoc, and went looking for Bill. He looked in at Lola's, at the Bounty, at the Hollywood Steakhouse, at the Chimu Bar, a sad gay cantina on Calle Coahuila. Going to these places made him feel claustrophobic. The good thing about pursuing a person who moves in a small orbit, though, is that you are sure to find him sooner or later; and sure enough, on his second night of looking, Barlow found Bill in the inner, darker room of the Bounty, where he was watching two American students, a man and a woman, play chess. They all looked up when Barlow came in. The male student must have recognized him, because he stood up and held out his hand. "Howdy, Professor. Didn't expect to see you here."

Had he taken one of Barlow's classes? Impossible to say. Barlow had a policy of forgetting his students' faces at the end of each quarter. "Hello," he said, shaking the hand. "Mr. Burroughs, I wonder if you have a moment? I've been thinking about the question you asked the other day, about the reliability of Díaz's source material." They stared at him. "We're just coming to the endgame here," Bill said. "If I don't give Gene the benefit of my experience, he'll be mated in a move or three." He winked to let Barlow know that *mated* was a pun. "I see," Barlow said. "I'll be out front, if you'd care to join me when your game ends." He went to the other room and ordered a glass of red wine, which the bartender poured from a half-empty bottle. It tasted like vinegar. But then Bill did come out and sat next to Barlow. Immediately Barlow took the bottle of morphine pills from his pocket and dropped it into Bill's pocket. "Thanks, Professor," Bill said, and stood up. "Wait," Barlow said, "that's it?" "How much?" Bill asked. "No," Barlow said, "just sit with me for a minute. I want us to be friends." He tried to explain what he had felt after Bill walked out, how they were both in some essential way unsatisfied. How he, at least, felt as though he had been born missing something that other people had, some film over the eyes that made things bearable. Like the membrane over the eye of a serpent, he said. "Did you know, I used to collect snakes?" "Really?" Bill asked with no interest whatsoever. "Yes, when I lived in Florida . . ." To Barlow's own disgust, he started talking about Cassia, and Howard. "Yes, *that* H. P. Lovecraft," he said. "I was in love with him, if you can believe it. It started with an exchange of letters about our cats . . ." Bill yawned. "Did I ever tell you about the cats we had, back in N'Awleans?" he asked. "There must have been a dozen of them, running wild in and out of the house. I used to tie their paws with string and drop them in the bathtub. You should have heard how they screamed. It was almost human. It got so they'd scream when they saw me coming, scream at me from the top of the stairs. Helen

Hinkle, that was Neal Cassady's girlfriend at the time, used to ask why I did it. *Why must you torture those cats, Bill?* I said to her, Helen, why does anybody torture anybody? Why did the Gestapo torture its prisoners? I'm trying to extract information. These cats know things, and, by gum, I'm going to find out what." "Howard also believed that cats possessed secret knowledge," Barlow said. Saying it felt like a betrayal. Howard had made an effort, however hopeless, to be human. Bill made no effort.

The more absent Bill seemed, the more he looked toward the back room to see what Gene and his female friend were up to, the more Barlow wanted to break into him. "I think you're going to be a great writer," he said. "I've met a few great writers in my life, and I can tell. A great writer gives off a special hum, almost like a musical note." "Is that right?" Bill asked. "I wish you could have met Howard!" Barlow said. "The two of you would have had a lot to talk about." Which was another lie, or maybe not. Howard could have talked to Bill about the icy clouds of the planet Neptune and the mountains of Antarctica, but also about the philosophy of Seneca, and Alexander Pope's acid wit. Barlow had a vision of the two of them becoming friends, and leaving *him,* which only made him more desperate. "Want to go for a walk?" he asked. "I ought to get back to my friends," Bill said. "But I was just thinking, I probably did read something by your Lovecraft fellow, when I was a kid. Story about a guy who reanimates dead bodies? Real juvenile stuff. I'm surprised you take such an interest in it, Professor." Bill went into the other room. Wait, Barlow wanted to cry after him, that was one of his minor stories!

He went back to the Bounty a few days later. Bill wasn't there, so Barlow waited at the bar, drinking wine. Finally, near midnight, Bill came in with the chess-playing student, a bearded twenty-year-old in an untucked red-and-blue-checked shirt. Even Barlow could see he was straight; his chumminess was obviously an isomer of contempt.

Spin it a few degrees and he'd spit in Bill's face. Barlow stood up. "Mr. Burroughs! And Mr. . . . ." "Hell, Professor, I'm just Gene," the student said. "I suppose you're wondering why I'm here," Barlow said. "I am recovering from the most unspeakably dull faculty meeting that has ever been held." Neither Bill nor Gene seemed curious about it. Finally, Gene asked, "Why do you go? It's not like anyone puts a gun to your head." "They don't have to," Barlow said. "If one wants to do research, one must teach. If one teaches, one must attend faculty meetings. It must be a natural law, because no one understands it, and no one thinks it's a good idea. Can I buy you gentlemen a drink?" "No, but really," Gene said, "I don't get cats like you. If you don't realize your freedom, why are you in Mexico? Why are you alive?" "I'll have a double tequila," Bill said. "You can ask the barman to deliver it to my usual table, in the back." "Oh, fine," Gene said, "rum Coke," and the two of them went into the other room. Barlow ordered the drinks with the sorrowful authority of a captain ordering a suicidal cavalry charge. He imagined Bill and Gene side by side, Bill's hand settling on Gene's thigh. Gene drunk enough, *on Barlow's drink,* not to move it away. The wine had upset Barlow's stomach; he went to the bathroom and took a shit. As he wiped his hands on the filthy towel, he thought of Bill unbuckling his pants. Stop! he told himself. Gene came into the bathroom. "You still here?" he said. He unzipped his jeans as if Barlow did not exist. "You know Bill is queer," Barlow said. "Yup," Gene said. "You know he wants to sleep with you," Barlow said. Gene laughed. "You know what Bill calls you?" he asked. "The Dust Fairy." Barlow couldn't speak. "Yeah, he has a whole routine about you. I bet he'd do it for you, if you asked." Gene shook his cock and zipped up his pants. "Are you going to buy me another drink?" "I'm sorry, not tonight," Barlow mumbled. He drove back to Azcapotzalco, thinking of ways to destroy Bill and Gene. He could report them to Dean Murray: that would be the effective way of getting rid of them, and it would put him on the right side of Murray. *That's right, Paul. I heard them making plans to recruit more of our students to their homosexual cause . . .* Then he was horrified and reproached himself: do that and you'll be as worthless as they are. He went to bed feeling virtuous. His reward was that he himself was destroyed.

There was a letter on Barlow's desk the next afternoon. It had no postmark; the secretary said a student had dropped it off. Barlow had the strange and, in retrospect, touching idea that it contained an apology from Gene, and he was partly right. The letter was from Gene. *Say, Professor,* it read, *Bill and I were thinking you might loan us $500 for a trip we want to take, to see a guy in Colombia. Bill says to tell you that this would be a trip for research purposes, so you should feel OK about funding it. We want to leave right away, so if you could bring the $500 to Lola's tonight, that'd be swell. Your pal, Gene. P.S. Your poo smells real bad.* Barlow tore the letter up; then he regretted tearing it up. It was evidence. But now that he was sober, going to Murray seemed dangerous: Why, the dean would ask, was Gene blackmailing *him?* No. Barlow had to fight the way Gene and Bill were fighting, darkly, without honesty. He thought of calling Dr. Márquez and buying Bill off with morphine pills. He thought of asking Juan, the Nahua boy, whether he knew anyone who would . . . but Bill carried a gun. He sat there for a long time, thinking, on the one hand, nothing, and, on the other hand, that his life had suddenly become exciting.

It was, at least, busy. The Carnegie Foundation wanted to send Barlow to the Yucatán, to take over for Ralph Roys,[*] who was approaching retirement. The position would start in the spring: good-bye, Gene! And good-bye, he supposed, Bill. What was more, his article on the Aspects of Tlaloc was, despite his total distractedness and frequent inebriation, almost finished; and near the end of it, he

---

[*] Roys (1879–1965) was a prominent anthropologist and historian of the Mayans.

had spied faint tracks leading backward out of certain codices toward as-yet uncharted chambers of the Toltec past. He sent letters to his correspondents in Paris, London, and Berlin, and looked again through catalogs and bibliographies he thought he knew by heart, but which yielded new surprises each time he returned to them. When he was doing this kind of work, Barlow couldn't help thinking of young Charles Dexter Ward writing to wizards in distant lands, looking for the formula that would reanimate the dust of the dead. And yet what a difference there was between that work and this. Howard, for all his erudition, had never known the awfulness of real scholarship: the cheats who sent false information to protect their embryonic studies of related subjects; the pages made illegible by copying errors that could never be fixed; the pages eaten by water; the pages eaten by fire. The dry half-life to which the dead, under the best of circumstances, returned, a two-and-a-half-dimensional existence that flattened back to nothing when you turned your head. The dead people who would answer one question; the ones who waited for you to think of the question to which they knew the answer. And yet! This was how it had to be done. And if someone wanted to know how to raise the dead, no Transylvanian wizard would be able to tell them. But they could write to Robert Barlow, care of the Department of Anthropology, Mexico City College . . .

One November evening, Barlow sat in his garden with a bottle of rioja, reading the photostatic copy of a Spanish codex which he'd just received from Berlin. It was a Jesuit's commentary on the correspondence between two priests, one at Tula and the other at Culhuacán, about the proper way to celebrate the *Atl Caualo,* the Ceasing of Water, a February ritual. The dancing and child sacrifices were not up for discussion, but, in the absence of paper, was it permitted to hang strips of cloth from the ceremonial poles? The Culhuacán priest thought it might be, but the Tulan disagreed. *Had they who ruled at Teotihuacan permitted it,* he wrote, *we would find some scraps of cloth on their poles even now; the fact that there is nothing proves that it was not allowed.* Which prompted the Jesuit Father to remark: *The sophistication of the Tulan's reasoning is out of keeping with any idea we have of the native intelligence. It is a Hebraic kind of reasoning, which lends credence to Fray Ramírez's claim that the pyramids at Teotihuacan were built by the Jews.* Barlow had to laugh, and groan. Here he was, trying to tell the story of the Culhua Mexica truthfully, but wherever he looked, he found a false floor of facts over a yawning basement of legend, the floor of which was also false. Beneath it was another legendary basement. The Spaniards got their information from the Mexica, the Mexica got *their* information from the Toltecs, and the Toltecs got theirs from the scattered peoples who survived the fall of Teotihuacan. About Teotihuacan itself, no one knew much. The pyramids had been there, massive, sinister, and abandoned, when the Mexica came down from the north. Who had the Teotihuacanos been? Why had they abandoned their magnificent city? Even if Barlow lived another hundred years, and read every Nahuatl codex in existence, the Teotihuacanos would still be shadows, dancing at the very edge of the fire. Poems ought to be written about them, he thought, not history. Barlow felt a tightness in his chest. He was trying to write truthfully about the dead, but was he himself living? Could he even *remember* living? He thought of Howard, plucking a blue flower from a tree in De Leon Springs. You're not supposed to pick the flowers, Barlow had said. I'm simply ruthless! Howard had replied. And Barlow had thought: yes, you are . . . But why had paper been in short supply, in Culhuacán, in the year Four Rabbit? A sound distracted him: Juan was raking up the sycamore leaves. It was a gesture only; he would not dispose of the leaves, and the wind would scatter them again.

"Juan!" Barlow called. *"¿Señor?"* "Come have a drink with me," Barlow said, in Nahuatl. Juan edged up to the table; some residual sense of respect prohibited him from walking directly. *"Señor,"* he said, "the bottle is empty." "Then get another one," Barlow said. "You know where I keep them." "I'll ask Rosa," Juan said, disingenuously. He shuffled to the kitchen and came back with a fresh bottle and a glass for himself. "Juan," Barlow said, "what would you do if I died?" "Are you ill?" Juan asked. "No, not at all. But I could be killed in an accident, or murdered by a thief." "I would be very sad," Juan said. "But what would you do?" Barlow asked. "Who would take care of you?" Juan blushed. "I'm not a baby, *señor,*" he said. "No one has to take care of me." He thought about it. "Probably I would go back to my father, and work for him." "Would you like that?" Barlow asked. "No," Juan said. "He would beat me, for having gone away." "Then why do it?" Barlow asked. "You could go to school. You could become a professor, like me." "I don't want to be a professor," Juan said. "If I went to school, I would study flying." "Flying?" Barlow laughed. "It's not funny," Juan said. "My friend's brother was in the air force for two years. He says that flying an airplane is a thousand times better than driving a car. It's better than women, better than marijuana. When you're in the air, no one can make you do anything. You have the radio, but," he turned an invisible knob, "if you don't listen, what can they do?" "I suppose they can do something, sooner or later," Barlow said. "Later, they can," Juan said, "but now you're totally on your own. You could go to Texas, or Cuba." "What would you do in Cuba?" Barlow asked. "I'd have sex with *las cubanas,* probably," Juan said. "And then fly back up, and make a circle in the clouds, and . . . what?" Barlow was giggling. "I'm sorry," he said, "I'm just trying to imagine you in the cockpit of an airplane. You'd have to lose some weight, wouldn't you?" Juan blushed with anger. "I'm sorry," Barlow said again. "I'm a little drunk. Would you like another glass of wine?" He poured him one before he could answer. Juan drank sullenly. "Juan," Barlow said. "I'm just thinking about your future. With an education, you could go places, more even than with an airplane." "Maybe," Juan said, in Spanish, "but I don't want to be a *maricón* like you." "What?" Barlow said. "You heard me," Juan said, and they sat there, looking at each other with hatred. "Why do you say I'm a *maricón?*" Barlow asked, finally. "*Señor . . .*" Juan said. He seemed embarrassed. "Everyone knows." "But everyone may be wrong," Barlow said. Juan shrugged. He drank the rest of his wine, got up, and went into the house. Barlow had to carry the empty glasses in.

This conversation took place the day before Barlow got the second letter. *Professor,* it read, *I really do need that $500. I'm sure you can spare it, seeing that you have such a plum job. Why don't you put the cash in an envelope, and leave it with Tom at the Bounty? That way we won't have to see each other, and maybe say things we don't mean. Hugs and kisses, Gene.*

8.

In the solar calendar of the Culhua Mexica, the last two-thirds of December were *Atemoztli,* the month of falling water. It was Tlaloc's month, and in his honor, Barlow threw a party and invited his guests—friends from the college, some students, plus a few Mexican artists whom he'd met long ago, through Martín—to come dressed as Aztec deities. Barlow himself dressed as Tlaloc; he summoned up his old art-school skills to make the costume. It had a papier-mâché headdress, with a snaky curlicue that came down over his nose, and a green cape hung with bronze discs, which he bought from an old Mixtec man in the Zócalo. Rosa sewed him a blue skirted tunic with a green belt. It was impossible to find a maize stalk in December, so Barlow made one from a mop handle and some corn husks. When that was done, he decorated the garden with green and blue streamers, and set out wicker baskets of popcorn: not quite authentic, but never mind. He bought green and blue lightbulbs for all his lamps. He was trying to make the Casa de Tlaloc into a magical realm, the way the Casa Azul had been magical, and when he looked over his creation, just before the party, he felt that he had done it. But the party itself was a drunken and somehow sordid event. At first, no one came, then Don Pablo appeared in evening dress but left a few minutes later for another party; and when the rest of the professors arrived, the only one who'd really embraced the costume idea was an English teacher named Wilkie, who came as Quetzalcoatl, a god whom he could not have resembled less. The addition of a feathered mask to his long, thin legs and potbelly made him look like a sunburned ostrich. True, some of the students wore costumes, but not with the respect Barlow would have liked them to show for the gods of the Culhua Mexica. The men read the invitation as an excuse to take off their shirts, and the women dressed as peasants or faintly surreal streetwalkers. There was nothing divine about any of them, except their youth. One girl wore green lipstick. They stood in clumps in the garden, drinking up Barlow's beer and gossiping. The colored lights, which he had meant to evoke the watery spirit of Tlaloc, merely made the scene look like a cheap student bar.

Barlow went from group to group, feeling less like the host of the party than like a beggar or prophet who'd come in from the street. Everyone complimented him on his costume, but not in a way that made him feel it was a success. Wilkie, the English professor, said it made him look *almost imposing*—and by the way, Dean Murray was up in arms about the Tennessee Williams plays. "Can you believe it, he had no idea Williams is queer," Wilkie said, which made Barlow cringe: he had voted for the idea. "Poor Murray! He views every day that passes as another brick in the road to Hell." "Fortunately, it's a long road," said a hook-nosed man who was standing next to Barlow's colleague Ignacio Bernal. "But who the fuck would pave a road with bricks?" "This is my brother, Rafael,"* Ignacio said. "Where'd you get that hat?" Rafael asked. "I made it," Barlow said. "Then I salute you," Rafael said. "That is one fucking amazing hat. Where are you from?" "Florida," Barlow said. "Miami?" "Not quite." "Miami is a fuck-

---

* The novelist Rafael Bernal (1915–1972), best known for his 1969 novel *The Mongolian Conspiracy*.

ing hellhole," Rafael said. "It's not a city, so much as one big fucking scheme to suck money out of your pocket, and pour it into the pocket of some Jewish gangster. Truly, they say we're corrupt here in Mexico, but the United States is just as corrupt. The only difference is that the United States has more criminals, so they also have better roads. In my opinion, and I've been everywhere, the only honest place in North America is Montreal." Rafael had studied there, and he spoke lovingly about its solid buildings and its women, who were surprisingly beautiful, he said, once you unwrapped them. But Barlow's mind was elsewhere: What were the students talking about? He wondered how many of them knew Gene. He wondered how many of them *knew*. The thought of people *knowing* was awful, not because Barlow was ashamed—he was not, and never had been—but because the facts of his life belonged to him. People had no right to know whom he loved, any more than they had the right to open his wardrobe and wear his shirts. Also, his headdress was punishingly heavy: papier-mâché had been the wrong idea. He couldn't take it off, though. Taking it off would have been a surrender. Barlow would not surrender.

It got late. The faculty went home, and the students moved Barlow's record player outside and danced to Artie Shaw's *Four Star Favorites*. Rafael Bernal had moved in on a female undergraduate, who tried to look pleased while signaling with her eyes for help. The smell of marijuana drifted across from the sycamore's shade. Things were falling apart: there was no society here. There was no world. Only some students with vacant, cruel faces laughing at a joke Barlow hadn't caught. Then, suddenly, awfully, he realized that Juan was watching him from just inside the gate. He had brought a friend, short, skinny, and dark, who laughed at something Juan had just said. How long had they been there? Barlow hurried to them. "Juan," he said, in Nahuatl, "tell your friend to leave, and go to bed." Juan didn't say anything, but his friend said: "Nice skirt, *señor*," in Spanish. The two boys tittered.

"You're on private property," Barlow said to the friend. "You were not invited. If you don't go, I'll call the police." "Call them," Juan's friend said. So Barlow turned toward the house, and the friend said, loudly, *"Maricón."* Barlow thought, or would think later, that he was protecting his guests, his students, from abuse. Also, he was a man, and you could not insult men in Mexico with impunity. Also, he was a god, and he had had enough. He swung his maize stick: it hit Juan's friend in the face. "Go!" Barlow shouted. Juan's friend doubled over, holding his eye. "You hurt him," Juan said, reproachfully. "I told him to leave," Barlow said. Everyone was staring at him. "Go to bed, Juan," Barlow said. "We'll talk about this tomorrow." "You're dead," Juan's friend said. Juan put his arm around him. "Come on, let's get out of here," he said. When they were gone, Barlow said, "It looks like we've had our child sacrifice! Please, go back to what you were doing." But no one could go back. Had Barlow just struck a child? Had he lost his mind? The students thanked him in the briefest possible terms and left. The last to go was Rafael Bernal, who grabbed Barlow by the upper arm. "Do you have a pistol?" he asked. "No," Barlow said. "Get one," Rafael said. "I'm serious. You want to be ready when those fucking kids come back."

The college went on its Christmas vacation. Barlow worked most of the day in his study, but just before sunset, he walked to the plaza at the center of Azcapotzalco, a vestige of the days when the suburb had been its own city. It had been a slave market under the Culhua Mexica; now it was a holding pen for the slaves of the office, the bus, the forty-hour week. Teenagers sat at the edges of the square in white button-down shirts, watching Barlow with a nonspecific mistrust which made his heart race. He thought in a lunatic way about trying to pick one of them up, but even if he had had the courage, he wouldn't have had the desire. Sometimes he went into one of the cantinas where he was *Señor Barlow,* virtuosically nondescript. He drank a mescal and listened to a few minutes of *futból* on the radio. When it began to get dark, he hurried home, driven by a child's fear of the night. He hadn't seen Juan since the party, and although he didn't think he would come back, he was still afraid. He locked the gate of his villa, which he had never done before, but it only made the fear worse. He ate quickly, drank too much, went to bed early. When he turned out the light, the dull green chaos of the air in his bedroom seethed with danger. If he took Seconal, he could fall asleep, but woke in the middle of the night, terrified and bereft, like the actual last person on Earth. Even the intricacies of the *Matrícula de Tributos,*[*] usually a comfort, didn't protect him. History was an empty corridor that led to other, equally empty corridors; the only sound in it was the echo of his own footsteps. He fell asleep just after dawn and woke when the roar of delivery trucks on the Calle Santander brought him back into a world toward which he felt, increasingly, only resentment.

Atemoztli gave way to *Tititl,* the month of stretching. On New Year's Eve, Barlow came home from his walk, and found Rosa waiting for him in the garden, clearly impatient to be gone. "There was a telephone call for you," she said. *"Señor* Murray." "Did he leave a message?" Barlow asked. "No, only that you should call him as soon as possible." "Thank you," Barlow said. He ignored the dinner she had prepared, went to his room, and lay on the bed. So Gene had decided he didn't need five hundred dollars after all, he thought. He would have to resign. He wondered if Murray would hound him, or if he would be able to work somewhere else. The Rockefeller job in the Yucatán would evaporate, that was certain. They couldn't afford to hire a known homosexual, not with McCarthy and Hoey[†] rooting around

---

[*] A sixteenth-century manuscript, which indicated what tributes the provinces of the Culhua Mexica paid to the emperor.

[†] Senator Clyde Hoey (1877–1954) had begun an investigation of "sex perverts" in the U.S. government in June 1950.

the government and everywhere else, looking for subversives. Don Pablo might find him something. Of course, he would be *the disgraced Robert Barlow*, but so what? Oscar Wilde had been *the disgraced Oscar Wilde*. Disgrace wouldn't change the meaning of the words he wrote, the words he had written. Would it? He rolled to the side of the bed and reached for the bottle of Seconal, but decided against it.

All that night, Barlow listened to the hiss and boom of fireworks, and thought about various things: the New Year's Eve he had spent with Howard in New York; the decline of the papermaking industry in Culhuacán; the fact that his record player was broken. He thought about Wandrei and Loveman, who were, so far as he knew, still spreading lies about him. He'd planned to sue them for libel one day, but now it was too late. A known homosexual would be laughed out of court. Why had he waited? He wished he had stayed in Lakeport, with Groo and Claire Beck, and started an artistic colony, as he had planned. Why had he given the idea up? Had it been required? Could he have found a way to stay in the world of writers and readers which was, in the end, the only world he had ever loved? He thought about the students who had come to his party, and a wave of bitterness washed over him. This was *their* world. Barlow's kind inhabited it secretly, the way Martín did, or lurked at its edges and played at being outlaws, like Bill. Or they froze, and froze, until they were frozen, like Howard. Why was there no other choice? Except there *was* another choice: a note, an empty bottle of sleeping pills, and then, finally, rest. It appealed so strongly that Barlow wondered if he had sought out his present disgrace so he would have an excuse not to outlive it. He thought of all the books he would never have to read. He would be merely a cloud of atoms, untroubled, unashamed. Wouldn't Howard be proud of him! "No," Howard said. "No?" Barlow repeated. "If we're all just atoms anyway, I can't see how it matters." "From that point of view, it doesn't," Howard said, "but think of what you'd be missing. Sunsets on the Moon

Pool! The clouds over the ocean! The stories told by certain inhabitants of remote corners of the Florida swamp!" "I thought you hated
those people," Barlow said. "Oh, well, I don't have much use for the
people," Howard said, "but I do enjoy their stories. Robert, you want
too much from life. Why can't you accept its small consolations? Ar-
chitecture, for example, and lighting, and the interplay between the
two." Barlow waited for him to go on, but he didn't. "That's it?" he
asked. "Be patient," Howard said. "Wait, and see what happens." "I'll
tell you what will happen," Barlow said, annoyed. "I'll go to prison."
"You know what I've been thinking about?" Howard asked, dreamily.
"The possibility that our minds could inhabit other bodies. Even after
death, I can't help thinking, there must be some way for our *patterns* to
return . . ." But already Howard was fading, and Barlow was alone in
Azcapotzalco. He rolled away from the window. If only it were so easy,
he thought, to come back as another person, in another time. If only it
were possible to escape from time altogether, to be alive everywhere,
and note the passing of cities and customs like the flicks of a watch's
second hand. To do that, and not to be alone. Then he thought, what
if there *is* a way? Soon Barlow's mind floated off to another place, a
soft-walled labyrinth which he could bend if he wanted to, or roll
up, so that one path touched another directly. He fell asleep smiling.

The first day of 1951 was bright and cool. Someone in the Calle
Santander was beating a rug. Barlow bathed and put on an old blue
suit that no one had seen him wear for years. He made a couple of
telephone calls, one to John French at the Canadian Embassy, and one
to Don Pablo. He pushed his notes on Tulan papermaking to one side
and typed a long letter, which he sealed in an envelope. There was no
practical need to seal it; but there was, possibly, a supernatural need.
Barlow was performing a ritual, and he wanted to do it right, in case
the gods were watching. He flushed the Seconal down the toilet, wrote
a note for Rosa, and pinned it to his door. *Do not disturb me, I wish to*

sleep for a long time. Then he went downstairs and smoked in the garden until he heard Don Pablo's car pull up outside. He climbed over the villa's gate: the key was on his desk, another probably needless gesture toward realism. Don Pablo looked distressed. "Robert," he said, "this is completely unnecessary. I will intervene with Murray. I know people who can talk to him. It's difficult to run a college in Mexico City, if you don't have any Mexican friends." "I don't want that," Barlow said. "Then what *do* you want?" Don Pablo asked. "Let's take a walk," Barlow said. They drove into the mountains, to the Desierto de los Leones, a place Barlow had always loved. Up there, you could see what the Valley of Mexico had been before the automobile, before Fanta: a pine forest, hills of dry grass, and clear, sweet air. Don Pablo parked by the convent, and they walked into the woods.

When they had gone far enough, Barlow told Don Pablo what he was going to do. "Dr. Márquez will draw up a death certificate," he said. "Tell him to say the body was cremated. And get some ashes to satisfy my mother. You can scatter them here." Don Pablo was horrified, then he laughed. "Excuse me for saying so, but I think you've gone back to writing weird fiction," he said. "Not at all," Barlow said. "In reality, this is the only way I can live. Because, even if you did talk to Dean Murray, he'd still know, and so would other people. I'd be like a piñata. And, eventually, I'd break . . ." They argued about it up and down hills. Don Pablo stepped in a stream and ruined his expensive English shoes, but in the end he was convinced that Barlow wouldn't change his mind. "What are you going to do when you get there?" he asked. "Rest," Barlow said. "I'd like to see that," Don Pablo said. "Seriously, what will you do? Study the Eskimos?" Barlow shrugged. "Maybe I'll paint. I've been neglecting that side of myself for a long time." "You know, Robert," Don Pablo said, "I have known many surprising people in my life, but I think you must be the most surprising of them all. How many sides do you have?" "Just one, right now," Barlow said. "I want to live in peace, and not be afraid of anything." "Yes, well," Don Pablo said, "you know you can always write to me, if you need money." "Thank you," Barlow said. They hiked back to Don Pablo's car and drove to the Canadian Embassy, where French was waiting.

9.

Barlow spent a month in Montreal, but he could not agree with Rafael Bernal: the city was *too* solid, too gray. He moved to Toronto, but it was the same as Montreal, only in an English way rather than in a French way. When the days got short again, he thought he might as well have killed himself in Mexico City, because he would never make it through another Canadian winter. His only consolation was the news he received from Don Pablo, who, with his infallible sense of what was needed, sent him reports on the anthropology department: Murray had named José Gaos as chairman; Horcasitas had taken over most of Barlow's classes. Everything went on just as it had before. Even the Student Life Committee had not been reformed: in the spring, they sponsored a production of Sartre's *No Exit,* and the actress who played Inès wore only a brassiere and a slip. The only really new thing was that some of the students were spies. Whether even Paul Murray was capable of instigating such lunacy, Don Pablo didn't know, but the FBI, responding to reports that the Mexico City College students were consorting with Communists and other degenerates, had sent a dozen agents to infiltrate the campus. The problem with this laudable scheme, Don Pablo went on, was that everyone knew who the agents were, because they wore their shirts tucked in and obeyed the speed limit. The real students found them entertaining. Imaginary revolutionary organizations multiplied; scrawls in the washrooms announced meetings in neighborhoods where it was certain no Mexico City College student had ever gone. *So we have the creative spirit here,* Don Pablo wrote. *Still, I am coming to think that you were wise to leave. The children do what they like, but this is not a place for free adults.* He sent no news of Gene, or Bill. Maybe, Barlow thought, they had gone to Colombia after all.

Barlow was just going into a café on Sherbourne Street when the science fiction writer Al van Vogt came out, holding two cups of coffee in his hands and, in his mouth, a sticky bun. He and Barlow had exchanged letters when van Vogt's story "The Black Destroyer" came out in *Astounding Science Fiction,* and they met once in San Francisco. "Bobby?" van Vogt said. The sticky bun fell to the ground. If Barlow had only turned away, it might have been all right: a case of mistaken identity. Instead, with instinctive pleasure—here was a friend!—he lurched forward, grinning, and said, "Al!" "I heard you were dead," van Vogt said. "Don Wollheim told me . . . hold on, wait a sec! Did you pull a Singleton* on us?" But by now Barlow had recovered himself. "I don't know what you're talking about," he said. "I'm sorry, I thought you were someone else." "What?" van Vogt said. "Don't play that with *me,* I don't care what you did." Barlow hurried away, counting to himself in Nahuatl as a way to keep his mind from making any more trouble. "Bobby!" van Vogt called after him. "What the *heck?*" The last Barlow heard of him was an embarrassed Canadian *sorry.* He turned the corner, furious with himself. He couldn't even stay dead! Now van Vogt would report that he was alive, and he would be doubly humiliated. Barlow the fairy who didn't have the balls to die. Even in the unlikely event that van Vogt didn't betray him this time, there would be a

---

* Earl Singleton (1916–1999) was the first person to commit pseuicide as a way to quit fandom.

next time, and even if there wasn't a next time there would be the constant dread of it. Barlow had thought he could make a life without fear, but really he'd just traded one fear for another. So he did what a fearful person would do: packed his suitcase and got on a bus heading north.

Two hours later, the bus stopped in Parry Sound. Barlow stepped out to use the men's room. While he waited for the last members of a fall-foliage-viewing expedition to get their luggage on board, he walked up Seguin Street; then he went back to the bus and told the driver he wouldn't be going any farther. It took him days to figure out why he'd done that, and when he'd figured it out, he laughed: Parry Sound looked like DeLand. It had the same broad streets, the same low buildings, the same feeling of being alive but asleep. It was as if *he* had become Howard, stepping off the bus, looking around for a Barlow to pick him up. He left his suitcase at the garage where the bus stopped and walked around. Halfway up Waubeek Street, he saw, in the window of a white clapboard two-story house, a handwritten sign: ROOM TO LET. An Englishwoman, Barlow thought, but she turned out to be an Australian, Lucy, who lived alone in this comfortable house and seemed totally unsurprised that Barlow planned to stay in Parry Sound indefinitely. What was even better, she had cats.

For a long time—three months, five—Barlow let himself be nothing. He got up at noon and drank cold tea from the pot Lucy had left on the dining room table. He ate toast. He walked to the Sound and sat on the beach, or pushed his way among blueberry brambles down the granite back of the coast. He ate codfish sandwiches in the luncheonette, crossed the river, climbed the fire tower and counted islands in the bay. He felt himself falling backward through time, not becoming younger, just headed the wrong way, turning his back on whatever it was that everyone else was looking for. Lucy's previous boarder had left behind some issues of *Galaxy*, and Barlow read them with abstract interest. Their future was the same one he'd read about in *Amazing Stories* twenty years earlier, only it had gone gray and gotten tangled up in ideas of universal law.

As autumn lit the hills again, Barlow realized that he had feigned death only to end up more or less dead. In order to live, he needed to put something *after* something else, which, for him, meant writing sentences. The tenant from whom he'd inherited the *Galaxy*s had also left behind a Royal typewriter, its ribbon dry as dust. Barlow put in a new one and typed poems, which he immediately burned, because they carried nothing anywhere. He thought of writing weird fiction again and shuddered. It rained. One morning in November, Barlow thought he might write something about Howard. By dusk he was ten pages in, and by the time he was halfway done with the first draft, he knew what he would do when it was finished. It was, in the end, such a simple reversal: all he had to do was stop thinking of himself as the sacrifice and become the priest. In his hand, a knife named *Howard*. He locked the growing typescript in his desk each night.

Barlow wrote all through the fall and winter. It was even harder to tell the truth about Howard than it had been to get ancient Tula right, hard to be clear without being clinical. The truth of Howard's life spooked at the first wrong word and flew off, leaving behind only its hooting call. He wrote and corrected and wrote again, and when he finished his story, on a warm March morning when the shifting ice creaked in the bay, he saw that he'd been working for nothing. The truth was too complicated and ambiguous; it would never be the weapon he was looking for. He burned the manuscript in the fireplace and might really have ended his life, if it hadn't been for Lucy, who made him tea and laughed at his despair. Lucy had lost her husband in a plane crash; her daughter had moved back to Melbourne; she, too, had gone to Melbourne for a while, but found that she no longer believed in it. It was just a place, covered by the word *home* the way a skin of ice covers a lake. So she came back to Canada and taught herself to shoot, to bake bread. She was unalterably alive, like a drum, which can sit in a corner for a century and still make a noise when struck. Barlow took her as a model. When the ice broke up and the lawn turned to mud, and boats with diesel engines pushed their way into the Sound, he went back to work, and this time he gave himself permission to lie.

It was like giving himself permission to live. In three weeks, Barlow had a draft of the *Erotonomicon,* and by the end of the summer he had the whole book, including an introduction and footnotes, which he composed gleefully. He typed a fair copy on carbon paper, and only then realized that he had no idea where to send it. Who would publish the scholarly edition of a pulp writer's diary, which was mostly about men and boys having sex? Once again Barlow despaired. To work as a weapon, his book had to be *read.* Nor did he dare send the *Erotonomicon* directly to one of his old friends in fandom; that would alert the people he intended to destroy. Who knew what powers of suppression Derleth and Wandrei still had? He considered various stratagems: He could plant the manuscript somewhere and wait for it to be discovered. He could invent a second persona who would discover the work of the first. He could invent a second persona who would found a publishing house, which would come out with the *Erotonomicon* only after it had put out certain other works, which would establish its prestige . . . Barlow ground his teeth in his sleep until one of his molars cracked. He went to see the dentist Lucy recommended, Dr. Brady, who had an office on Miller Street. Barlow sat in the waiting room while Dr. Brady performed surgery on some other poor patient. In the stack of *Maclean's* and *Chatelaine*s and *National Geographic*s left there almost certainly by mistake, he found a catalog for Boar's Head Books, which advertised *My Sister and I*, a recently discovered memoir by Friedrich Nietzsche. *A sensual and sensational work, which no other publisher would dare to print,* the copy read. There was an address in the catalog: P.O. Box 14110, Cooper Station, New York. Barlow copied it down. Then Dr. Brady was ready; he looked Barlow's teeth over and told him that he would have to sleep with a night guard.

"I could tell you the rest of the story," Barlow said to Charlie, "but you know it already. The *Erotonomicon* did even better than I hoped it would, and the only conclusion I can reach is that the world welcomes lies. Perhaps you're wondering whether I felt remorse, when I saw the harm I had done? I did not. It was infinitely less than the harm that had been done *to* me, for which no one apologized, ever. Also, I got a lot of pleasure from my book. Not only from writing it, but from knowing that people were reading it." "You liked being famous," Charlie said. Barlow shook his head. "Not that. Not that at all. After more than twenty years of trying, I had finally found a way to make Howard love me." "One last question," Charlie said. "Why Spinks?" "Why?" Barlow repeated, as if he didn't understand. "Why did you use his name? And what happened to the real L. C. Spinks?" "Oh," Barlow said. "Him. It's a sad story. Spinks was the previous boarder. A nice young man, heavyset, who fixed radios and washing machines. He came to Parry Sound from North Bay, after the war, and dropped dead one day while shoveling snow. Lucy tried to find his people, but no one knew who they were. Finally, she paid to have him buried, and that was the end of Mr. Spinks, except for the typewriter and those issues of *Galaxy*. It tickled me to think that he had been a fan, just like I once was. I had the feeling that a kind of fate was playing itself out. Spinks should have been alive, and I was supposed to be dead, and when I put his name on my manuscript, it was as if I had set the universe back in balance. It didn't occur to me that I would really have to *become* Spinks, later on. Is something wrong?" "No," Charlie said, "only that I looked for Spinks's death certificate, and I couldn't find it." Barlow shrugged. "Do you want to know something amazing? When I did become Spinks, I was sure I'd be caught. Someone who had known the real Spinks would point out that I was not him. But no one said anything. There was no father, no mother! Not even a friend! I thought that *I* had no people, but this Spinks had no one at all." Barlow coughed. "Now, Mr. Willett," he asked, "do you have what you need?"

Form No. 192
FOREIGN SERVICE
(Corrected April 1948)

Department of

AMERICAN FOREIGN SERVICE

REPORT OF THE DEATH OF AN AMERICAN CITIZEN

DEPARTMENT OF STATE

Consult Sections XIII-7, XIII-8, and XVIII-7 and Notes of the Foreign Service Regulations

Copy Form 192
to Treasury

Mexico, D. F., January 15, 1951.
(Place and date)

Name in full __Robert Hayward Barlow__   Occupation __Anthropologist__

Native or naturalized __Native__   Last known address

in the United States __unknown__

Date of death __January__   __2__   __unknown__   __1951__   Age __32__
(Month) (Day) (Hour) (Minute) (Year)   (As nearly as can be ascertained)

Place of death __Santander 27, Atzcapotzalco, D. F., Mexico__
(Number and street) or (Hospital or hotel)   (City)   (Country)

Cause of death __"Congestión visceral generalizado" as certified by__
(Include authority for statement)

__Dr. Enrique Márquez, Oriente 81-305, Col. Merced Balbuena, Mexico DF__

Disposition of the remains __Cremated and delivered to mother, Mrs. Bernice L.__
__Barlow__

Local law as to disinterring remains __Not applicable.__

Disposition of the effects __In possession of mother, Bernice L. Barlow__

Person or official responsible for custody of effects and accounting therefor __mother__

Informed by telegram:

NAME	ADDRESS	RELATIONSHIP	DATE SENT
Mrs. Bernice L. Barlow, Cassia, Florida		Mother	1/2/51
Everett Wayne Barlow, 1057 N. W. 97th Lane	Miami, Florida	Brother	1/5/51

Copy of this report sent to: Picked up Personally

NAME	ADDRESS	RELATIONSHIP	DATE SENT
Mrs. Bernice L. Barlow, Cassia, Florida		Mother	1/15/51
Everett Wayne Barlow, 1057 N. W. 97th Lane	Miami, Florida	Brother	1/15/51

Traveling or residing abroad with relatives or friends as follows:

NAME	ADDRESS	RELATIONSHIP

Other known relatives (not given above):

NAME	ADDRESS	RELATIONSHIP

This information and data concerning an inventory of the effects, accounts, etc., have been placed under File 330 in the correspondence of this office.

Remarks: __Death recorded in Book No. 1, Page 143, Entry No. 142,__
__of the Second Office of Civil Registry, Mexico, D. F., under date of__
__January 9, 1951. Passport No. 1235 FS 194335 issued by American__
__Embassy, Mexico, D. F., on March 9, 1948.__ (Continue on reverse if necessary.)
__cancelled and returned to mother.__

[SEAL]   002152
No fee prescribed.

W. John Wilson   (Signature on all copies)
Consul   of the United States of America.

(To be sent in triplicate to the Department of State; to be forwarded in sextuplicate when decedent is an American-citizen seaman, a beneficiary of or an insured by the Veterans Administration, or an officer or employee of the United States Government other than the National Military Establishment.)

U. S. GOVERNMENT PRINTING OFFICE   16—10800-2

IV.
A MUTATION AND
A MADNESS

1.

I remember how serene Charlie was when he came back from Parry Sound. It was as if he had already started to become the person he would be two years later: the person I had always hoped he might become, and whom I would learn to hate. It was late in the evening, late January 2008, when he slipped into our apartment, beaming. He put down his bag with unaccustomed gentleness and hung his coat on a peg. He was skinnier than ever, and somehow luminous, like a Tibetan lama. "Trip was good?" I asked. "So good," Charlie said. He opened a can of seltzer, which he drank with his hand pressed to the refrigerator, as though to express gratitude for its abundant contents. "Tell me!" I said. Charlie fluttered his fingers at me and belched. "The apartment looks nice," he said. "Did you do something?" I shook my head. Who was this Charlie who was looking at our apartment as if he hadn't seen it before? "My absence must become it," he said, and dropped his can into the recycling. Then he kissed me, and I kissed back. Parry Sound could wait.

For a month or so, Charlie shuttled between our apartment and the public library, fleshing out what Barlow had told him. He wrote a book proposal and found himself a literary agent, an esteemed dinosaur named George Arnold. George wanted sample chapters, so

Charlie quit his job at the *Voice* and worked day and night in his little office, with headphones on, humming to himself. Sometimes I'd get up in the middle of the night and hear him whisper, "Ssh! *Write!*" as though someone was there with him, and cackle at a joke I didn't get. I get it now: it's what Charles Dexter Ward whispers to his resurrected ancestor Joseph Curwen. It frightens me to think that, even then, Charlie knew what part he was playing. He sent the chapters to George at the beginning of March, and a week later George sold *The Book of the Law of Love* (as Charlie had called it) to HarperCollins for two hundred thousand dollars.

The first installment of Charlie's advance came in June, and he immediately wrote checks to cover his share of our May expenses. I was annoyed by how theatrical he was about it. Did he think that paying one month's bills would erase all the years when I had supported him? But my parents, my brothers, and even Grace had given me a lot of grief about supporting Charlie; I was happy to tell them that he was finally pulling his weight. And more. I'm embarrassed to admit how delighted I was when Charlie came home with a new pink-and-white-checked shirt and a pair of brown English shoes, which, he said, he had been coveting for years. He looked good in his new outfit, like an ad for a fancy vodka, or, at the least, like a well-to-do English professor. (Which was what his father had been when he was Charlie's age: a fact we both agreed to overlook.) That period, from the spring of 2008 through the spring of 2010, was the happiest in our marriage. Not that everything was easy: when Charlie was working, he was distracted and irritable, and when he couldn't work, on his *fishing boat days,* as we called them, he was despondent and irritable. But it was all set in a background of hopefulness. I'd had an idea about how to treat severe trauma: basically, I conjectured that the patient's inability to think about trauma as being *past* makes it impossible, paradoxically, for the patient to think of trauma as *real*. Now my supervisor was encouraging me to write a paper. Sometimes Charlie and I lay at opposite ends of the sofa and typed on our laptops, harmoniously, like two parts of the same person. We ate in fancy restaurants and fooled around like new lovers in the back of cabs. We bought a big gilt-edged mirror in an antique store on Atlantic Avenue, and Charlie hung it on the wall opposite our bed. "So I can see you coming and going, Mar," he said. "Don't be sleazy," I said, but I enjoyed it, too. I liked the multiplication, the feeling that we were numerous and at the same time indivisible. It was as if we were living in an enchanted zone; our savings account and our formidable fast-moving energy protected us from anything the world might throw our way.

The Book of the Law of Love came out in June 2010. To celebrate, I took Charlie to a cavernous Japanese restaurant in TriBeCa, where we were almost the only customers. We toasted to the book and kept drinking, while blue porcelain bowls arrived on our table, each holding a sliver of silver fish, or an exquisite fragment of a potato. Charlie was exuberant. "What *is* this?" he asked. "Did we just pay fifteen dollars for a bowl of bean sprouts?" He poked at them with his chopsticks. "On closer observation," he said, "I see they aren't ordinary bean sprouts, though. They were grown by Trappist monks, and educated under the Montessori system." "How can you tell?" I asked, foolishly. "Because they don't speak," Charlie said, "and they took their time showing up." He was irrepressible. But later that night he said, "Mar, I'm scared." "Of course you are," I said. "No," he said, "really afraid. What if I'm wrong?" "What do you mean?" I asked. Charlie told me that there were parts of Barlow's story which, for one reason or another, he'd been unable to verify. "You mean, you *intuited* them?" I asked. "No," he said. "I got them from Barlow. But I couldn't back them up with anything." The documents didn't exist; the relevant people were dead. For example, the Australian woman, Lucy, who rented Barlow a room in Parry Sound. What was her last name? Barlow didn't remember and Charlie couldn't find any trace of her. "That doesn't sound like a big deal," I said. "I guess not," Charlie said. "But my haters might disagree." Word of his book had reached the community of H. P. Lovecraft fans, and they weren't all delighted about it. A group called the Knights of the Outer Void, which probably consisted, Charlie said, of five or six teenagers, had threatened to sic Shoggoths on him: those being giant slug-like monsters from a Lovecraft tale. "I'm not worried about the Shoggoths," he said, "but still. What if I get creamed, like Barlow did for the *Erotonomicon?*" "Your book's not a fake," I said. "They hated him so much," Charlie said, "just for saying that Lovecraft was gay." "And guess what?" I said. "That was in the 1950s. Things have changed." "In some ways," Charlie said. I took his hands in mine.

And, in fact, when the reviews appeared, praising Charlie for the care with which he had exhumed this old and yet amazingly somehow still living story, when HarperCollins decided belatedly to frog-march Charlie through the bookstores of a dozen American cities, when the French expressed enthusiasm and the Germans came calling, and George Arnold was getting interest from *the coast,* when all those things happened, it seemed as if Charlie's fears had been totally unfounded, a last urge toward self-defeat voiced when it was too late to do him any harm. It's true that not everyone loved the book. Some Lovecraft fans sent emails, telling Charlie that he was a faggot and *a real Shub-Niggurath.*[*] The Knights of the Outer Void made a fuss on some blogs and found an unsurprising number of immature goons to spread their nonsense around. None of it bothered either of us much. In fact, Charlie

---

[*] Shub-Niggurath was, unfortunately, the name of one of Lovecraft's monsters.

created a page on Facebook—which he took to calling *The Book of Dead Faces*—where he reported ironically on the occult squawkings his story had aroused. The only time I heard him really worry was the night in July when he called me from Cleveland: shaken, he said, by an encounter with a woman who had caught her preteen son tongue-kissing his male best friend in their finished basement. When she asked what in God's name he thought he was doing, he mumbled something about the Ablo Ritual. "Lucky for me they weren't *really* doing Ablo," Charlie said. "I'd probably be in jail right now. Can you see the headline? *Black Pied Pederast Leads Local Youth to Lovecraftian Ruin.*" "Relax," I said, "kids try stuff like that all the time." "Yeah," Charlie said, "but now people are going to think it's my fault." "Are you indemnified?" I asked. "Am I what?" Charlie said. "Will your publisher cover your legal costs, if it comes to that?" "I don't know, I have to ask," Charlie said. "Mar, you know what really bothers me? The *Erotonomicon* is a fake. I say it over and over in my book. But somehow this kid and his friend just totally ignored that part. And now *I* feel like I perpetrated a hoax, like I tricked them, somehow."

But this unpleasantness was more than made up for by the public revival, the resurrection, you could almost say, of Robert Barlow. Critics wrote about his poetry, his weird fiction, his contributions to the history of the Aztecs. Barlow appeared on a Canadian TV program called *After the Fact* and spoke movingly about his life as a gay man in the 1930s and '40s. He apologized for the harm he'd done with the *Erotonomicon,* but that was so long ago, no one held it against him anymore. "Are you glad to have been rediscovered?" asked the program's host, a gruff woman named April Hoffmann. Barlow coughed. "The truth is, I'm happy just to be alive," he said. "You may laugh, but I don't feel in any way that I've reached the end of my life. If I could, Ms. Hoffmann, I would go on living and living and living." "I see,"

April Hoffmann said, around the lump in her throat. I assume there was a lump in her throat. There was certainly one in mine. "Charlie," I said, "you did it!" "Did what?" Charlie asked. "You saved someone," I said. "Took me long enough," Charlie said, but I saw that he was really pleased. We had no idea what was coming, or at least, I had no idea.

2.

At the end of August, Charlie was invited to speak at a convention of Lovecraft fans, in Providence. He was nervous about going. What if someone called him *the S-N word*? "They won't," I said. "And if they do, who cares? You'll stay cool, and it'll be good publicity for your book." "Fucking Gilles Baron is giving the keynote address," Charlie said. "Who's that?" I asked. Charlie said he was a French writer whose book *H. P. Lovecraft: Prophet of the Post-Human* had rippled the gloomy waters of contemporary philosophy some years earlier. "He's internationally famous," Charlie said. "My mom *knows* him. What if he comes to my talk?"

Charlie dealt with his anxiety by dragging Eric along. They left for Providence on a Friday morning, and at this point his story becomes two stories: the one Charlie told me when he came home Sunday night, and the one Eric told, under duress, a year later. In both stories, they checked into their rooms at the Biltmore, and Charlie discovered that he hadn't brought a change of underwear. They walked through the awful August heat to a nearby mall. To their amazement, it was full of goth kids with I ♥ CTHULHU pins on the lapels of their frock coats, acolytes in black robes, and eldritch beings with tentacled masks and bat-like satin wings. The really strange thing, Charlie said, was that these people were riding the escalators with shopping bags from CVS and Yankee Candle and so on, as if it were the most ordinary and natural thing for them to do. It was the Cult of Cthulhu! But now it was normal. Charlie and Eric joked about how they should approach the kids and say, *You know, I risked my life so you could wear that costume.* Charlie bought a three-pack of boxer briefs at Nordstrom's. (In Eric's story, a pretty girl with green hair sipped an iced coffee in the food court.) They went back to the Biltmore in time to catch a talk on "The Lengthening Shadow: HPL's Influence Today." It did, indeed, seem to be getting longer, Charlie thought, although like other shadows, it grew less dark as it stretched to cover more and more ground.

Charlie's talk was in the smaller of the hotel's two meeting rooms, and to his disappointment it was only half full. (But the green-haired girl sat in the second row.) He told the story of Lovecraft and Barlow, and worked up to what had become his customary conclusion: "It's true," he said, "that Barlow did some things it's hard to approve of, just like Lovecraft believed some things that I can't condone. But I wonder if in the end we maybe need our heroes to have feet of clay, or even of mud. Barlow was able to love Lovecraft, for all his flaws. And I want to tell you something he told me, when he was finished telling his story, which was, that although Barlow saw all the harm he'd done with the *Erotonomicon* hoax, he didn't regret it, because he'd made Lovecraft into a person who was capable of love. You don't have to agree with me, but I wonder if that's what stories *do.* I wonder if stories are our way of taking these imperfect humans we're stuck with on Earth, and making them into people who love us, and whom we can love in return." It was the line he'd used on *Fresh Air,* the line he'd given to the guys from *This American Life,* for their program about miraculous survival. It was a great line, and in Providence it got mildly enthusiastic applause. "I'll be happy to take questions," Charlie said, and hands went up all over the room. The Lovecraftians wanted to know more about how Charlie had found Barlow, and what Barlow was like, and whether Barlow might have in his possession unpublished Lovecraft stories, or letters, or anything at all. A gangly older man in a T-shirt that read I SCREAM, YOU SCREAM, WE ALL JUST SCREAM AND SCREAM pointed out that the Indian burial ground where Lovecraft and Barlow had an awkward moment in 1935 was actually a rather well-known place called the Fountain of Youth, and that the skeletons of Native Americans had been on display there until the Timucua tribe demanded that the remains be reburied, in 1991. "If you're looking for an idea for your next book," he said, "maybe you should write about Lovecraft and the Native Americans. I'd be happy to point you toward some fascinating material I dug up. So to speak!" "Thanks," Charlie said. They were out of time. Some people approached the lectern with copies of Charlie's book, which they wanted him to sign. (The green-haired girl was among them. "I'm so interested in your story," she said. "I'm looking forward to reading your book.")

When the others were gone, a middle-aged South Asian man with wiry hair, who looked like he had been awake for days, came up to Charlie. "I'm S. T. Joshi," he said. This was Lovecraft's biographer: Charlie had written to him, years ago, asking for information about Spinks and the *Erotonomicon*. "That was a nice talk," Joshi said. "Thanks," Charlie said. He fumbled for some appreciative words about Joshi's work, and made a crack about how funny it was that two brown dudes should have ended up writing about H. P. Lovecraft, which Joshi didn't even smile at. "I hope you don't think I did the wrong thing, writing about Lovecraft's sexuality," Charlie said. "Not at all," Joshi said. "I'm not a puritan, and anyway, it's 2010. Lovecraft scholarship has to keep up with the times!" He put his hands into his pockets and looked like he was about to walk away, then he said, "The truth is, your book made me uneasy for a different reason. "Have you been to the Old Burial Hill in Marblehead?" Charlie said he hadn't. "I've been there," Joshi said, "and you can't see much of anything from the top." "Oh," Charlie said, blushing. "Well, Barlow is ninety-one. He might have been confusing Marblehead with some other place they stopped on that trip." "He might," Joshi said, "but Marblehead was such an important place for Lovecraft, you'd think Barlow would remember what happened there. And then there's the whole business of the two of them looking out to sea, and talking about that island on the horizon. In your book, it leads them to talk about going to Europe. If they couldn't see any island, what were they talking about?" "I don't know," Charlie said. "Also," Joshi said, "I can't find any evidence that Barlow and Lovecraft went to Belknap's New Year's Eve party in 1934, but if they did, I'm one hundred percent sure Don Wollheim wasn't there, because he didn't meet Lovecraft until two years later. And that story about the spiked punch bowl has been told over and over. It's always at a different party, and I don't think it ever really happened." "Do you think Barlow was lying?" Charlie asked. "I don't think it was Barlow," Joshi said. "I'm not sure who you talked to, but Robert Barlow died in 1951." "He didn't," Charlie said. "And then there's the *Erotonomicon*," Joshi said. "What's the saying? Fool me once, shame on you? I didn't want to say it in public, but I think you've been tricked."

"Fuck!" Charlie said when Joshi was gone. "Don't worry," Eric said, "he's just being territorial. Like, you pissed on his lawn, you know? He's the H. P. Lovecraft *guy*." "I know," Charlie said, "but I'm worried about what he's going to tell other people." The two of them went to a bar on Peck Street, where Charlie ordered a Last Call of Cthulhu: gin, Chartreuse, Lillet, and lime, served up with an absinthe rinse. He drank it quickly, ordered another, and drank that one quickly, too, then he and Eric went to Gilles Baron's lecture. The Grand Ballroom was packed, not only with Lovecraftians but also with Baronians, who were identifiable by their small black notebooks and expensive shoes. Eventually, Baron, a diminutive man in a black blazer and white open-collar shirt, emerged from a concealed door and tiptoed to the lectern. His talk was about jellyfish, creatures which, he noted, Lovecraft rarely wrote about, possibly because they were so Lovecraftian that the master of horror saw little room for improvement. For a warm, stuffy eternity, Baron lectured the room on the biology of jellyfish, their diet, their habits, their peculiar *formal formlessness.* "Jellyfish thrive on our self-destructive policies," Baron said, "to the point where a reasonable person might speculate that humanity is *deliberately preparing the world for the coming of the jellyfish.*" The line got fewer laughs than you might think, Charlie said. This crowd wanted to prepare the world for something. "Lovecraft wrote," Baron said, "of the beings that will rise to power when humanity is gone, but if one considers the jellyfish, one might be excused for suspecting that those beings are here already." From there, by means of deft Cartesian footwork, he brought his lecture around to the point toward which it had always been heading, namely, that the jellyfish were the post-human incarnate; and that if we wanted to see the future of humanity, we had only to study these translucent creatures, which built nothing, plotted nothing, but merely floated, and stung. Then, smiling, Baron bowed, and declined to answer any questions. He would be happy to sign books, however.

Eric decided to get one of Baron's books, so Charlie said he'd get one, too. Would it be *Existinction* or *Phenomenology of the Switch*? No, in the end, Charlie picked up a second copy of *H. P. Lovecraft: Prophet of the Post-Human.* The green-haired girl was ahead of him in line. "Hi again," Charlie said. "Oh, hi," she said, turning. She really was pretty, in a sturdy, Central European kind of way, although her pale skin wasn't flattered by her choice of hair dye. She wore a cardigan over a purple T-shirt that suggested large breasts. Between shirt and jeans, a ribbon of white skin. "Are you a Baron fan?" she asked. "Sure," Charlie said. "Me, too," the girl said. Her name was Lila. She was from

Portland, Maine, where she worked in an animal shelter. She had read all of Baron's books; in fact, she wrote a Baronian blog, *Notes from After the End of the World*. Charlie promised to look at it. "Honestly, I think Lovecraft is kind of weird," Lila said. "But I loved your talk. Thinking about his stories in terms of that ambivalent sexuality . . ." "Thank you," Charlie said. "By the way, this is my friend Eric." Eventually the three of them reached the head of the line. Lila held out a worn copy of *Existinction* for Baron to inscribe. "I admire your work so much," she said. Baron turned to the stiff-haired publicist who sat beside him, and made a face. "I don't like this American edition," he said. "It shows dirt so easily." "Let me get another," Lila said, as if he'd spoken to her, but he was already signing the book. "Here you go," he said. "Thank you," Lila said. "I'm from Maine. We have a lot of jellyfish up there now, because of global warming." Baron looked at her blankly. "Well, thanks," Lila said again, blushing, and hurried off. Baron held out his hand for Charlie's book, but Charlie walked right past him. He caught up with Lila by the elevator. "What an asshole," Charlie said. "I guess he meets a lot of people like me," Lila said. "That doesn't make him not an asshole," Charlie said. Lila untangled the double negative and laughed. "Which way are you headed?" Charlie asked. "This is the top floor of the hotel," Lila said. "Right," Charlie said. "So, looks like we're both going down."

Eric couldn't, or wouldn't, say what happened after that. Did Charlie and Lila dine at the Providence Seafood Company, which offered special dishes to the conventioneers: Cthulhu Calamari, Innsmouth Fish Stew? Did they attend the Parade of Elder Gods, and the costume party afterward? Here's what I am reasonably sure of: Charlie hated being wrong, and Joshi had scared him. But he *loved* that he'd snubbed Gilles Baron. He loved that Lila was curious about him, and that she seemed to have nothing better to do—except drink iced coffee at the mall. "You had your eye on me at the *mall?*" Lila asked, laughing. "I'm glad you didn't notice me staring," Charlie said. "No," Lila said, "I did." They had a few drinks. Charlie had a room at the Biltmore and three fresh pairs of boxer briefs. He called me the next morning and said he'd missed his train. "I feel like I've found my people," he said, and I was so happy for him. I'd always wanted him to have his people.

3.

Did Charlie seem furtive when he came home that night? Did he act like a person with something to hide? The awful thing is that he did, but because I didn't want to be mistrustful, I pretended not to see it. Our fights, when we had them, that fall were about Adderall, which Charlie was still taking—which he *couldn't* stop taking, he said, because he had to perform so much. In October, he flew to a book festival in Atlanta and took the train to a symposium in Boston; in November, he spoke at colleges in California and Ohio and Vermont. (I wonder if Lila went with him on any of those trips. Charlie said she didn't, but by then I had stopped believing anything he said.) When he wasn't on the road, he went to literary parties, from which he came home drunk and stinking of cigarettes. When I asked if all that going out was really necessary, he got angry at me. "Mar," he said, "you have your career. Why can't I have mine?"

I didn't know what to say. The embarrassing truth is that I'd never thought of Charlie as having a career. This was, in fact, one of the things I loved about him: in a city of professionals, he was an amateur, in the old sense of the word, a person who did what he did out of love. One bright October morning, when we were eating brunch at a French restaurant on Dean Street, he told me he'd gone drinking with an editor at the *New York Review of Books* who wanted him to write an essay about James Baldwin. "Was she pretty?" I asked. Charlie looked at me as if I were the one who was acting out. "Is something wrong?" he asked. "Just that I know what happens when you drink," I said. *"He's sixty and bald,"* Charlie said, "and by the way, it's not my fault if a few people in New York enjoy my company. Anyway, it's not like *you* don't drink." I was so taken aback by that, I didn't know what to say. In what world was having a glass of wine before bed the same thing as coming home drunk night after night? "Forget it," I said. "I'm not going to write you any more prescriptions, though." "OK," Charlie said. "You're not the only doctor in New York." I heard something threatening in his voice. I wasn't the only a lot of things in New York.

That fall, Charlie bought a soft wool Italian suit and thick black-framed English glasses; he wore lavender shirts and experimented with pocket squares. His image started to show up in connection with things that weren't his book: Charlie Willett talking to Salman Rushdie at the National Book Awards after-party; Charlie Willett receiving an awkward kiss from Susan Sarandon outside City Hall. This new Charlie Willett, whom I barely saw, believed that love was more powerful than horror. He believed that in stories there was hope for our fractured nation and our divided souls. At the same time, ironically, he was getting into the work of Gilles Baron. He kept a copy of *Existinction* by the bed and read it on his infrequent nights at home. Baron, as you might guess from that speech about the jellyfish, was a materialist, who didn't believe that there was anything particularly interesting or special about human beings. Like Lovecraft, he thought of us as collections of atoms, organized by the laws of physics, chemistry, and biology, equipped with a consciousness that was mostly there to remind us of our limitations: our mortality, our frailty, our lack of freedom. Futility was our condition—so Baron argued—and extinction our goal. I don't know whether Charlie believed Baron's arguments, but he did repeat them to me, to annoy me, I thought. I'd be talking about something one of my patients had done, some sad repetition of an old trauma, and he'd say, "But trauma is our condition, isn't it?" And I'd have to argue with him, and point out that trauma was by definition something that *happened* to us and that it was also something we could recover from, which was the point of my whole practice. Charlie would just smirk and say, "Sure, but it doesn't make much difference in the end, does it?" And I'd say, "Maybe not, but there's a lot of living to do before you get to the end." I'd go back to *Sense and Sensibility,* or just roll over in bed and turn out my light.

It was hard for me to understand how the private Charlie and the public one fit together. Was Baron a sort of devil's advocate for him? Or did he really believe that nothing mattered, and was his public show of caring about people's stories just that, a show? The real answer is probably less profound: Charlie was fucking Lila. He was trying on her ideas, testing them out on me, seeing how they felt. In a small but disgusting way, he was becoming her. Anyway, Charlie didn't let his Baronian tendencies show in public. There he was all hope: he was biracial, post-racial, plural and undivided, a spokesman for the healing spirit that Obama was supposed to have brought to the United States. And he gloried in being that. He wrote an essay called "The End of Fear" for *New York* magazine and talked about it on *Fresh Air,* too. (My grandmother called to say what a nice voice he had. And when were we going to have children?) *Vogue* photographed him at home in his Italian suit, cradling his Darth Vader doll. Charlie flew to Austin to talk about forgiveness. He flew to Seattle to talk about survival. He was a Game Changer (*Wired*) and a Young Transformer (*Christian Science Monitor*). Which of course led him to ask: "Autobot, or Decepticon?"

With George Arnold's encouragement, Charlie started going through his old essays with an eye to assembling them into a book. He spent hours manufacturing *aperçus* (Charlie's word, alas) for his Twitter feed. He had the idea to collect love stories on Twitter, from *ordinary people* (his, too) and turn them into a book. Brief Loves, he said he'd call it. He was preoccupied with these and other projects, but reluctant to say much about them. Why did I need to know? Why did it matter that he hadn't told me photographers were coming to our apartment? I was at work all the time, anyway, and when Charlie *did* pay attention to me, it was almost worse. He wanted to know how my patients were doing; he was curious about my grandmother. Was she lonely, now that my grandfather was gone? A year earlier I would have been happy that he was taking an interest. Now I was wary. I imagined that Charlie was using me, for an article about an obscure psychotherapist, perhaps. That was a sad thought, and a worse one lay just behind it. What if Charlie had *always* been this way, and I hadn't seen it? He wanted to raise people up from obscurity, but, very possibly, the person he wanted to raise up most was himself.

My paper about severe trauma was published in January 2011. It attracted a lot of attention, and my practice filled up. My new patients were rape survivors, survivors of incest, an Iraq veteran. The world *they* brought to me was more terrible than anything in Lovecraft: a bleak landscape of cyclical emotions and terrible dreams, like a roundabout in Hell. My job was to take that landscape apart, and I could do it, but it took time, and often the gains we made, my patients and I, were undone by the smallest things: a fire on the subway tracks, a neighbor's barking dog. My patients had lost the ability to hope, so I had to hope for them. I had to stay with it. I was seeing ten or eleven hours of patients a day; I came home too drained to think about anything except how I was going to pull myself together for the next morning. I didn't think my new schedule would make much of a difference to Charlie, but it did. That winter, we went from being people who were shaping a life together to being people who shared an apartment and slept in the same bed, often not at the same time. When we did talk, we were like two old storytellers, repeating the lore of our tribe, the same old legends. Remember that time when we went to the Cape? Remember that stupid weekend in Connecticut? We spoke in fossils.

The nadir of this sad arc came one night in May when we went out to dinner with Grace and Eric at a Thai restaurant on Henry Street. Grace and Eric and I were talking about Lucian Freud when Charlie looked up from his pad thai and said, "You know, I think peanuts are the saddest nuts." "Why?" Grace asked, curiously. "I don't think they're sad," I said, although really I had no opinion about the emotional life of peanuts. "It's not that I don't like them," Charlie said, "it's just that they're so ordinary. It's like they're not trying." "I thought you liked ordinary things," I said. "I never said that," Charlie said. "Charlie, you're writing a book about ordinary people," I said. "What book?" Grace asked. "They aren't necessarily ordinary," Charlie said. "It's just whoever chooses to respond." "But you used the word *ordinary,*" I said. "I don't remember that," Charlie said. "You did," I insisted, even though there was no point. "Go easy, you two," Eric said. "I like peanuts," Grace said. "Charlie, do you think I'm an ordinary person?" "No more than anyone else," Charlie said. Grace glared at him. For a long time, no one spoke. It felt like a final rest: violinists, put down your bows. Then out of desperation I asked, "If you don't like peanuts, which nuts *do* you like?" "Seriously?" Charlie said. "Yes," I said, with inexplicable intensity. "Charlie Willett, what's your favorite nut?"

I need to mention something that I have left out of this story up until now, because it didn't seem relevant: My grandmother and grandfather, my father's parents, both survived Auschwitz. The work I did on post-traumatic stress was in their honor; it was, and still is, my attempt to bring kindness to a world that is too often cruel and unjust. When I felt Charlie slipping away, I had to ask myself, What matters? Who needs my help? I chose my patients because they had come to me, whereas Charlie wouldn't come to me. I chose my patients because, compared with them, Charlie was doing fine. I chose my patients because I had to, because that's who I am. I am telling all this too quickly because it is hard to tell. Really what I want to say is that I loved Charlie as much as ever.

4.

When Charlie's book came out, the Toronto *Globe and Mail* ran an article about it, which mentioned that Barlow had taken the name of the late Leonard C. Spinks, a resident of Parry Sound. In this way news of Spinks's death reached a Canadian World War II veteran named Horace Tudhope. Tudhope was surprised. He'd seen Spinks just the year before, as alive as ever. He wrote a letter to the *Globe and Mail*, respectfully suggesting that they had made a mistake, and his letter sat for nearly a year in a pile of unread mail. Then someone read it. On April 4, 2011, a reporter from the *Globe and Mail* gave Tudhope a call. Was he positive he wasn't mistaken about Spinks? Tudhope's answer was unprintable and brief. Leo Spinks was emphatically *not* dead. At that point, the reporter, whose name was, is, Darius Evans, started looking things up.

Other people besides S. T. Joshi had remarked on what you could and couldn't see from the Old Burial Hill at Marblehead, and the spiked-punch story, and some other things that Joshi hadn't pointed out: for example, there was only ever one post office in Cassia; why Barlow should have said there were two was mysterious. These were quibbles, but when Evans put them together with what Tudhope had said, he felt an inrushing exhilaration. What if Charlie's book was a fake? What if there was no miraculous Robert Barlow, just a clever, persistent L. C. Spinks? It was a great hypothesis and the kind of story that gets noticed. Evans drove up to Parry Sound, met Tudhope, and got from him a number of stories about Spinks, who, Tudhope said, had served with him in the Algonquin Regiment, at the beginning of the Second World War. Spinks was discharged for reasons Tudhope never learned; he returned to Parry Sound and went into the appliance-repair business. He never had a proper shop but worked out of his house on Waubeek Street. He was a nice guy who liked a beer and a good joke. The kicker was that Tudhope had a shoe box of photographs: Here was Leo Spinks in Thunder Bay, looking very smart in his uniform. He'd been on the regimental hockey team . . . Here he was in Parry Sound around 1960. He'd put on some weight, and his face was blurry, but he was recognizably the Spinks whose picture had been taken outside the CBS studio on a May afternoon in 1954. "Can I copy this?" Evans asked, and Tudhope said, "Sure, what the heck? I bet Leo got a laugh out of you thinking he was dead!"

Evans raced back to Toronto, and his story ran in the *Globe and Mail*'s Sunday supplement on April 17. On Monday morning, the eighteenth, Charlie's agent got a call from the CBC. They wanted Charlie on *After the Fact,* the TV show. They wanted Barlow, too, but they hadn't been able to reach him. "You have to do it," George Arnold said. "Otherwise no one tells your side of the story. By the way, what *is* your side of the story?" "My side is I don't know anything about this guy," Charlie said. "I have to talk to Barlow." "You haven't talked to him?" George asked. "I've been trying," Charlie said. "He doesn't pick up."

On Wednesday morning, Charlie flew to Toronto, and that afternoon he called me from Parry Sound. "Barlow's in the hospital," he said. The doctor said it was pneumonia, not life threatening, but they were keeping him for a few days to monitor the situation. "Did you talk to him?" I asked. "Just for a minute," Charlie said. "And?" "It's what

I thought," he said. "He's never heard of Horace Tudhope. Evans is obviously just trying to get some attention." "What about the photographs?" "Yeah," Charlie said, "there's this thing called Photoshop . . ." "But they're old, right?" I said. "Who knows?" Charlie said. "It's easy to make things look old. Mar, whose side are you on?" "Your side," I said, but I must have said it the wrong way, because Charlie said, "I gotta go. Car's waiting. Look for me on TV tomorrow at ten." "You're not coming back after the taping?" I asked. Charlie said, "Nope. The CBC is putting me up at the Four Seasons, and I got George to negotiate me an extra night. I think I deserve it. Don't you?"

I watched *After the Fact* alone on our sofa. And:

> *Horace Tudhope, a shrimplike man in a blue suit and unbecoming yellow tie, sits rigidly in an easy chair opposite CHARLIE, who looks relaxed and handsome. Next to TUDHOPE, DARIUS EVANS, thirtyish and already balding, fidgets with a CBC coffee mug. April Hoffmann, the presenter, sits between CHARLIE and EVANS. HOFFMANN is wearing a tan skirt suit that might have been fashionable in 1989. A copy of Charlie's book adorns the glass-topped table, along with three more coffee mugs.*

AH: Mr. Willett, let's start with you. In your book, you claim that the anthropologist and Mexican historian Robert Barlow impersonated Parry Sound resident Leonard Spinks, for somewhat complicated reasons.

CW: That's right. Spinks had been the previous boarder in the house where Barlow was living. He died of a heart attack, and Barlow borrowed his identity, to publish a book.

AH: Why didn't he publish it under his own name?

CW: Because he was supposed to be dead. You see, he'd been blackmailed in Mexico, and he faked his own suicide, to escape from what had become pretty intolerable circumstances.

AH: And before that, you say, Barlow was the lover of the horror writer H. P. Lovecraft, is that correct?

CW: Strange but true.

AH: Really amazing, Mr. Willett. But here we have Mr. Evans, who tells us that Leonard Spinks isn't dead.

DE: That's right, April. My story begins with a letter from Mr. Tudhope, here, who told me . . .

HT: Leo's fine! I saw him just a couple of years ago. It was during Parry Sound Days, you know, where they close down James Street to vehicle traffic, and folks come out to sell you hot dogs and soap and things like that. I came down to see what was what, and there was Leo, talking to a fellow in a clown suit. I talked to him, I mean Leo, for a few minutes. Asked if he'd been fishing over at Blind Bay. I caught half a dozen lakers . . .

DE: Horace, let's come back to that. Like I was saying, April, I went to see Mr. Tudhope, here, and he told me he's seen Spinks many times since his supposed death.

AH: Mr. Tudhope, you're sure the person you saw was Leonard Spinks.

HT: [*Laughs.*] Who else could it have been? There's not a lot of people like Leo in Parry Sound.

AH: Mr. Willett, can you explain this?

CW: I certainly can. Either Mr. Tudhope is confused, or he's not telling the truth.

HT: [*Deleted*] you, mister. Who the [*deleted*] do you think you are?

AH: Mr. Tudhope! Please, we're on television.

HT: He's calling me a [*deleted*] liar.

AH: As it happens, Mr. Tudhope, Robert Barlow was a guest on our program, and we have a video clip of him cued up on the screen right behind you. I wonder if you'd mind taking a look at it?

HT: Sure.

The clip plays.

HT: That's Leo. Looks like he was having some kind of joke on you, eh?

CW: How are your eyes, Mr. Tudhope?

HT: What?

DE: This is ridiculous.

CW: I'm just wondering how Mr. Tudhope can be so sure.

AH: We can replay it . . .

HT: It's Leo!

CW: April, it's been shown that eyewitnesses are notoriously unreliable. You've got a witness who says, That's him! And an innocent man goes to jail.

HT: Is Leo going to jail?

CW: I'm sure Mr. Tudhope is very sharp for a ninety-year-old. But people do make mistakes, and other people get hurt. Think about what happened in the States, after 9/11. Or with McCarthy . . .

AH: Mr. Willett, are you saying that Mr. Tudhope doesn't recognize a man he's known for fifty years?

CW: April, all I'm saying is, I'm just wondering if Mr. Evans might be using Mr. Tudhope for his own ends.

HT: Say that to my face, you little [*deleted*].

TUDHOPE stands.

DE: Stay cool, Horace.

AH: Mr. Tudhope, please, have a seat.

CW: I can't tell if you're lying, or senile. Or both.

TUDHOPE leaps at CHARLIE, knocks him out of his chair, and straddles his chest. For such an old man, he's surprisingly quick.

CW: Help!

A scrum of TECHS pull TUDHOPE to his feet. CHARLIE gets up. He holds his cheek.

CW: I stand by what I said.

It was great TV, but no way to contain the story. The next day, the CBC dispatched April Hoffmann to Parry Sound with a photograph of the man who had appeared on *After the Fact* and spoken so movingly about how he wanted to live. Was he Barlow, or Spinks? Hoffmann stood at the foot of James Street, determined to find out. But none of the people in the street—a German couple, a harried-looking woman on her way to the health food store—had heard of Robert Barlow *or* Leonard C. Spinks. "Not a lot of *After the Fact* viewers out today," Hoffmann said, wryly. She went into a store with the charming name Bearly Used Books, and the red-haired teenager behind the counter said, "Oh, yeah, I know that guy. He comes in all the time." "What's his name?" Hoffmann asked. "I have no idea," the teenager said. "He just buys, like, stacks of books." "What kind of books?" "Like, old books," the teenager said. "History and stuff." "Thanks!" Hoffmann said. The next shot was of Barlow's house on Waubeek Street. Hoffmann stood on the porch, waiting. "No one home," she said. "Let's go talk to the neighbors!"

So they went to the pretty little white house next door and a man in his thirties answered. "Hi, I'm April Hoffmann from the CBC," Hoffmann said. "Can you tell me who lives next door to you, in that house?" "It's that old guy," the neighbor said. "Do you know his name?" "Sorry, no," the neighbor said. Encouraged by Hoffmann and the camera's attentive gaze, he went on: "I asked him once if he could do something about his yard. He just *looked* at me, like I was some kind of insect. It's not neighborly, eh?" Next Hoffmann went to the across-the-way neighbor's house and rang the bell. Evidently no one in Parry Sound had anything to do, because this neighbor, too, answered the door right away: a mannish granny in a blue Maple Leafs sweat-shirt. "What's your name?" Hoffmann asked. "Gladys," the granny said. "Gladys," Hoffmann said, "can you tell me who lives in that house?" "That's Leo Spinks's house," Gladys said. "And is this Leo Spinks?" Hoffmann held up the photograph. "Sure is," Gladys said. "Is that from the TV?" "Do you mean to tell me," April Hoffmann asked, incredulously, "that you don't know what Mr. Spinks has been up to?" "What has he been up to?" Gladys asked. "He's been going around telling people that he is a rather well-known anthropologist named Robert Barlow," Hoffmann said. Gladys squinted. "What for?" "That is what we are going to find out," Hoffmann said. She turned to the camera. "I'm April Hoffmann, and we are *After the Fact.*"

5.

Charlie came home on Saturday afternoon with a black eye. With his wheeled bag still standing at attention in the hall, he got on the phone to his editor at HarperCollins. "I'm back," he said. "Listen, I was thinking, if we can get a camera crew to the hospital . . . What? But he *is* Barlow. I know! Let me talk to him again. I can go back up to Parry Sound, I'm sure there's something at his house. I don't know. I'll try. OK, on Monday morning." He set his phone on the kitchen counter and looked at me, perplexed. "They want to cancel the paperback," he said. I wasn't sure how much surprise he needed me to express. "That's terrible," I said. "I have to talk to George," Charlie said. His phone buzzed against the counter. "Hello?" he said. "Yes, speaking. No, I didn't know. I mean there wasn't anything *to* know. Because he's Robert Barlow! Yes, I'm serious." He hung up. "Gawker," he said, and shuddered. He was wearing a beautiful white dress shirt, which was soaked with sweat. "What we've got to do," he said, "is put Barlow on TV. He can tell his story. But no one can tell me when they'll let him out of the freaking hospital! They have him on antibiotics but apparently there's something going on with his lungs." "Charlie," I said, "have you looked at the Internet?"

In the twenty-four hours since April Hoffmann's second program, new evidence had turned up: photos of the young L. C. Spinks, a big and actually quite dashing man, who looked very much like the person Charlie had met in Parry Sound, and not at all like the young anthropologist who had once been friends with H. P. Lovecraft. It also came to light that Spinks had legally changed his name to Robert Barlow in 1991, but he hadn't told anyone in Parry Sound. He was Leo Spinks to the neighbors, Mr. Spinks to the shopkeepers, Leo to the hostess at Wellington's Pub & Grill. It was, I thought, as if he hadn't needed to convince anyone but Charlie. "Of course I looked," Charlie said, irritably. "And?" "I don't know," I said, "it just seems like, maybe he's not Barlow at all." "Please, Marina," Charlie said. "Hoffmann got *one* ID from a blurry photo. And her witness isn't exactly the sharpest tack in the box." His phone buzzed. "What? This is he. I don't know, I don't have anything for you now." "That was the *New York Times*," he said to me. For a moment he was himself again, a lost, hurt Charlie, his face as open as a child's. "Oh, Mar," he said, "I'm so fucked." Then he went into the little bedroom he used as his study and shut the door.

Charlie got Barlow—got *Spinks*—on the phone, eventually, and Spinks said not to worry. He had letters that Don Pablo had addressed to him in Montreal: proof that he'd survived his "death" and gone to Canada. "That's great," I said, although it seemed like scant evidence to me. Charlie said, "The problem is, he doesn't know where they are. This is Robert Barlow, the guy who left Lovecraft's estate in the basements of his friends. Fuck!" He spent the rest of the weekend looking for someone who might have known Barlow after 1951. He tried to find the Canadian consul, John French, and called dozens of Ohio numbers, looking for the descendants of the science fiction collector C. L. Barrett. He wrote to Mexico City College alumni, to librarians at Brown, and to the director of the Martínez del Río family archive. All in vain. Charlie wondered if Barlow might have tried to get in touch with William S. Burroughs, and wrote to the librarians at the University of Kansas, which has some of Burroughs's papers. On Monday afternoon, he flew to Lawrence to investigate a box of miscellany that had been deemed too unimportant—or was it *too revealing?*—to be itemized. He called me the next night from his hotel. "Guess what I found, Mar?" he said. "What," I sighed. It was a receipt from an auto mechanic in Sault Ste. Marie, dated March 11, 1978. "What I think," Charlie said, "is that Burroughs went to see Barlow. Sault Ste. Marie is on the way to Parry Sound, if you go north around Lake Huron. So, maybe they met by the lake. Kind of a nice scene, right? These two old guys, former lovers, walking on the shore, or sitting on the porch of some cheesy motel. Maybe they went fishing!" "But it's just a receipt, Charlie," I said. "OK, it's a receipt," Charlie said, "but listen. Burroughs doesn't write *anywhere* about going to Sault Ste. Marie in 1978, and nobody writes about him going there, either. I've put in a call to his biographer, but I bet he won't know anything about it. And why? Because, *Marina,* Burroughs wanted to keep the trip secret." Charlie's voice had gone all whispery, a voice from the bottom of the well, and I was afraid. "What are you going to do?" I asked. "I was thinking, I could hire a private investigator," Charlie said. "Some guy who can be my eyes and ears while I go after other leads. Ugh, Marina, can I call you back? I want to get right on this." It was ten p.m. "Sure," I said, sadly. "I'll be up for a while."

By the time Charlie came back from Kansas, he had decided the receipt was probably meaningless. He had a new idea: Could it be that the people of Parry Sound were conspiring against him? He'd made fun of Parry Sound in his book: the whole *remedial town* thing. More to the point, he was an outsider who had discovered something about Parry Sound that its citizens didn't know. So they had ganged up on Charlie and Barlow, beginning with that crusty old fucker, Horace Tudhope. They were all pretending that the real L. C. Spinks hadn't died of a heart attack in 1950 or whenever. "But there's no death certificate," I pointed out. "It got lost," Charlie said, testily. "So says L. C. Spinks," I said. I didn't care anymore about placating Charlie. I was on his side, but being on his side didn't mean agreeing with him. "If Barlow was impersonating Spinks," I said, "why did he change his name back to Barlow?" "He got tired of the charade," Charlie said. "He wanted to be his real self." "His real self!" I exclaimed. "Is that what you think? If he wanted to be his *real self,* why didn't he tell anyone who he was?" "He told me," Charlie said. "Yeah," I said, "and don't you think that's weird?" "What do you mean?" Charlie asked. "He was *waiting* for you, Charlie," I said. "He sat there in his house, waiting for you to show up. So he could pounce on you like some kind of spider." "Spiders don't pounce," Charlie said. "In Australia, they do," I said. "Whatever," Charlie said. "You're not completely wrong. Barlow *was* waiting for me. He wanted to tell his story to someone who would understand." "He wanted to tell his story to someone who would believe it!" I said. "Look at the facts. There's no record of Spinks ever dying. There's no record of Barlow ever changing his name to Spinks. What there *is,* is a record of Spinks turning himself into Barlow, and a lot of people who still know him as Spinks. Who do you think he is? Really?" "He's Barlow," Charlie said. "I was there, Marina. I heard his story. I know he was telling the truth."

I was happy to leave for work the next morning. That afternoon, Charlie left a message on my cell phone: an Ontario TV station was going to air a segment about *the Barlow thing* at six. I canceled my last two patients and hurried home. Charlie was lying on our bed. He was still wearing the SAVE THE LAST HUMAN FAMILY T-shirt and pajama bottoms he'd had on the day before. I sat on the edge of the bed and squeezed Charlie's arm. "It's going to be all right," I said. "For who?" Charlie said. "For us," I said. Charlie looked at me with so much incredulity, it was almost like hatred. "For the jellyfish," he said. "For them, this is no problem." "Hey," I said, "you know I'm going to love you no matter what happens, right?" "I have to brush my teeth," Charlie said. He shambled into the bathroom. When he came out, we watched the Ontario news on my laptop. The segment on Barlow—on *Spinks*—aired halfway through the program. "The strange story of a local literary hoax reaches its conclusion, we guess," was the lead-in.

The camera is trained on the entrance to the West Parry Sound Health Centre, a big tan brick box. A pudgy TV REPORTER in a blue button-down shirt holds a microphone.

TV REPORTER: We're waiting for Parry Sound resident Leo Spinks, who has become notorious as the author of a memoir called *The Book of the Law of Love*, which he apparently made up.

"The author!" Charlie groaned.

An old man comes out of the hospital's sliding glass doors: L. C. SPINKS. He's short, old, and frail. He walks with the help of a male NURSE, who holds his arm.

TV REPORTER: Mr. Spinks!
L. C. SPINKS: [*Turning.*] Eh?
TVR: Why did you do it?
LCS: What?
TVR: Why did you pretend to be [*consults notebook*] a Mexican anthropologist named Robert Barlow?
LCS: I don't know what you're talking about.
TVR: I think you do, Mr. Spinks! You've been all over the news. Why did you do it?

Just for a moment, SPINKS looks afraid. Then the fear vanishes. He steps toward the camera.

LCS: I'm not pretending.

TVR: OK, well, you wrote a book about how you're Robert Barlow, and you're not him. What would you call that?

LCS: You don't understand. I used to be Spinks. Now I'm Barlow.

TVR: If you're going to argue about semantics . . .

LCS: It's not semantics! I'm talking about souls.

TVR: What?

LCS: Souls moving into new bodies. I'm talking about possession.

TVR: Are you saying that you were possessed, Mr. Spinks?

At this point, the NURSE steps into the frame.

NURSE: [*To the REPORTER*] Stop upsetting him, eh? It's OK, Mr. Spinks. Let's get you in the van.

"Wow," I said, and shut the laptop. "He's psychotic." Charlie looked up at me. His skin had broken out; fresh red bumps rose among the faint purple acne scars on his cheeks and forehead. "But he really was convincing," I said. "He knew all that stuff. I would have believed him, too, probably." But I didn't believe it, and Charlie must have heard that in my voice, because he didn't answer. "Let's go out," I said. "I'll buy you a drink." "You go," he said. "I'm just going to sit here and contemplate my downfall." "This isn't your downfall," I said. "How do you know?" Charlie asked, suddenly fiercely angry. "Because it's not," I said. "You're a great writer. You're going to write another book." "Leave me alone," Charlie said. "*You're* going to be all right, no matter what happens. You and your rich daddy and his yacht." I didn't want to go out, but that quip hurt my feelings so much that I put on my coat.

How could Charlie think that I would be all right if he wasn't? And how could he imagine that my father made me *all right*? I took my purse and keys, but stopped at the front door. "I'm not leaving you," I said. Charlie just stared at me. In retrospect, I think he was afraid. He must have had some ideas of his own about what *I* knew, or suspected. "Forget it," I said. "I was just trying to help!"

I went out. There wasn't really anywhere I wanted to go, though, so I walked around Brooklyn Heights for a while, looking in the ground-floor windows of brownstones. People were eating dinner, talking on the phone, watching TV, cuddling, leaving the lights on in empty rooms. Why couldn't any of them be us? Why couldn't we step into their lives, and be OK? Of course, I had no way of knowing if any of those strangers were OK. For all I knew, they were heartbroken, terrified, up to their necks in marital problems of their own. Still, I had a violent desire to be someone else, to open a strange front door and call out, "I'm home!" I walked until my feet were sore, and when I returned to *my* home, Charlie was out. I got into bed and turned out the light, and as I lay there, not sleeping, it occurred to me that for just a moment I might have come close to understanding L. C. Spinks.

On May 2, the *Times* ran an article: THE OLD MAN AND THE CBC: QUESTIONS MULTIPLY AS A MEMOIR DISSOLVES INTO MYSTERY. The gist of it being that Charlie's book was certainly a hoax but no one could decide *whose* hoax it was. Had Spinks tricked Charlie? Or had Charlie been in on the trick all along? They quoted my husband, who said he wasn't ready to give an answer because he wanted to talk to Barlow first. *Barlow,* he said. Surely, the *Times*'s bemused book reporter asked, you don't still believe that he's Robert Barlow? At which point Charlie went all Baronian. What does it mean for someone to be someone? he asked. I mean, how does anyone know who they really are? The reporter must have wondered whether Charlie was insane or obfuscating; because the *Times* had given Charlie's book a good review, she chose the latter. *Mr. Willett may think he's playing a deep game,* the article concluded, *but even he ought to admit that the game is up.* As, indeed, it was. HarperCollins canceled Charlie's paperback. Other news outlets ran considerably less kind stories about the end of the deception. They compared Charlie with Jayson Blair, which infuriated me. Couldn't they see that Charlie had been fooled? Didn't they know how hard he had worked, to tell what he thought was the truth? Charlie, for his part, wasn't even surprised. "This is America, Mar," he said. "Of course they're coming after me with that." He got his old army jacket out of the hall closet and started wearing it, with a wool cap pulled down over his ears. "Homeless Vet Chic," he said. "New for the spring of 2011."

On the Internet, pseudonymous strangers accused Charlie of being a liar and a sociopath. They imagined that *he* had tricked *Spinks* into impersonating Barlow, which, I suppose, was how it might have looked from a distance. It was hard to believe that the frail old man who'd confessed on TV had thought of the whole scheme, that he had taken Charlie in—even if Spinks was the author of a previous hoax. The trolls supposed that Charlie had done it for the money, or the fame; they decided that all his talk about love and hope had been bunk. In fact, the virtues Charlie had professed to believe in only made people attack him more viciously. There was nothing more satisfying than watching a saint get his comeuppance, or giving it to him. ANOTHER UTOPIAN BULLSHITTER BITES THE DUST was the headline of Gawker's story about the scandal, and the theme of many ugly comments, on Gawker and Buzzfeed, Salon and Slate. Which was bad enough, but for those places it was just one story among many. For the readers of fantasy and horror, Charlie's scandal was *the* story of the summer. The fans who had trusted Charlie howled their outrage at having been tricked, and the ones who had hated Charlie's book from the beginning trumpeted their correctness. *Only a moron could have believed that crap,* a person called Tsathoggua wrote on the blog *Modern Tentacles. HPL hated sex, and thank Gawd for that. If he'd had a love life, he would be ordinary = boring.* To which someone else replied that everyone has a love life, as Freud had "proved." A person called NoKindredOfMine wrote that the problem with Charlie's book wasn't that it gave Lovecraft a sex life; it was that Charlie had failed to condemn Lovecraft's racism.

> **Has anyone read Lovecraft's poem "On the Creation of Niggers"? If not I recommend you take a look. How a black writer could feel sympathy for the author of that poem, much less express it, is beyond my comprehension.**

Tsathoggua replied that he didn't care what the social justice warriors thought. Lovecraft's work was good.

> **I get why Willett likes Lovecraft. What I don't get is how he could be so fucking gullible and arrogant.**

And NoKindredOfMine:

> **Probably because he was trying to please assholes like you.**

The fight grew fast and large. Charlie pretended to take it ironically: *Kids will be kids,* he tweeted, which didn't help. But I saw that he was furious. He *knew* that Lovecraft was a racist. He'd tried to understand him anyway. "If I give up on all the racists, there won't be anyone left!" he said, which made me wince. "No one, Charlie?" He was supposed to respond gracefully but he just mumbled something and turned away. He posted the James Baldwin quotation *Love takes off the masks that we fear we cannot live without and know we cannot live within* on his book's Facebook page and was savaged for it. Either he had failed to take off enough masks with his quote love unquote, the trolls wrote, or he'd been wearing a mask himself, and either way, would he please have the good sense to shut up and die? George and his publisher both urged Charlie to make a public apology. It wouldn't save *The Book of the Law of Love,* but it might save him. Charlie refused. What was he supposed to apologize for? Caring too much about someone else's life? Trying to express a complex point of view? The way he talked about it made me think that, even then, he didn't entirely believe that Barlow was Spinks. I didn't disagree with him, because he needed me to be on his side; but when I thought about Charlie in the privacy of my mind, I was afraid for him, and even a little afraid *of* him.

Then, in the middle of July, a person called StarseedMom posted a comment on *Modern Tentacles:*

> I don't know about social justice but I wish my son had never read Willett's book. It taught him how to kiss a boy.

It was the woman who'd come to Charlie's reading in Cleveland. She got a quick response from Tsathoggua:

> Wait, what?

and told her story to the blog. HideousGelfling, the moderator of a widely read fantasy subreddit, tweeted a link to it:

> @charliewillett's book is a manual for pedophiles? #barlowhoax #inexcusable

At which point the online clamor became something nightmarishly new. It was as if Barlow's miraculous survival had been a dam behind which a lake of indignation had pooled. Could Charlie really have written a sympathetic book about an adult man in love with a teenage boy? Had people really been obliged to admire it? Well, no one was obliged any longer, and with the word *pedophile* came a flood of revulsion. Strangers who had never read Charlie's book, or even heard of it until then, accused Charlie of being a pedophile himself. He ought to be investigated by the police, they said. Was anyone looking into destroying the unsold copies of *The Book of the Law of Love*? Would someone put pressure on the publisher to surrender them? A petition snaked from in-box to in-box until fifty thousand people had signed, and meanwhile, well-meaning individuals organized support groups for those who had been hurt by Charlie's book, and other do-gooders investigated Charlie's previous articles for traces of falsehood—which, of course, they didn't find. The righteousness of their activity was terrible, like watching a monster do therapy on its victim. But the things written by the unrighteous were worse. I mostly refused to read their spew, but one morning a patient canceled, and I thought I'd see what Twitter had to say about Charlie, so I could be more empathetic toward his situation. Right away, I found WilburWhateley12's suggestion that

Someone should get child pOrn onto @charliewillett's hard drive and tip the FBI.

To which RandolphCarterDreams replied:

@WilburWhateley12 Too bad @charliewillett doesn't have kids. The porn cld be of THEM.

Which gave WilburWhateley12 another idea:

@RandolphCarterDreams Especially if it was snuff pOrn.

I was glad, then, that Charlie and I had never returned to that conversation about having children. It wasn't just that I would have been afraid for their safety. I didn't want to bring new people into this world.

When I was starting out in private practice, I treated a patient who convinced herself that I was not the *real* Dr. Marina Willett. What had I done with the real Dr. Willett? What would I do to *her*? She made out her checks to "Marina Willett *or so she says,*" and I deposited them without blinking, but the insane things she wrote on some rate-your-doctor sites have haunted me for years. That was upsetting, but this was different. The quantity and inventiveness of the hatred that came Charlie's way seemed to have no limit. It was like the torchlight mobs of old, but enormous, shapeless, impossible to defend yourself against. It was, in fact, just what Charlie had been afraid of: a replay of the scandal of the *Erotonomicon* in the 1950s. It made me wonder what people were, really. Were they individuals to be loved and puzzled over, or were they *a species,* as Gilles Baron said, *bent on its own destruction?* At the same time, the outpouring of hatred made me love Charlie more—or, maybe I should say, it made me love him again. He so clearly didn't deserve to be treated like that, and he was so clearly being destroyed by it. He stopped sleeping and asked me to write him a prescription for Ambien, which I did, but it gave him nightmares, so he went back to drinking. He stayed up late in the little second bedroom, hunched over his laptop with a glass of Scotch, following the news of his *downfall.* I told him not to read it, but he said it was the only thing he still found interesting. He lost weight. He smoked too much, and had panic attacks. He was afraid to go outside. What if someone recognized him? I couldn't blame Charlie for being afraid. I knew about *doxing,* about *swatting.* My heart rate went up each time someone climbed our building's stairs.

That summer Charlie and I lived like criminals on the run. We disconnected the landline, and ordered takeout under false names. We went out late at night—Charlie was still wearing his stupid wool hat, despite the heat—and bought groceries at the bodega. I wore big black sunglasses to work and hurried home at the end of the day to make sure nothing awful had happened. For the first time in years, I could count on Charlie to be there. We kept the blinds down and huddled on the bed, watching DVDs of *The X-Files.* It was awful, but wonderful, too: we were in terror together. We were Scully and Mulder, looking for the truth, which was still out there. We were Bonnie and Clyde, Harriet Vane and Lord Peter Wimsey. Meanwhile, as the summer wore on, the world lost interest in Charlie's book. Even fandom was now preoccupied by the larger question of Lovecraft's racism: Was it OK to read Lovecraft, to celebrate him? What about the trophies given out at the World Fantasy Awards, the grotesque little busts of Lovecraft? With surprising speed, Charlie's hoax cooled from an outrage to a curiosity.

In August, a graduate student at the University of Copenhagen asked if he could interview Charlie about the literary strategies of his deception, and *This American Life* invited Charlie back to tell them how it felt to be exposed as a fraud. George urged him to do the radio program. It could be the start of your second act, he said. Charlie refused. He wasn't ready for a second act. Besides, he was still angry about being compared with Jayson Blair. When he told his story, if he told it, he said, he'd be the one to do the telling. Great, George said, send me a proposal! Charlie didn't do that, either. He had enough money from foreign sales of *The Book of the Law of Love* to last a year at least. I'll make my comeback then, Charlie said. I didn't point out that a come-back might take time, and that neither of us might be happy to go back to the days when Charlie was living off my income.

What Charlie did do was to start playing Dungeons & Dragons again. Eric had a weekly game night, and he attended it religiously. His character was a thief, he said, a half-elf with a cruel sense of humor and a tragic family history. And the world! They had begun by chip-ping a gem out of the statue of somebody's god, and now they were caught up in some big political machination and who knew what was in the balance. "Eric is a dungeon master's dungeon master," Charlie said, tugging at his recrudescent beard in a way that made me think of the person I'd met at Grace's party, years before. I thought: Charlie came through this once, when his father died. He was a kid then and he had fewer resources than he has now. He didn't have *me*. I thought: we're going to make it. I picked up the dirty clothes Charlie left on the bedroom floor, threw his leftovers away, sponged cigarette ash from the windowsill, held Charlie when he wept. Slowly, things got a little better. Charlie drank less and started eating again. Dorothy Sayers had launched him on a mystery kick; he read his way through Dashiell Hammett and James M. Cain. We went to the Cape for a week in August, and I wanted us to go to Connecticut for Labor Day, to show my parents we were all right, but Charlie begged off. Eric had invited him to Vermont for a gaming weekend, he said. The whole group was going. With the help of some bottles of Lagavulin, they were going to finish their campaign. "We're fighting gods, at this point," Charlie said. "You don't want to deprive me of the opportunity to kill a god, do you?" "No," I said, "you'd better do that."

The gamers left on Friday afternoon, and by the time I came home from the office that night, I'd had second thoughts about seeing my family. I couldn't remember the last time I'd had a weekend to myself. I called my mother, who expressed disappointment; but disappointment was her ordinary mode of being. I ordered takeout Chinese and sprawled. *Northanger Abbey* fell asleep in my lap. The next afternoon, I wondered if it might be pleasant to leave the house. I'd heard that there were parks in Brooklyn, although I couldn't remember the last time I'd seen one. I put on running shoes and sunglasses and jogged into the brilliant autumn. The still-green streets of Brooklyn Heights welcomed me eagerly: someone who hadn't gone away for the weekend! I jogged in the shade, marveling at all the beautiful old houses that had somehow escaped the city's self-consuming greed. When I passed the building where H. P. Lovecraft had lived, on the corner of Clinton and State, I gave it the finger. Fuck you, Mr. Lovecraft! This city is all right. Your horrors were all in your mind. I crossed Atlantic Avenue and turned left on Pacific, with the vague idea that I'd run to Prospect Park. Where there was, I thought, a farmer's market! I stopped at a red light to stretch my aching hips. "Hi, Marina!" Grace said. She and Eric were waving from the far corner of Smith Street. Eric held a canvas shopping bag. The light changed and I ran to them. "What are you doing here?" I asked. "We're having a picnic," Grace said. "I would have invited you, but I thought you were out of town?" "I thought *you* were out of town," I said to Eric. "Um," he said. "Our plans changed. Last minute." "Did Charlie go?" I asked. "Go where?" Grace asked. "Uh, yeah, he did," Eric said. "That's funny," I said. "I didn't know you could play without the *dungeon master.*" Oh, I knew what I was talking about. I'd been around Charlie so long I was an expert. "Where's my husband?" I asked.

6.

I ran home and googled *Lila, animal shelter, Portland*. A puffy-faced girl with a pit bull pup. I read the latest posts on *Notes from After the End of the World*, looking for the smugness you'd expect from a woman who was fucking another woman's husband, but there was only the usual Baronian hand-wringing at the folly of all these people who didn't know they were doomed. I wondered, wildly, whether Lila was having an affair with Charlie in order to make the world more Baronian. To make her little tear in the human fabric, to nudge humanity toward its final disorganization. Then, bring on the jelly-fish! They were hermaphroditic and immortal, and adultery meant less than nothing to *them*. I envied them. I went to the bathroom and tried to throw up, but I couldn't. With that third-person feeling you have sometimes in dreams, I observed myself in the kitchen, still wearing my stupid running tights, opening a bottle of sauvignon blanc, and arranging Triscuits on a yellow Fiestaware plate. I returned to my laptop, took a sip of wine, and looked at pictures of Lila again. She had a man's jaw, a muffin-top. Charlie had been reading Baron in our bed because *she* liked him! I threw a Triscuit at the wall. I contained tears, and let them out. I thought it might be fun to revisit the awful things people had written about Charlie online, so I could agree with them. *Rape his wife and make him watch. Cut off her head. Cut off his head.* I should have felt honored to be included. They weren't planning to rape Lila. *He better change his name. I can't wait for his next book. Lynch him*—ugh. Very soon, I had the impression that what I was reading was no longer the transcription of human speech or human thought, but just a barking from the bottom of a pit, faceless creatures calling for food. *Does anyone know of anyone Willett has raped?*

I was five pages into the search results when Charlie's old articles surfaced. "The Native Speaker." "Whiteout: Or, How a Black Man Stood on Top of the World." "Five Reasons Why *Firefly* Is the Most Brilliant TV Show, Ever." It was dark by that point, and my dream of exercise had turned into a pot of pumpkin ravioli and a third glass of wine. Under its maudlin influence, I read every story Charlie had ever published, in order to recover the man I loved. The strange thing is that I did. Reading Charlie's eager sentences—so many exclamation points in those early pieces, so many dashes!—I heard him as he'd been when we met, a very young and not very reformed nerd, utterly in love with the strange textures of the world. Oh, Charlie, I thought. Come back. I called his phone but there was no answer. I poured myself another glass of wine and tried not to think about what he might be doing at that very moment. I composed an email to Lila asking her to please send my husband home but wisely didn't send it. I lamented everything. The whole human condition, the fact that one thing leads to another, and the ten thousand years of progress that had enabled a horde of toxically regressed strangers to camp out on my laptop's screen. Then it occurred to me that I hadn't read Charlie's story about the Happy Rabbit. I searched for it: nothing. I googled *Happy Rabbit, Memphis, William Lee.* I remembered every detail. The Chinese immigrant prepared for a plausible future. A strange idea that could have saved the world. Nothing. Had Charlie researched the story but not written it? I googled *golden rabbits* and got a cascade of irrelevance. *Happy Rabbit?* Internet, please? *Memphis rabbit restaurant?* Finally, I realized that Charlie had made the whole story up. Right at the beginning, and how could I not have seen it? What kind of restaurant would serve only rabbit meat? I asked the obvious question: What else had he made up? Horrified, I packed a week of clothes and went to stay with my brother in Westport.

I had been lied to before, of course. Everyone's been lied to. When I was eight, my father told me he was going on a business trip and he'd be back in a week. He was gone for six months. For most of them, he lived in Fairfield, practically next door to my quietly furious mother. He came back shortly after my ninth birthday: I tumbled off the school bus and there he was, rising from an armchair, reaching out to me in wonder. "Look at you!" he said, as though I were the one who had gone away. Then he said, "How about an iced tea?" We never talked about why he had left, but it didn't take much sleuthing to figure out that he had run off with another woman. The greater mystery was why he had come back, and I never solved it. Nor did my mother ever really become less furious. The episode vanished from our family history to the point where my brothers claim they don't remember it; the few times I've brought it up, they looked at me with total incuriosity, as if I were telling them about a dream. But those six months are still there; they can never stop being there. I see them in the way my brothers clown around on our family vacations, as though to keep my father in his seat. I see them in the adult-education classes my mother takes, on everything from Gemology to The Modern Middle East. Nothing, but nothing, will ever catch her off-guard again. And naturally I see the consequences in myself.

By the time Charlie called me, Eric had already talked to him.

"I'm so sorry, Mar," he said. "I ruined everything." "Yes, you did," I said. "I owe you an explanation," Charlie said, "but I don't completely understand it myself." "See a therapist," I said. "OK," Charlie said. "OK. You're angry." "Charlie, I'm not angry, I'm *done*," I said. "That's not true!" Charlie said. "You can't leave me just like that, over this one thing. Marina, you can't leave me *now*." "Watch me," I said. But Charlie was right; we weren't done. I saw him a week later: late September, everything blue as can be. I was renting a studio on the Upper East Side, and we met on the East River promenade, amid joggers and nannies with kids and forlorn people taking the Sunday *Times* for a walk. Charlie looked fifty years old. His hair was threaded with gray, and his expensive English glasses magnified the dark bags under his eyes. His army jacket smelled like a bar. He held out his arms to hug me and I stepped away. "I'm going to fix this," Charlie said. "Grace gave me the name of a therapist." He laughed. "The curious case of Charles Willett." It was such a stupid thing to say that I didn't answer. "I love you, Mar," he said. "I don't want to hear it," I said. Charlie lit a cigarette and turned to look at the river. "I went back to Parry Sound," he said. "You *what?*" I said. "I wanted to understand," Charlie said. "Oh, my god," I said, "don't you ever learn?" "I *did* learn," Charlie said. "You know what Spinks is?" "A monster," I said. "He's like the DMV guy, Mr. Rational Language," Charlie said. "He's someone who had to start again from zero. And the thing is, it kind of worked." I was speechless. "You can't be serious," I said. "Totally serious," Charlie said. "The truth is, in a sick way, I admire him. He helped me to figure something out . . ." "Will you fucking *stop?*" I shouted. I thought he had finally and truly lost his mind. People turned to look at us, and looked away. Just another young, or not-so-young, couple, having their weekend meltdown. "OK, chill!" Charlie said. "I'll tell you about it another time." "Tell me never," I said. I had to get away from him, so I started walking. "Marina!" he shouted. "Hey, come back!"

. . .

I didn't see Charlie again until the last day of December, when he emailed that he was sorry, he missed me, and he promised he wouldn't talk about L. C. Spinks. I met him at a bakery in Cobble Hill. He was worn out, hunched around himself, around the place where he used to be. I felt the loss, too. "How are you?" I asked. "My life is a sad joke," he said, "only there's no one to laugh at it." "What about Lila?" I asked. "That's over," Charlie said. "Too bad for you," I said. "Please, Mar," he said. "You have no idea what this is, not having anyone." I wanted to touch his hand but I told myself it wasn't time yet. Then he told me he'd tried to kill himself with his leftover Ambien, and I told him that he should check himself into a hospital, and he did. Six days later he was gone.

7.

Charlie died to me then, the same as he died to everyone else. I wept and mourned and participated in the rituals of grief, the most terrible of which was surely the memorial service Charlie's mother held in her faculty apartment in Morningside Heights. It happened on a Sunday in February, one of life's low points. Something that was almost snow drifted wetly out of the clouds. Indoors, two dozen people stood around a nearly bare living room, the only things in it a purple sofa, a white rug, a dozen bottles of cheapish Malbec on a sideboard, and a card table on which a thoughtful relative had arranged a basket of bagels, tubs of cream cheese and olives from Fairway. The last time I visited, on Charlie's mother's birthday the year before, the apartment had been imposingly full of books: volumes of German philosophy and art history and Greek and Latin Loebs. Their absence was almost as shocking as the occasion on which I was seeing it. Without the books, the apartment looked dingy: the plaster patched and painted too many times, the crown molding missing here and there, in accordance with some previous professor's bygone scheme. Charlie's mother—close-cropped gray hair, black turtleneck, round black glasses—circulated through this desolation like a zombie bride. Eventually, she approached me and asked if I was all right. I said I was as all right as I could be, under the circumstances. "What happened to your books?" I asked. "I got rid of them," Charlie's mother said. "Don't you think the apartment looks bigger without them?" "Absolutely," I said. "I rented a U-Haul and took them to the Strand," Charlie's mother said, "and when I got there, they said I had so many books, *they* would have sent a truck to pick them up! Let that be a lesson to you, Marina. Call ahead." "I'm going to get a drink," I said. Charlie's mother looked at me vaguely. "Why don't you come over for lunch, sometime?" she asked. "I'd like that," I lied. "Wonderful," Charlie's mother said. "I'll look at my calendar, and my secretary will give you a call." I slipped past an awkward knot of Charlie's Princeton friends, and two cousins from Philadelphia who stood with their backs to the radiator, talking about basketball in an undertone. A man in a gray tweed jacket, a philosopher, I assumed, was searching for a cheese knife. There were plastic knives on the table, but he seemed unable to accept the absence of the correct tool, knowing that there *were* cheese knives in the world. I watched him for ten seconds, then I slipped out of the apartment, and in the elevator I thought of what a miracle it was that any living human being had emerged from such a place, let alone Charlie. Who was no longer a living being, I had to remind my-self. Outside, I started crying, but with all the slush falling from the sky no one could tell.

But you have to keep living; so, in March, I moved back into our apartment in Brooklyn Heights. There were beer bottles in the sink, newspapers on the kitchen counter, piles of unopened mail, ashtrays full of cigarette butts, and black dust on the windowsills. I was furious at Charlie for leaving me with one more mess to clean up: even in death, he'd found a way to make me his maid. I threw out the trash but couldn't bring myself to sort through Charlie's things. Sometimes, in the evening, or on a weekend afternoon, I leafed through the com-position books in which he had made notes for his projects. I wasn't looking for anything; I just wanted to revive my memories of Charlie, to touch his handwriting, his smart-kid print. Inevitably, I found the notebook he'd used for his conversations with L. C. Spinks. My instinct was to set it in the sink and burn it: this book was dangerous. But I don't believe in burning books, any books, and even if I did, I could never have brought myself to burn Charlie's handwriting. Out of morbid curiosity, I leafed through the notebook one wet April night, but it didn't tell me anything I hadn't already known. There was no record of Charlie's last visit to Spinks, no suggestion of what my husband might have *figured out*. Which was strange, because Charlie took notes on everything. You never know what's going to be useful, he said, when I teased him about it, and he'd often been right. I looked for the missing notes in the bag that had come back from the hospital, but they weren't there. Nor were they in the sealed plastic bags the Stockbridge Police Department had finally sent me, containing Charlie's shoes and pants and jacket. (No T-shirt, though. Had he worried about his chest getting cold?) It was possible that there *were* no notes, because Charlie had either thrown them away or never made them in the first place. It was possible, though dreadful to think, that he had taken the notes with him into the lake. More likely they would turn up in a closet or a bag that I hadn't yet searched. Life is full of loose ends. My patients get tangled in them all the time; I'm supposed to help them see meaningful patterns in their lives, but I spend a great deal of time pointing out that some things are meaningless. Anyway, I told myself, it didn't matter. Spinks was a liar. What could he possibly have told Charlie that would make any difference?

Then, on March 24, someone texted me a photograph of an indigo ocean. I didn't recognize the number, and I was about to delete the message, when I had a wild thought about what it might mean. I remembered the note Charlie had left in the hospital: *Do not disturb me, I wish to sleep for a long time*. It was the note Barlow had pinned to his door before he killed himself, and I had moaned with pain when I heard about it, because it was so terrible to think that Charlie's last words had been a quotation. But what if he had slipped away, like *his* Barlow? How insane that would be, I thought, and how infuriatingly stubborn. Which is to say, how Charlie-like. My heart beat hard as I called the number back. It rang four times, and just when I thought it would go through to voicemail, someone picked up; then the call dropped out. I called back and the phone rang and rang. It was a New Mexico number but possibly a cell phone, so the call could have come from anywhere. I saw a patient, and wasn't much use to him; then I called again. This time I got a computerized voicemail. "It's Marina," I said. "Whoever this is, please, call me back." I called ten more times that night and left ten messages that all said the same thing.

I told myself it was a wrong number, but here's the thing: Being a psychoanalyst is in some ways like being a detective. You follow the trail of symptoms and dreams and memories back to the buried crimes of childhood. And like a detective, I'm very stubborn. I'm like Charlie in that regard. I kept my phone on all the next day, hoping the ocean person would call me back. That night, I forwarded the text message to Eric, who, I figured, owed me a favor. I asked him to use his big computers to figure out where the photo had been taken and whose number it was. He wrote back half an hour later. *No information about the number. You probably need a subpoena for that. But according to the meta-data, the photo was taken at Latitude 29.186460 North, Longitude 80.986413 West, 1.5 meters above sea level.* Ask a programmer, I thought. I wrote back: *Where in the world is that?* Eric replied: *Daytona Beach.* Oh, I thought. Daytona was near Cassia, where Barlow had once lived. And I recalled Charlie's dumb fantasy of working on a fishing boat. The next day, I called the Daytona marina—yes, Marina called the marina— and asked them to put up a picture of Charlie and my telephone number. I called tour-boat companies and fishing charters. I emailed

Charlie's face to dozens of strangers. I also thought about the photograph: the ocean, at night. Was whoever sent it pointing me to "The Night Ocean"? Barlow's story was about an artist who rented a cottage by the sea to recover from a grueling project. Did that mean Charlie was resting? The story was also about fish-men who carry swimmers away. Should I be on the lookout for fish-men? For fishy men? Inevitably, I thought of L. C. Spinks. What had Charlie *figured out* when he went to Parry Sound in September? Where were his notes? Even as I was looking for them again in Charlie's closet, I told myself, this is magic. You're doing a ritual. When you're done bothering random Floridians, maybe you can put Charlie's photo on a shrine and light a candle to it every day until you get sick of magic and move on.

Then I emailed Lila. *I doubt you want to hear from me,* I wrote, *but I think Charlie might still be alive, and I'm wondering if you know anything about that. You'd have to be a monster to know, and not to tell me.* I deleted the last sentence and pressed send. Lila wrote back that evening: *I used to think the same thing,* she said. *Now, I'm not so sure. Call me if you want.* So I called her. I pictured her in some crappy room in an apartment in a part of the country where everyone has a house. Old linoleum, particle board, fluorescent loop on the kitchen ceiling. Lila's voice was painfully young. "Thanks for making time," I said, as if she were the busy one. "That's OK," she said. Either she thought she *was* the busy one, or she was good at irony. "The truth is," she said, "I want to apologize. I feel really badly for what, um, happened. I was never in love with Charlie, and I don't think he was in love with me, either. It was just, like, a thing that happened. I think, maybe he was lonely? And confused? And maybe he was going through some kind of midlife crisis?" For a Baronian, her psychology was dismally ordinary. "Lila," I said, "why did you think Charlie might still be alive?" "Well," she said, "*someone* updated his Facebook page on, like, January eighth." "They did?" I couldn't imagine how I'd missed it, except that I was too distraught, and I had stopped looking at Facebook. "Yeah," Lila said, "it was just one word—*Whoosh*. But, I thought, who could have posted it, if not Charlie? And there was another thing. Charlie was reading this book, *The Long Goodbye*. It's about this guy, Terry Lennox, who fakes his own death. And the lake where Charlie disappeared is right near Lenox, Massachusetts. Lennox and Lenox. I thought, maybe that was a sign?"

Oh, god, I thought. Lila *was* in love with my husband. Nothing but love could occasion such fantastic hermeneutics. Which made me wonder what *I* was doing, but never mind. "You don't think that anymore," I said. "No, Mrs. Willett, I don't," Lila said. "I think probably his Facebook page was hacked by somebody who was messing with him. Those Knights of the Outer Void people knew he was in the hospital." Once again, I was angry at myself for not paying attention to what had happened online. "They knew?" "Yeah," Lila said, "they were tweeting about it. It was so ugly." "Lila," I said, "when was the last time you saw Charlie?" "In November," Lila said. "That was when we broke up. But like I said, we weren't ever really in love or anything." *Whatever,* I thought. "Did he leave a notebook at your house?" "A notebook?" "Yes, a composition book with a black-and-white marbled cover. College ruled." If she even knew what that was. If she even lived in a house. "No," Lila said, "I don't think so. I guess I could look?" "Please do," I said. "If my husband left behind anything with writing on it, I want to know." "I'm not sure I like you telling me what to do, Mrs. Willett," Lila said. "I feel bad about what happened but it doesn't make me, like, your servant." "It's *Doctor* Willett," I said, "and I don't give a fuck what you like." I hung up. The satisfaction I felt was short-lived.

Talking to Lila made me angry at Charlie again. How dare he have seen her ugly house, and read a novel in her presence? How could he have drowned himself? And if he *hadn't* drowned, if, like stupid Terry

Lennox, he'd faked his death, that would make Charlie the worst person ever. One evening in early April, I went to the liquor store and collected an armful of empty boxes. I filled a box with Charlie's shoes; I filled a box with his shirts. I sat on the sofa doing nothing at all for a long time, then I called L. C. Spinks. I thought his number would be disconnected, and I was surprised when he answered the phone. I told him who I was, and he said, "Ah, Dr. Willett. What can I do for you?" His voice was hoarse but warm. "You talked to my husband in September," I said. "I want to know what you told him." There was a silence, then Spinks laughed. It sounded like a radio leaving its station. "That would take quite a long time," he said. "Your phone bill would be astronomical." "I have unlimited minutes," I said. "Well, *I* don't," Spinks said. "OK," I said, "just tell me what you talked about, generally." "The transmigration of souls," Spinks said. "I have some thoughts about it. Your husband seemed interested." "OK," I said, for lack of a better response. "Was that the last time you talked to him?" "It was," Spinks said. Then I couldn't help myself: I asked, "Do you have any idea where he might be now?" Spinks hesitated. "Dr. Willett, are you telling me that Charlie is alive?" He sounded almost eager. "I'm not telling you anything," I said. "Well," Spinks said, "in answer to your question, I don't know. But I wonder if I might be able to help in another way. If I could share with you a few of my ideas . . ." "No, thanks!"

I got off the phone quickly and bristled at Spinks's arrogance: How dare he offer to *help*? It was like the knife offering to help the wound. I wondered what was happening in his mind, and how he'd become the person he was. Some early trauma? Abuse, neglect? Then I resolved not to perform pro bono psychotherapy on L. C. Spinks's phantom and set him aside, or tried to. I soon discovered something that Charlie must have understood a long time ago: Like certain books, certain people are hard to put down. Charlie was one of those people, and

Spinks was another. Why did he talk to Charlie about the transmigration of souls? What did Charlie *figure out*? In the weeks after I talked to Spinks, my mind circled his mystery to the point where it became disturbing. Finally, I did the only thing I could think of: I wrote out the story of what had happened. Which brings me, novelistically, back to the present, but with an un-novelistic weight in my heart.

Charlie is gone. Looking back on what I've written, I see that the Daytona photo isn't a clue to anything but the extent to which a smart person can fool herself. Either it was meant for someone else, or it was a cruel prank played by a troll who got my mobile number. I shudder to think how close I came to believing that there was more to the story: that Charlie might return. But, sadly, I do still think about L. C. Spinks. Charlie fell under his spell; he believed his lies once, and even when he knew what a monster Spinks was, he went back for a second helping. How close I came to being drawn into the same unreality! Even now, when I ought to know better, I wonder: Why did Spinks deceive my husband? As a Freudian, I'm not supposed to use words like *evil;* my business is with instinct, memory, and desire. Nevertheless, I've been wondering, lately, whether evil might exist. If it does, I've been thinking, it might be like what Freud called *the navel of the dream,* the place where all the lines of meaning the analyst has so carefully traced through the patient's life vanish into the unknown. But where the navel of the dream is an essentially harmless phenomenon, a point where the dream's meaning is sufficiently understood, and further interpretation would be pointless, evil is a mystery with power. It reaches up into the world and makes everything mysterious.

When faced with such a phenomenon, what can you do? For me, the answer is clear: You walk away. You get back to your life and make meaning where you can. So I've been trying to concentrate on my patients, whose suffering is as great as mine, or greater, but has the advantage that I can do something about it. I haven't given up on myself, either. I've started seeing my old therapist again; she reminds me to be patient, no pun intended, and to accept my fantasies about Charlie's being alive as just that, fantasies, built on the foundation of old long-ings, old fears. I run in Prospect Park on weekends, and I'm thinking about adopting a dog. My grandmother wants me to start dating, but I'm nowhere near ready. Let me take my August vacation, I tell her, and we'll see what happens in the fall. I don't tell anyone about the useless thought that I keep pushing away, but which keeps coming back, like a stick of driftwood on the tide, and I'm sorry if the simile is too spot-on: It's late July, and Agawam Lake is as warm as it will get. But Charlie's body has not been found.

V.

A NIGHTMARE AND
A CATACLYSM

1.

L. C. Spinks's house was larger than it looked on TV, and wilder. The lawn was a miniature prairie, through which, as I watched, a black and white cat undulated. The rusted-out frames of lawn chairs stood among the weeds like goals in some forgotten game, but the bird feeders that hung from the eaves of Spinks's porch were full of seed. Wondering what kind of person would both keep cats and attract birds, I threaded my way up the path to the front steps, just as Charlie must have done four and a half years earlier. The gray-painted wood creaked underfoot. A wind chime hung silently from the porch eaves. I saw, with surprise, a brass mezuzah, screwed into the jamb just over the doorbell. I rang, and, not for the first time, the idiocy of what I was doing caught up with me. Why had I squandered my vacation on a trip to Parry Sound? Why had I thought for even a second that Spinks might have anything useful to tell me? Then Spinks came to the door. He looked younger than he had on television, and more vigorous. Despite the August heat, he wore a peach-colored dress shirt and brown polyester slacks. He really had been handsome, once, I thought. High forehead, strong round jaw. His nose dented like it had been broken long ago. "If you're here about the book," he said, "I don't give autographs." I was about to impersonate an autograph seeker and vanish, when Spinks said, "Dr. Willett?" "Yes," I said. "Please," Spinks said, "come in."

I sat where my husband had once sat, in the kitchen, which was warm and stuffy and smelled of cat fur. Spinks fussed around, looking for a special tea which he insisted I try. There was no villainy in his fussing, no sinister aura to the chipped blue cup he set before me. Only a feeling of time having gone by. Yet Spinks had impersonated Barlow, and in the end, he'd let Charlie fall. I pushed the cup aside, and I was about to speak when Spinks asked, "Are you a Freudian?" It wasn't a question I'd expected. "Sort of," I said. "More like a post-Freudian." "But you believe in talking cures," Spinks said, "generally speaking?" "I do," I said. "That's good," Spinks said. "I don't like the doctors who try to cure everything with pills. We need words. We *are* words, really." What were we talking about? I wondered. "Now, Dr. Willett," Spinks said, "please tell me, why have you come all this way to see a very old man?" "My husband said he figured something out, when he talked to you," I said. "I want to know what it was." "I don't know," Spinks said, "I can only tell you what I told him." "And what was that?" I asked. "Well," Spinks said, "understandably, your husband wanted to know why I had, from his point of view, impersonated Robert Barlow. I explained that I hadn't *impersonated* Barlow at all. I *became* Barlow. I *am* Barlow." "I see," I said. I was glad to have a therapist's reflexes for this kind of conversation. "You don't believe me," Spinks said. "I'm listening," I said. Spinks laughed. "It's all right! Charlie didn't believe me, either. So I told him how it happened." "And did he believe you, after you told him?" I asked. "I'm not sure," Spinks said. "I think he did. But it's a very difficult thing to believe if you haven't experienced it yourself." "Why is it difficult?" I asked. "Let me find that tea," Spinks said. "Where could I have put it?" He stuck his head in the pantry closet. "Did you have a good trip up from Toronto?" I didn't say anything.

"The roads can be crowded, this time of year," Spinks said. "Lots of people going to and from their cottages. Ah, here it is."

From a cupboard over the stove, Spinks took down a brown paper bag and emptied some of its contents directly into the steaming kettle. He turned off the gas. "I'll just let it steep for a moment," he said. "Where are you staying in town?" "At a hotel," I said. "Yes," he said, "I meant, which one? Well, it doesn't matter. I'm sure it's nice. They all are, these days. Not like when I was a child . . ." He enfolded the kettle's handle in a crocheted pot holder and poured tea into my mug. "Aren't you having any?" I asked, suspiciously. "Yes," Spinks said, "of course I am." He took a second mug from the cabinet, where it hung from a tiny brass hook, and filled it. "Really, I'm becoming very absent-minded!" he said. We sat there for a while. Finally, I took a digital recorder out of my bag and set it up on the table, with its little tripod. "I'm ready," I said. "For what?" Spinks asked. "For you to tell your story," I said. "Aha," Spinks said, mildly. He sipped his tea. "Will you excuse me for a moment, first? I have to take care of my old plumbing." "Go ahead," I said. He went to the bathroom, and I sniffed the tea. It didn't smell like Spinks was trying to poison me, or to drug me into believing him. On an impulse, I opened one of the kitchen drawers. It contained the usual collection of string and matches and scissors; also a sewing kit in a worn red velvet case. The clutter was sort of sad, and I had to remind myself that I was not there to empathize with Spinks. All I wanted to know was what he had told Charlie, and whether it might mean that my husband was still alive.

It seemed as though Spinks was taking an awfully long time in the bathroom, but on the other hand, I didn't know anything about his old plumbing. Finally, I heard the toilet flush, and a minute later, Spinks returned. "You must promise me that you'll let me tell my story from beginning to end," he said. "If you interrupt with questions, my old brain will just get tangled up." "I promise," I said. It was strangely peaceful in the kitchen, with butter-yellow light coming in through the chintz curtains and birds cheeping in the backyard. I took a sip of tea. It was sweet and smoky, and I was sure I'd had it before, but I couldn't remember when. "This is a horror story," Spinks said.

2.

I was born in Hungary, in 1922, Spinks began. My family was very rich. My father, if you can believe it, had been the Hungarian ambassador to Uruguay, and my mother's family were bankers. We had a house in Budapest, and a vineyard near Lake Balaton, where we lived in the summertime. There was a tennis court, and a boathouse with many little sailboats. Practically the only thing I remember from that time is that I wanted to go out in a boat, but my mother wouldn't let me. My older brother had drowned on the lake just the year before. Then, when I was four years old, my parents were murdered by thugs. I don't know why. They were rich Jews—maybe someone envied all they had. Conceivably, it was political. My father was an adviser to the would-be king, Charles the Fourth, and he had many enemies. It doesn't matter, they were dead, but no one thought to murder me. I was sent to Paris, then to London. A charity organization found a home for me in Canada, with a young couple who had no children of their own. Their names were Walter and Charlotte Spinks. Walter was a Quaker; Charlotte was from a wealthy family in Montreal. Her family manufactured corset stays, and like the stays, they were a little stiff. Walter and Charlotte wanted a child badly but when they couldn't have one they decided to do something good for the world, and took in a European orphan. They met me at the Toronto train station with gifts: a German-English dictionary, which was doubly useless, because I couldn't read, and I didn't speak German; and a box of caramels, which were then, and remain, my least favorite candy in the world. I carried a bouquet of daffodils which had wilted on the train from Halifax, and when I saw my new family I burst into tears.

I cried again when I saw Parry Sound. It was so small! I don't know what you think of our town, but to me it seemed like the end of the Earth. But I soon appreciated how lucky I was. Charlotte was an excellent cook; Walter was a gentle disciplinarian; and Canada, safe Canada, stretched out for hundreds and thousands of miles all around me, and beyond it was the ocean, and the people who had murdered my parents were almost unimaginably far off. I went to school in our old one-room schoolhouse, where I learned English and quickly made friends. In the summer, like the swallows and the Amazons,* we'd sail off to an island and camp, and not come back for days. In the winter we played hockey, and to everyone's surprise, I was good at it. When I was eleven, I joined the Parry Sound Juniors as a defenseman. Which, by the way, was the position Bobby Orr played for Parry Sound in 1959, when *he* was eleven. The Bruins scouted him the next year; I had no such luck. What I did have was science fiction. I was thirteen when my friend Gregory loaned me a copy of *Amazing Stories*, with a story about a scientist who attaches human heads to the bodies of dogs. Well! It was like someone had taken off *my* head and sewed it onto the magazine. And I guess you'd say the operation was a success.

It was in this way that I discovered the work of H. P. Lovecraft. *At the Mountains of Madness, Astounding Stories,* February 1936. It filled me with weird excitement: Lovecraft wrote about aeons-old civilizations,

---

* The reference is to Arthur Ransome's novel *Swallows and Amazons* (1930).

beings that had vanished from the Earth. Well, I had been something else, too, before I was a Spinks. I knew about old worlds. Even the language Lovecraft's cultists spoke, *Ph'nglui mglw'nafh Cthulhu R'lyeh wgah'nagl fhtagn,* and so on,[*] reminded me of the mother tongue which I was rapidly forgetting. Also, Lovecraft's stories were about books. The *Necronomicon,* the *Liber Ivonis,* the *Culte des Ghoules,* the *De Vermis Mysteriis:* ancient and forbidden tomes full of knowledge that drove men mad. It was just like my father! He was always locking himself away in the library of our villa, to read. Lovecraft's stories were so evocative for me that, little by little, they took the place of my memories: the few that I had carried with me from Europe, and the many I had lost on the way. When I read Lovecraft, I felt as if I were learning about my oldest and truest self.

Weird Tales was banned in Canada on account of Mrs. Brundage's covers,[†] so I wrote to fans and collectors in the States, and got them to send me the forbidden issues with Lovecraft's stories in them. Eventually, I started a mimeographed magazine, *Pickman's Vault,* in which I published lists of the stories I was looking to buy or trade for. I mailed it to the people I had corresponded with, and they passed it on to *their* friends, and soon my magazine became well known. I got to be friendly with Lovecraft fans all over North America, and, in fact, that was how I first heard of Robert Barlow. He was notorious in those days for having absconded with Lovecraft's books and manuscripts. All kinds of rumors circulated about him: that he was hoarding dozens of unpublished Lovecraft stories, that he had burned those same stories, that he was queer and had disgraced himself by making a pass at Howard

---

[*] An incantation from Lovecraft's story "The Call of Cthulhu" (1926).

[†] Margaret Brundage (1900–1976) was notorious for her illustrations of almost-nude women, which appeared on the cover of *Weird Tales* between 1933 and 1938. It was rumored that her daughter posed for most or even all of these pictures, which only added to their notoriety.

Wandrei.* He sounded interesting, so I got his address and sent him a friendly letter, but Barlow never replied, and I soon forgot about him.

I had other things to think about. When I was fourteen, I wrote my own *Necronomicon:* I filled a notebook with nonsense words and bits of would-be spells that I found in histories of religion and books by Aleister Crowley. I wrapped the book in black cloth, and for a while I kept it under my mattress, adding to it now and then as abominations occurred to me. Then suddenly that wasn't enough; I had to go up to the attic and sit cross-legged among trunks full of Charlotte's out-of-season clothes; I had to chant my spells softly, and see what would come. Sometimes I saw black stars dancing in the corners of my eyes; sometimes I felt a weird presence hovering just out of reach. Once I thought I saw a green light floating over Mr. Lewis's house. All of which would have been foolish enough, but that summer, I got Gregory to join my cult by promising that it would make us rich. I spoke about the *Necronomicon* in such terrible terms that by the time I allowed him up to the attic, and unwrapped the book's black shroud, he was, I think, really afraid. We chanted and chanted, and the strange thing was, after a while, I *did* feel as though we had made contact with something, as though some invisible presence had heard us, and was coming closer, closer . . . Then Gregory broke off and kicked at the flour pentagram we'd drawn on the floor. "It's not working," he said. "This is just nonsense, isn't it?" "No," I said. I told him that we'd summoned a demon, and it had already penetrated the veil between worlds. It was on its way to us on giant invisible wings. Gregory went home in terror and told his mother everything.

I had to answer to Walter, who was as furious as he ever allowed himself to get. I had tricked Gregory! And my head was full of dark

---

* Howard (1909–1956) was Donald Wandrei's brother. An artist and writer, he lived in New York.

nonsense about creatures from beyond the stars, black magic, and doom. Hadn't Canada, hadn't *he,* taught me anything at all? He took me to Gregory's squalid little house on River Street and made me apologize to him in front of his parents; and when *that* humiliating exercise was finished, Walter took me to the top of Belvedere Avenue. "Look around," he said. "What do you see?" "Houses and the water," I said. "Some trees." "And what do you think, when you see those things?" "We're in Canada." "So we are," Walter said. "Are you glad to be here, Leo?" "Yes," I said, honestly. "Me, too," Walter said. "So tell me, why do you need all that made-up stuff? All those monsters?" I thought about trying to answer honestly but I was afraid I'd hurt his feelings. Neither he nor Charlotte liked to be reminded of where I had come from. "I don't know," I said. "Well, think about it, Leo," Walter said. "You're getting a little old for made-up stories." "I guess so," I said. "That's the spirit," Walter said. Then we went home, and he took my *Necronomicon* and all my pulp magazines to the backyard, doused them with gasoline, and set them on fire. If Walter hadn't done that, I might have done as he asked, or tried to. I might have gone to college and become a scientist, or an engineer, or headed north to work for the Forest Service, as Gregory eventually did. The pyre made those lives impossible. As I watched my magazines go up in smoke, all I could think was that I would never accept a life of rocks and houses and trees. I would have my old, weird world, and I would make Walter pay.

Walter kicked at the ashes of my book, scattering them. "I think that's about that," he said. "Come on, Leo. Let's go see what Charlotte's got in mind for dinner." She was cooking roast chicken and crispy potatoes, my favorite. It was her way of making up for what had just happened. Walter, too, was apologetic. "How about if we walk over to Calder's and sample their wares," he said, when our quiet meal was finished. "Leo, would you object to a peppermint or two?"

"Walter, we must have chocolate," Charlotte said. "All right," Walter said, "chocolates all around. How's that strike you, Leo?" "Sure," I said. I got a sack of chocolate nonpareils and ate them methodically on the way home, but I was not appeased. I had, however, discovered in myself a talent for writing forbidden books. And here I am. Here I am.

3.

Through *Pickman's Vault,* I had begun corresponding with a group of fans who called themselves the Futurian Literary Science Society. This was Donald Wollheim, Fred Pohl, John Michel, Doc Lowndes,* and a few others, all of whom would go on to be very well known. Back then, Wollheim was the only one who had published anything in a professional magazine, but in the world of fandom, they were titans. For a Parry Sound kid to be exchanging letters with them was very exciting, even if my new friends in the States asked odd questions: Was it true that some people in Canada had only one leg, and faces in their stomachs? Did they really play *hokey* with the vertebrae of dinosaurs, and use strips of elk meat for currency? I answered with great candor, and my responses delighted the Futurians so much that they urged me to visit New York for the First World Science Fiction Convention. So, of course, *of course,* I went. With silent apologies to my adoptive parents, I stole twenty dollars from the cash register of Spinks Hardware and hitchhiked to Toronto, where I got on a bus. It was the summer of 1939, and I had just turned seventeen.

---

* Like Wollheim, Frederik Pohl (1918–2013) and Robert "Doc" Lowndes (1916–1998) would go on to be notable science fiction writers and editors; John B. Michel (1917–1969) was a science fiction writer and essayist.

Pohl was the one who had invited me, so I went to his apartment, on Dean Street, in Brooklyn. I arrived at about ten in the morning. Through the door, I heard the most unbelievable noises: it sounded like somebody was being machine-gunned, while somebody else shouted at a moving train. I knocked and knocked, and finally, a chubby, mustached person with buck teeth opened the door. He was wearing a violet satin dressing gown and one blue slipper. "Mr. Pohl?" I asked. "I'm Lowndes," he said. "Who the fuck are you?" I had sent a telegram from Toronto, saying that I was on my way, but it hadn't arrived yet. I introduced myself. "Holy shit," Lowndes said. "It's the Canadian!" From somewhere farther back in the apartment the reply came: "Ask if he can use a sewing machine!" "You might as well come in," Lowndes said. "You couldn't possibly make things worse than they are presently."

The apartment was hot and dark, like a tomb dug into the base of a volcano. In the living room, two young men in shirtsleeves wrestled with a bolt of silver fabric, most of which had unrolled on the floor. There was, in fact, a sewing machine in the room, but what they were doing seemed to have no relation to it. A can of silver paint was balanced on the radiator, with the handle of a brush sticking out of it. "The Canadian," Lowndes said, as if it were my title. "This is Fred, and this is Johnny." In the gloom it was hard to tell which was which. "What are you doing?" I asked. "Isn't it obvious?" one of them said. "We're making space suits." "Wouldn't it be easier if you turned on a light?" "It *would*," the same one snapped, "except the electricity's been turned off." "Not the h-h-heat, though," the other one said. "Welcome to N-n-new York." The person who would turn out to be Pohl banged on the floor with the handles of a pair of scissors. "God dammit! I told you we should have done this last week." "I told *you* Doris should have d-done it," said the one who would turn out to be John Michel. "Fuck you," said Pohl.

I watched them with horror and amusement. "Maybe if you lay it flat on the floor, and double a length of it over," I suggested. They did this. "Now," I said, "if you have a pencil? We can trace one of your bodies, and then cut out the shape." "Too dark to see a pencil outline. Doc, lie on the floor. We'll cut around you directly." This, too, was done. Lowndes cried out only once: "My ear!" But feeding the doubled shape into the sewing machine was impossible. "What if we scratch the suits and just wear the helmets," Michel suggested. "We could be visitors from a planet with more or less terrestrial conditions, but a slightly different atmosphere." "Without the suits," Pohl said, "we'll just look like people with fucking bowls on our heads." And, in fact, next to the pot of paint there was a stack of four deep wooden bowls. "We could paint our clothes silver," Lowndes offered. "And be what, spacemen who wear ties?" countered Pohl. "No. It's hopeless. We're going to give up the whole fucking thing." "Excuse me," I said, "but what's this for?" Even in the darkness, I could tell that the Futurians did not think I had asked an intelligent question. "For the convention," Lowndes said. It began the following afternoon.

Pohl took the cutout fabric to the window and sewed up the legs of Lowndes's suit by hand, but we had all overlooked the fact that Lowndes was three-dimensional. He hopped around with one leg in the space suit, one out. "What are you people doing?" asked Wollheim, who had just come in. He had been in Pohl's bedroom, typing up a leaflet with the Futurians' demands, to be handed out at the convention. "We need a steamroller to flatten Lowndes," Pohl said. "We need s-s-someone who knows how to s-sew," said Michel. "Forget the costumes," Wollheim said. "No one cares if we dress up or not. What we've got to do is crush the viper, Moskowitz." "Moskowitz?" I said. Michel, Lowndes, and Pohl all told Wollheim at once that the Canadian had arrived. "*Now?*" Wollheim said. "Well, put him to work." He handed a mimeograph stencil to Michel. "I figure we need two hundred copies." Over by the window, Pohl dropped a cigarette into the paint can. "Is paint flammable?" he asked no one in particular.

I began to form new ideas about the Futurians: they were more frightening than I had expected. "Is he talking about Sam Moskowitz?"* I asked. Lowndes took it on himself to explain. The convention had been organized by a fascist dictatorship which consisted of Moskowitz, Jimmy Taurasi, and Willy Sykora,† whom they referred to as "Dirty Willie." All three of them hated democracy and freedom of expression and basic human dignity. They were trying to turn fandom into an extension of the militaristic scientific establishment which was leading the world to the brink of another catastrophic war. "A plot which we must resist, with our lives, if necessary," Lowndes said, striking his chest, which made a hollow sound. "We'll definitely resist with *your* life, Doc," Pohl said. The cigarette seemed to have gone out. "We're fighting for the future of civilization," Michel said. "It's as simple as that." But a moment later he was dissatisfied with his own answer, and asked, "Have you read Marx's *Kapital?*" Here I made a terrible mistake: "I might have seen it in *Amazing Stories,*" I said. The Futurians laughed until they began to choke and cough. "Jesus, you *are* a spaceman," Pohl said. "I was joking," I said. I wished that I had stayed in Parry Sound, but then it occurred to me that if the Futurians were really intelligent, they wouldn't be working in the dark. "Does this building have a roof?" I asked. "No, it rises infinitely into space," said Pohl. "Let's take the suits up there," I said, "and see what we can do."

The space suits *were* hopeless, but we carried the mimeograph machine to the roof and spent the rest of the day running off leaflets. From the rooftop, I had a view of countless buildings, more than I had ever seen in one place before. There was the Williamsburgh Savings

---

* Samuel Moskowitz (1920–1997), a prominent fan from Newark, New Jersey.

† James Taurasi (1917–1991) and William Sykora (1913–1994), both from Queens, were also notable figures in the microcosm of 1930s fandom.

Bank Tower, and, behind it, the Empire State Building with its zeppe-
lin mast, and Manhattan rising to the north and south of it like a vast
windowed wall; far in the west was New York Harbor, a silver squib
from which the Statue of Liberty poked up like a nail. Cars honked on
Flatbush Avenue. Someone was playing Caruso on a record player.
And there I was, with four of the best-known fans in fandom, printing
up antifascist propaganda to save civilization! "You guys, this is fun!" I
said. But the Futurians were sullen and busy. In the light of day, they
looked like young gargoyles: Pohl had a high forehead and an overbite;
Lowndes, who had changed into black trousers and what looked like a
red pajama top, had buck teeth and bandy legs. Michel's cheeks were
pocked with old acne scars, and fresh pimples dotted his chin. His right
arm was in a sling. The wind blew some pages to the edge of the roof,
and Pohl shouted for someone to get them, so I got them. I ran down
to Pohl's apartment for a stapler, and on my way back up, I passed a
perplexed-looking old woman in a sea-green housedress. "Roof re-
pairs," I said. I went up and down, carrying finished leaflets and new
stencils, until it was dark outside, and completely lightless in the apartment. Wollheim and Michel went home, and Lowndes, Pohl, and I ate
beans cold from the can. Then Lowndes went to sleep on the sofa, and
I lay on the hard, dirty floor, thinking about how lucky I was.

The convention did not mark the start of a new era. What happened was, we arrived early at the Midtown hall which the fascists had
rented from the Baha'i: it was decorated with green sunbursts and mu-
rals depicting the succession of the prophets and the unity of all mankind. "Lo, the future is upon us!" Michel exclaimed. And so it was.
Moskowitz and Taurasi waited outside the upstairs auditorium, and
they wouldn't let us in without consulting Willy Sykora, who hadn't
arrived yet. We went downstairs; we went upstairs again. Someone
called the police, but Moskowitz told them everything was all right.
They said they would come back in an hour. We loitered peaceably

downstairs, distributing leaflets entitled "People of Earth! Beware of the Dictatorship!" to puzzled fans. I had been in New York for only a day, but already I felt like an insider. "Don't let the fascists make the rules!" I implored teenagers in high-waisted pants and propeller beanies. "Scientific socialism *is* the future!" A photographer from *Time* magazine took my picture. Isaac Asimov arrived and asked me, "Who *are* you?" "Who are *you*?" I asked him back. Of course, he wasn't Isaac Asimov, not *the* Isaac Asimov, yet. Two girls arrived. One was from California, and the other was Pohl's girlfriend, Doris. She was surprisingly beautiful—very surprisingly, considering how Pohl looked. She had auburn hair and high-arched eyebrows and a cruel mouth, like the Dragon Lady in *Terry and the Pirates*. I offered her a leaflet. "Where's Fred?" she asked. "Upstairs," I said. "Sam Moskowitz won't let us in." "And a big strong kid like you is afraid of Moskowitz?" Doris said. "Phoo."

Well. Michel and I hid our pamphlets under a radiator and followed her upstairs. Wollheim and Pohl were standing outside the auditorium, along with some Futurians whom I hadn't met. "He wants us to promise that we won't disrupt the convention," Pohl said. "How can we promise that?" Wollheim asked. "What if we go in and one of us has a seizure?" Moskowitz, a large youth with slicked-back black hair, who did, actually, look like a fascist, grimaced. "Just promise that you won't mess things up on purpose," he said. "That's undemocratic," Pohl said. "If we promise, then everyone who goes in should have to promise. You can't hold us to a different standard." "Well, *I* promise," Doris said, and for some reason she looked not at Pohl but at me. "Are you coming?" I would have liked to follow her, but I didn't want to disappoint the others. Moskowitz was scowling. "I guess . . ." he said, but just then Sykora came up the stairs. It was immediately clear why his nickname was "Dirty Willy." Everything about him was gray, except his fingernails, which were edged with black. He stood there like a sad, short human pyramid and shook his head. "You know what I found in the lobby?" he asked. "Communist propaganda!" "I wonder who could have left it there," Wollheim said. "You know what you guys are?" Moskowitz said. "You're a bunch of liars." "We are n-n-not," Michel said. "You're the l-l-liar, S-s-s . . ." He stopped, breathless. "He can't even say it," Moskowitz said, laughing. Michel stepped toward him, and Moskowitz took a step back, surprised, and almost lazily pushed Michel, who fell to his knees. That wasn't fair, I thought. Michel was half Moskowitz's size. I approached Moskowitz, intending to reason with him, and also to shield Michel from further harm, but Sykora, misunderstanding, shouted, "Help! Police!" and the police, who were just then on their way up the stairs, seized my arms and escorted me down to the street. Wollheim and Pohl ran after me, shouting, "He didn't do anything! Don't touch him! We'll sue!"

We spent the afternoon in a cafeteria near the Baha'i hall, handing out leaflets to hungry fans. Asimov came and put an entire hard-boiled egg into his mouth. "You fellas missed a lot," he said. "Charlie Hornig[*] gave a great speech about the future of science fiction! He says it's all going to be nuclear physics, and we have to educate everyone to do math." "Shut up, Isaac," Pohl said. "The hard sciences are going to take over the so-called soft sciences," Asimov went on, undeterred—it was impossible to deter him. "Even the brain is just chemistry!" Cyril Kornbluth[†] came in, a short, dour kid with curly black hair, who reminded me of the cigar-chomping infants you see sometimes in cartoons. He and Pohl had just been to the World's Fair, and they got into an argument about whether the automated highways in the Futurama exhibit would make traffic better or worse. I entered into a daydream in which I hip-checked Moskowitz, shoved the heel of my hand in Taurasi's

---

[*] At the time, Hornig (1916–1999) was the editor of the science fiction magazine *Wonder Stories*.

[†] Kornbluth (1923–1958) was a member of the Futurians, and would go on to be one of the great science fiction writers of the mid-twentieth century.

face, and slid into the auditorium. What did I find inside? Goodness. Doris. In reality she did not appear. When it got dark, we walked down Lexington Avenue, whooping and kicking trash cans. "Did you see Sam Moskowitz's face when the Canadian muscled in?" Lowndes asked. "Sheer terror." "Where'd you learn that move, Canadian?" Wollheim asked. "Hockey," I said. "But I didn't do anything really." "Didn't you?" Wollheim said. "Spinks, you're all right." He took my arm and we skipped together down the street. Wollheim sang,

> From nineteen thirty-nine to eight hundred thousand, seven hundred
>   and one,
> The Futurians' work is never done,
> First we'll annoy, then we'll destroy,
> Every last Eloi,
> From Brooklyn to Washington!

The others joined in. Then, changing key, they continued,

> Arise, ye prisoners of Earth!
> Arise, ye hungry hacks!
> For Science thunders in your guts,
> It's time to take a crap!
> Away with all your inhibitions,
> And god-damn Gernsback's eyes—
> Piss on all scientifictions!
> Futurians, arise, arise!

to a tune that sounded vaguely familiar. "What song is that?" I asked. Wollheim let go of my arm. "Spinks," he said gaily, "we must educate you." He went into a Western Union office and tried to send a telegram that said FUCK YOU to Moskowitz, but the clerk rejected it, so he sent one that read THE BANISHED SEND THEIR REGARDS TO THE TYRAN-NOUS TRIO. Then Wollheim went back to his parents' apartment on the Upper West Side, and the rest of us took the subway to Pohl's.

Pohl's mother was asleep, so we went up to the roof. We lay with our backs to the low parapet and talked about whether humanity would ever travel to other stars. "We've got to," Pohl said fervently. "It's the only way we're going to escape extinction." Kornbluth was skeptical: "How many people are you planning to squeeze onto that spaceship, Fred? And how many generations is it going to take before they've all got webbed fingers and Habsburg lips?" "What you could do . . ." Pohl began, but then Michel said, "Hold on, who's *that?*" He pointed across the courtyard at a lit window where two girls were preparing for bed. One of them took off her dress, and—"My God," Michel said, "that c-can't be r-real." "I think it's underwear," Lowndes said. He had worked in a Civilian Conservation Corps camp in Connecticut, and claimed great knowledge of sexual matters. "We'll see," Asimov said. He produced a small device from the inside pocket of his blazer. It looked like a cross between a telescope and a kazoo. "It's called a Wonderscope," he explained. "It uses X-ray filters to see hidden objects." We took turns looking through it, but could see only colorless blobs which, Pohl said, were probably on our own eyeballs. The girls had put on dressing gowns and were daubing their faces with cold cream. One was tall and fair, the other short and dark. Neither was anything like as beautiful as Doris. "Courtesans, doubtless," said Lowndes. We lay on the parapet, watching, until their window went dark, then we rolled onto our backs and looked up at the few faint stars. "Say," I told Michel, "I'd like to read that book you were talking about, *Kapital?*"

4.

To the Futurians' surprise, and to my own, I did not go back to Parry Sound. Instead, I moved into Pohl's apartment, with the understanding that I would contribute five dollars a week toward the rent. I slept on Pohl's sofa and spent a lot of time with Pohl's mother, a small, sharp woman, who worked as a substitute teacher, and seemed frightened by her brilliant but erratic son. Pohl had just quit his job as a messenger for an insurance company, and he spent his days looking for work and his nights writing poems and teaching himself to play the guitar. I looked for work, too, but more often than not my search took me over Brooklyn Bridge, as people said in those days, to the used-book shops on Fourth Avenue, where I spent hours leafing through volumes of Lord Dunsany, Arthur Machen, Algernon Blackwood, and M. P. Shiel.* One day, while I was ogling a locked bookcase of weird rarities in Dauber & Pine, on Fifth Avenue, a youngish, baldish clerk in a black jacket and high-collar white shirt came up and asked if I was looking for something *in particular*. "Do you have any Lovecraft?" I asked. He laughed. "Not much," he said, and pointed out a back issue

---

* Edward John Moreton Drax Plunkett, aka Lord Dunsany (1878–1957), Arthur Machen (1863–1947), Algernon Blackwood (1869–1951), and M[atthew] P[hipps] Shiel (1865–1947) were all writers of weird fiction, whose work Lovecraft admired.

of *Weird Tales,* which I already owned. "Are you a fan?" he asked. I informed him that I was the editor of *Pickman's Vault,* which, I said, was one of the best-known magazines for Lovecraft collectors in all of North America. "Is that so," the clerk said, amused. He told me his name was Samuel Loveman, and he had been Lovecraft's friend. "You *knew* him?" I squeaked. "What was he like?" "Howard was a gentleman," Loveman said. *Howard!* I could hardly speak. Loveman asked what I was doing in New York, and I told him about the convention. "I know Donald!" he said. "He came to a party at Belknap's apartment, once." I knew who Belknap was, but I'd never thought of him as having an apartment. As if by magic, names were turning into people. The only name I hadn't heard before was Loveman's. "Do you write stories?" I asked. He shook his head. "I am a poet," he said. He made it sound very grand.

Loveman told me that if I came back the next day, he'd show me some of *Howard's* poems, in a rare letterpress edition. "Just to look at, not to buy, you understand." I grinned and told him I couldn't buy them, anyway. I didn't have five cents for the subway back to Brooklyn. "Is that so?" Loveman asked. "Why don't you come talk to Mr. Pine?" So I did: an old disconsolate Einstein of a man, unevenly poured into a purple cardigan sweater. He hired me to shift stock in the back of the store for seven-fifty a week. After paying rent to Pohl, it would leave me two-fifty for food and car fare; but I figured Pohl's mother wouldn't let me starve, which turned out to be more or less true. I started immediately. The *back room* was actually a basement, and the *stock* was countless boxes of moldy books that Dauber or Pine had bought from the estates of individuals who had died, judging by the look of the books, in the late nineteenth century. My first task was to make pathways so the boxes in the back could be reached. Have I mentioned that the basement was cold and wet? It was cold and wet. And in its corners, the spoor of what I hoped were unusually large mice.

I wouldn't have lasted even a week there, except that Loveman and I became friends. When I looked especially hungry, he took me to Fleischmann's Vienna Model Bakery on Broadway, where my nose tingled with familiar yet unplaceable smells. Over pastrami and coffee and Linzer torte, he told me stories about *Howard* and the many other famous people he had known. Loveman had been friends with the poet Hart Crane—had I heard of him? And with Ambrose Bierce, too. In fact, he said, Bierce had written to him from Mexico in December 1913, asking Loveman to please send a copy of Giambattista Vico's *Scienza Nuova* to him care of the Hotel Imperial. Bierce went missing in the desert just a few weeks later, and Loveman had often wondered whether the book was a clue to where that great man had gone: whether, having spent his life tearing down hypocrites and imbeciles, Bierce had decided to create himself anew. "I still dream of going to look for him," Loveman said. "Wouldn't he be very old?" I asked. "Ninety-seven," Loveman said. "But he had a remarkable vitality." He shared with me a theory that he had been toying with for the last several years, that some people, not all, but some, are equipped with an extra soul, the way some people have an extra digit, or webbing between their toes. "An accident of metempsychosis," Loveman said. "They may not even know it. But gradually, as one soul ages, the second awakens from its dormancy and becomes ascendant." "What's *metempsychosis?*" I asked. "It means, *reincarnation,*" Loveman said. "The transmigration of souls from one body to another." "Oh," I said, "like in that story where they sew that one guy's head onto the other guy's body." "Yes," Loveman said, smiling. "Sort of."

I was curious about Loveman's famous friends, but far more curious about Pohl's girlfriend, Doris. The Futurian Society had weekly meetings in the Flatbush Young Communist League's hall, upstairs from a deli on Kings Highway. The meetings were part lecture and part shouting match; they were very entertaining, and Doris came to nearly all of them. She stuck close to Pohl, but sometimes I managed to talk to her, and I had the impression that she liked me. Once, when I got into an argument with Wollheim about his proposal to start an American Futurist Party—it should be the *North American Futurist Party*, I insisted—Doris was the only one who took my side. Another time, I read aloud a story called "World Peace," which was just the reflections of a brain in a jar. The Futurians hated it, but when the meeting ended, Doris asked me where I had got the idea from. I said it had come to me in a dream, which was true. "It's so sad," Doris said. "Maybe," I said, "but did you like it?" Doris just looked at me. "What are you doing here, Leo?" she asked. "I'm fighting for the future," I said. "Of people?" Doris asked. "Or of brains in jars?" She walked away before I could answer.

From Pohl, subtly, I learned that Doris was an art student at The Cooper Union, and that she lived with her parents—her mother was some kind of minor aristocrat—but she was nagging Pohl to move out of *his* mother's apartment and go to college. She refused to see what was so clear to Pohl, namely, that college was at best a waste of time, and at worst an indoctrination into the ovine values which he and the rest of the Futurians were working so hard to eschew. Worse, she wanted Pohl to go with her to Mississippi, to educate Negro farmworkers: a harebrained project if there ever was one, Pohl said. Not that he had anything against Negroes or farmworkers, but *why* couldn't Doris see that the future had to be won here, in New York City? They'd been fighting about it, but, Pohl said, "It's like fighting Lilliput. Stomp your foot and all the little Dorises run away. But go to sleep for a minute, and they tie you to the ground." I wanted to tell Doris that *I'd* go to Mississippi with her, but I didn't dare. I made do with looking at her sidelong, while Wollheim raged against the fascists, and Asimov delivered an interminable speech about Cro-Magnon Man, and Pohl talked about the lessons of Spain. Sometimes I caught Doris's eye. Sometimes, for an ecstatic second or two, she did not look away.

In the last week of August, Wollheim organized an expedition to the beach. The Hitler-Stalin pact had just been announced, and the Futurians were aghast: the future was taking shape, it could not be denied, without us. The expedition was Wollheim's way to make us feel better, those of us who were still around, anyway. Michel, who suffered from osteomyelitis, had gone into the hospital to have an operation on his bones; Lowndes had long since gone back to Connecticut; and no one wanted to invite Asimov. So the expedition party was Wollheim, Pohl, me, Doris, and her friend Rosalind Cohen, a heavy girl with brown hair whose father ran a catering business. Rosalind owned a Plymouth convertible with a top that was permanently down: "It's nice in the summer," she said in response to my compliment. She drove us to Coney Island and talked the whole way about the strange letters she had received from Doc Lowndes. He had begun by proposing marriage, she said; then, when she turned him down, he sent her a series of poems, some of which he'd written, and some of which he'd copied from a book of French poetry; and these, when translated, turned out not to be love poems at all. One was about the Pope and some airplanes, and another seemed to be about trains and a Ferris wheel. "But the ones *he* wrote are disgusting!" Rosalind said. "I think your friend is very sick." "Why do you say that?" Wollheim asked, innocently. "He admitted to being a necromancer," Rosalind said. It soon became clear that she was confusing *necromancer* with *necrophiliac*. Fortunately, by this point we were at the beach. Art Deco stands sold caramel popcorn and stuffed animals, and the bright crinkled water of the harbor stretched out on the other side of them, dotted with pink bathers. A weathered sign warned of dangerous currents, but no one paid it any attention. Doris spread a blanket on the sand, and Rosalind set down a hamper of food. We removed our outer clothes. Doris was wearing a white bathing dress which accentuated the rise of her breasts and hugged the curve of her stomach. Pohl took off his shirt and sat on the sand with his arms around his knees.

I said something about flying cars, and Wollheim explained why flying cars were a stupid idea. "The *big* problem," he said in his high, nasal voice, "would be traffic. Can you imagine? If cars could go up and down, you'd have to have signs everywhere. No climbing. No descending. And cops. The sky would be full of cops." "Well," I said, blushing, "maybe you wouldn't have them in big cities. But in the country, a flying car would come in handy!" "We have those already," Wollheim said. "They're called *airplanes*." "But what's the point of the future," I asked, plaintively, "if they don't have flying cars?" Pohl and Doris rose from their blanket and went to splash around in the surf. I watched Doris's legs, her wide white thighs. Suddenly Pohl pushed her into a wave, and she disappeared under the lip of the water. The wave broke but Doris didn't reappear. I stood up, my heart racing. I could see one of Doris's feet. Then Doris shot out of the water and knocked Pohl onto the sand. "Ah, young love," Wollheim said, unpleasantly. Rosalind opened the hamper. "We have pastrami, we have meatballs, we have egg salad," she said. "Who's hungry?" This was more food than I had seen in weeks, but I said, "Maybe in a minute." Pohl and Doris were coming back from the water. Pohl grabbed the blanket and dried himself with it. Doris continued past him into the dunes. All of us watched her go—it was impossible not to. "Fred," Wollheim said, "what do you think about flying cars?" "I think they can go fuck themselves," Pohl said, distractedly. "I'm going to get a beer." Rosalind got up to visit the ladies' room, and I was alone with Wollheim. I knew that he, too, had met Lovecraft, and I wanted to ask him about their friendship, but Wollheim did not look like he wanted to be questioned. "Maybe you're right," I said. "We should think more about what all these new gizmos would *mean*." "Thank you, Spinks," Wollheim said. "If you really believe that, you're just about the only man in America who does." "In *North* America," I said reflexively. Wollheim glared at me. "Think I'll go for a walk," I said. I left him sitting alone on a pink towel, staring out at the water with a fixed unhappy expression. If you were going to make a painting of the last man on Earth, I thought, it would look like Donald A. Wollheim at Riis Park. I followed the path until he was out of sight; then I cut across into the dunes.

Doris was walking in a shallow valley parallel to the path that led to the changing house and the restaurant. She had taken off her bathing cap, and her auburn hair stuck out from the sides of her head. She wasn't especially happy to see me. "Are you all right?" I asked. "Yes," she said, "are you?" "Well, of course I am," I said. "I was just worried that you were upset." "Don't worry about it," Doris said. I walked along beside her without talking for a moment. "I wish there was something I could do to make you happy," I said. Doris laughed. "Leo," she said, "you don't even know me. Why does it matter to you if I'm happy or not?" She picked up a stick and hit the dune grass as we walked farther from the shore. "I'm tired of New York," she said. "I want to go to Paris. I want to meet Picasso and Gertrude Stein and Alice B. Toklas. I want to meet Gertrude Stein's little white dog. I want to drink red wine all day and sleep in a garret. I want to starve, and hunt pigeons for food." There was something Pohl-like about the way she spoke, and I could see why Pohl wouldn't like it. The last thing Pohl wanted was another Pohl. "I want to go with you," I said. Doris stopped hitting the grass and looked at me, finally. "I suspect you do," she said. "But unlike Fred, I don't need fans." "I don't want to be your fan," I said. I was terrified. If Nazi frogmen had come out of the surf with submachine guns, I would have been relieved, but they didn't, and I still had to act. I put my hand on Doris's waist and kissed her.

Doris folded against me briefly, and stepped away. "Leo, you're very nice, but I'm not going to run away with you," she said. "You already have," I said. "We must be half a mile from our blankets by now." Doris laughed. "Well," she said, "if we're runaways, we'd better have a destination in mind." "There," I said. I pointed to the top of a sandy hill. We climbed up. From the top we could see the beach and the ocean; in the other direction lay Canarsie and Brighton Beach. I sat on the sand, and Doris sat beside me.

There was something terrible about the moment. It was so perfect that any change would ruin it, but doing nothing wasn't interesting. "Who's Gertrude Stein?" I asked. "She's the person who said, Rose is a rose is a rose is a rose," said Doris. "I've never heard that before," I said. "Well, it's true," Doris said, laughing. She stood up. "That was quite an escapade, Mr. Spinks," she said. "What do you have planned for us next? Maybe we'll stow away on the ferry and visit Staten Island?" "I don't know," I said, "but if you tell me your telephone number, I'll call you." "My father's name is Hans Gustav Baumgardt, with a D," Doris said. "If you know the alphabet, you can look me up." She started walking down the hill, and I stood up to follow her. "Hold on there," she said. "It's better if I go back first, alone." "How long should I wait?" I asked. "As long as you want," Doris said. She ran down the hill, slid, fell, got up, and turned onto the path without looking back. I stayed where I was. The sun got low in the sky, and over by the changing house, a band started playing. Chains of white lights came on up and down the beach. I had no desire to move. This is the pinnacle of my life, I thought, and nothing that happens to me, however great or grand, will ever delight me more than having kissed Doris Baumgardt at Riis Park on August 26, 1939. Finally, I walked back. I expected the Futurians to have left, but when I returned to their spot on the beach, I found Wollheim and Doris dancing before a driftwood fire, snapping their fingers and laughing while Rosalind clapped and Pohl watched with an intense expression, as though he were trying to remember everything so he could write it up later in his report to some unforgiving authority. I sat next to Rosalind on the blanket. "Is there anything left to eat?" I asked. Silently she handed me a plate of egg salad.

5.

Back at Dauber & Pine, I asked Loveman about Gertrude Stein. "Miss Stein? I know her slightly," he said. He told me that she had come to speak at the Algonquin Hotel in 1934. She'd given a lecture about how enjoying was the same thing as understanding, and how there was no such thing as a normal American. Then she and Loveman and Max Bodenheim* had gone for a walk in Greenwich Village, and when they came to Washington Square Park, Bodenheim had said, "Pigeons on the grass, alas!" Which made Miss Stein laugh, because it was a line from one of her plays. "Why do you ask?" Loveman asked. "I was just curious," I said. Loveman beamed. "You're becoming a modernist," he said. At the end of the day he took me to the Brittany Hotel for a drink. In the tranquil gloom of the bar, he told me a story about the time, in the summer of 1922, when Lovecraft had come to Cleveland, and Loveman introduced him to Hart Crane. The meeting did not go well. Hart had just discovered the Symbolists, and he wouldn't stop talking about Rimbaud's "Sonnet of the Asshole." "It was childish," Loveman said, "but on the other hand you could see Hart growing into himself, stretching his *ailes de géant,* so to speak."

* Maxwell Bodenheim (1892–1954), poet and novelist.

Lovecraft was quietly outraged. "Howard, the New England gentleman! He let Hart talk, and when he was done, Howard said, 'That reminds me of something interesting which I read the other day, about the possibility that Pluto has one or possibly several moons.'" The conversation ended icily. "Which was tragic," Loveman said, "because Hart and Howard were both such great artists, and they had the same tendencies." "What tendencies?" I asked. "The same tendencies," Loveman said. "And *that* was where Howard stumbled, and Hart flew. A poet can't be afraid of what people think. He must *speak*. Don't you agree?" He put his hand on my knee, and I shifted away. "I guess," I said. "Hey, can we order some sandwiches?" Loveman smiled bitterly. *"Chacun à son goût,"* he said.

I walked back to Brooklyn that night with the feeling that a curtain had been lifted partway. Clouds hung over Manhattan's tip; beacons blinked in the harbor. Everything was somber and mysterious. Loveman was certainly queer, I thought, but what about Lovecraft? The possibility that he, too, had had those *tendencies* didn't bother me much—I knew a couple of homosexuals in Parry Sound, and nothing about them was remotely alarming—but I did feel that I was passing from a child's understanding of things to an adult's understanding. I wondered what I would say to Loveman the next day at Dauber & Pine, but when I got back to Pohl's, I found him sitting on my sofa, smirking. "Spinks," he said, "you'll be pleased to hear that Doris and I are getting married." He told me he'd found a job, editing two magazines for Popular Publications, and on the strength of it, he'd signed the lease on a house south of Prospect Park. He and Doris would move in at the beginning of September, three days hence. "You're welcome to stay here and keep my mother company," he said. "The rent is twenty dollars a month." I had been paying all of it.

The next morning, heartbroken, I moved into the Ninth Street YMCA, and from its lobby I placed a collect call to Parry Sound. It was the first time I'd called home in three months, but when Charlotte answered, it was as if we'd never been out of touch. "Leo, thank god," she said. "You can't imagine what has happened." Walter had had a heart attack. No one knew if he would recover. "Come home now if you want to see him," Charlotte said. "If you wait even until tomorrow, he might be gone." She wired me thirty dollars for the bus. In a daze, I packed my clothes in my Scout knapsack and collected the money from Western Union; then I went to a phone booth and called three H. Baumgardts before I got Doris. We agreed to meet in the Forty-Second Street Cafeteria. It was a hot, hazy evening, and my shirt was soaked by the time I got to Midtown. Doris was already there, looking cool as usual. She asked about my father. "He's not my father," I said. I told her where I had come from, and what I remembered of that. Doris listened with interest. "Do you speak any foreign languages?" she asked. "French," I said, "and English." Doris laughed. "Leo," she said, "you're a surrealist without trying." Then we talked about the war which had just begun. "Are you going to enlist in the Canadian Army?" Doris asked. "I don't know," I said. "I guess I could wait to be drafted." "They'll never draft Fred," Doris said. "He tried to volunteer for the Lincoln Brigade and they laughed him out of the office." "Anyway you're getting married," I said in a rush. Doris's fine black eyebrows went up. "Where did you get that idea?" she asked. "From Pohl," I said. "Fred and I were engaged for about a day and a half," Doris said, "and to tell you the truth, I think it was only because he thought I was going to run off with *you*." "Oh," I said. "Well, aren't you going to live together?" "Nope. Fred is on his own." "Oh," I said again.

I had thirty-five dollars in my pocket. It wasn't enough for Europe, but surely it would have bought us two bus tickets to someplace interesting. I wonder what my life, what our lives, would have become, if I had asked Doris to run away with me; but I didn't ask. "I have to go," I said. "My bus leaves in an hour." "Then you should go," Doris agreed.

She looked at me sadly. "Here," she said, "I brought you something to read." She gave me a paperback copy of *The Autobiography of Alice B. Toklas*. I paid the check and we went outside. The haze had turned to drizzle, which had a lustering effect on the Broadway asphalt. Across the avenue, an electric billboard made of thousands of lightbulbs blinked an animated cartoon, in which a humanoid blob swung a hammer at a catlike blob. We watched in wonder as the cat got out of the way. "Lo," I said, "the future is upon us." "Not yet it isn't," Doris said. She took hold of the lapels of my jacket, pulled herself onto her toes, and kissed me. Her mouth tasted of coffee. Then she hurried to the subway. I stood there for a while longer, watching the cat dodge the hammer, then I walked to the Greyhound terminal on Fiftieth Street and began the book Doris had given me. It took me a long time to figure out that it had not been written by Alice B. Toklas, and an even longer time, a vastly longer time, to understand why.

The next afternoon I was in Parry Sound. Clear, wholesome water washed the pebbled shore. Sailboats strained at their moorings—I had been in the city so long, I'd forgotten there was such a thing as a sailboat. Even the sky looked verdant after New York. And in the house on Waubeek Street, Walter was all right. It hadn't been a heart attack after all: just heartburn. I was furious. "How could she say . . . ?" "It's the business of doctors to imagine the worst," Walter said, gently. "Now tell me about New York. Did you see the World's Fair?" I hadn't. "The Empire State Building?" Only from a distance. "What *did* you do?" I began to tell the story of how I'd nearly hip-checked Sam Moskowitz at the World Science Fiction Convention, but Walter looked puzzled and closed his eyes. "I'll rest now," he said. "Go down and see if your mother needs help." Charlotte had taken most of the pans out of the kitchen cabinets, in preparation to make one of several dinners, none of which she ended up making. "Oh, *chéri*," she said, without turning to look at me, "you can't imagine how frightened I was. They said your father could die if he picks up one paper clip." "But it was heartburn," I said. "They said *maybe*," Charlotte said. "He has to go to Toronto for more tests." She didn't ask me about New York. "Hug me, Leo," she said. "I couldn't live if I lost both of you."

The next day Walter was up and about, with Charlotte standing by him, making frightened inhalations every time he picked something up, which couldn't have helped. In two days we were all sitting at the dining room table, eating Charlotte's roast chicken with the windows open and a sweet breeze coming in from the bay. "Now, Leonard," Charlotte said, "you're going to have to help your father in the shop. You'll be in charge of the inventory, and he'll be in charge of the . . . of the books. Am I right? *Inventory* and *books*?" As if she hadn't been married to Walter for nearly twenty years. I couldn't tell her that I'd only come for a visit. Weeks passed. Poland fell. In the middle of October, I heard from Wollheim that he and Michel had moved into the house Pohl had rented, and so had Doc Lowndes. Kornbluth joined them in December. In June, France fell to the Germans, but in New York City, everything went on the way it had before, more or less. I thought, I really thought, I could go back whenever I liked. Then, in August 1940, Pohl married Doris Baumgardt, and I enlisted in the Canadian Army.

6.

"Excuse me," Spinks said. "Plumbing." He was gone so long that I
started to worry about him; then he came back, settled into his
chair, tugged at the creases of his pants. On September 4, he said, I
was ordered to report to the Parry Sound high school. It was a muggy
late-summer day, and I wore a short-sleeved shirt and a pair of tan
slacks which I hoped would look military. I took extra care polishing
my shoes. When I got to the school, I found two dozen recruits idling
on the football field. We stood there for half an hour, joking around,
then a furniture-moving truck pulled up to the edge of the field, and
Roy O'Halloran from the dairy came out of the school building in a
sergeant's uniform and ordered us to get on. The truck drove us to
Huntsville, about forty miles away, and deposited us at the sports
arena. O'Halloran informed us that we'd be there for a few days.
"Where are we going to sleep?" asked a weaselly kid named Horace
Tudhope, whom I knew from Parry Sound. He had nine brothers and
sisters, and he used to run away from them periodically and get drunk
and pick fights. O'Halloran pointed at the bleachers. "What the fuck,
Roy? Can't the army put us in a hotel?" O'Halloran took a step toward
Tudhope and raised his hand, then he let it drop. "Private," he said,

"you don't know anything about the army." That was true. None of us knew anything about it.

The army didn't know much about us, either; nor did it care. We drilled in the rain until the wet grass wore out our shoes; we marched with wooden rifles and garden spades. We didn't have blankets, and the nights were already cold; we lay on the bleachers in our civvies and froze. After a couple of days of that, we boarded a train for Camp Borden, outside of Barrie, Ontario, where I learned that I had joined "A" Company of the Algonquin Regiment. I was given a uniform and a pair of boots. Otherwise, Borden wasn't much better than the sports arena. The huts where we slept had no beds, and the whole camp reeked of bleach. I quickly grew tired of parades and inspections, the fanatically pointless rehearsal of activities which had nothing to do with any war I could imagine. I drowsed through lectures on gas-mask maintenance and venereal disease, and wrote cynical letters to Wollheim about my instructors, who were a bunch of fascists if I'd ever seen one. But I also learned to shoot, and I was surprisingly good at it. Before long, I was the second-best marksman in "A" Company. The best was a phlegmatic ogre named Kip Drummond, who'd worked in lumber camps in the North Bay before the war and enlisted only because the army looked like easier work. We became friends, and I dizzied him with my ideas for science fiction stories, and enlightened him about the coming revolution of the proletariat. Unlike the Futurians, Drummond thought I was very smart.

At the beginning of October, our regiment moved to Port Arthur, at the western end of Lake Superior. We stayed there for nine months. I joined the regimental hockey team, which had an undefeated winter on the Lakehead circuit. Drummond and I trained as scouts, and when the snow fell, we took a winter-fighting course. Gliding around on skis with a rifle slung across my back, shooting the occasional squirrel or fox, I felt very Canadian. So it was with real surprise that I received a letter from Charlotte with another letter inside it, heavy with foreign stamps. Charlotte told me that it had come from the agency in London, that I shouldn't feel obliged to read it, and that she loved me very much no matter what. The enclosed letter was postmarked from Budapest and addressed to someone I had never met: *Mr. Levente Rozen, care of the Jewish Children's Aid Society, London, England.* "Dear Cousin," the letter began,

> Warmest salutations! You will perhaps remember me from your fourth birthday party—I was the tall fellow whose neck you found so amusing. Very much time has passed since then, and I think you must be grown up. I wonder, what profession do you practice? I am a physician, specializing in stomach complaints. As you must know, however, the laws here forbid Jews to practice medicine, so I am working in a sawmill! Dear cousin, I need your help. Will you go to the Emigration Office in London, and inform the officials there that you desire me to come live with you? Tell them that you have work for me, it doesn't matter what, and ask them please to send this information to the English Consulate in Budapest, so that I may obtain a visa. Keep receipts for any fees you may incur, and I will repay you, when I am settled in your country.
>
> I hope that we will be reunited soon. You will have the pleasure of meeting my wife, Sara, and our two lovely children, Lili and Sandor, whose name remembers that of your late father.
>
> Your affectionate cousin,
> Mihaly Rozen.

It took me a remarkably long time to figure out that *I* was Levente Rozen. I'd never asked Walter or Charlotte the name of the child who arrived in the Toronto station fourteen years previously; nor did the name *Levente,* which they had kindly naturalized, summon up any former selves, at first. When I read the letter, I was merely annoyed. Why was this stranger asking me for help? A little later, I thought: Where was Mihaly Rozen when my parents were killed? Surely I could have used *his* help. I put his letter in my trunk and tried not to think about it, but the letter had its own ideas about what it would do. Night after night, it flew from the trunk into my dreams: I was walking up a steep street at sunset, when my father said to look, the river below us was coral red. Or else it was summer, and my beloved brother was sailing on the lake. I was playing in the grass; I was holding someone's hand, whose hand? *Levente* was struggling to make himself known, but still I did nothing.

It was around that time, too, that I learned something more about Robert Barlow. I'd been corresponding not only with Wollheim, but with other Lovecraft collectors whom I knew through *Pickman's Vault,* and from one of them I heard that Robert Barlow had moved to California and set himself up as a publisher. He was going to put out an edition of Lovecraft's essays. He'd also written a book of poems, but according to my correspondent, they were very abstruse and not Lovecraftian at all. Still, I felt a pang of envy. If only I'd been born in a different place, in a different tongue! I, too, could have been living a romantic life of letters. So I was pulled in two directions, toward Mihaly Rozen and toward Robert Barlow, the family of my blood and the family of my imagination. But for the time being, Barlow's influence on me was faint.

The winter ended. The snow melted; the ground turned to sticky mud. In the woods, blackflies swarmed. In April, Kip Drummond married a Port Arthur girl, and he asked me to be his best man. I gave a toast and afterward he told me how grateful he was for my friendship, while his new wife looked coolly on. "Leo's going to be famous," Drummond said. It was embarrassing. But the wife wasn't bad looking, I thought. It was amazing how beautiful women found their way to these homely men. I thought of Pohl and Doris. I hadn't dared write to her since I left New York; all I knew was what I'd heard from Wollheim, that she was living with Pohl in Greenwich Village: in a *very bourgeois* apartment, Wollheim said. Meanwhile, Drummond's admiration had stirred my conscience. I got a day pass from the company C.O., Captain Kennedy, and went to the Port Arthur town hall, where I mazed from office to office, until finally a clerk in the Lands Agent's office explained that what I wanted was impossible. Only farmworkers could immigrate to Canada, and for Jewish farmers a special permit was required. Did I own a farm? Well, then. I was far more disappointed than I'd expected to be. I went back to camp and told my story to Drummond, who had a low opinion of foreigners and Jews, but received my confession solemnly. "What should I do?" I asked. Drummond sucked his yellow teeth. "Tell your cousin to sit tight," he said. "We'll be there soon enough." He was wrong. In June, we went west to Manitoba, and in the fall of 1941, we came east again to guard the Welland Canal. Then we shipped out to Newfoundland. We landed at St. John's in February, and a month later we moved to Botwood, a village at the north end of the island, with one gravel street. We patrolled the harbor and took part in endless emergency drills: rushing off in the middle of the night to secure bridges and roads against an invasion that never came. Or *mostly* never came.

One warm afternoon in March, I was on patrol with a corporal named Bob Ellenwood, beating the brush up by the Bay of Exploits, when we heard distant voices. We belly-crawled over a ridge of granite and scrub pine, and there, incredibly, was a U-boat, riding at anchor. On its narrow salt-streaked deck, two sailors in white shirts were doing something to the deck gun. I shouldered my rifle, took careful aim, and fired. The sailors were at most two hundred yards away, and I could hit the bull's-eye at a thousand, but my shot went wide: probably I'd failed to account for the rise and fall of the submarine. The Germans vanished belowdecks. "What the *fuck*?" Ellenwood hissed. The two of us ran up the ridge, and we kept running, five and a half miles back to camp, where Ellenwood breathlessly informed Roy O'Halloran that we'd spotted a U-boat and I had fired on it. "He did, did he? Spinks, wait in barracks. Corporal, come with me." I heard shouting and the rumble of vehicles rushing out of the camp. I knew I'd made a mistake, but I had no idea how serious it was. Weren't the Germans the enemy? I was sure O'Halloran would forgive me after I'd had a chance to explain myself.

It wasn't O'Halloran who asked for an explanation, however, but Lieutenant Colonel Hay, our battalion C.O. Hay's office was in a Quonset hut at the western end of the camp. The sound of typing came through the partition. "Very serious offense," the colonel said, "breach not only of procedure, but really of discipline. And, just, stupendously bad judgment. We might have captured that U-boat yesterday, if it hadn't been for your stupidity. Do you want to explain yourself?" "Yes, sir. I thought . . ." I felt like I was being strangled. "It was my intention to engage with the enemy . . ." "Don't be ridiculous, Spinks. You were on patrol. What could you have been thinking?" I was asking myself the same question. What would I have accomplished if I'd hit the German? What had I hoped to accomplish? When I looked in my heart, all I found was a violent calm, like a wave of perfectly clear water. All my useless waiting had fed it. And underneath it, somewhere, was Mihaly Rozen, and his wife and two children. No, I couldn't bring myself to regret shooting at the German. I did regret having missed. "I failed to appreciate the situation," I said. "Sir, I regret my error deeply. Please let me have a chance to make up for it." The colonel shook his head. It did seem, however, as if my words had convinced him of something. "Did you really think you could sink a U-boat with your rifle?" he asked. "No, sir," I said. "Then why did you shoot?" "I'm very sorry, sir," I said. "I don't know." "The riddle of the Spinks," the colonel said. He looked down at the papers on his desk. "Well. It looks like we ought to court-martial you. There's a chance you'll be shot. More likely you'll spend the rest of the war in the digger. What do you think of that?" "Sir, it's not for me to say." "Sergeant O'Halloran says you're a defenseman. Is that right?" "Yes, sir." "Hate to shoot a good defenseman. I think what we'll do is discharge you from the service." "Sir?" "You're going to be a civilian again," the colonel said. "I'm sure your mother will be pleased."

7.

Two weeks later, I was back in Parry Sound. And the terrible thing was, Charlotte *was* pleased. "Oh, Leo, how *could* you?" she asked. "We'll have to keep you out of trouble, now we know how dangerous you are. But, really, it's just as well that you're here. Walter hired Kevin Prince to help out in the shop, and he's stealing us blind. I've told your father he has to fire him, but you know how he is. And with his heart"—she put her hand to her own—"I don't dare to insist." I emptied my duffel onto the floor of the attic room and lay on the too-soft mattress. My mind was numb with disappointment, and meanwhile, my body was ready to jump up and run to a waiting Jeep, to cover in the brush by a bridge and wait for the all-clear. My arms wanted to lift a box of ammunition. All that first night, I listened for footsteps on Waubeek Street, as if I'd been posted there, as part of the defense of Parry Sound, but there was nothing. Then the Canadian Pacific freight crossed the viaduct at the end of the street and my body froze in terror. After the train was gone, I fell asleep, but I was up again at four thirty, awakened by a bugle no one had blown. I went downstairs and made coffee on the stove. For the first time in my second life, I felt entirely alone.

Such was my war: sitting in the living room, with Walter, my poor

Quaker father, listening to the news. I cried with rage at the report of the Dieppe raid, where the Canadian Second Division was slaughtered on the beach, unable, with thousands of men, and tanks, and bombers roaring overhead, to get as far inland as a child with a pail of sand could toddle in a minute and a half. Why hadn't it occurred to anyone that tanks couldn't climb the seawall? In my mind, Pohl said, *What if you equipped the tanks with a kind of ramp? You could carry it on top of the turret, and it would double as a shield* . . . But I had no idea where Pohl was now. And where was Mihaly Rozen? The English-language newspapers said next to nothing about Europe's Jews, but Charlotte had *Le Devoir* sent from Montreal, and they reported that Jews in Poland were being rounded up and sent to ghettos. I read with incredulity about the Nazis' plan to ship them off to Madagascar. It was the kind of thing the Futurians would have dreamed up, but evil.

Autumn came, and the bay darkened with clouds. Snow mounded on the curbs of Waubeek Street. The summer of 1943 found me in the same chair, my stomach bigger, as the Canadian First Division fought its way through the mountain passes of Sicily. That winter, the First Division was stranded on the Italian littoral; in the spring, I cheered when the Allies breached the Hitler Line and Rome lay before them. "Go, Canadians!" Walter looked up from the *Globe and Mail*. "Those are your friends dying over there. Are you sure you should be cheering?" "It's different units," I said. "And we won, so yes, thank you, I'll cheer." I felt contempt for my father's weakness. "If everyone was like you," I said, "we'd have Hitler parading down Sherbourne Street." Walter said nothing. "Actually, pacifism is just about the same thing as treason," I said. "Is that really what you believe, Leo?" Walter asked. "You bet," I said. "If I was in charge, I'd treat the pacifists like Hitler treats the Jews." I knew that what I was saying was hateful, but I had to speak. Finally, Charlotte ordered me upstairs, where I listened to the war on a smaller radio.

In June 1944, I was drafted. I thought the letter must be a mistake, but it wasn't. So Charlotte saw me off again, and wept again, and I went back, as if in a dream, to Camp Borden, which had grown immeasurably since I was last there. I took a course on mine detection and removal which, in its brevity, gave me an idea of what fate Canada had in mind for its draftees. My unit, the 273rd Engineers, was sent to England, where we sat out the winter in a camp on the South Downs; then, in April 1945, with the war almost over, I was posted as a munitions specialist to the RAF's 84 Group. After four and a half years of waiting, I crossed from Dover to Antwerp on a breezy blue morning and saw that the harbor was full of sunken German warships. That was my first intimation of what the war really was: a tremendous, chaotic destruction. Compared to it, my anger was nothing. The city itself had been wrecked by German rockets, V-1s and V-2s, which had smashed the buildings like giant fists, leaving behind caved-in heaps of beams and pools of black water. I saw old women with infinitely bitter faces hauling buckets of water, and men in suits lifting the body of a horse onto the bed of a truck. To my relief, we drove straight out of the city, and that night we camped in a field. There was a red light on the horizon; our C.O. said it was the city of Essen, burning. We convoyed east for days, through Holland into Germany, on the heels of the Second Canadian Army. The towns we passed through had been shot to bits; the air smelled of burning trash and dead flesh. The Germans ran from us like a race of crabs, ash-colored crabs, their eyes dark with hatred. Sometimes we'd come upon a scaffold where, in its insanity, the SS had hung deserters: most of them not regular soldiers, but old men and children, who had been called up to reduce the number of living Germans at war's end to an absolute minimum. So these were the fascists, I thought. I wanted to tell Wollheim that we'd been fighting the wrong people, but I supposed he already knew. And perhaps we hadn't been fighting the wrong people after all.

Eighty-four Group was bound for Celle, at the southern edge of the Lüneburg Heath. We got there three days after the war ended. The spring had taken firm hold of the land by then; the fields were green, with a speckling of small white flowers. The town, too, was very pretty. At the center of it was a white-and-pink Baroque castle, where, in happier days, the philosopher Leibniz had shot billiards with the Duke of Lüneburg. The castle was surrounded on three sides by a park, with a lake fed by meandering streams. On the fourth side was the *Altstadt,* the old town, with cobbled streets and half-timbered houses with peaked roofs. It was like a town sprung from a cuckoo clock. Eighty-four Group was stationed at the Scheuen airfield; our job was to inventory the various assets that the Luftwaffe had left behind in the region. I drove our platoon commander, Lieutenant Yale, to airfields and offices and POW camps, where he interviewed irrelevant personnel in his bad German. You didn't have to speak any German to know that our activity was pointless. The Luftwaffe's planes had all been shot down or blown up; the hangars were empty; any piece of equipment that might have been useful had been stolen or sabotaged. When I wasn't on duty, I hiked on the heath, which reminded me of the land around Muskoka, a rolling plain of heather and eerily regular stands of pine. Hiking was more fun than wandering around Celle, enduring the citizens' quiet, orderly hatred. And when I heard that there was a concentration camp in the forest, and that some people from 84 Group were going there to bring supplies to the liberated inmates, I volunteered right away.

On an overcast May Sunday, Lieutenant Yale and I drove around Celle, banging on the doors of frightened civilians and demanding their overcoats "for inspection," a ruse that the Germans obeyed with strange alacrity. In no time our Jeep was full of fine winter coats. We joined the relief convoy and drove into the heath. Swaths of pine forest had been burned by the British to flush out German snipers, but even here, remarkably, a green fog of life clung to the ground; wildflowers with red bell-shaped blossoms grew at the feet of black limbless trees. But the air smelled foul, like a latrine trench, and as the convoy crunched up the road, the smell got worse. We seemed to be approaching a zoo. By the time we came to the camp's gate, a single bar hung across the path; the odor was nauseating. The words to describe it, I realized, with uneasy surprise, came from Lovecraft: a *mephitic blast,* or a *nameless stench:* words that have no particular power to terrify, until you find yourself in the presence of the thing to which they refer. Until you discover that there *is* a thing to which they refer. The head of our convoy, a Canadian officer named Aplin, ordered the soldier on duty to lift the gate, and we went into the camp.

I soon learned that what I saw was far from the worst of what Belsen had been. By the time we arrived, the dead had been cleared from the streets, and buried in mass graves the size of football pitches. The camp had running water again, and heroic Australian sappers were digging up the clogged sewer lines. Many of the sickest inmates had been moved to the hospital at the Panzer Training School in Hohne, three or four kilometers north of the camp. But what I saw was terrible enough. Belsen was inhabited by emaciated creatures with yellow skin, wearing bathrobes and pajamas or long coats, their shaved skulls covered by kerchiefs and hats. Their eyes were set deep in their heads, and their teeth, when they smiled, seemed unusually large, because their gums had retracted. They walked in twos and threes, up and down the street, as though they existed in a completely different sort of time than us. Even as they approached our convoy, their eyes darted left and right, to see who might take from them the things they hadn't received yet. It was a scene from a horror story, and I was in it, and what I felt was not thrilling in the least. It was, above all, sadness and repugnance, and not a little anger at the insane people who had made this place. I wished I hadn't come; I wanted what I saw never to have been. Still, what could I do? Belsen existed. I was there.

"Coats!" I cried out, gamely. The crowd came toward us and stood in solemn silence, looking at what we'd brought. An old man with a black fedora asked me for a cigarette, but Aplin had warned us not to give them out. If you gave an inmate a cigarette, he said, the others would fight him for it, and they'd all get hurt. I said that I didn't smoke. The old man shrugged skeptically and turned away. The rest followed; they didn't want winter coats in May. They mobbed a Jeep whose wiser crew had brought toothpaste and stockings. In a minute everything was gone, including, I discovered, our spare tire and gas can. Someone asked if we wanted to visit the hospital, and Lieutenant Yale said no, not today. "Spinks, I think we'll go home now, and return when we have something these fellows need." So I drove us back past the mounded graves and barbed wire, into Lüneburg Heath, which I thought would be a welcome change from the camp, but now that I knew what it hid, I felt only nausea and sorrow. As soon as we got back to Celle, I went to our hotel and bathed, then I got drunk. I tried to fit what I had seen into my consciousness, then I tried to squeeze it out, but I couldn't do either. It was there, singular and awful, like a hole in the world. But as terrible as that was, it wasn't as terrible as the thought I had later, when I was trying, uselessly, to fall asleep. The man who asked for cigarettes had spoken Hungarian, and I had answered him in the same language.

8.

Here, in horror's heart, I had found my people. Only, what people they turned out to be! Shamblers, moochers, living corpses with terrified eyes. Angry women and stealthy children. Vacant people set like stones at the feet of trees. A broken race in borrowed clothes, feigning politeness while the British were looking, and breaking out in fights when their backs were turned. I felt my kinship to them in waves of contradictory emotion: horror and pity and terrible rage. I thought about going down to the Rathausplatz in Celle on market day and opening fire on the Germans with a tommy gun, but what would that accomplish? The only thing I could do was go back to Belsen and help as best I could.

With Lieutenant Yale's blessing, I returned on my own the next Sunday, with a cargo of pots, pans, knives, and spoons commandeered from the locality. These were a success; the inmates took everything, and asked if I could bring them rolling pins, ladles, teapots, coffee, tobacco, rain boots. I did what I could. Helping was a way to conquer the horror of what had happened. And I had another purpose, too. There were many Hungarian Jews in the camp; they had survived in such numbers because they'd been the last to arrive. I wondered if one of them might know my cousin. In halting Hungarian, I asked around, and discovered that everyone had heard of Mihaly Rozen. They had seen him alive! For a cigarette or a chocolate bar, they would tell me where! But when I gave them what they asked for, it turned out that they were thinking of Mitzi Rozen, or Michel Bloch, or some interesting object that had appeared far behind my left shoulder, which they hurried off to investigate.

The only positive result of all my looking was that I became friends with a Hungarian schoolteacher named Luiza. When we met, she might have been forty-five; but as the months passed, I would have the strange privilege of watching her age in reverse until she was twenty-six. In addition to her native language, she knew Czech, German, French, English, Yiddish, and a little Russian. She had the decency to tell me that Mihaly Rozen was probably dead. "So many from Budapest died," she said. "It was better for the Jews in the countryside. Not that the peasants loved them more. Just that they were harder to round up. Because, more dispersed. And, of course, the Budapest Jews all went to Auschwitz." I had heard the name of that place, but not much else. Luiza had been there. She told me everything. Nowadays we know what Auschwitz was, sometimes I think we know to the point of forgetting; but for me, hearing, for the first time, about the gas chambers and the selection lines, the children taken from their parents and burned up, it was as if I'd passed from one horror into another, still more horrible. I believed Luiza, how could I fail to believe her, but I felt dizzy, as if I were falling into some kind of terrible chasm. "It makes you wonder, doesn't it," she said. It certainly did. "Wonder what?" I asked, anyway. "What is underneath," Luiza said. She scratched the back of my hand with an unevenly bitten fingernail. "Whether you could ever know." She threw her cigarette on the ground and a moment later a kid who looked all of nine picked it up and ambled off with the dignity of a priest. "Would you like another?" I asked. "No, thank you," Luiza said. "I must be careful of my complexion."

I drove back to Celle and wept for the family I would never meet, and also for the one I had lost when I was a child. By then I had remembered them as much as I ever will: my tired, gentle mother; my father in his study, which smelled of the Turkish cigarettes he smoked to cure his asthma; and my brother, who sailed and played with older boys and told me I didn't have enough courage to be an Indian. I even remembered Mihaly Rozen and his gentle blond wife, Sara, and a chorus of other cousins who had come to stay with us in the summers, bringing with them trunks and maids and strange dogs. It was infinitely worse than if I had never got Mihaly's letter. I felt as if everything had been taken away from me, and every hope had been extinguished. I thought about shooting myself, but it seemed ridiculous. How could I do that when the inmates at the camp, who had endured infinitely more terrible things than I had, were so determined to go on living?

A few weeks later, I ran into Luiza again. I offered her a cigarette; she shook her head coyly. So, chocolate? Not that, either. "What I want," she said, "is books." "Books?" "Yes. Look at us. We are the people of the book, here, and yet we have *nothing to read*." This was in early June. The concentration camp's wooden huts had been razed, and the inmates had all been transferred to the Panzer Training School, an enormous campus of identical white-stuccoed barracks, which looked, to my Canadian eyes, like sinister ski lodges, their ranks punctuated by neat parade grounds. Luiza and I stood by the Roundhouse, a grandiose neoclassical pustule where the Germans had had their officers' mess and cinema. Now it housed the British post office and the clothes distribution center, which everyone called Harrod's. "What are we supposed to do, in the night?" Luiza asked. She looked at me with disinterested curiosity. "With nothing to read?" she clarified. I blushed. "Of course. Stupid of me not to have thought of that." "Oh, you have so many things to think about," Luiza said. "You have all of us, and yourself, too. Whereas we survivors think only of ourselves." She held out a thin hand and I shook it gently.

I went round the *Altstadt,* banging on the Germans' cuckoo-clock doors, demanding *Bücher.* I got Goethe and Schiller in black letter; when I brought the books to Luiza the following week, she looked aghast. "No!" she said. "Take them away!" "It's what they had," I said apologetically, to Luiza's back. In the days that followed, I canvassed the Brits and Canadians, and got a hoard of adventure novels; then I drove to Bremen and hit up the Americans. By this point, everyone knew what Belsen was. British cameramen had filmed the bulldozers push-ing bodies into the pits; the newsreel played all over the world. The Americans were all too happy to fill canvas sacks with comic books and paperbacks. Among them, I noticed with pleasure, was an Armed Services edition of Lovecraft's stories: Lovecraft's fame had grown to the point where he was a ration, a war supply, like chocolate or ciga-rettes. I delivered my haul to Luiza in the middle of June. It was a beautiful day, and the parade ground beside the Roundhouse was full of people sunning themselves. "Leo!" Luiza said. She'd never before called me by my first name. "These are all in English, which is a prob-lem. But some have pictures. In short, it could be worse." She re-cruited two American artillerymen from a vaccination table, and together we carried the books into the Roundhouse, and set them up on shelves in a former Nazi janitor's closet. Luiza had written a sign on a cardboard square: LIBRARY, in Yiddish, Hebrew, German, English, French, Polish, Hungarian, Czech, Russian, Latin, and Greek. "Any-thing else?" I asked, gallantly. "Yes," Luiza said. "Books in languages we can read. Also, leather wingback reading chairs." "Wingback?" I asked. "Yes," Luiza said. "I think they would look nice in here." *In here* being the circular hallway that ringed the Roundhouse's interior rooms. Luiza looked very happy. She had put on some weight, and the color was returning to her skin. She had on bright red lipstick: some genius had delivered a case of lipstick to the camp, and all the women were wearing it. "I'll see what I can do," I said. "You will get them!" Luiza said. "It's an order."

All the leather wingback chairs in Celle had been commandeered by our officers, but it didn't matter. The library was abolished before it had begun. It happened so quickly, Luiza told me, in tears. First, a mob of children came to claim the comic books, and dispersed with them to the farthest corners of the camp, where the English speakers translated the dialogue for the rest. But, of course, they were seen doing this, and right away a representative of the Jewish Provisional Committee confronted Luiza at the door to her closet and told her that it would not do. These children had not survived the greatest atrocity in history to become comic-book readers! They deserved *Jewish* books, by *Jewish* authors. "So he got a *Kommando* of disgusting barbarians, and they took all my books and locked them in one of the equipment sheds." "Is that all?" I said. "I have a friend, his name is Mr. Crowbar. He can help us out . . ." "You don't understand!" Luiza said. "They are cracking down. Everything must be done the way the committee has decreed it. It's like the Nazis all over again! I don't know why they didn't just burn the books and make us all watch." "Probably because they aren't Nazis," I said, as gently as I could. Luiza was still trembling with anger. I had imagined that *I* was angry, but I was nothing in that department, not compared with her. She had seen every kind of horror, and her rage was without measure. "I can still bring you books," I said. "The Provisional Committee will never know. I'll smuggle them to you inside of oranges." Which was a joke on several levels: oranges had not been seen in Northern Europe since the war began. "I don't want your small books," Luiza said. She led me to the closet, which was empty now. "Break the shelves," she said. "What?" I said. "Break the shelves," Luiza said. "I don't want this closet to be used for anything, ever again." I didn't bother pointing out that shelves were easily built. While Luiza stood guard outside, I broke up the shelving with an entrenching tool. Splinters hit my face and cut my hands, but when I was finished, the closet was impressively wrecked, a memorial to Luiza's broken hope. "Thank you," she said. "My poor library." Indeed, I felt bad for it, too. It was what I thought of, years later, when it came time for me to describe Yoh-Vombis.

9.

That summer, visiting Belsen became a kind of fad for British and American troops. Every day two or three transports arrived, driven by grinning privates or grim sergeants or young, visibly drunk officers, who all said the same thing, that they'd *heard what happened,* and they *wanted to do something.* None of them had consulted anyone; they'd just taken whatever was nearby and diverted it to Belsen, where they pulled up at the gate with the eager look of schoolboys who'd brought something unusually interesting to show and tell, and unveiled their cargo of soup, or tents, or, in one case, enormous spools of copper wire. Because no one else wanted to do it, I helped them unload whatever it was into a shed, added it to the list of the shed's inventory, then—this was the tricky part—I tried to get the visitors to leave without taking the tour to which they felt themselves entitled. Everyone wanted to see the concentration camp; they were disappointed to learn that it had been burned. I did my best to keep them away from the displaced persons camp at the Panzer School, but I was often outranked, and the whole situation lay outside the scope of my orders. So I acted as a guide, leading the Brits and Americans on quick tours of the DP camp. Here was the cinema, here the post office, here was Harrod's. I was appalled by how many of the visitors expressed disappointment. "Hell, it's just like the University of Indiana," an American major said. I tried to protect the inmates from such morons. "Keep back, please, they're easily startled," I said, although the opposite was true. The inmates would accost anyone, even in the absence of a mutual language, to ask for newspapers, stockings, nail scissors, thread, whatever they'd run out of. Sometimes, shamefully, I said the inmates were contagious. Typhus, you know. "Oh!" was the usual response, and more often than not, I thought, the visitors were relieved. They had done their duty; they'd seen Belsen! Story for the grandchildren. Now back in the truck, and on to some less unsettling part of the peace.

The truth was that the inmates were recovering. No one had thought they would. The psychiatrists who passed through the camp in April estimated their chances of returning to anything like normal human life at nil, but already in early June, young men were playing soccer on the parade grounds, and promenading up and down between the barracks in smart summer clothes. It was possible to hear laughter in what had been Belsen. It's true that most of the survivors were young, between eighteen and thirty-five, and many of them had arrived at the concentration camp just a few weeks before liberation. Also true that many were not well and that, among those who appeared to be mending, there were many who, when a door slammed or a work crew dropped a mallet, retreated to some terrible place from which they were slow to return. But life was turning out to be more powerful than any psychiatrist had guessed; life was winning. When I saw children kicking a ball, or a young man sitting under a tree, reading a book—books *were* making their way into the camp, thanks to a Jewish organization in New York—I could almost believe that the horror I had seen in April had been only a dream.

Luiza, too, was getting better. When she talked about the library, it was as if the whole thing had been a joke. "Can you imagine, we really put all those terrible books in a *closet?*" She was campaigning to be elected to the permanent committee of liberated Jews that would be formed in the fall. She told me about her conversations with Yossi Rosensaft, the head of the DP camp's Provisional Committee: a small but massive man who'd survived the mines at Dora, where the Nazis built their rockets. "He wants me to do something in education," she said. "I told him, no!" "Why?" I asked. Luiza laughed. "I am sick of being a teacher! You have no idea how hard it is. You come in, *Hello class,* and there, you have all these dull little faces looking up at you, like puddings. You work and work, and still, they are puddings!" "You're not a pudding," I pointed out. "I was *never* a pudding," Luiza said. "The world is divided that way. Puddings and not. It isn't fair, but I don't see why I should have to fix it." "What will you do?" I asked. "I want to be in charge of dances," Luiza said. "Dances, and parties. For example. Soon, it will be winter. I want to make a huge mound of snow in the banquet hall"—the former officers' mess, in the Round-house—"and let the children sled down it. Wouldn't that be wonderful?" "I suppose," I said. "But why not just get a heap of snow together outside?" "Because, foolish person, I do not want the children to be *cold.*" She tapped my arm with a nail: manicured, and painted deep red. "They have suffered enough, don't you think?" I said that it was very inventive of her. "I know," she said. "I just thought of it now! I am going to tell Yossi, before I forget." She was off.

I don't know whether Luiza was in any way responsible for it, but there *was* a dance that June. It was held upstairs from Harrod's, in the former officers' beer hall, now a nightclub called the Coconut Grove. It was a strange affair, the young women in their new best dresses, but still very thin, dancing with big, sheepish servicemen who handled them like porcelain teacups. There was no liquor, at least, not offi-cially; but many of my brothers in arms had smuggled in their flasks, and I think, on the civilian side, there had been some distillation of *slivovitz* and potato vodka. I was sober but I don't know, I'll never know, if Luiza was drunk. I danced with her. Charlotte had taught me the steps, although it turned out that what I knew was only their dead form; Luiza spoke the living language. Under the guise of following, she flung me around the room like a toy duck on a string. Then, abruptly, she let me drop. "That was nice," she said. "Now I want to sit down." I said I'd keep her company, but another girl sprang up and beckoned. "Private! You dance very nice." I was there to help. I tried to keep track of Luiza, but it was impossible; the party had heated up. Many people were drunk. At the tables, couples kissed, and their hands groped under cover of the white tablecloths. There was a lot of shouting.

I left around ten o'clock and walked across the parade ground. It was a clear night, with no moon; thousands and thousands of stars pointed out that ours wasn't the only planet, and that whatever mess we'd made here was, from another point of view, nothing but a speck of light. But the Earth didn't seem like a mess. The air smelled of pine needles and heather and clay. They'd opened the windows in the Coconut Grove, and the music came softly out. Just as I was beginning to enjoy myself, though, I remembered what had happened here. Then I was furious: as if the pines and the stars had tricked me. I was going to borrow a Jeep and drive back to Celle, when I bumped into Luiza. "There you are, Leo!" she said. "I was wondering when you would ever come out." She took my hand and we walked away together. "Did you dance with many girls tonight?" she asked, in Hungarian. By then we'd spoken it enough that I could have a clumsy conversation. I said that I had just been doing my duty. "Of course you were," Luiza said. "You're a very kind person, Leo." "I'm Canadian," I said. "Yes, Canada," Luiza said. "Tell me about it." I talked about Parry Sound, its church dances and candy stores, its public library and movie theaters, and the great excitement everyone had felt when I was a child and the Mail Car

Bandit stole Mrs. Laird's car and ran it into a ditch. I think I must have spoken for quite a long time, as much to remind myself of Canada as to inform Luiza about it, but she did not lose interest. When I was done, she said, "It sounds lovely." "It is," I said. I hadn't realized how much I missed it until then. "What about Budapest? How was it before the war?" Luiza squeezed my hand. "Another time," she said. We had walked to the edge of the forest, the familiar, terrible forest. "Leo," Luiza asked, "am I your friend?" "Of course you are." "Good," Luiza said. "Will you marry me?" I liked Luiza: she of the indoor sledding hill. I did not love her, not the way I loved Doris. But I thought she and I could be happy together, and I imagined that by marrying her I might undo some of the war's destruction. Spending the rest of my life with Luiza would be my way of rebuilding; it would be my way to make a future that was better than the past. "All right," I said. "Wonderful!" Luiza said. "Now, I am going to bed." She kissed my cheek and ran into the dark.

We were married in the middle of July, at the DP camp's synagogue, a repurposed room in one of the barracks blocks. It was decorated for the occasion with scarlet rowanberries and blue lupins. Luiza carried a bouquet of white flowers which grew all over the heath that summer, a cross between white lilac and hydrangea. I don't know what they were called. Her friends had baked cakes, and the Red Cross in Brussels sent a bottle of champagne. Yossi Rosensaft made a speech. The newspapers took pictures of us coming out of the barracks; then we got into a black Opel and drove out of the camp for three days' honeymoon. We were going to stay in Hanover, but as soon as we'd got out of view of the DP camp, Luiza told me to pull onto a side road, and we made love on the Opel's creaky backseat. "Now shall we go to our hotel?" I asked, afterward. "We will not go to any hotel," Luiza said. "We will not give one cent of your money to any German." And we didn't. We spent our wedding night on the heath, and commandeered our coffee and bread the next morning from a surly farmer. "Congratulate us!" Luiza instructed him. "Congratulations," he said. Luiza put her arm around my waist. "We are going to have many Jewish children," she told the farmer. "OK," I said. "OK?" Luiza said, sharply. She'd taught school, all right. "It is OK with you, Leo?" The farmer turned away in disgust. The rest of our honeymoon was more or less the same. I couldn't blame Luiza for any of it. Things will be better when we get home, I thought.

My repatriation papers came in October, but because of a bureaucratic mix-up, Luiza's visa wasn't ready, and we couldn't leave until December. In that time, the DP camp became a fully living place. Just as Luiza had foretold, the Provisional Committee elected a Central Committee, with Rosensaft at its head, and they began the serious business of lobbying England for permission to emigrate to Palestine. They opened a library, too, the bulk of which was twenty thousand volumes of Jewish writing that the Nazis had cached, with characteristically boundless perversity, in Berlin. The inmates had what they wanted: Torah and hundreds of volumes of commentary, but also Sholem Aleichem and Sholem Asch, Thomas and Heinrich Mann, Franz Werfel, Jakob Wassermann, Stefan Zweig, Max Brod. I was amused to see that while wiser books stayed on the shelves, the novels were almost always on loan, romances in particular. It made me think that what the world needed was not wisdom, but stories. Some of the books I'd brought to the DP camp had escaped destruction, too; now and then I'd see a kid furtively leafing through a comic book, and once I even saw a bespectacled Polish boy sitting on the bank of the Meissen, reading Lovecraft. At the time he looked to me like the first green shoot poking up from a burned forest, although when I think about that scene now it seems quite monstrous.

Luiza and I stayed in London long enough to spend my back pay on hotels and dinners and clothes. Just before Christmas, we took a ship to Halifax, and from there we took the train to Toronto, and on to Parry Sound. Walter was dead. Of a heart attack, ironically, just as I first drove Lieutenant Yale through the gates of Belsen. Luiza and I made our way through high snowdrifts on Avenue Road, and when we came to the house on Waubeek Street, *this* house, we found an evergreen wreath on the door. Charlotte skipped out of the kitchen to greet us, wearing an apron over a shiny new dress. "Leo!" she gasped, "you look like a soldier!" And, turning to Luiza: "So, this is your *wife!*" They took stock of each other. Unfortunately, Luiza was better dressed than Charlotte, more simply, but more elegantly. Nothing about her appearance had been disturbed by our walk through the snow, whereas Charlotte, who had been cooking, was flushed; strands of gray hair clung to her forehead. "It is a pleasure to meet you," Luiza said, and she stepped toward Charlotte to kiss her cheeks. Charlotte, who had rarely failed to embarrass me by kissing my friends and their parents and near strangers in the street, held out her hand. *"Enchantée,"* she said. "I would linger, but I am making a Christmas goose; in fact, an entire Christmas feast." She hurried back into the kitchen. Luiza and I sat in the parlor, drinking leaden eggnog by the Christmas tree until the meal was ready. It was, indeed, a feast: a goose with cranberry sauce and a bacon-chestnut stuffing that glistened with fat; roasted carrots; mashed potatoes; and a *tourtière,* a pie stuffed with roast pork and more potatoes. And to begin with, a platter of Prince Edward Island oysters on ice. "Charlotte," I murmured. *"Quoi?"* Charlotte said. *"Qu'est-ce qu'il y a?"* *"Mais rien,"* Luiza said. *"On vous est très reconnaissant."* She inclined her head formally. *"Il n'y a pas de quoi,"* Charlotte replied, beaming. *"Vous êtes de la famille!* Leonard, you are the man of the house now. Will you say grace?" We bowed our heads. All through the meal, Charlotte pretended to be delighted by Luiza's French. How had Luiza learned it? Was it true she was a teacher? Did she know that there were many French people in Canada? By the time we got to dessert—a steamed plum pudding with suet—my wife was on the verge of tears. "Please," she said, "I will go and lie down." I helped with the dishes. "She's very nice," Charlotte said. "But so frail! Of course, considering . . . No, I'm very happy for you." And Luiza, upstairs: "Leo, your mother is a monster!" "Ssh!" I said. "She *is!*" Luiza said. "We must leave this place, as soon as we can."

I couldn't leave, though. I had just come home. Everyone had just come home; everyone was looking for work. I was lucky to have a job in the hardware store. "But we can go anywhere!" Luiza said. "To Saskatchewan, if you want! There must be work *somewhere.*" I said she wouldn't like Saskatchewan. She said she didn't like Parry Sound. She missed streetcars and pastry and concerts, all the things she'd promised herself when she knew she was going to live. We fought in whispers in my childhood bedroom. Then one day in February, Luiza called my mother a Nazi and said that she wouldn't live under her roof any longer. "Leo," she said, "are you coming?" "Where are you going?" I asked. I'd said *you.*

Even so, Luiza didn't leave entirely. She moved into a room at the far end of Church Street and started giving French lessons. "This woman amazes me!" Charlotte said. "She hardly speaks French!" In fact, she spoke it very well, but with an accent. Luiza returned to our house for supper every night; sometimes, when she'd eaten well and life seemed less intolerable than usual, she came upstairs with me, and we nestled in my bed. She had become very thin again; I think supper was often her only meal. We didn't make love. Instead, Luiza whispered her dreams at me: She was going to Toronto, to become an actress. She was going to open a hat shop in Parry Sound. She was going to become a radio announcer. Her dreams had nothing to do with her abilities, or with what the world wanted from her. They were built haphazardly out of parts that didn't go together, like the indoor mountain of snow. Her genius was for knitting them into a coherent story and defending them in the face of everything. "When I have my radio program," she whispered to me, as we lay squeezed together, "I will invite on it all the generals, and they will explain how it took so long to liberate the Jews. And they will tell why the Jews still cannot go to Palestine, why they must stay in their camps." "Good question," I said. Luiza hit my chest. "I am serious!" she said. "I will talk to Churchill, and I will change his mind. Everyone will go to Palestine." "I hope so." "We will go, too, Leo," she said. "We'll have a farm." "I thought you wanted to live in a city?" "No, on a farm! We'll have sheep, and roses." "All right," I said.

The Canadian Pacific rattled over Waubeek Street. Downstairs, the radio was still on, playing classical music. Charlotte must have got into the habit of leaving it on, after Walter died, so she wouldn't feel alone in the house. I felt guilty about not having come home sooner, although I couldn't have come home any sooner than I did. I wanted to be a good son, a good husband, but, in reality, I was living the life of an automaton, running the hardware store by day, and by night, giving Luiza a safe place to deposit her dreams. Luiza knew it. One afternoon in March, she came to the store. It was sleeting, and her umbrella was sheeted with ice. She shivered. I went to hold her, but she stepped back. "Leo," she said, "will you do a favor for me?" "Anything," I said. "The drainpipe over my window is broken," she said. "Water is coming through the top of the window. It's making a mess!" I said I would come by as soon as the store closed. Luiza hesitated, and then said that would be all right. She kissed my cheek. "I am lucky to have married you," she said. I wondered if that meant things would get better. I wondered how long it would take to save up enough money for us to move to Toronto. At the end of the day, I shuttered Spinks Hardware, gathered up some tools, and went to Luiza's house. Her room was empty, except for a note on the bed, which said that she had gone away, and not to forget her, please. She would remember *me*. I went to the window, as if she might still be nearby, but the street was deserted. The drainpipe was, in fact, broken.

Two weeks later, Luiza sent me a postcard from Edmonton. She had fallen in love with a dentist, she said. They were going to be married. Strangely, she didn't ask for a divorce—maybe the idea of bigamy appealed to her. Maybe it didn't even occur to her that it would be a problem. She'd started over so many times, she'd learned not to think too much about what she left behind. When I told Charlotte what had happened, she patted my hand. "Poor Leo," she said. "Life can be very disappointing, sometimes. And poor dentist!" I wanted to hit her. I went to the station and bought a ticket for Edmonton. The train didn't leave for several hours, so I went over to the Belvedere Hotel, and while I was sitting at the bar, eating peanuts and wondering whether I was making a terrible mistake, Horace Tudhope came in. He'd just come back from Europe. He told me that he had stayed in the Algonquin Regiment until the end of the war. Just about everyone else from the beginning was dead. Dozens had been slaughtered in Normandy, when a misread map sent them to a hill five miles behind German lines. Others died crossing the Leopold Canal, a body of water with two channels, each about thirty feet wide. It was incredible that so many people could have died in so little space, and *for* so little space. "That's war," Tudhope said. "You spill ten guys' blood to get across the fucking street."

Despite his aversion to danger, Tudhope had ended up with one of the war's riskier jobs: driving a crocodile, a flame-throwing tank. "The Mof were *scared* of those fuckers, and for good reason," he said. "We grilled 'em by the dozen. In houses and out-of-doors. You don't even know what can burn until you've shot the cannon of a crocodile." "What about Kip?" I asked. "Drummond?" Tudhope sucked his teeth. "Well, that stank. We were up by Rastede"—a town in northern Germany, through which I had also passed—"when we got word to stand down. We were most of us too fucking tired to care. But Drummond said, I'm going out to organize us drinks. He walked into the woods and some Germans in the next valley shot him. They hadn't heard the war was over, apparently." "Oh." "What about you? Sink any more of the German Navy?" Over many drinks, I told Tudhope where I'd been, and what I'd done. Tudhope grinned. "Fuck me, Leo, you're the luckiest man I know."

10.

Spinks stretched his interlaced palms toward me and cracked his knuckles. "I've been sitting for quite a long time," he said. "My physical therapist would be furious." He took his cane from where it was propped by the windowsill, and stood up slowly. The room was dim. The sun had set, and the last red-gold light was draining out of the sky over the bay. "He wants me to walk for thirty minutes a day," Spinks said, "but the truth is, even that is getting to be too much. Will you join me?" I followed him down the shadowy hall, out of the house, into the street. The air was pleasantly warm. Barn swallows swooped around, vacuuming up bugs. "What happened to Luiza?" I asked. "Did you see her again?" "Remember your promise, Dr. Willett," Spinks said. He squeezed my forearm. His grip was very strong. We kept on and stopped at the top of a hill that led down to the water. "I think this is as far as I go," Spinks said. Far out in the bay, a motorboat threw up a violet wake. We watched it for a while, then Spinks said, "I'm sure your husband is alive." "How are you sure?" I asked. "Because that's the kind of person he is," Spinks said. "He struck me as someone who was unlikely to give up on anything." Well, that was true. Charlie hadn't even given up on Spinks. Suddenly, I was uneasy. "I should go," I said. "I have a ticket for the sunset cruise." "Ah, the sunset cruise,"

Spinks said. Clearly he knew I was lying. "Too bad. I was hoping you might stay for dinner." "No, sorry," I said. "It's all right," Spinks said. We made our slow way back, and at the foot of his porch steps, Spinks stopped again. "Come earlier tomorrow," he said. "I still have a lot to tell you." He went up the steps and vanished into the house.

I walked up Waubeek Street and climbed Belvedere Avenue. There was a little park overlooking the bay, its multitude of islands black against the sunset. A seaplane came in for a landing and taxied to the dock. It *was* a pretty town, I thought. I ate dinner in a fancy-ish restaurant overlooking the mouth of the Seguin River, and went back to my B&B, which was unfortunately situated beside the Canadian Pacific viaduct. I checked my recorder to be sure I had captured Spinks's story, and wondered again what Charlie might have learned from it. I thought about going through the recording and making notes, but I was too tired, and anyway, I thought, it would be better to do that in New York, when I had some literal and figurative distance from L. C. Spinks. I slept badly. Part of it was the train, which thundered overhead like a war; but I was also frightened by Parry Sound and what I was doing there. I felt like I had put myself in danger, although I couldn't say what the danger was. As soon as it was light, I jogged down Gibson Street to the bay. I ran past a pizza restaurant and the Bobby Orr Hall of Fame, a modernist metal barn with an ambitious parking lot; then I picked up a walking trail that cut through the woods on the town's western shore. A hundred yards down the trail, there was a monument to the soldiers of the Algonquin Regiment who had died in the war. I scanned it for the names Spinks had mentioned and found them: Robert Ellenwood, Kip Drummond. It was strange to see Spinks's story fact-checked in stone. I realized, after a moment, that I was relieved: I *wanted* to believe Spinks. And that, I thought, was the danger.

At eight thirty, I was back at the house on Waubeek Street, all business. Spinks let me in. He, too, looked as though he'd had a bad night. His cheeks were unshaven and purplish, like maybe he had been drinking. But he was wearing a fresh outfit, a navy shirt with a Byron collar, and pressed white slacks. I followed him down the hall, past the intriguingly open door of his book-filled study, to the kitchen. "Would you like coffee?" Spinks asked. I held up my to-go cup. "Some eggs? I make very good scrambled eggs." "No, thanks," I said, then I felt bad for being so curt. "I went for a run this morning," I said. "I saw the Algonquin memorial." "Yes, they just put it up," Spinks said. "People here still make a fuss about the war, probably because so little has happened since." He sat in his usual place at the kitchen table and rubbed his temples. "Shall we begin?" he asked.

That spring, Spinks said, I began to see Parry Sound the way Luiza had seen it. I lived in a small, provincial town, full of sober Scotch-Irish shopkeepers whose great misery was the unplowed snow in the streets, and whose great delight was the annual fur sale at Florence's Finery. It would have been cruel to bring my wife back from Edmonton. Charlotte tried, tactfully, to show me all the ways in which my situation had improved now that Luiza was gone. I could get a good night's sleep! I could go to the Saturday concerts at Hagan's Hall! She didn't go so far as to suggest that I take *her* to the concerts, but if I had invited her, I think she would gladly have accepted. I dreamed of writing stories again, but didn't write a word. By day, I worked mechanically in the hardware store; at night, I lay awake, listening to clods of snow thunder off the roof and detonate in our backyard. I might have gone on like that forever if I hadn't received a letter from Wollheim. The Futurian Literary Science Society had broken up, he wrote. He wouldn't bother me with the details. Suffice it to say that some of the ex-Futurians were very angry with him, even though the situation was all their fault. They were mailing defamatory letters to everyone in fandom, and Wollheim worried that I might have got one. I wrote back that his reputation in

Canada was unsullied, and by the way, had the breakup left any of the Futurians with an extra room? Wollheim's reply was brief: If you're thinking of coming to New York, he wrote, why don't you get in touch with Doc Lowndes? I regard him as a traitor, but I hear he's looking for a roommate. He was; and in early May, I told Charlotte I was going back to New York. She pretended to think it was for the best: "You have so many friends in New York, Leo!" Then she implored me not to stay away too long. Her health was poor. She had terrible constipation, and arthritis in both knees. I shrank from her last selfish kisses and got on a southbound bus.

The city I returned to was very different from the one I had left seven years earlier. The buildings were grimier; instead of the auto-mated expressways of the Futurama exhibit at the World's Fair, a somber parade of whalelike vehicles crept along West Street. Doc Lowndes lived on Eleventh Street, in Greenwich Village. He, too, had changed: the red-shirted gypsy of 1939 was now a chubby bachelor with pipe and dressing gown, who lived among stuffed armchairs and Axminster rugs. He edited a magazine called *Crack Detective,* listened to classical music, and swore the Communist Party was a plot to turn healthy Americans into robots. Four times a week, he went to see Dr. Fish, a Reichian analyst on Twelfth Street, who was teaching him how to liberate his body from the psychic armor in which it was im-prisoned. He told me the story of the Futurians' rupture: Wollheim had expelled Pohl for being too bourgeois, and Kornbluth quit. The end came when Wollheim ordered Johnny Michel to break up with his girlfriend, a fellow Futurian named Judy Zissman, on the grounds that she was a Trotskyite. Judy called the society's remaining members to arms, and they expelled Wollheim on the grounds that *he* was a ma-nipulative bastard who wanted everyone to be as miserable as he was.

Now the Futurians were scattered: Wollheim and his wife, Elsie, lived in Forest Hills, where, it was rumored, they had a sunken living room. Asimov was in Boston, teaching chemistry and becoming famous. Michel was on Fourth Street. Pohl lived on Grove Street, with a Florida girl named Dorothy, an ex-WAC who wanted to make it as a screenwriter. "What about Doris?" I asked. I was so excited, it was like being afraid. "Remarried," Lowndes said, "to an *artiste* named Owens. They have produced an offspring and retreated with it to the wilds of Long Island." "Oh," I said. "When did they get married?" "I believe it was in Forty-two," Lowndes said. "In love with Doris, were we?" "No," I said. In 1942, I had been stationed in Newfoundland, guarding the Botwood harbor and getting drunk on a vile local distillate called *screech*. How could Doris have fallen in love with someone else when I wasn't in a position to do anything about it? "Don't bother denying it," Lowndes said. "Analysis has made me keenly empathic. And besides, who wasn't in love with Doris?" "What should I do?" I asked. "My dear," Lowndes said, with a smile so tender that it could only have been contemptuous, "remember, you are now a resident of the Village."

So I was. I consoled myself for the absence of Doris in all the bars within staggering distance of Lowndes's apartment, and there were many. In six weeks I dated a painter, an ex-dancer who had married an accountant, and two NYU students, one of whom was studying French and the other, anthropology. I caught gonorrhea and lost the last traces of my Canadian prudishness. All in all, I wasn't much happier than I had been in Parry Sound. I had hoped that I'd be able to write in New York, but when I sat at my little desk in Lowndes's back bedroom, I had no idea where to begin. Anything I could invent would be too flimsy, and everything I remembered was too sad. I tried to see Wollheim, but he was working at Avon Books and didn't have time for me. Pohl didn't return my calls. I did, however, manage to see Michel, by the simple expedient of visiting him in person. His building was, like all the others on his block, gray, with the rudiments of a grocery downstairs and silver cans of uncollected garbage huddled by the stoop. He answered the door with an angry "What?" but when I told him who it was he opened right away. "Leo! *Hermano!* I'd shake your hand, but I have to be careful. G-germs." I was surprised at how much he had aged. His sandy hair had climbed his forehead, and his face had swollen up and turned an unhealthy pink. His two-room apartment was neat to the point of sadness: bare floor, tidy piles of books pushed against a wall on which hung one of Michel's own paintings, of a red square balanced on a swerve in a landscape of lightly crackled white. The tabletop squeaked under my finger. "It does me g-good to see you," Michel said. "Spinks of the old days. *In thirty-eight the sky was red, and Gernsback rumbled overhead,*" he half sang, forgetting that I hadn't been around in 1938. He poured us each a drink. "Where have you b-b-been?" he asked. I answered briefly. Michel was impressed. "What we need, Spinks, are more people like you, who say what they mean and aren't afraid t-to fight."

We got through the bottle, and I was ready to go home, but Michel threw on a corduroy jacket and insisted that we go for a drink at Goody's, on Sixth Avenue. The bar was nearly empty, and we took a table at the back. Michel talked angrily about how science fiction was dead. "It's pure bullshit, emphasis on *pure,*" he said. "I'm not kidding myself. I write aviation stories now. Tom Trouble and His B-big B-b-bomber. I save the political stuff for Mike Gold at *New Masses.*" He coughed. "I wonder if anything would have been different if we had won." "Won what?" I asked, perplexed. "Jesus, Spinks, the c-c-convention. You were th-there." I listened with amazement while Michel unreeled his theory. It was a given, he said, that for the last decade, science had only been catching up with science fiction. We had the atomic bomb already, and television, and the Radar-Range. Next would be ray guns, space rockets, space suits. "Not flying cars?" I asked. "Who cares?" Michel said. "The underlying situation won't be any d-different. We'll all be slaving away, saving up to buy the new gadget. Does your flying car have V-venusian leather seats? Does it have a three-speed f-fan? Did you know Pohl is an a-adman now?" I hadn't heard that. "He works on Madison Avenue," Michel said. "It makes me s-sick to think of what we *could* have been."

If only the Futurians had seized control of the World Science Fiction Convention in 1939, he said, we might have changed the world. "You really think?" I said. "Of course I think!" Michel said. He was furious. "Who *reads* science fiction, Leo? Scientists! They g-get their ideas from *us!*" To hear Michel tell it, if we had defeated the fascists in 1939, we wouldn't be living under their iron heel now. "I thought we *did* defeat the fascists," I said, doubtfully. To me, too, it seemed that our victory had been less resounding than it might have been: we had won the war, but we had not been able to restore some vital quality that the world had lost. Michel smirked. "I'm sorry," he said, "haven't you h-h-heard of J. Edgar Hoover? Jesus, Spinks, we're probably under surveillance right now." He told me that the members of the Communist Party were all being wiretapped, and had been for months. "Any d-d-day now they're going to r-round us up," he said. "They'll p-p-put us in the internment camps where they had the Japanese." He smacked the table. "Leo, we f-fucked up!"

I saw Michel again a couple of weeks later. As before, we ended up at Goody's, and we were talking about more or less the same things when a pallid man in a trench coat crept up on us. "Are you gentlemen interested in some atemporal fun?" he asked. I had never heard a dope pusher use the word *atemporal* before. "What have you got?" I asked. He stuck his hand into his pocket and it came up with two yellow cardboard tubes. "Morphine syrettes," he said. "Four dollars each." "Take a hike," I said, but Michel stopped him. "How about f-five dollars for b-both," he said. "Sold," the stranger said. Michel looked in his wallet, which was empty. I paid the stranger and took the syrettes. "What's with that?" I asked. Michel grinned. "I've got a b-bad b-b-back. Come on." We went into the men's room, which smelled of urine and sweat and something old and entombed. Michel pulled me into a stall and shut the door. "How do you use it?" I asked. The syrettes were like tubes of toothpaste with needles on the cap; you pushed a pin down through the cap, stuck the needle in your arm, and squeezed the tube. Almost immediately, there was a loose feeling in my calves, which spread up the back of my legs. I felt like I was floating in warm salt water. I pulled the syrette out of my arm and pressed my finger on the blood that welled up. Michel hadn't got that far. He leaned against the stall with his eyes closed. "Johnny." I took out his needle and pulled down his sleeve. "You all right?" "Mm," Michel said. "You faggots finished in there?" someone asked, not unkindly. I flushed the syrettes and got us back into the bar. The stranger in the trench coat sat with us. His name was Lee, he said. He told us that, in his opinion, the purpose of morphine was to escape from the system of human time, which, like psychoanalysis, advertising, and the Ford system, was intended to keep human beings in chattel slavery. He talked and talked, and what he said must have made an impression on me because in the end I did escape from time. I was sitting on the shore of a lake, looking for the shadow of a boat. My eyes hurt. My brother was out there, on the water, and my mother was standing beside me, wearing a brown dress. She, too, was looking at the water. Then she turned and hurried back up the path. "Where are you going?" I asked, but she didn't answer. And my brother, where was my brother?

I wanted to sleep, but someone had to keep watch. I forced myself to sit up. I was in the back of Goody's, and Michel slumped against my arm. Lee was gone. We were going to have trouble getting home, I thought. We would have to take a train to Antwerp, and wait for a ship. Then we'd take another train . . . "Hey!" I shook Michel's shoulder. "What," he said. "Are you all right?" I asked. "I don't know," Michel said. "We should go," I said. I tried to stand up, but all I could do was sit and hope that my brother would come by. I looked anxiously at each person who went past our table. These, I thought, were the dead: a parade of the dead. The god who rules the underworld had ordered them to march past me. "You can have anyone you recognize," he told me, laughing. I sat up as straight as I could. If I closed my eyes for even a moment, someone I loved might pass, and I would lose that person forever. But the parade was endless. Why did I agree to this deal? You can't bargain with the god of the underworld; he always wins! What was worse, to make sure that I didn't save anyone, the god had given each dead person a false name, which was very terrible indeed, because names, as I understood, in that moment, are the channels by which spirits move from one body to another. You can't have anyone back unless you know his name. I watched and waited and finally I fell asleep. When I woke up, Michel lay with his head in my lap. There was a puddle of vomit on the floor and streaks of it on the legs of my pants and my shoes. Amazingly, it seemed to be only ten p.m. I groaned. "Johnny. Wake up." With the Negro busboy's disgusted help, I got him to his feet. Sixth Avenue was as black and vast as the space between the stars. I carried Michel home and deposited him on his bed. I tried to untie his shoes, and gave up. I went home and found Lowndes in an armchair, reading manuscripts. Elgar came mournfully from the record player. "Good grief," Lowndes said, rising. "Leo, where have you been?" "Tell me your name," I said. "Robert Lowndes," Lowndes said. "No, your real name," I said. I lay on the sofa and closed my eyes.

11.

I bought morphine from Lee once a week, then twice a week. I roamed ancient kingdoms of waste; I swam in cold oceans and climbed desolate hills strewn with bodies and skeletons. It was a kind of underworld, but what made it endurable was my certainty that my lost family could be found somewhere within it, and that if I played by the rules, I could have them back. All I had to do was keep going. For that, though, I needed money. After some searching, I got a job at a French laundry on Fourth Street: the owner, an Italian named Esposito, was looking for a Frenchman, and my secondhand Québécois passed muster. When that wasn't enough, I stole books from Lowndes's library and sold them in the used-book shops on Fourth Avenue; and it was in this way that I ran into Sam Loveman again.

He had his own store now, on the second floor of a building on Tenth Street. It was bright, tidy, and spare, the opposite of what Dauber & Pine had been. Either he had forgotten how our last meeting ended, or it didn't matter to him. He was happy to see me and paid me generously for poor Lowndes's books. His shop was mostly poetry and obscure French and British writers from the beginning of the century, but there was always room, he said, for a little fantasy. But when I brought him Lowndes's copy of *Marginalia,* a collection of Lovecraft's miscellaneous writings, which Arkham House had published, Loveman made a face. "I don't think so, Leo," he said. "I don't think I can." "Why not?" I asked. "I've learned some things about Howard," Loveman said. He told me that he'd seen Sonia Greene, who had been Lovecraft's wife, when she came to New York, in 1945, to shop around an idea for a book called *The Private Life of H. P. Lovecraft.* She had somehow just learned that Lovecraft was dead, and in the freshness of her grief, she was unloading stories about him in every direction. So she confided in Loveman that Howard had been an anti-Semite. He'd always disparaged the Jews, but at first Sonia had imagined he was just repeating thoughtlessly what so many other people said. Over the years, though, she became convinced that Howard wasn't speaking thoughtlessly at all. He never spoke thoughtlessly about anything. Howard *hated* the Jews: he'd told Belknap, in her hearing, that he wished a whiff of cyanogen gas from the tail of some passing comet would exterminate the inhabitants of the Lower East Side. "That's horrible!" Sonia had said. "You can't mean it!" "Why not?" Howard had asked, mildly. "But Howard . . ." Sonia hadn't been able to understand him at all. "Do you want me dead?" she'd asked. "Certainly not," Howard had said. "I'm speaking of a population, not of individual people." "But Howard," she'd said, making the obvious point, "what do you think a population *is*?" By this time, Sonia told Loveman, she was already worried about Howard's mental stability. "But I don't think his stability had anything to do with it," she'd said. "I think that was what he really believed." Loveman, for his part, was horrified by the personal betrayal. "He pretended to be my friend," he said, "but all the while, he must have been thinking, *There's Sam Loveman, that dirty Jew . . .*" It was unforgivable. Loveman could no longer support Howard or his work, not even in the form of a used book. I, too, was horrified. From Luiza, I knew that the Germans had used a cyanogen gas in Auschwitz. There might have been a big gap, an enormous gap, between wishing the Jews dead and actually building the gas chambers, between the words *cyanogen gas* and the barrels of Zyklon B that the Nazis put to their inhuman purpose, but I didn't see it. From that moment on, I could only think of Lovecraft's work as evil, and I was ashamed that I had ever admired him.

Learning the truth about Lovecraft drove me further into despair; but, strangely, despair drove me closer to revelation. What, I wondered, if the trips I made to the kingdom of the dead could be made by others as well, and in the other direction? One day in the late summer of 1946, I went back to Loveman's shop and asked if he really believed in the transmigration of souls. "I believe in it poetically," he said. "What about practically?" I asked. "If the dead were to come back, how would they do it?" "You short-story writers are always looking for manuals," he said, but the question pleased him. He danced through his shop, pulling from the shelves volumes I couldn't possibly afford: Blavatsky's *The Secret Doctrine,* Flournoy's *From India to the Planet Mars,* the *Tibetan Book of the Dead,* Pythagoras and the poems of John Donne. I copied down the titles and went to the Public Library on Forty-Second Street, and there, in the cool vaults of the Reading Room, which seemed to me a kind of vast mausoleum for the living, a chamber that floated, silently, between the city's noisy life and the rosy Heaven painted on the ceiling, I read about the mysteries of death and the miracles of life after death, of life after life after life. Most of what I read was gibberish and some of it was cynical trash; but here and there, I found sentences and paragraphs that rhymed with what I myself had experienced. It became clear to me that these books were describing the same thing under many names: transmigration, reincarnation, metempsychosis, and even possession, all meant but one thing, which was, that under certain circumstances, the soul could move from one body to another. What I wanted to know was how it happened—and how you recognized an old soul in its new flesh. I didn't get far with the first question, which had been answered too many times in too many different ways, but I did acquire some interesting notions about the second. The new body, I read, might look completely different from the old one, but the soul that lived there would sign its name somehow: with a familiar gesture, a way of holding the head, even a purse or pin or tie, repurchased by the new person to remind him or her of a cherished item that had been lost a century earlier.

I hadn't really understood anything yet, and what I believed was close to madness; but it was scarcely less mad than anything anyone else in the Village believed, in 1946. On the advice of Dr. Fish, Lowndes had bought himself an orgone box, a kind of phoneless wooden phone booth in which he sat, naked, for half an hour every morning, while cosmic energy accumulated at the edges of his skin. Meanwhile, over on Grove Street, I heard that Pohl and his new wife were training white mice to follow telepathic commands. And Michel and Wollheim still believed in Stalin! Why shouldn't I hope for the return of the dead? I looked sharply at certain people I passed in the street, wondering if they might be emigrants from my earliest memories. Could that long-necked fellow on the Number 6 train be Mihaly Rozen? What about the lady walking a toy poodle in Bryant Park: Had she been the friend of my mother's who came to stay with us in the summer, the one whose dog—a schnauzer, I think—tried to nip my arm? And was her averted gaze a sign that I had seen more than she wished me to know? Never mind that the lady in the park had, by the look of her, been born thirty years before my mother's friend was exterminated by the Nazis; the arithmetic of ages and dates didn't interest me. What mattered was that souls could move. The lady in the park might, for all I knew, be one of what Loveman had called the double-souled: people hiding within other people, just as, in their former lives, they had hidden in attics.

My visit to Loveman had another consequence, too, which was that I leafed through *Marginalia* before I put it back on Lowndes's shelf, and discovered that it contained a memoir by Robert Barlow, of the time he and Lovecraft had spent together in Florida. Once again, I felt a pang of envy: it was as if Barlow was living the life I ought to have lived. I had to remind myself that Lovecraft had been an anti-Semite, and that I was lucky *not* to have known him. Anyway, I thought, Lovecraft had been queer, and Barlow was probably queer, too. I wondered if Barlow had been Lovecraft's lover, which was something I would never have wanted to be, not under any circumstances. Then I put Barlow out of my mind again—although not before I'd noticed that, according to his memoir, he was living in Mexico City, and wondered, with another pang, what he was doing there. His life sounded very exotic and colorful, the opposite of gray New York.

After that, I got high more and more often. Lee had run into trouble with the law and gone home to his family in Saint Louis, but I bought morphine and later heroin from other Village pushers. Sometimes the high was strong and I was catapulted into the pen-sketched waves at the edge of the map. Sometimes I ended up in the kingdom of the winds. On no occasion did I rediscover the lake, or any of the people I had ever known. I heard children crying in the apartment above Lowndes's. I heard the faint, dull thrum of the subway. I heard coughing and scraping, and saw a few stars framed by the top of the light well. One night in November, I woke up on the floor of my bedroom, the needle still in my arm. Lowndes was standing over me. "Jesus, Leo," he said. "What?" I said. I felt fine. I took the needle out and dropped it on the night table. "Look at my rug," Lowndes said. There was a spot of blood on the oval rug he'd loaned me as a welcome-back-to-New-York gift. The spot was the size of a palm, and I told him not to worry about it; I'd bring the rug to Esposito's and get it out. "OK, but what about you?" Lowndes asked. I said that I was not dry-clean-only. A shower would put me right. And maybe some toast. I'd developed a thing for toast. It was enough like food that it fooled my body into going forward. "You need to see a doctor," Lowndes said. "Look at my arm," I said. "I'd go to jail." I didn't know if that was true, but I didn't think a doctor would be much help with my peculiar problem. "I'm going to make you an appointment with Dr. Fish," Lowndes said. "He cured my asthma, you know." "You never had asthma," I said. "It was psychosomatic. Aside from your buck teeth, there's nothing wrong with you." Lowndes blanched. "Don't be hateful," he said. "It'll only make you more sick." I said that I didn't care. Then he discovered that I'd been stealing his books and threw me out of his apartment. I didn't care about that, either. I moved into the YMCA at the west end of Jane Street, where plenty of other addicts lived. Any day now, I thought, I'll find what I'm looking for.

I would probably have died looking, if Esposito hadn't leased a new Bendix washer for the laundry and its motor hadn't burned out. Esposito called a repairman, and I helped him install the new motor; he was impressed by how well I knew my way around the machine. "What are you working *here* for?" he asked. He introduced me to his boss, an old Czech Jew named Hungerleider, who had an office in Queens. The front was a garage for the repair truck, and the back was like Frankenstein's laboratory, heaped with electric motors and hoses and couplings and mare's nests of red and blue wire. Hunger-leider was short, neatly dressed, and extremely solid—*warrantied for life,* he said. He shook my hand like he was pulling me from the water. He had me change the seal on a pump, and was interested to hear that I had been in the Canadian Army. When I told him about Luiza, he blew his nose into a handkerchief, and said I could start the next day. It wasn't charity, Hungerleider said. He had more business than he could handle. All over Queens, people were buying washing machines; in Manhattan, they were buying stoves and refrigerators to replace the ones they had nursed through the war years. His repairman, Gus, was overwhelmed.

I helped Gus for a few weeks, then Hungerleider decided my apprenticeship was over and explained his actual plan. Nassau County was where I would work, he said. New houses were going up by the hundreds, in what had been onion and potato fields. New houses meant new appliances, which would need to be repaired. Hungerleider bought a second truck, and day after day I drove to Wantagh, Plainview, Massapequa, Levittown, an eerie landscape of identical white houses on seventy-by-a-hundred plots, each with its white tongue of driveway and its huddled garage, bare trees, and brown lawn crusted with patchy snow, set, one after another, on roads that curved gently in order to efface their incredible monotony. I made five or six calls in the morning, four or five more in the afternoon. I was a great success as a repairman. I was polite, clean-shaven, a veteran. I drove under the speed limit and signaled my turns. And, nightly, I stuck a needle in my arm and went looking for people I knew in the kingdom of the dead. That was my life, until one soggy March afternoon I rang the bell of a brick-and-vinyl Cape Colonial in Lynbrook, and Doris came to the door. "Leo?" she said. She was wearing slacks and a paint-stained old sweater. "Washer on the fritz?" I asked. "Oh, my God," Doris said. "Leo!"

She was a mother now. Her daughter, Margot, was out with her grandparents, but had left behind, for the entertainment of the adults, many blocks and balls and a wooden chicken that pecked when you pulled its string. "I'm afraid she's going to grow up to be a farmer," Doris said ruefully. "She's already got her eye on a patch of the yard." Her husband, Tom Owens, sold tombstones. It was either a fitting job for a war hero or a crushing humiliation, and most days, Doris said, Tom thought the latter. What he wanted to be, what he *was*, was a painter: he'd done the portrait of Doris that hung over the sectional sofa, in oils, in Florida, against a backdrop of suggestive pink blossoms. But he also wanted to live decently; he and Doris had had their fill of hovels during the war. "Sheds, practically, and tents, too. Tom had it worse than I did, on those jungle bases." He'd flown B-25 bombers over the Pacific, dropped countless tons of explosive on Japanese positions. He had a box of medals and was a legend in the community, now dispersed, of Pacific bomber pilots. "What it comes down to," Doris said, "is that he wants to believe he was fighting *for* something. That we deserve something, now that the war's over. So, this." The vast room in which we stood had a freestanding fireplace and a picture window that looked out on the backyard. The radio was tuned to a classical station. "No down payment for veterans," Doris said. "The opportunity of a lifetime. Would you like a drink?" She poured us each a glass of red wine. "I'd offer you whiskey, but Tom keeps track." She was as beautiful as ever, I thought. More beautiful, now that she was a little heavier, and a little more worn. "Please tell me that you don't live on Long Island," she said. "In the Village," I said. "With Doc Lowndes, actually." I didn't want to tell her where I really lived. "With Doc!" Doris was enchanted. "Is he still editing *Crack Detective*?" I said he was. "Good for him," Doris said. "Tell him I say hi. And tell *me* about New York. We get over there about once a century."

The sun came in through the picture window and turned the wall-to-wall carpet red. The trees on the horizon turned black. Eventually, inevitably, I took Doris's hand. It was rough, from gardening, she said. Even in the winter there was work to do. I leaned over to kiss her, but she slid away. "Margot will be back any minute," she said. "I'm sure she'd be thrilled to meet you, but I don't feel like doing that much explaining." "I'm sorry," I said. "It's all right," Doris said. I stood up. "I'd better take a look at your washing machine." Doris laughed. "Leo! Don't be offended. I want to be your friend. I'm terribly lonely out here, actually." I opened the washer. A wire in the timer had been shaken loose, and I soldered it into place. "You're all set," I said. "Thank you, Mr. Spinks," Doris said. She walked me out, and in the driveway, in full view of any neighbors who happened to be watching, she kissed my lips. "Tell Doc I'm going to send him a story," she said. I got into my van. The sun had dropped below the roofline of the house; Doris was a blue shadow, waving to me, the only moving thing in that landscape. But all of Long Island came to life with her wave, and I was alive in it, too.

12.

I saw Doris perhaps half a dozen times that spring. If work took me anywhere near Lynbrook, I'd think, why not stop in? Or I'd finish my rounds early and find myself heading west on Highway 27. I suppose it was a form of addiction. But Doris was happy to see me, too. She confided in me that she was writing a novel about army wives, called *Penelope*. Was the title too obvious? Oh, she didn't care. She was too old for subtlety. It was going to be a powerful book, a war novel for women. She had the outline of it in her mind but was flummoxed by how hard it was to get it on paper. Either too much was happening or too little, and always in the back of her mind there was a thought about Margot. Did the silence mean she was asleep, or had she gone outside? Was she eating bulbs out of the flower beds? "She did that, you know. I had to take her to the hospital." Did Margot think Doris was a good mother? Did Tom think she was a good wife? "Then I smoke a cigarette, and poof, the day is over." I didn't try to kiss her again. I was happy just to sit at the dining room table with her, swapping memories of other days or listening to her stories about the horrors of Long Island. Did I know that Levittown was *systematically* rejecting applications from Negroes? Even veterans. It was disgusting. Doris had joined an anti-segregation league, and she wanted me to join, too. "Leo," she said, "you can't live unless you *do* something." "I am doing something," I said. "I fixed a refrigerator today, and two electric ranges." Doris made a face. "That's sad. You're running away." "No, I'm not," I said. "Leo!" Doris was really angry. "Do you even know what's happening in the world right now?" It was June, and Truman looked to be starting a war with the Russians in Greece. Levittown was a disaster and a model for the future of the United States. "You can't run away," she said. "We need your help." I didn't want to listen, but Doris made my old hopes stir in their sleep. Maybe the world could be fixed after all.

I stopped using heroin, which was easier than I'd thought it would be. I moved into my own apartment, on East Fourth Street: a basement apartment, with a view of a cracked gray courtyard. I bought a potted ficus tree and put it in front of my window. And one day I picked up a box of Anti-Segregation League leaflets from Doris and slipped them into mailboxes as I made my rounds. It didn't take much effort on my part, and it made Doris happy. "That's the spirit, Leo! Now, I want you to come to one of our meetings. You'll meet a lot of interesting people."

I did go to the meeting, and I met her interesting people, but then something new happened: I thought of a story. It concerned a bank messenger in New York, who must deliver an important document to the European city of S. He takes a ship to Hamburg, and from there various trains conduct him farther and farther into what is, to him, a completely unfamiliar continent. The strange thing being that, when he gets to S, he has the feeling he has been there before. And, in fact, when he leaves his hotel and goes for a walk around town (it's Sunday afternoon, so he can't deliver his package yet), he finds his way without trouble to the city's various landmarks: the tower where S's last king performed his disastrous experiment with a pair of artificial wings; the park with its white gravel paths and its carousel; even a certain alley which leads first to a restaurant (you have to climb a single, high step to enter) decorated in blue and gold, then to a comically small piazza with a cinema. How does he know these things? What's stranger, when he returns to his hotel, weary and perplexed, a message is waiting for him from a woman named D., whom he has never met, inviting him to dinner. D. lives in a far-off part of S, with her sister. After some preliminary conversation, D. reveals that they belong to a revolutionary organization, which is working to overthrow the government of S and reinstate the heir to the throne. Will the bank messenger help them? He hesitates—he is, after all, just a bank messenger. Why, he wonders, does D. want his help? He asks if he can take a day to think it over, and D. says, One day, but no more. The bank messenger returns to his hotel, and, moved by an intuition which is no stranger than anything else that's happened in the story so far, he unwraps the package he is supposed to deliver. It contains a sheaf of documents. On the first page of the first document, the word *inheritance* catches his eye, and he reads on. The heir to the throne of S, it turns out, is him.

I had never written anything like that before, and I have not written anything like it since. It seemed to me that my entire life had assembled in the waiting room of my imagination, so that one memory after another could enter my story's magical translation machine and appear in the pages I pulled from my typewriter. The Futurians were there, and so were Walter and Charlotte, and Miss Ditchburn who taught Canadian history, and after those people, or before them, I found a blue rug, a wooden table with a glass top, an old woman in a white hat, a ball, a bridge, a pony, a bowl of soup, a wool sock that itched my calf, a haul of scraps which did not, in themselves, amount to a world, or even a coherent suggestion of one, but which gave me hope that there was more, and maybe much, left to salvage from the wreck of what I had originally been. It was, I thought, the opposite of my gloomy search for my lost people on the subway; although now I see that the story grew out of the searching, that it was, in fact, the only form the searching could really take. I wrote for an hour or two a night, all through the summer, and by fall my story gave signs of becoming a book. I wanted to show it to Doris, but I was afraid she would say I was running away again. Also, I worried that she wouldn't like it. It wasn't like anything that anyone I knew was writing, or reading. Finally, I called Wollheim and asked if he would look at it. He said he was too busy, but if I liked, I could read some of it to his new club, the Arisian Society. They were much livelier, he said, than the Futurians had ever been. So on a Saturday at the beginning of October, I took the subway out to Forest Hills. Wollheim came to the door in slippers, tweed slacks, and a white shirt open at the collar. "Spinks!" He looked at me mistrustfully. "You haven't changed a bit," he said.

Wollheim led me to a big sunken living room with low book-shelves on two walls and windows on the third. His wife, Elsie, was in the kitchen, sprinkling crumb topping onto an unbaked coffee cake. And there, on the lip of the living room's pit, sat the Arisians: a dozen or so children who slouched in flat-fronted pants and shirts with the sleeves rolled up, and packs of cigarettes rolled into them. They might have been the same age as we had been in 1939, but to me they looked extremely young and not very bright. Two of them were building a house out of crackers while a third thumbed through an issue of *Action Comics*. They picked at their pimples and gave off a sweet, flatulent miasma. Wollheim introduced me: "The well-known Canadian fan, Leo Spinks," he said. "He used to edit a magazine called *Pickman's Vault*, which some of you may have heard of." The Arisians nodded noncommittally. "He's back from the war, and he wants to read us a story. Leo?" I took out my pages and read.

When I finished there was a long silence. Then one of the Arisians said, "Hamburg?" "It's a port in Germany," I said. "I know where it is," the kid said. "I just wonder why the ship would take him there." "I guess because it's the closest place to S," I said. "Is that in Germany?" another kid asked. "No," I said. "I think more like Central Europe." "You don't *know*?" the kid asked. The Arisians laughed. "Also," said the first kid, "why a bank messenger?" "Couldn't they send a cablegram?" "Or send it airmail?" "It's too important to send airmail," I said. "They have to send a messenger. They have to send *this* messenger." "Why?" "Because they know who he is," I said. It hadn't occurred to me until just then. But the Arisians were pitiless. "They? They who?" "The bank *knows* it's got a king working for it? Hoo-ey!" I waited for Wollheim to come to my defense, but he sat with his hands clasped around his crossed knees, his face a smiling mask. It occurred to me that he was afraid. He was like a man feeding pigeons: he didn't want to startle them away.

The next story was by a grubby, black-haired, paperboy-looking kid named Wilsey. It concerned a man who thought he had been buried alive and clawed his way out of the crypt, only to discover that he wasn't alive at all: pure secondhand Lovecraft. Halfway through, I excused myself and went to the bathroom. I washed my face but that wasn't enough. I wanted to wash my face *away*, to become nothing, a blank. I found a bottle of prescription cough syrup in Wollheim's medicine cabinet and drank it. The Arisians were still talking about Wilsey's story when I came out. Crusted blood under the fingernails was a nice effect, someone said, but would a thousand dead rats really smell like ammonia? Wilsey said they would, in a hollow voice that implied a thousand dead rats were the least of the things he'd smelled. "I wish there was some cannibalism," another Arisian said. "Why?" Wollheim asked, mildly. "I don't know," the Arisian said. "I just think it would add to the effect." "What do you think, Leo?" Wollheim asked. I remembered something Loveman had told me, long ago: that a poet can't be afraid to speak. "I think Wilsey's story is shameful," I said. "He wants to write like H. P. Lovecraft, and I guess he does an OK imitation. But who was Lovecraft? Do any of you know that he hated the Jews? Do you think that's something you should be imitating? Do you hate the Jews?" "I'm Jewish, actually," Wilsey said. "Go easy, Spinks," Wollheim said. "Don't tell me to go easy, you coward," I said. "I saw Belsen. Thousands of unburied bodies heaped up in the street. That was horror. And Lovecraft, the rat, would have liked it." The Arisians replied, in chorus, that that couldn't be true. "But it is," I said. I told them what Loveman had told me. "You don't know anything. You just want a good thrill. But Lovecraft was a monster!" I was shouting. "And you just sit there!" I stood up. "Don, you asked for my opinion," I said, "and that's it. Now I'm going home." I walked to the door and found myself in the kitchen. Elsie was on the phone, murmuring something to the sea-green handset. "Where's my hat?" I demanded. Then, apparently, I threw up on the coffee cake and passed out.

Later, I heard that Wollheim was telling people I was dangerous, unreliable, a drug addict, as he'd heard from Michel, and a madman. In retrospect, evidence of my insanity was everywhere: I'd showed up unannounced at Pohl's mother's apartment, I'd nearly punched Sam Moskowitz, and I'd been unable to stop leering at Doris! I even heard that Wollheim and Pohl had made up their differences in order to agree that *I* was a monster. I didn't care. All I wanted was to finish my story. But, unfortunately for me, the Arisians' criticism had taken root: Why *did* the bank send its royal messenger? Where *was* S? I struggled on, full of doubt; soon the bank messenger was imprisoned in the castle dungeon, and I couldn't figure out how to free him. When I wasn't working for Hungerleider, I folded myself into a rickety chair at a too-small table and filled my wastebasket with useless typing. I stopped going to see Doris. She found my number and called to ask if she'd done something to upset me. "Not a thing," I said. "I just need some time alone." "Leo, you have *plenty* of time alone," she said. "You need time with me." But I didn't go back. I don't know why. Maybe I still wanted too much from Doris, and I couldn't afford another disappointment. Or maybe I was just stuck in the basement of the castle.

In December 1947, Cyril Kornbluth came back from Chicago. He hadn't heard about my disgrace and so he knocked on my door early one Sunday afternoon. He invited me to come with him to the Bronx Zoo, where Pohl was apparently going to demonstrate his telepathic control of rodents. I said I was working. "Writing the great Canadian novel?" Kornbluth asked. "Don doesn't think so," I said. I told him what had happened with the Arisians. "Wollheim is a rat," Kornbluth said. "You can't pay any attention to what he says. Mind if I take a look?" He sat on the bed, a cigarette between two plump fingers, and read my typescript quickly. Then he stood up and cracked his knuckles. "It's interesting," he said. "Glad to see you getting away from all that Lovecraftian gunk." "But what happens next?" "You get up," Kornbluth said. He sat at my desk, looked at the page in the typewriter, and licked his thumb. Three minutes later, he was finished.

Kornbluth had written:

"Good news," said the warden. "You're going to be put on trial."

"I am?" said the messenger. His heart leaped. If he had a trial, then at least he could send a message to the conspirators who were surely wondering what had happened to him. He just needed to think of a suitable code. "When will it happen?" he asked, timorously.

"Now," said the warden.

"Now?"

The warden held out a pair of handcuffs. "I can trust you to put these on yourself, I think."

His mind racing, the messenger closed the cuffs on one wrist, then on the other. The warden unlocked the door to his cell and motioned him out. They made a little procession: first a guard, then the messenger, and, bringing up the rear, the warden of the castle, who hummed a pretty song to himself—it seemed to the messenger that he had heard it before, when he was a child, perhaps. They climbed a flight of stairs and came by way of a little-used door into the courtyard of the castle. It was sunrise; all the castle's western spires were rose pink, and the eastern ones all blue. Rose . . . the messenger thought. Suddenly he realized what message he could give his friends, as soon as he was allowed to speak. His heart was twisted by a violent hope.

"Wait up," said the warden.

"Here?" the messenger asked. "Shouldn't we go on to the courtroom? I'm eager to prove my innocence."

"Not just yet," the warden said. He drew his pistol, and shot the messenger in the back of the head.

FIN

"Now come on," Kornbluth said. "Let's go watch Fred make a fool of himself."

I burned my story in the bathroom sink that night. I was done with stories, I thought. I was done with everything. The only thing I could still imagine wanting was revenge.

13.

Three years passed. For two of them I worked in Hungerleider's shop, then I got a job as a salesman for General Electric. I worked in a showroom on Park Avenue, selling ranges and dishwashers guaranteed to last a lifetime or more, and I was so good at it that in the winter of 1950 the company invited me to join a team that was going down to Mexico, to teach their local salesmen how to sell stoves to the Mexicans. Apparently, people in Mexico still liked to cook on coal stoves, as though the twentieth century had never happened. We were supposed to know the secret that would change their minds. Of course, we didn't. The GE ranges were so beautiful and modern, so much a part of what Americans wanted back then, that they sold themselves. On the plane to Mexico City, I took the things Michel had told me at Goody's and tried to turn them into a pitch. What we were selling, I said, when I got there, was the future. People had been dreaming of this stuff for decades, and now here it was, in white enameled steel, with buttons that lit up in different colors, like the controls of a spaceship. It would have been a great pitch if the Mexican people had grown up reading *Amazing Stories,* but if they had grown up reading *Amazing Stories* they would have been the same as the Americans, and selling stoves would have been no problem.

When our day of pitches was over, we went to the hotel bar and drank beer with the Mexican team. Ed Armstrong, one of my fellow salesmen, suggested that we find a whorehouse and show them our *automatic Calrods*—that was the name of a GE stove. It was the kind of joke we had been making all afternoon. What can I say? We were the future, but we were disgusting. I told Ed I was too tired, and walked alone down the Paseo de la Reforma. I got lost, doubled back, passed a hospital and several parks. Finally, thirsty and footsore, I went into a bar to get a drink of water. It was a shabby place, just a counter with a few beaten-up stools and an ice chest full of beer, and bottles of Coke and orange soda. After a while, I realized that the two men next to me at the counter were American. One was tall and skinny, with damp light brown hair pushed this way and that on his head. He had on a light tropical suit and a dirty white shirt. He was talking to a short, swarthy friend who wore a lot of silver jewelry, rings and so on. "It's no use going to a Chink," he said. "Even if he writes you a script, no one will fill it." "I don't know about that," the friend said. "What about a Chinese pharmacy?" The taller one laughed. "I went to a Chinese pharmacy, once. I put down the stomach ulcer routine. You know what I got? Powdered rhinoceros horn. I cooked it up, and it nearly killed me. The real mystery, though, is where they find all those rhinoceri. There can't be enough in Africa to stock every Chinese pharmacy in New York, let alone in China. I asked an acquaintance about this, a jazzman named Clark. He told me they breed them in captivity. But apparently, and this is quite interesting, the rhinoceri won't mate unless there's music playing. That was how Clark knew about it. He did a six-month bid on a rhinoceros farm in Rhodesia, playing Glenn Miller to put the lady rhinoceri in the mood." "Excuse me," I said. "Is your name Lee?" The tall one swiveled around to look at me. He coughed. "Wel-l," he said, "that's a hell of a long way to come for a score."

Bill was his real name, he said. He'd gone by Lee in New York to dodge the law, but here there was no law to speak of. In the heat of the Mexico City winter, he looked luminous and irritable, like a vexed angel. He introduced me to his friend, whose name was Dave, and asked if I could buy them a drink. When I said I could, he said we should go to a restaurant. The place we were in served only beer, and Bill and Dave were in the mood for tequila. They led me down the Calle Durango, to a steak house on the corner of the Avenida Oaxaca. It was two stories tall and full of Mexicans eating steak in the middle of the night. "This place all right with you?" Bill asked. I nodded. General Electric was paying us too much, and I would have spent even more if I'd gone to the whorehouse. "Might as well eat as long as we're drinking," Bill said. We got a table on the upper floor, looking out on a round plaza where there had been a market earlier in the day. Now there was just the empty scaffolding for the awnings, and a couple of sanitation men pushing brooms around. To my surprise, Bill remembered some things about me. "This guy was in the real war," he told Dave. "He must have shot fifty Germans." I hadn't said anything of the sort, but I was happy to let Bill lie on my behalf. "He got a medal for killing a German with the butt of his pistol," he said. "Clubbed him on the head. Kaputt!" They each ordered a porterhouse steak and a tequila and a beer. "We could use a brave guy like you," Bill said. "We're thinking of going on a dangerous trip." He told me that he and Dave wanted to travel south to Ecuador to score a drug called yage, which was supposed to be better than heroin. "Bill wants to go," Dave said. "I'm not going." "That's the kind of friend Dave is," Bill said. "He'll eat your steak but he won't put up with any hardship." "That's right," Dave said. The food came, and he cut into his meat and filled his mouth. "How about it?" Bill asked. "We could head out anytime you like. Hop a plane down to Guayaquil and get a train of mules." "Mules?" "To head into the jungle," Bill said. "The reason we'd need a train is that most of them will be killed by venomous serpents. The worst is the fer-de-lance. I know a guy who got bitten by a fer-de-lance, right on his johnson . . ." I wanted to go to bed, but Bill and Dave kept ordering more drinks. Dave ordered a shrimp cocktail and a baked potato. "You better not leave us with the check," he growled. "We've got a whole operation here. Our boys will track you down and take it out of your skin." "That's right, we have boys," Bill said dreamily.

I asked how he had ended up in Mexico, and he told me he'd been busted for heroin in New Orleans, and he'd come here to escape prosecution. "They'll put you away for life," he said. "For life and more. They have a prison beneath the regular one, where Cajun witch doctors collect the souls of the deceased prisoners and bottle them up in soda pop bottles. Not like in Mexico. This country is *open*. A man can do what he wants. What's more, he can do it with whom he wants. You can do it with gentle Mexican boys, although actually not. Did you know, these Mexicans are some of the most bloodthirsty people on Earth?" Dave got up to use the toilet, but Bill, who seemed, as he spoke, to be releasing himself from some kind of terrestrial bondage, kept talking, about the Aztecs, whose proper name, he said, was the Culhua Mexica, the people from Culhuacán, where they had learned to farm and build temples and cut out the hearts of anyone they felt like. "That's the way to do it," Bill said. "Right to the heart. Rip it out. Feed it to the gods, they're hungry for our hearts." Outside, the plaza was clean. Two girls were tugging a man away from the restaurant, or possibly holding him up. "Is he talking about that Aztec shit?" Dave asked. "He won't stop. With the, what do you call it?" "Culhua Mexica," Bill said. "That's the proper name. The problem with you, Dave, is that you don't want to learn anything. Whereas *I* am a student. I'm always learning." Bill told me that he was enrolled at Mexico City College. Most of the classes were crap, but their Aztec specialist was pretty good. "A little fairy called Barlow." "*Robert* Barlow?" My heart jumped. "Goes by Bob," Bill said. "Why, do you know him?"

On our second day in Mexico City, a psychologist from Fairfield asked us to play a game, in which we wrote on a slip of paper the name of a household object with which we identified. "It can be any ordinary thing you might find around the house," the psychologist said. "How about a wife?" one of the Americans asked. The psychologist raised a heavy professional eyebrow. "Do you identify with your wife, Mr. Davis?" "Just kidding, Doc." I wrote AN URN and folded my slip neatly in half. In the second part of the game, we each had to say something about our object to our Mexican counterpart, and he had to guess what it was. "I hold ashes," I said. My partner beamed. "Ashtray!" "No." Ten minutes later he gave up, and I unfolded my paper. "Urn . . . What is that?" His object was a dish towel. I got it in two guesses and felt bad for him, but not as bad as I felt myself. I told my partner that I was going out for some aspirin, and found a bus that went to the Colonia Roma. I made my way to Mexico City College, on the Calle San Luis Potosí. It was in an ordinary commercial building that looked like the back office for something that was sold elsewhere. There were iron bars on the ground-floor windows. I located the anthropology department, where an indifferent secretary told me I was in luck: Professor Barlow was in that day. She told me where to find him.

Barlow's office overlooked the college's interior courtyard, where students sat at tables under gaudy striped umbrellas; but the office itself was gloomy and cramped. Earthenware pots stood on the bookshelves; a serape was tacked over the window like a curtain. Everything was dusty and mixed up: pens in the ashtray, a crumpled napkin on the bookshelf, stacks of paper on the rug. Robert Barlow sat at his desk, looking at a fountain pen as though he were trying to hypnotize himself. I had expected him to have an extraordinary presence, like the old magus Joseph Curwen in *Ward*, but, in fact, he looked like a rather prim professor. He had a broad forehead, a narrow chin, and protruding ears. His wire-rimmed glasses were big around and very thick, and they magnified his brown eyes. He had a sparse little mustache. "Can I help you?" he asked. His voice was surprisingly deep. "Professor Barlow? Just wanted to say hello." I came in, my hand outstretched. "Leo Spinks. I used to edit a magazine called *Pickman's Vault*." Barlow stared at me. "L. C. Spinks?" he said, after a while. "That's right," I said. Belatedly, he shook my hand. "You don't look at all the way I pictured you," Barlow said. "What are you doing in Mexico City?" I told him. Barlow found it amusing. "It's true," he said. "I bought a gas stove last year, but my cook won't use it. She won't use the tin pots I bought, either. She says they make the food taste bad." "Do they?" I asked. "I wouldn't know," Barlow said. "I've never eaten anything out of them." He smiled. "I wish you luck, but this is a very conservative country. In some ways." "What brought *you* here?" I asked. "Anthropology," Barlow said. "I seem to be enchanted by the stories the Aztecs left behind." "The Culhua Mexica," I said. "Yes," Barlow said. "Are you an anthropologist, too?" "I just sell stoves," I said. "Well," Barlow said, "it's nice to meet you, L. C. Spinks. I'll have to look at home and see if I have any copies of your magazine." He held out his hand and I shook it again. "It's nice to meet you, too, R. H. Barlow," I said, not letting go of his hand. Barlow looked at me and I looked back. "How long are you here?" he asked. "Until tomorrow afternoon," I said. "Why don't you come to dinner tonight," Barlow said. "I have some Lovecraftiana that might interest you." He wrote the directions to his house on the back of one of my business cards. "Come around eight." I thanked him and went out, exulting. It would be easy to get Barlow to tell me what he and Lovecraft had done in Florida, I thought, and I would use that story to destroy Lovecraft's reputation once and for all. In the courtyard, the students were

14.

Spinks made a sound, a rattling. I'd worked enough emergency room shifts to be alarmed. "Are you all right?" I asked. He clutched his chest with one hand and the table with the other. "Are you having a heart attack?" I looked for a phone and realized I had mine in my pocket. I called 911, and while I talked to the operator, I tried to look in Spinks's mouth, to see if his airway was blocked. I felt his neck for his pulse, which was strong and even. So, not a heart attack. Something respiratory. I thumped his back. I tried to get around behind him, to squeeze his diaphragm, only, what could he have choked on? Neither of us had eaten in hours. When the paramedics arrived, I was sitting on the floor, with Spinks slumped in my lap. "Breathe," I was saying, fairly uselessly. The paramedics got him up on a stretcher and put him on oxygen. One of them asked if I wanted to ride in the ambulance. I said no. Who was I to Spinks? Not kin. Not even a friend. The paramedic shrugged and they wheeled Spinks out. The ambulance was lit up on Waubeek Street; they loaded in the stretcher and it wailed off.

I went back into the house and turned off the lights. I thought: the cat. I opened the kitchen window partway, filled the cat's food dish, and set out a bowl of water. Then I had to pee. I remembered that

Spinks had used a bathroom in the hall, and it wasn't hard to find: first door on the right. A big room, practically the kitchen's twin, with a curtained window looking out on the backyard and a deep porcelain tub. A silver grab bar ran around the tub and continued to the toilet. There was a white wicker hamper, and a rank of prescription bottles on a shelf above the sink. I was going to see what medications Spinks was taking, but then I noticed something else: a black ring binder, which had been stuffed into the hamper. So it goes in the homes of the old, I thought. I lifted the binder from its nest of towels, and I was going to return it—to where?—when it occurred to me that it might not be there by accident. I looked inside. The binder contained a sheaf of printed-out pages; at the top of the first page, in blue ballpoint, Spinks had written MY LIFE. It was the story he had been telling me. I was baffled, indignant, amused. Spinks must have wanted to give me the impression that he was speaking from memory, but no one's memory was that good, certainly not at Spinks's age. So he'd hidden his notes in a location that he could visit frequently, without arousing my suspicion. Poor vain Spinks, I thought. What if he never came back from the hospital? A stranger would go through his things, and I would never hear the rest of the story. I decided to borrow the binder. I left Spinks's house with it tucked under my arm, and called the hospital, and they told me that Spinks was in stable condition. For an hour, I walked aimlessly around Parry Sound. I took the sunset cruise and saw several dozen of Georgian Bay's thirty thousand islands, dotted with houses where Canadian vacationers could play at being the only people in the world. I ate dinner in the same riverside restaurant and drank three glasses of sauvignon blanc. Finally, I went back to my room and read Spinks's notes.

Without Spinks's voice to animate it, the story was abrupt, like a film in jerky fast-forward:

December 21, 1950. Dinner at B.'s villa in Azcapotzalco.
Chicken with beans and rice, all cooked over charcoal.
A bottle of Burgundy which B. brought back from Paris.
He was there in 1948 to study Mexican mss. in the
Bibliothèque Nationale. A gloomy place, he says. He
has come to think that any place devoted to books is
necessarily gloomy. After dinner B. shows me the
notebook in which HPL composed "The Shadow Out
of Time." HPL's handwriting is small, spidery, thick with
deletions and amendments. It's thrilling: as if I've
followed a river back to its vine-tangled source.
Or its heart of darkness.

Lovecraft's story concerns an economics professor, Peaslee, whose body is possessed by the mind of a member of the Great Race of Yith, a creature from the distant past. After five years, the Yithian departs, and Peaslee embarks on an expedition to Australia, where he discovers a mysterious underground city . . .

Drawn in against my will. Realize: *This is how
transmigration works*. Words take you over. And you may
inhabit others in the form of words. First time I have
seen it so clearly. I put down the notebook in a hurry.

What did Spinks mean? I wondered. Did he believe that books are souls, that writers live on in the bodies of their readers? It seemed like a very Lovecraftian idea of reading, to say the least. But on the other hand, I couldn't feel that he was entirely wrong.

Casually, I ask B. about his friendship with HPL. He tells
me some things I already know, and repeats the line from

his memoir: HPL was a *closet Quetzalcoatl*. What does
that mean? I ask. B. gives me a look. It's a long story, he
says. Then he tells it. Says he loved Howard but Howard
did not love him back. B. has 3 ideas re: HPL. (1) HPL
did love him but was too shy and fearful to express it;
(2) HPL diverted his love into his work; (3) HPL was
incapable of love. B. has believed each of them at one
time or other. He thinks they may all be correct. People
are full of contradictions, he says. Asks if I have read
Alfred Kroeber.

Spinks had come to destroy Lovecraft, but now he wasn't sure he
wanted to. He had to remind himself that Belsen had not been a
dream. There was evil in the world. Without hinting at the purpose
that had brought him to Barlow's villa, he repeated

what Loveman told me re: cyanogen. B. admits that HPL
said some terrible things. B. won't defend him. Thinks
HPL was human, and that, compared to some people,
he did little harm. I say it still seems unjust that he should
be so admired. B. says yes, but remember, Howard isn't
here to enjoy it. His fans are enjoying it, I say. Shouldn't
someone tell them the truth? B. says he felt the same way
after Howard died. When Wandrei and Sam Loveman
spread lies about me, he says, I fully intended to sue
them for defamation of character. Then it occurred to
me that, although I might be able to hurt them, and I
might even enjoy doing so, hurting them would not
restore what I had lost. Howard was dead and his friends
would never welcome me again. I wanted justice, but
what I needed was company.

So: San Francisco, Berkeley, the poets, Kroeber, and, finally, Mexico City. Slowly, Barlow's hunger for justice had waned. He'd even forgiven Derleth, and had sent him all of Howard's manuscripts, except this one, which he kept as an indulgence.

You're not angry? I ask. I'm furious, B. says, but not about that. He says Mexico City College is run by villains who either don't care whether the students are learning anything, or don't want them to know anything that was not known in 1911. This even though many of the students were in the war and know in their scars and bones that the old way of doing things is a ruin. Worse, two of B.'s students are blackmailing him. If he doesn't pay they will expose him as a homosexual. I'll lose my job, B. says, and what then? Who will hire me in manly Mexico, or in America the fearful? But if I *do* pay I condone their vileness. I ask why he is telling me this. B: Because I can trust you. Anyway, what did I just say? People are full of inconsistencies and contradictions. It's no wonder history is so hard to piece together.

December 22, morning. We take the bottle of cognac down to the courtyard. Tile floor, canvas folding chairs. The blue-green air smells of woodsmoke. B. says he is thinking of leaving Mexico City. The Rockefeller Foundation has offered him a job studying Mayan inscriptions in the Yucatán. He giggles. Imagine the look on the Dean's face when I quit! B. is less impressive in the courtyard than he was upstairs, maybe because he's drunk. Still I admire his courage in telling me so much. How can I think about revenge, still? Why can't I be more like B.? I start to cry. B.: What's wrong? Me: I have no idea how to live. B.: A question to which I, too, have given much thought. Me: So, what's the answer? B.: Maybe this. He rises from his chair, kisses me on the mouth. There, he says. Now we've both got what we wanted. I am perplexed. B. clearly doesn't think I wanted to kiss him. Does he know why I came? If so why did he tell me about HPL? I want to ask about this but am afraid. B. is much braver than I am, I think.

The sun comes up and it gets hot in the courtyard. B. gets up, gathers some papers, begins to work. Never enough time, he says. I take a picture of him, shirtless, editing a poem. I don't want to leave. Fear that when the night's spell is broken there will be absolutely nothing left. But in the taxi, on the way to the hotel, I feel that a new life is beginning. I think of Doris.

On the flight back to New York, Spinks flirted with a stewardess. As soon as he'd got his bag through customs, he took the train to Lynbrook and caught a taxi at the station.

Lynbrook, the Friday before Christmas. Everything white and all the identical houses strung with identical lights. Doris's house too. I ring the bell and Tom Owens opens.

He insisted that Spinks stay for dinner. He wanted to meet more of Doris's friends, he said. So they had an awkward meal, macaroni and salad, Doris keeping all the Christmas food in reserve.

Sherry, wine, Scotch. All of us hopelessly drunk by the end of it, emphasize *hopeless*. At the end of the night

Owens tells me in confidence that he is thinking of
moving out. Can you imagine what it's like, living seven
days a week with *that*? he asks, indicating blackboards,
buttons, boxes of leaflets, heaps of typing paper,
ashtrays, books, banners, thumbtacks, and bits of tape,
and not a single dish removed from the drainboard. I say
it sounds terrible. Go on! Owens says. You're not much
of a liar, Spinks. But think twice before you get involved.

On Boxing Day, Spinks called Doris from work.

I tell her I want to run away with her. D. says, Finally!
What do you mean, finally? I ask. Leo, D. says, you were
supposed to ask me eleven years ago.

The question was, where to go? And Spinks thought, why not go back
to Mexico City? He could introduce Doris to Barlow. They were two
of the most remarkable people he'd ever met. He bought tickets on
Aeromexico, for the sixteenth of January, figuring that Doris needed
time to get things in order.

January 15, 1951. I call Barlow to tell him we're coming.
His brother answers. Who is this, he wants to know.
Who is *this*? I ask. After some more of that he tells me
that Robert is dead, almost certainly a suicide. No funeral
to attend—thanks for asking! Ashes interred in a city
park. And me, still with two tickets for the 16th.

15.

Spinks and Doris went to Mexico City. They stayed six nights in the Hotel del Prado; they visited Chapultepec Castle and the Zócalo and the ruins of Tenochtitlán. They made love, finally, but mostly they argued. Doris walked faster than Spinks did. She was always leading him around, always asking men for a light, always flirting with them, or so it seemed to Spinks. She wanted to sketch strangers, which Spinks thought was very rude.

> Finally D. asks me, Leo, have we come here to be free, or
> not? And I say, yes, we have, but not like this. Then like
> what? D. asks.

Spinks didn't know. Barlow's suicide had cast a shadow on his thoughts. He wanted to know how someone so wise could have done something so rash. While Doris went to the National Museum by herself, he returned to Azcapotzalco and met Barlow's secretary, Lieutenant Castañeda, who was busy typing up a report of the circumstances of Barlow's death. Spinks also met the gentlemanly Don Pablo, who had come to collect some books he had loaned Barlow years earlier. Neither of them was surprised by how Barlow's story had ended.

No one asks *how could he have done it?* They grieve but in their sorrow I hear resignation. Confirmation from Rosa, the cook, who hasn't left yet, probably in the hope of collecting further wages. *El señor Barlow,* I ask, in my bad Spanish, *¿Cómo fue? ¿Triste?* Well, I get my meaning across. Rosa nods. *Triste, sí.* I go back up to Barlow's study, to ask Castañeda something (what?) but he is not there. B.'s papers have been sorted into piles: college work here, scholarship there, miscellaneous correspondence on the sofa. It takes only a moment to find the letters HPL wrote to B. I put them in my briefcase and go out.

While Doris went by herself to the opera, Spinks went to see Barlow's friend George Smisor.* He brought a bottle of good mescal, and they talked late into the night. The picture Smisor gave him was of a man who had always known that he would kill himself.

Smisor says B. worked too much. He never let himself rest. But on reflection S. not sure whether that was cause or effect. If S. knew he would die at 40, he might work harder too! Although not as hard as B. did. The truth is that B. accomplished more in his short life than most people do in longer ones.

As to the root cause of Barlow's melancholy, Smisor could only speculate. His homosexuality had something to do with it, but Smisor believed there was another, deeper cause. A long-ago hurt? A loss of

---

* George Smisor (1906–1982) was the head of the microfilm laboratory at the Benjamin Franklin Library in Mexico City, and Barlow's literary executor.

love, a lack? Lovecraft, Spinks thought. What would Barlow have become if Howard had lived a little longer and loved him back? What if Barlow had at least been allowed to keep his place at the head of Howard's estate, and not had it stolen from him by Wandrei and Derleth—could he have lived?

> I wonder if what B. told me re: justice was wrong. After all look what happened to B. Maybe the answer *is* to fight.

Spinks and Doris were certainly fighting. Mexico City was no good for them. Spinks wanted to try their luck in Oaxaca, where there were more painters and fewer people to paint. Doris wanted to go home. Running away wasn't the answer, she said. She pretended that she had *never* thought it was the answer. She missed Margot, her friends, her committees. If they were going to have a life together they would have to make it in New York. So, on January 24, they flew home. Spinks returned to East Fourth Street, and Doris went to Lynbrook. Tom had moved out; he'd taken all the liquor, the car, and the portrait he'd done of her in Florida. "What he wants that for, I don't know," Doris said. She had Margot back, and when Spinks went out there one Friday evening, she would hardly talk to him. Did Margot want a snack? Did she want Mommy to read her a book? Spinks stood uselessly in the living room, holding a bouquet of winter roses. He had an intimation of how Tom must have felt. He went out and hauled some bundles of old newspapers from the garage to the curb. He and Doris and Margot ate leftovers, then Doris put Margot to bed, and Spinks rubbed Doris's shoulders. They made love in what had been Doris's marriage bed, and was now a palimpsest, a bed of many beds, stuffed with ghosts and the ghosts of hopes. Spinks stayed until Monday morning.

So this *was* a new life, he thought. He saw Doris every weekend.

He played Candy Land and Uncle Wiggily with Margot; she called him *Leo*. He built a fence to keep the deer out of Doris's vegetable garden, and she made him coq au vin and raspberry chiffon pie. He and Doris talked about moving together into an apartment in the city. Spinks could afford it. After the memorable sales speech he'd given, he was promoted to an office in General Electric's headquarters in Fairfield, where he was supposed to come up with ways to sell stoves in the farthest corners of the world. It was strange, this path by which he had arrived at his ideal life: truly unforeseeable. But he was happy in it, or at least he would have been, if it weren't for Barlow. Each time Spinks thought about him, he experienced a dull tension, a feeling of there being work to do. Which was appropriate; if Barlow haunted you, it would surely be in the form of a need to work. But what work? Spinks read and reread Barlow's obituaries, his weird stories, his memoir of Lovecraft. With a certain reluctance, he deciphered Lovecraft's letters to Barlow, all three hundred–odd pages of them. If you read between their spidery lines, you could hear the story Barlow had told, of a young man in love with an old writer, and an old writer who couldn't love him back. It was very sad, but not as sad as the stories Barlow had written, which Lovecraft had revised.

> "The Night Ocean" pretends to be a story about how
> little we matter to a world that will go on without us
> but in fact I think it is about how without love we must
> despair. The creature in the ocean is Barlow, and the
> artist on the shore is HPL, looking bleakly at a world
> of delight which he fears to enter.

Spinks wanted to help, but how? Lovecraft was dead and so was Barlow. They could not love; there was nothing for them anymore,

except the desolation of the last lines of "The Night Ocean," which
Spinks had intended to quote to me:

> Silent, flabby things will toss and roll along empty shores,
> their sluggish life extinct. Then all shall be dark, for at
> last even the white moon on the distant waves shall wink
> out. Nothing shall be left, neither above nor below the
> sombre waters. And until that last millennium, as after it,
> the sea will thunder and toss throughout the dismal
> night.

There seemed to be no point in doing anything at all. Then, one Friday
evening, Spinks made a strange acquaintance:

> March 23, 1951. On the train to D.'s house, I sit across
> from a man who looks familiar. Double chin, sad, narrow
> eyes. Realize with a start that it is Whittaker Chambers:
> his face was in all the papers two years ago. He sees me
> looking at him and says sadly, Yes. Tells me he is going to
> see his mother who lives in Lynbrook. He was just in
> New York for a press conference. Alger Hiss has gone to
> prison and the world wants to know what Chambers
> thinks of that. What does he think? Chambers thinks it is
> good, if it makes people aware of the character and
> reality of Communism. But he is afraid it will merely
> make Hiss into a living martyr. He sighs. If only the
> world knew, he says, how much *he* has given up! He had
> a job with *Time* magazine that paid thirty thousand a
> year. But it was his duty to bear witness, he says. He asks:
> Are you a religious man? Me: My father was a Quaker.

Chambers, warmly: As am I. He says secular people can't fight Communism. Doubt cannot prevail over belief. Only belief can prevail. We get off the train together. D. waiting for me with Margot. Jesus, she says, do you know who that was? She covered the Hiss trial for Transradio Press. I say, I know, we talked on the train. About what? D. asks. I say mostly about Quakerism. D: My, Leo, the company you keep.

Soon afterward, for reasons not mentioned in his notes, either because he knew them by heart or because he didn't know them at all, Spinks wrote the *Erotonomicon*.

Explain that at first I have no idea of publishing. Writing the diary is a private act, an act of piety. I start in April, finish in June. Am delighted. I feel that I am doing magic: in a small way I am altering the course of history. I show it to nobody, not even D. Whom could I trust with this most forbidden of books? No one, I think. But the story has its own desires; it wants to be known.

So:

May 19, 1951. In Loveman's shop, leafing through an 1855 issue of the *Revue Spirite*. L. joins me in admiring it. Asks if I am still writing stories. I say I have mostly been reading. Then can't help myself. I found something you might be interested in, I say. And pull a story from the air: I was in Columbus on GE business, I say, & ran into the collector Charles Barrett. He had me to his house in Logan. Motorboat on the lake, steak in the

deep-freezer: an American man of means. Bought from
him a bound vol. of *Weird Tales* which he bought from
Robert Barlow's mother, after B.'s death. And found,
bound into it, a plain notebook, a diary, its entries written
in a spidery hand . . . Guess whose? L.: Howard's. Me:
Correct. His Polished Loathsomeness, in person. And
what a person, Sam! You remember how you told me he
didn't act on his *tendencies?* Well, I'm here to tell you that
he *did*. In this diary of his, which, by the way, he calls the
Erotonomicon, he tells all. If Barrett had thought to *open*
the *WT* volume, instead of sticking it on his custom-
made mahogany bookshelf, all fandom would know by
now who Howard really was. Lucky for us it ended up in
my hands, huh? L.: Can I see the notebook? Me: Sure, I'll
bring it to you. And now I have to produce it. Fortunately
I know a girl named Violet Schmidt, who does
handwriting. I go to a stationers' on East 50th, which
does so little business that it has become a *de facto*
museum of stationery. Buy a few old notebooks, &
bottles of black Skrip ink.

June 24. I have the notebook. It's beautiful. I ring
Loveman up in the evening and he says to meet him at his
shop. It's just the two of us sitting there on stools in semi-
darkness. L. in bifocals, turning pages and sighing. He
doesn't imagine for a moment that the *Erotonomicon*
might be a fake, even though he knew HPL! I am so
impressed by what I've accomplished that I keep quiet.
Figure at worst L. will tell some of Howard's friends and
they'll gossip about it for the rest of eternity. Finally L.
closes the notebook. Frowns. I had no idea that Howard
was so friendly with Hart, he says, but it figures.

Howard didn't tell me the truth about anything. Me: I bet
some of Howard's fans would be interested to know the
truth, though. L., slowly: They might. I suggest that the
two of us print up the *Erotonomicon* in a little book.
Letterpress, limited run. A collector's item. Bind it in
black leather stamped with seals and sigils. It's L. who
finally says, I have a better idea. Me: What's that? L.: Can
you come back tomorrow? There's someone I want you
to meet.

Loveman introduced Spinks to Samuel Roth, the infamous booklegger, whose illegal editions of *Lady Chatterley* and *Tropic of Cancer* he
had been selling under the counter for years.

Describe Roth. Middle fifties? Balding, thin mustache.
Red bow tie and gray pinstriped suit. The look of a
certified accountant and the heart of a fanatic. He talks
for an hour about the novel he just wrote in prison. It's
about a Jew who is best friends with Yeshea, i.e., Jesus.
The Jew is of course Roth under an assumed name. In a
way, he reminds me of Luiza. Are you Jewish? he asks.
Originally, I say.

Roth was wary of Spinks's book. He'd published a novel about homosexuals, *A Scarlet Pansy*, but those were adult homosexuals. Robert Barlow had been a child. Spinks assured him that Barlow had been very
mature for his age,

and anyway, I say, you can't libel the dead. R. not
convinced. Loveman tells him that the book will sell.

He knows two hundred people who will buy it the day it comes out. He talks about how popular HPL is, and how his fans love forbidden books. R. has never heard of HPL and this argument doesn't move him much. I tell him the *Erotonomicon* is a love story. Not because it describes sex acts but because it extends the domain of love to include these difficult people. Because it loves the unlovable. R.: You say this Lovecraft is well known? L.: Very well known. R.: OK, we'll do it, but you have to scholar it up. I go home and add dozens of notes. Takes me a week.

The *Erotonomicon* was published in March 1952. The U.S. Postal Inspection Service declared it obscene three months later, and the police raided Roth's office on Lafayette Street. Spinks was alarmed, but Roth reassured him. He'd been raided before. He'd been to *prison* before. "These are the sacrifices we make in the service of a better world," he told Spinks. "I don't want to go to jail," Spinks said. "Chances are, you never will," Roth said. "Meanwhile, your book is selling like hotcakes! Sam Loveman can't keep it in stock. Don't worry, you're going to come out fine."

Doris said the same thing, more or less. (He'd told her the same story about the *Erotonomicon* as he told Loveman, except that she knew he hadn't been to Ohio, so he said he'd bought the volume of *Weird Tales* through the mail.) "Courage, Leo!" she said. "You told the truth, now let the dogs bark." So Spinks didn't worry. He didn't even worry when Violet Schmidt threatened to expose the *Erotonomicon* as a hoax. He cut her in for ten percent of the royalties, and the problem was taken care of. He didn't need the money, anyway, and he liked the idea that Violet's mother would get a new washer. He even told her which one to buy: a Constructa front-loader. It was German, but he figured that with a name like Schmidt, she wouldn't mind. Then:

July 22, 1952. Two FBI agents visit my office. One looks like a barber and the other like a quarterback. Am I the author of the *Erotonomicon,* they want to know. What do I tell them? They've already raided Roth. I assume they know everything. The editor, I say, and hold out my wrists. The agents laugh. Let's take this one step at a time, the barber says. We want to ask you some questions about your book. He pulls a copy from the pocket of his raincoat. There are some words in here that we don't understand, he says. What's the Ablo Ritual? I am dumbfounded. The barber asks if it's a sex act, and I say yes, it probably is. Barber: A sex act between a white man and a Negro boy? Me: Yes, I think so. Still they don't arrest me. What about this word here, the barber says. Yogge . . . Sothothe, I say. I think it refers to masturbation. Barber: Is that so? What about this here, the Aklo Password? We go through the whole book like that. Thank you, the barber says. Now will you tell us why you wanted to publish this disgusting piece of smut?

He clearly hopes to catch me off guard, but I've had time to think. Me: Gladly. Barber: And? Me: It's simple. I wanted the world to know who HPL really was. I think history will thank me for it. Children should not read the work of such a man. Barber: Huh. Quarterback (first time he's spoken): Hm. Barber: Mr. Spinks, are you a homosexual? Me: I am not. Barber: Are you now or have you ever been a Communist? Me: Are you kidding? I work for General Electric. Quarterback: Answer the question. Me: I am not and have never been. Strangely, the agents seem to believe me. Thanks, Mr. Spinks, the barber says. If we need anything else from you, we'll be back in touch.

Spinks was terrified. He *had* been a Communist. Under John Michel's influence, he'd joined the Young Communist League and got his Party card in the name "Howard P. Fightcraft," a joke that looked all too transparent, in retrospect. He didn't know what the FBI knew, or what they could find out; but he did know that under the McCarran Act, any member or former member of a subversive organization could be deported. He didn't want to go back to Parry Sound. He didn't want to lose his job or stop seeing Doris. He wished he'd never written the *Erotonomicon* and thought about admitting that it was a fake, but he couldn't see how that would help him now. He couldn't see how anything would help.

When August Derleth testified before HUAC, in October, and named names, Spinks assumed that he would be deported. He was so dismayed that he didn't anticipate the obvious result of Derleth's testimony, which was, that his old friends blamed *him:*

> November 20. Letter from Elsie Wollheim: Why on earth did I publish HPL's diary? Do I know that Don has an FBI man sitting in his office at Ace Books? They eat lunch together, and the FBI man asks him to match [Communist] Party names to real people. Don has a lung embolism which she says is my fault. I am the most perfidious person in the history of perfidy, she says. I am worse than Sam Moskowitz, with whom, by the way, Don has become friends.

All the Futurians were ruined. Pohl and Judy Zissman—now a couple—moved to New Jersey and raised chickens. John Michel fled to a tiny town at the edge of the Catskills, where he made table decorations out of wire and glass. Even Asimov was investigated, and nearly lost his job at Boston University. As for Lowndes, who had never shown Spinks anything but kindness:

> November 22. I run into Doc at the Waldorf Cafeteria.
> He can't bring himself to avoid me. Says he is out of
> *Crack Detective*. No one will touch him now that he has
> been questioned by HUAC. He has joined the
> Episcopalian Church and tells me he is thinking of taking
> orders. I ask what Dr. Fish thinks of that. Doc says he
> can't afford to see Dr. Fish. Why did you do it, Leo? he
> asks. I say I never would have, if I had known that
> Derleth would rat us out. I only wanted to tell the
> truth about HPL. The truth! Doc laughs. He sounds
> like a bellows with a hole in it. His asthma is back,
> he says.

The encounter left Spinks hurt, angry, and still afraid. He had underestimated the madness of his age, he thought. He waited for HUAC's subpoena to arrive, but it never did, probably because he wasn't a U.S. citizen. Instead, he got the FBI:

> November 25. Barber and quarterback have more
> questions for me. Did I know that Robert Barlow
> was a Communist sympathizer? Am I sure I was never
> a Communist? Do I know an individual named
> John Michel?

It was easy to guess that Michel had told the FBI about him. Spinks wasn't surprised. All of them—Michel, Wollheim, Pohl, even Doc— had made him out to be the villain all along. He saw no reason to hold back.

> I admit everything. I *was* a Communist. Of course I knew
> Michel. We were in the same chapter of the YCL, the
> Flatbush chapter. But I've repented of that folly, and
> some others, too. Barber: That's good. Now would you
> mind telling us who else was in the Flatbush chapter
> with you?

Spinks named them. It was the opposite of what he'd once dreamed naming might do; instead of bringing people to life, he was condemning them to poverty and oblivion. To which they'd already been condemned, he told himself. Still, Spinks thought he'd sunk to the lowest depths; but the agents weren't finished with him yet.

> Barber: What about Doris Baumgardt? Was she a
> Communist? Me, reluctantly: Don't you already know?
> Quarterback: Answer the question. Me: I'm not sure.
> Barber: You aren't sure if she is? Or if she *was*? Me: I
> think she may have been. She does belong to the
> Levittown Anti-Segregation League. Barber: Thank you,
> Mr. Spinks.

After they left, Spinks wanted to call the FBI and take back what he had said, but he was intelligent enough to know that there was no going back. He would have to fight his way through, which meant thinking of something to tell Doris. He thought about it all night. His best course of action, he decided, was to admit that he had been afraid, but he never got the chance to take it.

> November 26, 1952. 7:05 train to Lynbrook. D. not at
> the station. I take a cab to her house. D. won't let me in.
> Shouts, Go away, you traitor, you creep! Please, I say, let
> me explain. D.: No! Me: Please! *Ad absurdum*. Or rather
> thrice. Then D.: I'm calling Tom! Because she can't call
> the police. In her estimation the police are now on my
> side. I walk back to the station because my cab has
> already left. The next day—which happens to be U.S.
> Thanksgiving—I have a cold.

Spinks wrote her a letter. Michel was the one who had given the FBI her name, he said. He asked her to call him, so they could talk things through. He waited a week, a month. Almost exactly two years after he first asked Doris to run away with him, he wrote again. He'd made a terrible mistake, he said. Could she forgive him? He loved her! He'd only ever wanted to stay in the United States, to be near her. He would retract everything. He'd quit his job and picket GE headquarters. This time he got an answer:

> Dear L. C. Spinks,
>
> I no longer wish to have anything to do with you. It's
> none of your business, but I'll tell you anyway: no one
> has ever managed to betray me as viciously as you have
> just betrayed me, or to wound me more deeply than you
> have just wounded me. Do not attempt to contact me. If
> I see you anywhere near my house, or my child, I'll shoot

you myself. It would be worth the probable consequences.

Spinks couldn't help but marvel at the wording. *Do not attempt to contact me.* Clark Ashton Smith had written almost the same thing to Barlow, fourteen years earlier. Spinks was devastated, but at the same time, he felt that his life was converging with Barlow's in a way that he didn't entirely understand.

General Electric fired Spinks in February 1953. They said he was a danger to the safety of company property—as if he might sabotage one of their indestructible stoves! Spinks wondered what he was supposed to do next. Retreat, like Barlow, to some remote place and study a vanished civilization? He knew how that story ended. No. Spinks would fight. It was too late to save anyone else, but at least he could save himself. He wrote an article for *Galaxy,* denouncing Lovecraft, and another for the Red-baiting magazine *Confidential,* which he placed with the help of Whittaker Chambers. He attended a cocktail party at William F. Buckley's apartment on the Upper East Side, where he met Walter Winchell. He spoke passionately about the things he'd seen in the war and the dangers of anti-Semitism. He had the idea that he was doing what Barlow ought to have done. He felt Barlow's soul in him, urging him on. Writing the *Erotonomicon* hadn't been an exorcism, he realized. It had been an invitation.

16.

From 1953 to 1954, Spinks moved in strange circles. He dined with Winchell at the Stork Club and said hello to Roy Cohn when he stopped by their table. He saw Cohn again at the 21 Club, where he was eating dinner with George Sokolsky, a columnist for the Hearst papers:

> Cohn invites me to join them for a drink. To my
> amazement, he says he read my article in *Confidential*.
> Terrific stuff, he says. We can't let our kids read this pro-
> queer crap. Right, Sok? Go get 'em, Roy, Sokolsky says.
> Cohn points at me with the butt of his spoon. What you
> gotta do, he says, is broaden your approach. You nailed
> Lovecraft, OK, great. Don't stop there. Who were his
> friends? Did he know Hammett? Or what's her name,
> Kay Boyle? Me: I don't think so. Cohn: So, who? Me:
> Well, there's Clark Ashton Smith. Cohn: Never heard of
> him, but OK. Me: And . . . Lovecraft exchanged letters
> with Robert E. Howard. Cohn: The *Conan* guy? It figures.
> You gotta go after them all, get 'em off the fucking
> shelves. Me: How? Cohn: Sok? Sokolsky: I could help you
> out, sure.

The next thing Spinks knew, he was writing for Hearst about "perverted horror" and the need to get the works of Dunsany and Machen and even Poe out of North American libraries. He was amazed by the response he got. It wasn't just from anti-Communists like Buckley and Cohn; ordinary people all over America sent him letters, thanking him for telling the truth about those terrible books, which were giving their children bad dreams. He became a regular in the Stork Club's exclusive Cub Room. He and Cohn and Cohn's friend David Schine took a weekend trip to Montauk, where they ate fried clams and drank beer, and Schine picked up a waitress. They drove back to Manhattan drunk, and when the cops pulled them over, Cohn talked to them gently, and the cops vanished.

Was this what Barlow's spirit wanted Spinks to do? He thought maybe it was. Live, he told himself, live as much as possible! The problem was that the more he lived—the more he drank, the more notable people he met, the more places he visited—the more Spinks felt unreal. It was as if there were some inverse proportion between reality and experience. Who was he at the Stork Club? In Washington, DC? In Spokane, where he gave a speech on Wholesome Horror to the American Book Publishers Council? Was he Barlow, or Spinks, or some completely other person, who was often hung over and always tired, who had trouble moving his bowels and woke up at four in the morning, night after night, terrified of an unspecified event which somehow never happened?

To anchor himself in the world, Spinks returned to the faith not of his fathers, but of his father. He went regularly to Quaker meetings at the Society of Friends on Fifteenth Street, and although the spirit did not move him to speak, he felt buoyed by the familiarity of the meetinghouse. He could almost imagine that he was a child again, sitting with Walter Spinks while gentle, frowsy people stood up to bear witness in a language he did not yet entirely speak. As soon as he left, though, he felt dizzy, as if he'd gone too long without eating—which, sadly for his waistline, was never really the case. He told Cohn about his problem, and Cohn sent him to his doctor, who gave him a shot of vitamin B_{12}. That, too, made Spinks feel better for a while. But:

> January 19, 1954. In Providence for a conference of Writers for Freedom. The usual talk on the Lovecraft Cult, &c. Afterward, restless in my room at the Biltmore. Out for a walk, and, naturally, up College Hill. Without meaning to I find my way to HPL's old house at 66 College Street. Someone has scratched COMMIE QUEER in the door's green paint. Signs too of something white—toilet paper?—having mostly been scrubbed off the sidelight windows. Well. Justice. But I can't help thinking that Barlow would not have been pleased. I walk until dawn, & stand on Prospect Terrace, overlooking the statehouse dome & the red and black city. No sensation of beauty, only of loss.

That Sunday, Spinks went to the Society of Friends as usual.

> January 24. Stand up in meeting & try to talk about what happened in Providence. I have a friend who believes some terrible things, I say. He told me about them in confidence, but I couldn't keep his secret, and now my friend's friends have turned on him. I ask the meeting, did I do right, or wrong? Then I get into this bit about the name *Providence* and how perhaps everything that happens is right because it accords with the divine plan. It sounds very abstract, even to me. The silence after I sit down is ordinary but devastating.

Spinks went on with his campaign to save the world from the horrors of Lovecraft. In February, he wrote an essay for the *Saturday Evening Post,* in which he let all the horror writers have it, all the disciples, all the villains. As usual, grateful letters from parents and clergymen flooded in. Librarians were taken to task—and what about comic books? Spinks's readers wanted to know. *Tales from the Crypt* was full of gore and queer innuendo. Shouldn't somebody do something? The public's enthusiasm for wholesome horror was gratifying, but Spinks was finding that kind of gratification less and less sufficient. Had he done right? Had he done wrong? He went to see Loveman, who had been totally unaffected by the *Erotonomicon* scandal; indeed, he was still selling copies of the *Erotonomicon* under the counter of his shop. Spinks wanted Loveman to absolve him— he wanted Loveman to say he'd done what a poet would do. But, in fact:

> L. will hardly talk to me. Says he's in a hurry, he has to
> meet a friend for lunch. Who? I ask. Just a friend, L. says.
> First time he has ever failed to mention the name of one
> of his friends. I hang around the shop for ten minutes,
> buy a first edition of Besant's *Thought Forms.* L. wraps it
> up, and asks me not to come back. He doesn't want any
> trouble, he says. I walk up to Union Square. A loudspeaker
> truck blares Give, give to Israel. I stop at a newsstand to
> pick up the *Journal-American* and browse the paperbacks.
> Ray Bradbury has a new book, *Fahrenheit 451.* And in a
> tawdry Ace double, *Junkie: Confessions of an Unredeemed
> Drug Addict.* So much for wholesome horror, I think. Leaf
> through it. To my amazement, it's by Bill.* Give, give to
> Israel! I sit on a bench. I have accomplished nothing.

---

* Spinks doesn't mention it, but *Junkie* was published by Donald Wollheim. Another of those coincidences that make fact as rich and as strange as fiction, I guess.

Ten days later, Spinks wrote to Don Pablo Martínez del Río, inviting him to expose the hoax. That summer, he left New York for the last time and returned to Parry Sound.

> May 24, 1954. I climb the steps to this house which I shall never really leave again. Charlotte is just getting out of the bath. Leo, you're so fat! she says. It's good that you came home, you were letting yourself go in New York. She strokes my cheek. Her love is more forgiving than forgiveness itself, and more terrible, too.

The hardware store was long gone, so Spinks went into the appliance-repair business. At least there he knew what he was about. Charlotte put him on a diet, and he went on and off it. He swam in the summer and skated in the winter. He slept nine or ten hours a night. Even so, he didn't feel any more real in Parry Sound than he had in New York. What he felt, more and more, was angry. He'd tried to bear witness, and what happened? The United States had made him into a monster. Yes, that was what he had become: it was like at the end of Lovecraft's story "The Outsider," where the hero looks in the mirror and realizes that the horror is *him*. But what else could Spinks have become? On the day he read his story to the Arisians, he'd lost the chance to be anything else. It was maddening. He had tried to *speak,* but the idiocy of those kids was too strong for him. The American id could not be educated, Spinks thought. It needed horror in order to stay awake and to justify its most pleasureful pursuit, the destruction of helpless people who had never done anything wrong.

> America is truly Lovecraft's country: fearful because it cannot love.

Spinks wanted to set the record straight about Lovecraft and Barlow, but if he spoke out, who would believe him? For many years, he fixed radios and washing machines and television sets. But something was coalescing slowly in the innocent air of Parry Sound; a thought was taking shape. If L. C. Spinks was unreal, then who could say he was really Spinks? Who was really anyone? Souls were words.

No reality but in books.

So Spinks hit on the idea of telling the true story of Lovecraft and Barlow, but *not as himself*. He would have to become the one person whose knowledge of the story no one could doubt. He tried on the name *Barlow* the way a transvestite might try on a stocking. Then the other leg, then the dress, the makeup, the wig. It took him years to master the facts of Barlow's complicated life, but it gave him an enormous, private satisfaction. He was proving the power of love to the only audience that could still hear him, i.e., to himself. In the privacy of his study on Waubeek Street, he demonstrated that with great love and hard work and enormous attention to detail it was possible to bring a human being back to life. It was a kind of reincarnation: an invitation to Barlow's soul to possess Spinks's living flesh once and for all. He didn't dare to hope that someone would discover his new identity, but he did dream of it: of the day when he would be able to tell the truth. He owed that much to Barlow's memory, and to Wollheim and Lowndes and Pohl and even to sneaky Michel. Most of all he owed it to Doris Baumgardt, who had died of lung cancer in 1970, at the age of forty-nine.

17.

was up all night, reading. In the morning, I took a cab to the West
Parry Sound Health Centre. Spinks was in a semi-private room, the
other half of which was unoccupied. He lay propped up on a hospital
bed, wearing an oxygen mask. His eyes were closed. In his blue hospital gown, he looked smaller than he had the day before, and I had the
strange thought that telling his story had literally shrunken him, as if
he had parted not only with words but with his own substance. His
arms were thin and mottled. Strands of dyed hair clung to his forehead. I sat down by his bed, prepared to wait until he woke up, but he
must not have been sleeping, because he opened his eyes right away.
"Hi," I said. "You scared me yesterday. Are you all right?" Spinks slipped
the mask down over his chin. "Don't do that!" I said. "It's all right,"
Spinks said. "I can breathe on my own for a few minutes." "I brought
you flowers," I said. I'd bought them in the hospital gift shop, an after-
thought. "How kind," Spinks said. "Put them over there." He pointed
at the radiator. I thought of how my grandfather's hospital room had
looked by the end, how there wasn't room for another carnation, another card. Here, there was nothing. How happy Spinks must have
been, I thought, when Charlie called him up out of the blue. I, too,
might have impersonated someone, just to have the company. "How

are you?" I asked. "I have a pulmonary fibrosis," Spinks said. "It's not new, but it does seem to have gotten worse." "Are you taking steroids?" I asked. "They should have you on steroids." "Thank you, Dr. Willett," Spinks said. "I'm sure if my doctor thinks steroids would be a good idea, he'll prescribe them." I blushed. "Did he say how long you'll be here?" "Two or three days," Spinks said. "Can you stay? I want to tell you the rest of my story." I thought about informing Spinks that I had already read the rest of his story, but decided not to. "I'll try," I said. "If you can't stay, then you'll have to come back," Spinks said. "Provided I'm still here!" "OK," I said, "let's see what your doctor says." "Good idea," Spinks said. He put his mask on again and closed his eyes.

I sat there, watching him breathe. Now that I knew his story, it was hard for me to hate Spinks, or to fear him. It was true that he'd done terrible things, in the distant past and in the recent past, too, but mostly I felt sorry for him. He'd so rarely been happy or loved. Except by Charlotte—and by her, too much. In his way, Spinks had even tried to be good. He wanted to help the Futurians, and Luiza, and Doris; it wasn't his fault that the world's currents had wrecked him on the rocks when he was just a child. The person he ought to have been was Levente Rozen, and I couldn't entirely blame him for impersonating Barlow. After the age of four, his whole life had been an impersonation. Poor Levente! He never had a chance. Strange to say, I was angry *for* him.

After maybe five minutes, Spinks opened his eyes. "You're still here," he said. "Yup," I said. "Why?" he asked. "Why what?" I said. "Why are you here?" I thought about it. There were many things I still wanted to know, but none of them explained why I was sitting by L. C. Spinks's hospital bed, watching him sleep. Nor did I really expect to learn them from Spinks anymore. The story was over, I thought, but the person was still there. He deserved something. "I didn't want to leave you alone," I said. Spinks reached out with surprising speed and took hold of my hand. His grip was as strong as ever. "Thank you," he said. Then he lay back and closed his eyes again. He was still holding my hand. I let him hold it until the nurse, Denise, came in. "Why, hello," she said, "you must be family!" "Just a friend," I said. "Dr. Willett is one of my admirers," Spinks said. "Look, she brought me flowers!" "Aren't those pretty," Denise said. "I'll get a vase so they don't wilt."

My flight didn't leave until the next morning. I took a cab back to my B&B and looked at the flyers downstairs for local attractions. Each looked more dismal than the last. I had used Parry Sound up; now I wished I could fall asleep and not awaken until it was time to leave for the Toronto airport, but I wasn't tired. With a feeling of total arbitrariness, as if I were a molecule bouncing through the humid August air, I walked up Gibson Street, toward the center of town. There were two bookstores on Seguin Street, one new and one used. The used one looked more inviting, so I went in. On a whim, I asked the gray-ponytailed manager whether she had *The Book of the Law of Love*. She made a face. "I think we got rid of it," she said, "but if not, it will be in local history." She pointed me to a slim section between Spirituality and Gardening. Charlie's book was, indeed, not there, which was just as well. I leafed through *Up the Great North Road: The Story of an Ontario Colonization Road*, by John Macfie, who had compiled a great deal of information on the subject. "It was Man against Nature in its most primary form," the introduction told me, "bareknuckled roadbuilders and homesteaders attempting to transform a rugged landscape containing the most ancient rock on the continent." I wondered if that was really the most primary form the contest could take. What about the contest between a person and his own nature? What about the ancient rock of the id? Stop analyzing, I told myself. I put *Up the Great North Road* back and pulled out another book, also by John Macfie. Half the books in the local history section were by him, I realized, with wonder. After three days, I thought the town had nothing more to tell me, but here was someone who had found in it an inexhaustible supply of stories, about loggers and homesteaders and trappers and ships and fires and weather and Indians and trains. And wars: I opened *Sons of the Pioneers: Memories of Veterans of the Algonquin Regiment,* and glanced at the table of contents. Spinks's story was not listed, which wasn't surprising; he'd only served in the Algonquins for a short time. But Horace Tudhope was there, good old Horace Tudhope, the weaselly kid who'd picked fights and burned up Germans in a flamethrowing tank. I read his story. Spinks wasn't in it anywhere. With a little flutter of anxiety I flipped to the index. No Spinks, L. C.

I took the book to the register. "Is John Macfie alive?" I asked. I pronounced it *Mac-FIE* and the manager corrected me: *Mac-FEE.* "He is," she said. "He came in just the other day." "He lives in Parry Sound?" I asked. "Yes," the manager said. Of course he did. I went outside and found his phone number on the Internet. A woman answered. "Hi," I said, "I'm trying to reach John Mac-FEE." "Oh," she said, "John!" He came on. I told him that I was the widow of the man who had written *The Book of the Law of Love,* and that I'd just spoken with L. C. Spinks. He took a moment to understand what I was talking about, then he asked, "What can I do for you?" Everyone here is so helpful, I thought. "Mr. Spinks was telling me about his life," I said. "He said he was discharged from the Algonquin Regiment for shooting at a German U-boat, in Newfoundland. I was wondering if you know anything about that?" "No," Macfie said. "I've never heard that story before." I'd been walking as we talked, and now I found myself on James Street, which was closed to traffic for a festival. There was almost no one in the street, though, just a few lonely booths offering to check your blood pressure or sell you cell phone service. "Well," I said, "do you think it could have happened, anyway?" "It's not why he was discharged," Macfie said. "There was another reason for that." "Which is?" I asked. Macfie hesitated. "I wonder if it would be easier to talk about this in person," he said. An impossible red vehicle rolled past, a cart pedaled by a dozen people all wearing the same aqua T-shirt. The back of each shirt read TOGETHER WE CAN. I have no idea what was on the front.

Macfie lived at the other end of town, in a white ranch house with a steepish front yard. He was wearing a yellow T-shirt, cargo shorts, and slippers with socks. He was as old as Spinks, but tall, rangy, rumpled, and in better shape. He showed me to his office, which was in the basement, a chilly low room cluttered with photographs, farm implements, glass telephone resistors (I asked), and other tangible evidence of Parry Sound's past. He showed me a photograph of the Algonquins at Camp Borden and pointed out Spinks in the second row. "There's your man," he said. "He was discharged because he was a homosexual. I think they caught him fooling around with a First Nations boy up in Thunder Bay." "No," I said, "that can't be right. He was married to a woman named Luiza. He met her in Europe, at the end of the war, and brought her back to Parry Sound." "I'd be very surprised if Leo Spinks was ever married," Macfie said. "She was a redhead," I said. "A teacher, from Budapest. She gave French lessons!" "I've never heard of any such person," Macfie said. "But here, I dug this up." He handed me a manila folder labeled PARRY SOUND UFO HOAX. It held two tawny newspaper clippings about exactly that: in the winter of 1938, a local youth had frightened the town's residents by driving around with a loudspeaker, announcing that invaders from Mars had landed by the Nobel munitions plant and were heading south. The youth was, of course, L. C. Spinks. The article noted that he'd made the loudspeaker himself, by taking apart his parents' radio. "He's always been like that," Macfie said. "Kind of a pain in the ass, pardon my French. I worked for the Forest Service, after the war. Leo would haul old tires out to a clearing in the middle of God knows where and set them on fire, and we'd have to send our trucks out for nothing. Things like that. We had a big carnival for the town centennial, in 1967, and he sneaked in a day early and set off all the fireworks. Leo's one of those fellows that can't take anything seriously." Macfie reflected. "Maybe because he never fit in here," he said. "Being, you know. Liking men." "Plus, he was adopted," I said. "That can't have helped." Macfie just looked at me. "Where'd you get that idea?" "Oh, no," I said.

Macfie tried to interest me in his wife's homemade jam cookies, but I said I wasn't feeling well. I walked back to the center of town, through the festival, and continued on to Spinks's house. The front door had locked itself, so I climbed through the kitchen window. The room smelled of dust and cat food, which the cat hadn't touched. Probably it had gorged itself on birds. I went into Spinks's study and switched on the light. Three black bookcases lined the room's far wall, and dozens of books were stacked on the desk and on the floor, next to a ratty green armchair. I looked at the ones on the desk first. Ben Shepard, *After Daybreak: The Liberation of Belsen 1945*. Joanne Reilly, *Belsen: The Liberation of a Concentration Camp*. Leslie Hardman, *The Survivors*. G. L. Cassidy, *Warpath: the Algonquin Regiment from Tilly-la-Campagne to the Kusten Canal*. John Macfie, *Sons of the Pioneers*. Whittaker Chambers, *Witness*. The books were all there; or, rather, I thought, everything was books. Histories of Greenwich Village and Mexico City and the Futurian Literary Science Society and the First World Science Fiction Convention and the integration of Levittown. Books by and about Wollheim and Pohl and Asimov and Kornbluth and Doc Lowndes and Samuel Roth and William S. Burroughs. S. T. Joshi's biography of H. P. Lovecraft in two volumes and the five volumes of Lovecraft's *Selected Letters* and a thick green volume of his letters to Barlow. The *Obras de Robert H. Barlow*, eight volumes in Spanish, and a study of Barlow's weird fiction and poetry, and a half dozen volumes of reminiscences of Lovecraft by friends and fans, and what looked like a complete run of the journal *Lovecraft Studies* and a few worn volumes of Barlow's journal *Tlalocan*. There was even a book about Diego Rivera, and a book about Trotsky in Mexico. The amount of time Spinks must have spent preparing for his roles was staggering. *Roles:* first Barlow, then L. C. Spinks. Oh, he'd told me a horror story, all right. The horror was that I had believed it. I'd entered into it as if it were real life, and now what I felt was a great dying-off. All the people who had talked and fought and loved in my imagination for the last three days were vanishing back into the pages of the books from which they had been summoned; they were turning to mere bits of black ink on yellowed pages, lifeless and faceless and impossible to keep in mind.

If Spinks's only crime had been to bring all those people to life, only to let them die like that, I would never have forgiven him for it. But there was worse. Impelled by a desire for completeness, which, I think, I must have learned from Charlie, I woke up Spinks's computer. The browser was open on the big old monitor, and it displayed a page I'd seen all too many times: my professional home page. Spinks had visited all my links. He'd read my biography and my publications. He had searched for my grandparents. Creepy, I thought, then I understood what it meant. Spinks had prepared his role with me in mind. He'd told a story that *I* of all people would be likely to believe, because it touched on things I knew about, and loved. He'd seen Belsen because he knew it would move me; he'd invented Luiza and then married her on my account. I wondered what else he'd done for me. Had he loved Doris Baumgardt because he thought I'd enjoy a love story? Had he gone to New York because I lived there? The more I thought about it, the more everything crumbled to dust: Doris and New York and my grandparents and the entire world. I cried out with horror then, and ran down the hall, out of that evil house, into the street where it was already dark.

Downtown, the festival was turning into something new, a block party for tourists and cottagers. I found a taxi on the edge of it and went back to the hospital. Visiting hours were over, but I told the floor nurse I'd forgotten something and went into Spinks's room before she could object. Denise was there, taking his blood pressure. My flowers stood by the black window. "Hey," Denise said, "you can't be in here now." "Yes, I can," I said, "I'm a doctor!" I sat by Spinks's bed, and in my calmest and most therapeutic voice, I said, "I talked to John Macfie. He told me there was no such person as Luiza." "I'm calling security," Denise said. "He didn't know her," Spinks said through the mask. "She kept to herself." "Leo, I looked in your study," I said. "I know you made everything up." "No, I didn't," Spinks said. "You never went to Belsen," I said. "You weren't married. I'm guessing that you weren't in love with Doris Baumgardt, either. Why did you tell me all that?" Spinks said something, but it was lost in the noise of Denise consulting with the floor nurse. He looked confused and scared. It was an expression I'd seen before: the one he'd worn when the TV reporter cornered him outside the hospital. It was also, I realized, how he'd looked when Edward Murrow interviewed him sixty years ago. "You don't have to be afraid," I said. "You can tell me. I'm listening." I wanted to scream at Spinks, or just to run away and spend the rest of my life trying to forget that I had ever met him, but I needed his answer: I needed to touch bottom. With the feeling that I would pay for it later in ways I did not yet understand, I took Spinks's hand. "Here I am," I said. It was as if something settled in his chest, a scared bird. He whispered into his mask. I took it off. "I hated them," Spinks said. "Who?" I asked. "Hated them," Spinks repeated. "I heard you," I said. "Who did you hate?" Spinks looked at me. His eyes were big and soft. "All of you," he said. "Everyone in the world." The security guard put her hand on my shoulder. "You have to go," she said. "Right now." "I'm going," I said, and left.

VI.

THE NAVEL OF
THE DREAM

1.

I don't know the true story of L. C. Spinks's life, just the facts about him. Here are a few: He was born to Walter and Charlotte Spinks, of Parry Sound, Ontario, on July 9, 1923. He attended the Parry Sound High School, where he got fairly good marks. He played defense for the Shamrocks, the Parry Sound junior hockey team. He published twenty issues of a fan magazine called *Pickman's Vault*. In September 1940, he enlisted in the Algonquin Regiment, and he was dishonorably discharged two years later. He returned to Parry Sound and repaired small appliances. In 1952, Spinks published the *Erotonomicon* and was briefly famous as an anti-Communist crusader and champion of "wholesome horror." He lived for a time in New York—not on East Fourth Street, so far as I can tell; more likely he stayed at the Statler Hotel, next to Penn Station. His hoax was unmasked by Don Pablo Martínez del Río in the summer of 1954, and I doubt very much that Spinks had anything to do with it. When I look at the pictures of him from that era, at dinner parties with Roy Cohn and Whittaker Chambers and so on, I see the person Spinks wanted to be: handsome and jovial and sociable; above all, *seen*. I bet he never wanted to go home. But he did; in the summer of 1954, he was back in the house on Waubeek Street, with Charlotte. For decades nothing happened. Then

Charlotte died, and Spinks inherited enough money that he didn't have to work. He closed up his business. He bought a lot of books. In 1991, he legally changed his name to Robert Barlow, although most people in town still knew him as Leo Spinks. So far as I know, he is still alive.

I can find no evidence that Spinks and Barlow ever met. They probably knew *of* each other, through the small world of Lovecraft fandom. Spinks surely heard that Barlow had run off with Lovecraft's papers, and he probably heard the rumor Samuel Loveman was spreading, that Barlow was gay. It would have been easy for him to find out that Barlow lived in Mexico and what he was doing there. What a dream that must have seemed, to Spinks. Not only did Barlow have lovers, but he was living an adventuresome life in a foreign country, far from his mother. I imagine Spinks on a winter night in Parry Sound, starving for what he thought Barlow had: sun and boys and the world's respect . . . But I am not going to give Spinks more life than he already took. Back to the facts. It *is* likely that Spinks met Donald Wollheim, not in New York, but in Toronto, at the Sixth World Science Fiction Convention, in 1948. What happened there, I don't know. I called up Wollheim's daughter, Betsy, and asked if her father had ever talked about L. C. Spinks. She told me that her father had, indeed, mentioned him. Decades after it had been forgotten by nearly everyone else, Wollheim was still angry about the *Erotonomicon* hoax, which had nearly cost him his job and his health; but in his more philosophical moments, he acknowledged that the FBI would probably have investigated him anyway. He didn't renounce Communism until the mid-1950s. I asked Betsy if she knew why Spinks might have perpetrated the hoax, but she had no idea. Her father had only ever spoken of Spinks as an *idiot* and a *jerk*.

Donald Wollheim, Betsy said, was remarkably unprejudiced against gay people, but Spinks might not have seen it that way. And, prejudiced or not, Wollheim was notoriously prickly. I imagine Spinks meeting him in Toronto: A pass. A snub. A snicker. Then years of revenge. To make so many people pay such a high price for so little seems inhuman, but Spinks *was* inhuman. He was a biographical vampire, a person who stole other people's lives because he had no life of his own. What made him that way? Charlotte's smothering love, or Walter's chilly pacifism—if he was, really, a pacifist? I don't know, and I'm trying very hard not to care.

2.

I went back to my practice after Labor Day, but I was haunted by the feeling that nothing was true. My patients talked and talked, but I couldn't hear the reality in what they said, the ancient rock. They were animated stories that had spun themselves up out of nothing, which might return to nothing at any moment; and I was reading to them from a list of things a psychiatrist might say. The entire world was a story told by L. C. Spinks: a planet-sized hoax, which he'd cobbled together from books, and told, and was telling, for obscure and hateful reasons of his own. The only thing I was certain of was that no story would lead me to my husband. He was gone, sunk in the muck at the bottom of a lake in western Massachusetts. I boxed up his things and put them in storage: I wasn't ready to give them away, yet.

I talked to my therapist about my Spinks thoughts, and she suggested I follow them back into the past, where, as we both knew, I'd find the old story: my father vanishes and comes home six months later, and I am left to wonder whether anyone can be trusted. And how did that make me feel? I tried to do as she said, but it didn't help. My father is not the answer to Spinks's riddle. Nothing in my life is. I thought it might be helpful to write down all the things Spinks told me in Parry Sound, and I have done so, checking my facts as I go, even though I no longer trust facts, and in a way, I no longer even believe in them; but writing has only made me aware that, beneath my fear of unreality, there lies another, deeper fear. What if Spinks has taken me over? By means of words, I mean. I certainly spent enough time listening to him. What if, by listening, I let Spinks into my mind, into my body—what if he lives on in *me?* I can't help noting that in Lovecraft's novel *The Case of Charles Dexter Ward,* the character who finally defeats the evil magus Joseph Curwen is a physician named Marinus: Marinus, Marina. *Mwahaha.* I've talked to my therapist about this, of course. She expresses concern. Could my fear of being possessed by Spinks be related to some earlier incident which we haven't analyzed? Do I want to try an antidepressant? I don't know, maybe not just yet. For the time being, I am still hoping to defeat Spinks on my own, even if there is no real way to defeat him, and no real Spinks to defeat . . . But ssh, Marina. *Write!*

In December, I got an email from Lila. She hadn't found Charlie's notebook—nice of her to tell me!—but she *did* find a strange number in her phone bill, which turned out to belong to Jessica Ng, the woman who picked Charlie up outside the hospital. Lila saw this as a major clue. Charlie must have arranged for Jessica to meet him, maybe with a change of clothes. Then they left Charlie's old clothes by the shore of Agawam Lake and went off somewhere together: a conclusion that was *supported* (Lila's word) by the fact that Jessica wasn't returning her calls. Lila's thinking seemed delusional to me. Sure, Charlie might have arranged for Jessica to pick him up, although you couldn't dismiss the possibility that her appearance that night had been a coincidence. But would the two of them really have run off together, and stayed away for a year, in hiding, in silence? Fool me once, I thought, and I wrote back to say thank you, but please don't investigate any further on my behalf. Still, out of a desire for completeness, I emailed Eric to ask if he could tell me anything about Jessica Ng. This time it was

Grace who replied: *Marina, you have to let go. Remember how Charlie was, at the end. Remember that whole thing about William S. Burroughs's gas station receipt?* I wrote back: *I know, but can Eric answer my question anyway?* Eric sent me a link to Jessica Ng's page on the Book of Dead Faces, which I could have found on my own in two seconds. She was a pudgy post-teen in bulbous black sunglasses, enjoying some kind of happy life in Santa Fe. Her interests were spirituality and film and nonviolent video games. Not a word about Charlie. I messaged her, but she didn't reply.

A couple of days later, my family took its annual vacation. My father booked us rooms in a fancy hotel at the north end of Miami Beach, far from the shops but close to the water. The weather was cool and windy, but my relatives went through the motions of swimming in the hotel pool, running on the footpath by the beach, drinking tropical drinks on the terrace. It had been almost a year since Charlie went into the lake, but they still treated me with more kindness than I wanted or could do anything with. My brothers, ordinarily loud and obnoxious, spoke quietly when I was around, or looked reflectively at their BlackBerrys. My father wanted to take me sailing; fortunately, the weather didn't cooperate. My mother urged me to get a massage, a salt scrub, a back facial. She wanted to take me on a tour of the Art Deco houses of South Beach, but I demurred. My grandmother didn't do much of anything, which was a relief. She had brought along an enormous hardback thriller, and, day by day, she lay fully dressed on a beach chair by the pool and worked her way through it. I kept her company, me and *Daniel Deronda,* which I couldn't read. But I liked being near my grandmother. She held out the possibility that there was happiness, or at least contentment, on the far side of grief.

So I felt almost betrayed when, one night, as we were finishing our salmon (which we ordered instead of shrimp or lobster out of respect for my grandmother, who, I think, could not have cared less), she, my grandmother, leaned across the table and took my hand. "It's sad to see you doing so little with your vacation, Marina," she said. "What do you mean?" I asked. "I mean that we've been here for five days, and you haven't even put on a bathing suit!" my grandmother said. It was true. I'd gained some weight and I felt self-conscious about it; anyway, the weather was too cold for swimming. "Marina can do what she wants," my mother said, forgetting that she'd had her own designs on my time. "Of course she can," my grandmother shot back, "but doesn't she want to *meet* anybody?" We all stared at her. "Come on, Ma," my father said. "Give Marina a break." "Well, I'm sorry," my grandmother said. "Marina, I love you. I just don't want you to be lonely." "I love you, too," I said. "I'm just not ready to meet anyone new." "That's all right," my grandmother said, "but you don't want to get to *my* age and have nobody! Don't you want children?" The anguish in her voice ignored the fact that I have two brothers who are both likely to reproduce. It came from someplace else, someplace older. It made me think that the difference between me and my grandmother, in terms of anguish, was that she mostly hid it better than I did. "Let's talk about something else," my father said. "Who wants to rent a Jet Ski with me tomorrow?" "Nobody," my mother said. "Don't shut me down, Ellen," my father said.

As soon as the meal was over, I went outside. It was a windy night, and the tops of the palms were hissing around, like they were grabbing for something. The ocean was frothy and faintly luminescent. There weren't a lot of people out, on account of the weather, just a pair of late-night joggers and a couple of kids who were making something weird out of driftwood. I took off my shoes and walked down to the waterline. I let the white surf cover my still-pale feet. There was a jellyfish-warning flag up by the lifeguard station, and sure enough, there they were, the jellyfish, translucent blobs stranded at the high-water mark, and floating, as I saw, when my eyes adjusted to the darkness, on the inky blue water. The night ocean, I thought. And the *silent, flabby things* that will still be here when all of us are gone. Against my will, I thought again about L. C. Spinks. If he had really hated everyone, as he said, how could he have imagined them all so warmly? I wondered if his final words to me were also an act, if he had merely pretended to hate everyone because he thought that was what I wanted to hear. I wondered if there was love underneath his hatred, and underneath the love, a terrible loneliness. He was someone who had never found his kind, possibly because there wasn't anyone like him. No wonder he'd thought the only place you could find life was in books. But, ugh, there I was, analyzing Spinks again. I told myself, Let him go. He's just a jellyfish, waiting to sting whoever comes by. Not evil so much as inhuman. I remembered what Charlie had said when we met on the East River promenade: that Spinks had started again from zero, and that it had worked. He'd been partly right, I thought, gloomily. Spinks *was* zero. He was whatever he made up. I thought again about that September afternoon, the next-to-last time I saw my husband: wind coming off the river, dogs sniffing around, the waves hoisting plastic scraps onto the slimy black rocks of Manhattan. And suddenly I knew, or thought I knew, what Charlie had figured out. Making things up was a way to survive, to give your wrecked life a second act. What if *that* was why he'd run away from the hospital? Oh, what if. What if he'd faked his death, after all, and come down to Florida with Jessica Ng, or, as I preferred to imagine, without her? What if he'd got a job on a fishing boat? What if he had texted me that photo of the ocean the way Spinks planted the matchbook in the Cassia house, as a clue, to see whether I *wanted* to find him? What if he knew I would seek Spinks out, what if he wanted me to meet Spinks, so I would go through what he had gone through, and feel what he had felt? Well, I did it. I felt everything. Now what? If I made the right signal, would Charlie come running? I jumped in the air. I waved my arms like a castaway. Of course, no one came. I'd let myself get carried away by a fantasy. Annoyed, I stepped farther into the surf. Waves parted at my shins and soaked my thighs. I hadn't been swimming since I got to Florida, hadn't, as my grandmother observed, even put on a bathing suit. Why not have a little fun? I thought. I went out of the water, stripped to my underwear, waded back until the waves came up to my hips, and dived in. The ocean was unpleasantly cold, though not dangerously so. I rolled onto my back and stroked out a little ways from shore. The hotel was lit up yellow and red and green for the holiday; up and down the beach, other hotels shone in similar colors. Condo towers rose to the north, like balconied hives. I swam a little farther, a little farther still. My body was getting used to the water temperature. It would have been easy to keep going. I am a strong swimmer; when I was a kid I scared everyone with the distances I could cover in Long Island Sound. I turned for a few strokes of crawl and wondered what Charlie had felt when he paddled into Agawam Lake. Mostly cold, I thought, then warm, or nothing. How long had he remained conscious? And what did he think about? His father, Spinks, Lila, me, the people who were hounding him on the Internet, Lovecraft, Barlow. Tlalocan was the paradise of the drowned. Who knew what might be down there? Sympathetic maidens, an endless party, a family that never fell apart. Whole streets under the water, a whole development going on, down there. A better world than the one he'd hitchhiked out of. I want to say that I was tempted to swim down and find it for myself, but not really. I'm too cautious, too hopeful, too bent on living. Still, it was peaceful in the ocean, a hundred yards or more past the breakers, and I might have floated there for a long time if two things hadn't happened more or less simultaneously: my leg brushed a jellyfish and lit up with pain; and I saw someone on the beach, waving his arms, shouting in a familiar voice, calling my name.

Acknowledgments

I'm profoundly grateful to the Dorothy and Lewis B. Cullman Center for Scholars and Writers at the New York Public Library, and to its staff: Jean Strouse, Marie d'Origny, Paul Delaverdac, Julia Pagnamenta, and Caitlin Kean. This book could never have been written without the Center's generous support. Thanks also to Virginia Bartow and Whitney Berman in the NYPL's Special Formats Processing unit, who shepherded me through their collection of amateur periodicals, which includes issues of Robert Barlow's little magazine, *The Dragon-Fly;* to touch the pages that Barlow had touched was a kind of archival magic. Not to mention all the strange little dolls that were lurking in the Special Formats office . . . Truly, if you are looking for wonder in this world, just ask a librarian. Lorna Toolis and Mary Canning at the Judith Merril Collection, in the Toronto Public Library, also provided invaluable help; as did Dr. Thomas Rahe at the Documentation Centre at the Bergen-Belsen Memorial, and Christopher Geissler and the staff of the John Hay Library at Brown University.

ACKNOWLEDGMENTS

The Night Ocean is a book (mostly) concerning the dead, but many of their children and grandchildren are still living. Heartfelt thanks to Margot Owens Pagan for enlightening me about her mother, Doris Baumgardt; and to Betsy Wollheim for telling me stories about her father, Donald—and for allowing me to copy a sheaf of unpublished letters from H. P. Lovecraft to the young Wollheim. Thanks to Emily Pohl-Weary for telling stories about her grandparents, Frederik Pohl and Judith Merril. I'm also grateful to Hugh Pierson, the British liaison officer at the Lager Hohne, who emptied his car of houseplants in order to give me a windshield tour of the former DP camp at Belsen; to Jarett Kobek, for his talk on R. H. Barlow at the NecronomiCon 2015; to Mark Rich, for sending me hard-to-find pages of John Michel's unpublished novel about the Futurians; and to Joseph Quinn, James Wilkie, Richard Wilkie, Lyle Brown, Don Dumond, Oriol Pi-Sunyer, and Michael Schuessler, for sharing stories about Mexico City College in the 1950s. Thanks to S. T. Joshi, Ursula K. Le Guin, and John Macfie for being themselves. I hope they won't be displeased to find their names in these pages. And thanks to Robert Kelly, for telling me about Barlow in the first place. Of course the characters in *The Night Ocean* are fictions, and I take responsibility for any and all discrepancies between my creations and the facts.

For their shelter and support while I was writing *The Night Ocean,* I am fervently grateful to the MacDowell Colony, the Corporation of Yaddo, Ledig House/Omi International Arts Center, and the National Endowment for the Arts. Eben Klemm gets credit for the Last Call of Cthulhu, but don't try to make it at home—who knows what might rise from the depths of the glass? Many, many thanks also to the friends who read and corrected drafts of this book: Betsy Bonner, David Lida, Elliott Holt, Noah Millman, Herb Wilson, and Jeff Zacks. I owe boundless gratitude, and as many Last Calls as they would like, to my sanity-preserving agents, Gloria Loomis and Julia Masnik, and to my all-seeing editor, Ed Park.

I might never have finished this book if Kit Reed hadn't told me that I could do it.

And to my in-house dramaturge, Sarah Stern, who has believed in *The Night Ocean* all along: dog, heart, sparkly heart, sparkly heart, fat red exclamation point. Or, as Lovecraft would have put it: *Umph.*

OGTHROD AI'F

GEB'L—EE'H

YOG-SOTHOTH

'NGAH'NG AI'Y

ZHRO!